PROGRESS
SOVIET AUTHORS LIBRARY

VERA PANOVA

SELECTED WORKS

PROGRESS PUBLISHERS
MOSCOW

Translated from the Russian by Olga Shartse and Eve Manning

Illustrated by Tatiana Tolstaya

Вера Панова
Избранное
На английском языке

First printing 1976
© Издательство «Прогресс» 1976.
© *Translation into English. Progress Publishers 1976.*
Illustrated
Printed in the Union of Soviet Socialist Republics

П $\dfrac{70302\text{-}473}{014(01)\text{-}76}$ 83-76

CONTENTS

Rostov-on-the-Don, the town where I was born and where I grew up, was not particularly beautiful or clean in those days, but it was a lively, bustling town, a rebel town, a hard-working town with a great sense of humour.

A motley crowd of people filled it—there were Russians, Ukrainians, Armenians, Georgians and Azerbaijanians. The market places were piled high with fish from the Don, the Black and the Caspian Seas, and fruit from the Caucasus. I remember the spring fairs held in front of St. George's Church on the dusty common trampled by thousands of feet and littered with sunflower-seed husks; the suburban holiday crowd with the women wearing pink and blue scarves; barrel organs and concertinas playing different, discordantly shrill tunes; the merry-go-rounds with their streaming tinsel ribbons; tent shows with gaudily painted clowns, and the Chinese conjurers, those wizards of my impecunious childhood, who sat on their small rugs and performed their miracles right there, on the dusty ground, under the very nose of the keen-eyed spectators, pressing close round the rug, determined to see through the trick and admitting defeat with good-humoured admiration of the magicians' skill.

I have loved town since childhood, I love the contours, lights, sounds of town, and the hot breath of its life. For me the smallest street happenings are full of meaning and poetry, and in books, too, I like to read the descripton of towns and street scenes, especially "crowd scenes" in the open, although I myself have never learnt to render such scenes and I don't know if I ever will.

I was born in 1905. My father, Fyodor Ivanovich Panov, was an assistant accountant at the Mutual Credit Society's bank in Rostov. He worked for our living, but his heart lay in other occupations. He built canoes and yachts: with his friends who were as keen on boating he founded two yacht clubs in Rostov. First, the one which in my childhood was called the Rostov Yacht Club on the right bank of the Don. Very soon, however, the town's rich, bored with other

amusements, swooped down on the club which offered
something entirely novel. They arrived in their own carriages, with champagne suppers and cabaret girls. The
modest sports club which several enthusiasts had built with
their own hands, was turning into a society playground. And
then my father and his friends quit this club and built a new
one on the left bank, a long distance away and not easily
reached— you had to go over a wooden bridge and then wade
ankle-deep in sand. This clapboard structure on piles was
called the Nakhichevan Yacht Club, after the working-class
district Nakhichevan-on-the-Don.

I know about my father's hobby from my late mother,
Vera Leonidovna, and as for the Nakhichevan Yacht Club I
remember it perfectly myself — I remember the large verandah, built high on piles, under which the canoes and paddles
were kept, I remember the peculiar, hollow sound of
footsteps on the floorboards of this verandah built over a
void, and the smell of pitch on a hot day — till this day the
smell awakens memories in me that are as remote as a dream.
I remember the sand all round, and the shrubs growing in this
sand, I don't know what the plant is called, but it's a tall
shrub, as tall as a man, with long, pliant boughs, long and
slender leaves and plain little mauve flowers that look like
potato flowers — and all this generously flooded with
sunlight, as with golden honey.

(In *Sentimental Romance* I described these sands under the
honey-gold sun, these shrubs, and the whole of this quiet,
golden spot. The scene is forever alive in my memory, it still
has the power to move me, although, one would think,
what's so wonderful about it compared to the scenic beauties
I have seen since.)

My father died at the age of thirty. He was drowned in the
Don.

I was five then. We were left without any means, in dire
poverty. My mother found employment in an office. A friend
of ours, an aged schoolteacher whose name was Anna
Fadeyevna Prozorovskaya and who, I think, was the best
teacher fortune could have sent me, wished to teach me. I
owe her a debt of gratitude for giving me all the elementary
knowledge I possess, and above all else for installing in me a
passion for reading. When I was seven, I read Goncharov's
Frigate "Pallas" aloud to Anna Fadeyevna, learning geography from this book of travel impressions in South Africa,
Malaya, China and Japan. We also read *Askold's Grave.*
Placing her small, wrinkled hand on the book, my teacher

would interrupt the reading to tell me about ancient Rus, about Oleg, Olga, Svyatoslav, and Vladimir and other Russian princes. And, while on the subject, she would take another book down from the shelf and read aloud for me Pushkin's poem *The Lay of Prince Oleg*, rendering it beautifully. She had a real gift for developing a child's imagination. She made me give thought to hundreds of questions which without her help would never have occurred to a girl of my set and my upbringing. I dreaded her displeasure more than anything in the world; I thought it was because of her strictness, but actually it was because I timidly worshipped her spiritual superiority, that beautiful world into which I was initiated. To my great sorrow my wonderful teacher died suddenly, and I had only had a year of her guidance.

I remember how frightened, dismayed and helpless I felt when, coming for my lesson one day, I was told: "Anna Fadeyevna has died."

My father had a small book-case. On the bottom shelves he kept his various tools and blueprints rolled into tubes, and the two top shelves were filled with books, among them Pushkin, Gogol and Turgenev—my early spiritual nourishment, the true legacy of my father. At eight I had read Gogol's *Evenings Near the Village of Dikanka* and Turgenev's *Spring Torrents*; at nine I'd read Gogol's *Dead Souls*, and at eleven I knew chapters from *Yevgeny Onegin* by heart. What beautiful worlds sparkled before me, and how I thank fate that no one took an interest in my reading, because had anyone seen that I was reading books beyond my age I would have been promptly deprived of them. Anna Fadeyevna was dead, and there was no one to stand up for me.

I also read textbooks, not regularly of course, but now and again I'd read a textbook on natural history or geography, I also attempted to read science but it was beyond my grasp and there was no one to explain things to me. What I loved best, and still love, was reading history textbooks, even poorly written ones.

There was no money for my schooling. I did start going to a grammar school, but the fees were more than my mother could afford and I had to leave it before the end of my second year there. I cannot say that I was in despair (I was quite glad, really, because I'd have more time for reading), but still the thought that I'd be left an ignoramus gnawed at me. And so I did my best to fill in the blanks in my education by reading textbooks.

I started writing prose and poetry when I was eight or nine, trying to imitate one writer or another. It was all very funny, of course. The grownups read my masterpieces and laughed. Their laughing hurt me and estranged me from them, although I could see for myself that my ineptitude was disgraceful. After that I wrote on the quiet, carefully hiding my work in various caches. I gave up writing poetry quite soon, when I was still in my 'teens, realising that poetry had to be written very well or not at all.

But I knew already then that I was going to be a writer. I could not imagine being anything else. With my mother working, I had to take on the household chores—cleaning, cooking and washing—at a very early age. I remember we had two huge bedspreads crocheted from thick cotton thread with an overall pattern of little balls the size of cherries. Even when dry, a bedspread like that weighs a ton, and when soaked in a tub you can hardly turn it over. I washed these monsters as best I could, and as I struggled with them I invented the titles for the books I would write some day. I never wrote one of them. When I entered real, active life, it overwhelmed me with different impressions and suggested different plots. As a matter of fact, I did not become a writer as quickly as I planned.

*   *   *

At seventeen I was taken on by the newspaper *Trudovoi Don*, and until 1946 I was a newspaperwoman, a correspondent.

In *Sentimental Romance* I described my first editing job and my first steps in this career. I learnt everything as I went along. I was assistant district organiser of worker correspondents, a reporter, a feature story writer, and a publishing editor. If a feuilleton was needed, I wrote it. If a story was wanted, I wrote that too. Among the newspaper staff, or rather its top crust, was Nikolai Pogodin, the future playwright and author of *The Kremlin Chimes.* He demanded of us, raw beginners, that we should master the profession of newspaperman seriously, developing into proper journalists and not pot-boilers. He used to say that a newspaperman who cannot write quickly and well is not worth his salt. In later years Alexander Fadeyev, then a very young man, appeared in Rostov. In the basement of the Workers' Enlightenment Club where young writers and newspaper people used to gather, he read us chapters from his *Rout* which he was then working on. We lived in that nutrient medium where a young person with any sense at all could enrich himself spiritually with every day.

A newspaper correspondent goes everywhere and sees a lot. I remember the enterprises of the early NEP period, the children's homes and clubs of the time, and the schools where both young and old were taught how to read and write. Although the town I described in *Sentimental Romance* is not Rostov but a collective image of a town, the novel was naturally based on my Rostov impressions and the people I had encountered there. The youth of Stepan Bortashevich (from my novel *Seasons of the Year*) apparently also passed in Rostov.

Later, I saw how the "Gigant" state farm was organised, and how Rostselmash (Rostov Farm Machinery Works) came into being, one of the firstborn of the initial five-year plan. I saw the events described by Sholokhov in *Virgin Soil Upturned*. I attended the trial of a group of kulaks for the attempted murder of Akulina Brileva, a village correspondent. They had fired from a sawed-off gun and wounded her. She had crawled to her cottage, leaving a trail of blood behind her. Luckily she was made of strong Kuban stuff, she recovered and came to the trial with her husband and children. The assizes were held in the modest district club, the total collectivisation of farming had just been launched, and passions ran high. I wrote a brochure about Akulina Brileva. My Maria Petrichenko in *Sentimental Romance* does not look like her, but she would not have come into being had there been no Akulina Brileva and had not the newspaper sent me to cover the inquest.

Years passed in newspaper work. The more observations and thoughts I stored up, the more passionately I wanted to get down to some fiction writing.

In 1933 I started writing plays, and wrote quite a number of them. For some I was awarded prizes, some were staged, practically all of them were published eventually, but I felt cramped in this form of literature, and did not know (and still don't) how to fit in everything I wanted to say into the limited medium of a play. Novels, I thought, would give me more elbow room.

In 1944 I lived in Perm, in the Urals, working on the regional and railway newspapers and also on the radio. While in Perm I wrote a story about a working-class family. It was the result of a newspaper assignment. The children's homes were overcrowded with war orphans, and families had to be

found who would take at least some of the children in. My
assignment was to find out how the campaign was proceed-
ing, and I came across cases and characters I terribly wanted
to describe in a story. Later, I polished up this immature
endeavour and published the story under the title of
Yevdokia. It was dramatised for the screen and produced by
Tatiana Lioznova.

Also in Perm I began work on my novel *Kruzhilikha.*

I used to go to the plant and the township on newspaper
business, and little by little my novel became peopled with
characters who took up abode in it, and acquired flesh, voice
and also a past, present and future. Although I had already
had some writing experience, I realised for the first time
what it was to be a writer, how difficult it was and yet how
delectable. I re-wrote every sentence dozens of times in a
striving for accuracy, I changed my constructions, combina-
tions and comparisons countless times for greater expres-
siveness. And I delighted in these painstaking, interminable,
and never fully satistying strivings. I had done half of the
novel when suddenly the Perm branch of the Union of Soviet
Writers gave me an assignment to write about a hospital
train.

...A beauty of a train stood on the farthest tracks beside a
long fence. The freshly painted dark-green coaches had red
crosses on a white ground; the hand-embroidered linen
curtains on the windows were dazzlingly white. I could not
have known when I walked into the staff car with my tiny
suitcase how much this train, or rather the people there,
would mean in my life. They had been living in the train for
three and a half years since the first days of the war, and
performed their noble work with honour and impeccable
honesty. This hospital train No. 312 was one of the best in
the Soviet Union, and the administration of military hospitals
decided that the personnel ought to write a brochure about
their work to hand down their experience to others. I was
sent to help them as a professional journalist: I was to be the
pen which would take down their stories and arrange them in
the proper order.

I was accommodated in a compartment of the pharmacy
car where there was a small writing desk, painted white, and
where everything was spotlessly white and washed with
carbolic, because this was where the wounded had their
dressings changed. (I have never again lived in such sterile
surroundings.)

Every morning at 8.30 sharp, members of the staff started

coming in—trained sisters, ward nurses, train-maintenance men, etc. They came one by one, sat down, and recounted in detail and without haste their life in this mobile hospital during the war, their pre-war life, their interests, and their expectations. They had long told everything to one another, and were glad to have a new listener. They showed me photographs of their families, and photographs with touching inscriptions given them by the patients. They mourned their dear ones, killed in battle. Some sang their favourite songs to me. Needless to say, all this took place when we were travelling empty. When the train was carrying the wounded there was no time for interviews, but then I saw with my own eyes the selflessness with which these people worked. I took down what I saw myself, I took down their stories and tried to preserve their characteristic intonations and convey their individual personalities in my rendering.

I made four trips on this train—two trips travelling empty and two with a load. The first time we went to collect the wounded at Dvinsk, and the second time at Chervonny Bor. What this newspaper assignment meant to me personally was that it was while living among those wonderful people that I understood that I was indeed going to be a writer, because I simply had to tell about their daily dedicated effort. I would tell it as I witnessed and understood it. And that would be my modest contribution to literature and life.

Putting aside my *Kruzhilikha*, I wrote *The Train* while the impressions were fresh in my mind. I never wrote anything so easily and quickly. The story took me eight months to write and it was published in 1946.

I finished *Kruzhilikha* and published it in 1947. My story *Bright Shore* came out in 1949, the novel *Seasons of the Year* in 1953, a cycle of stories about a little boy named Seryozha in 1955, the *Sentimental Romance* in 1958, and the stories *Valya* and *Volodya* in 1959. Besides this, I wrote several screenplays based on my prose works, also several short stories and plays.

*   *   *

Readers often ask me:

"Why did you write about a hospital train and not a regular hospital? Why don't you write a story about teachers, students, weavers, a paper mill, an iron and steel works?"

I think that a book gets written when the material which the author has accumulated and reflected upon clamours for expression. This is how it was with me in the case of *The Train, Kruzhilikha* and *Seasons of the Year.*

The soul of a child was revealed to me, the revelation engendered reflection, my reflections became clothed in images—and there appeared *Seryozha.*

The impressions of my youth, only marshalled by me years later, weighed down on me like a burden and when I wrote my *Sentimental Romance* I was free of it.

The stories *Valya* and *Volodya* which became shaped in my mind during the war took a very long time to ripen. My original intention was to write a novel, but instead I wrote two stories, keeping the main substance, the concentrate, so to speak.

I think that boys and girls like Volodya and Valya could have also been weavers, paper makers, and metal workers. And that there are women like Yulia Dmitrievna among the teachers, scientists, Party and Government workers, and anywhere else. It does not matter what trade union a particular personage belongs to. The question is how correctly his or her human essence has been revealed.

For this present collection I selected the stories which to my mind are the most successful in this respect. True, in our business success is a very relative thing: the author always dreams of greater things than he can achieve. There are no recipes to follow, each story is a try-out, a reconnaissance of strange territory, a start from scratch. In our work we are forever exploring and our apprenticeship never ends.

1962

V. Panova

SELECTED WORKS

THE TRAIN

Chapter One

DANILOV

Danilov could not sleep. He got up, pulled aside the thick curtain and lowered the window. The heavy window frame slid down without a sound. Everything in this train was of excellent quality and made to last. All the fittings were a pleasure to handle.

The wind rushed into the window. The sky and the fields were ashen pale, without any colours. It was a white night. And very still.

The summer came late this year and was unlike any previous summer. It was sweltering in the daytime, and cold at night. Danilov was chilled as he stood at the window. Perhaps he had been standing there too long? He could not tell.

He pulled on his breeches and tall boots. That fat nurse in the white gathered cap had again brought him a pair of carpet slippers. What a sight he'd make in breeches and carpet slippers! Would she have her husband going about like that, he wondered?

No excuse for looking sloppy even if it was night. He put on his tunic and tightened his cool, creaky belt. And he picked up his cap.

After all, somebody had to be an example to the crew, damn it all.

The wide windows in the corridor of the staff car glowed with an ashen light. Not a soul. The quiet had a tinge of that peculiar nocturnal sadness. The sky and fields sailed past, pale, without colours. Danilov wondered if Dr. Belov was asleep. He slid back the soundless door into his compartment, and looked: the head doctor was sleeping in his trousers and socks, his short legs drawn up in the manner of children. His hands were folded and pressed to his chin, as though he were praying.

The door of the next compartment was opened, and Dr. Suprugov came out into the corridor. He had on a blue hospital robe and carpet slippers.

"You also can't sleep, I see," he said.

"No, I have slept," Danilov replied.

He lied because he did not want to be like Suprugov in anything. If Suprugov could not sleep then he, Danilov, could. And vice versa.

"I've had all the sleep I want. And you?"

"Sleep just won't come, you know. I suppose it's the strangeness of the whole situation."

"What's so strange about it?" Danilov asked. "We're travelling in a train, that's all."

"Yes, but going *where*?" Suprugov snickered. It was a disgusting habit he had. Good people either smiled or laughed out loud, and he snickered.

"To the front, Comrade Military Surgeon."

Danilov studied Suprugov from his magnificent six foot height. You're funking, doctor, you're in a terrible funk. It isn't the same as receiving patients in your consulting room: 'Breathe, please. Once more, and more deeply....'

"D'you think we might get into trouble?" Suprugov asked.

"It's very likely. We have an even chance, haven't we?"

Suprugov raised timid eyes. Danilov's gold-capped tooth glistened in the ashen light. Suprugov assumed a stern expression.

"I cannot understand it," he spoke quickly and irritably, quite changing his tone. "It's a crime sending a train like this one to the front. Fainna says that all the windows will be blasted from the very first explosion."

"What Fainna is this?"

"The head nurse."

"Oh, is her name Fainna?" The name brought back the forgotten smell of a woman's wet, heavy, silken hair. Dammit, what a thing to remember. It was almost twenty-five years ago. Twenty-two, to be exact. And the head nurse's hair was short and frizzly. Fainna, indeed!

"It is definitely a crime," Suprugov said, and mournfully lit a cigarette.

"And what do you propose?" Danilov asked, and clamped his jaws angrily. Suprugov would have seen fury in Danilov's grey eyes had he looked, but he was engrossed in his cigarette which had gone out for some reason — there was probably a tear in the paper. "Pull the emergency brake? Or send an express telegram to the People's Commissar saying: 'Save the cars, they're being driven to slaughter!'"

Suprugov was terribly offended now that he realised that Danilov was mocking him. After all, he was a doctor, not an orderly.

"I do not propose anything. But I may have my own opinion. Like you, I am also going to certain death."

"Think so?... Oh well, before we're dead I'll go and check the crew and the posts, with your permission."

Pulling futilely at his cigarette, Suprugov followed Danilov out with his eyes. He cut a dashing figure, this commissar of theirs. The robe and carpet slippers were unfortunate, Suprugov thought. It was all his own fault, of course. He shouldn't have tried to draw Danilov into an informal chat. It was all right with Fainna and the girls, but not with the commissar—not under any circumstances. One had to be on one's guard with that one.

*　*　*

All the right side windows were opened in the nurses' coach, and still it was stuffy inside. It hadn't taken the girls long to give the place a homey look what with those mirrors, mascot dollies, and photographs of their boy-friends tacked to the wall above their bunks. Danilov hoped they hadn't brought any bedbugs in together with their boy-friends' photographs. He'd have to make sure.

Lena Ogorodnikova had the lower right bunk. She was a funny little woman with the look of a boy who had some prank up his sleeve. Even in sleep she looked impish. A mirror in the shape of a palette hung over her bunk. So tomboys also needed mirrors, it seemed. Opposite Lena slept Iya—what a name for loving parents to give their daughter! Her powerful arms were flung out dramatically, and her breathing was tempestuous and noisy. Good for the girls— all of them had on men's jerseys or T-shirts, not one wore a flimsy nightgown. The night before last, when making his rounds, he found Iya sleeping with bare shoulders, so he had wakened her and given her an extra fatigue duty. What shamelessness! He wouldn't stand for any immodesty in the girls.

The hospital coaches were ready and waiting to receive the wounded. The bunks with the dark-blue flannelette blankets were smartly made. A towel, folded into a triangle, lay on each of the snow-white pillows.

There was a smell of sulfur, potash, varnish, and that elusive and nameless odour which is common to trains and railway stations in general and which cannot be destroyed by either painting the premises all over or fumigating them.

These ordinary second-class sleeping cars were intended for the ambulant wounded, and a soldier was on duty in every car. A dark figure with a rifle and with the tiny flame of a cigarette in his mouth came forward down the corridor at the faintest click of the door.

Smoking in these cars was forbidden, but Danilov did not scold the sentries for breaking this rule. Men weren't robots, after all. The train was heading for the front, carrying its red crosses like a banner. But no one on that train deluded himself with the hope that the red crosses would protect them. Everyone knew that they were precisely what the enemy would aim at.

The man on duty in coach 9 was Sukhoyedov—a squat man with square shoulders and a large head with practically no neck. Barring Dr. Belov, he was the oldest person there. Danilov knew that in the Civil War Sukhoyedov had fought against Yudenich, in the Finnish campaign he had joined up as a volunteer and had been wounded in action. On June 22, the day war was declared, he went straight to the enlistment office and demanded to be assigned to combat duty at once. His age and the state of health made him ineligible, and so he was assigned to this hospital train instead. He had the bitterly hurt look of a man who has been done out of a reward. In peacetime he had worked at a coal mine near Moscow, and the pores and wrinkles on his face were clogged with coal dust, the swarthiness making his clear blue eyes all the bluer and innocent like a child's.

Sukhoyedov remained standing at the window and only turned his head for a second and beckoned to Danilov. For once his expression was neither hurt nor embittered. He had the look of a hunter on the trail of a beast.

"That's where that German plane is, see?" he said softly.

A strange light wavered on the horizon, behind the low and dark line of a distant forest. Suddenly the beam of a searchlight shot into the sky and began to swing right and left unhurriedly. And then a second beam shot up a little distance away, the two crossed and stood still for a moment, and then they parted to search the sky.

"We're searching for that plane," Sukhoyedov said grimly. "Can't you hear anything?"

"No, nothing."

Sukhoyedov cocked his ears and listened.

"They're bombing like mad somewhere," he said grudgingly. "Bombing like mad...." He took a pouch from his pocket and rolled a cigarette.

"Want a smoke?" he asked, holding the pouch out to Danilov.

"Thanks, I don't smoke."

"And quite right, too," Sukhoyedov said. "Smoking gives you a terrible cough in the mornings, I wouldn't wish it on anyone. And then a non-smoker has it twice as easy at the front not having to worry about tobacco. It's a real worry, you know. So don't start. Once you get the habit, you're a finished man."

Danilov smiled, and said:

"I've trodden this earth for thirty-eight years, and I won't start smoking now, seeing I haven't acquired the habit in all that time."

"Can you be thirty-eight?" Sukhoyedov raised his eyebrows in surprise.

"I was thirty-eight in the spring."

"You look younger," Sukhoyedov said thoughtfully, looking closely at Danilov. "I'd say you were thirty, or maybe thirty-two at most. Was your life so soft, or what?"

"I don't know if it was so soft, but it was a good life, I'd live a hundred such lives and never tire."

A silence fell between them. And then Sukhoyedov said very strangely: "You won't be killed."

The beams in the sky crossed again, and hung there in a motionless, slanting cross.

Danilov knew without being told that he would not be killed. His life could not be cut short just like that. Everything had only begun, nothing was done yet, only put off for a time. The only thing that was done with was his feeling for Fainna. But then, stranger things have happened, and they might meet again some day. She would stand before him and, arching her back and shaking out her heavy, wet hair, would say: "Comb it out, will you, Vanya..." What stupid, childish rubbish, he mustn't admit even thinking such silly thoughts, let alone confide them in anyone....

* * *

After the cars for the ambulant wounded came the pharmacy car. Nobody knew why it was called that, since the pharmacy proper occupied one small compartment in it, while the rest of the space was divided up into a dressing station, a shower room, and an airing room. In the service compartment a desk had been installed for the medical secretary. There was such a post in the personnel list, but nobody filled this post. Neither Danilov nor anyone else knew what a medical secretary was supposed to do, and so Danilov did not appoint anyone when the staff was being made up.

Danilov liked the pharmacy car best. He had fallen in love at first sight with its whiteness, nickel-plate, linoleum, airtight doors, and the small collapsible tables and seats, fitted to the walls. Cleanliness and convenience were a passion with Danilov. He had a jealous regard for his favourite car, and the first thing he did on entering it was to rub the window panes with his handkerchief to make sure there was no dust. The pharmacist had contrived to spill some iodine on the bluish-white, newly painted table her first day there. When Danilov saw the stain, he turned pale from distress. Poor Klava Mukhina, a ward nurse, was quite run off her feet in an effort to maintain this impossible cleanliness demanded by the commissar.

Klava was in the shower room when Danilov came in. Wearing a gauze turban on her dark-auburn hair, she stood at the table stitching a length of bandage into a kind of frill. The windows were curtained, and a lamp was burning overhead.

"What on earth are you doing?" Danilov asked her.

She turned her white, freckled, good-natured and sleepy face to him.

"I'm making a lampshade," she replied with a weary sigh.

"One more? For the lamp here?"

"No, for the spray."

"What spray?"

"The shower."

She was sleepy and inarticulate, but he knew what she meant and liked the idea.

"I see," he said. "When the shower is not being used it has one of these lampshades put on it to make it look pretty, is that right?"

"Yes, only it's a pity it's gauze. Silk would be better. Pale blue or pink."

"Silk would certainly be better," Danilov grinned. "But silk we have none, Klava. You might dye the gauze with bluing, you know."

"And if we had some red ink we could dilute it in water, and then we'd have a pink dye," Klava said, and glanced trustfully into Danilov's face.

"We'll buy some red ink," he promised. "We'll buy some at the first shop we come to."

The girl had cheered him up, and he smiled as he crossed the rumbling gangway into the next coach.

The Krieger cars for the gravely wounded were like spacious hospital wards without any partitions. Everything was painted white. There were three tiers of suspended bunks on either side of the car. There were small hanging bedside tables, and chaise longues in the aisle. This place felt too much like a hospital, and Danilov wanted to hurry past these suspended bunks with the raised net sides like in baby cots.

He came to the tail car which housed the isolation ward and the electric power station at the far end. This was, in fact, his destination, the main purpose of his tour of inspection, for here he suspected trouble.

There was no sentry in the isolation ward now.

Danilov stood for a moment before the door of the electric power station. He heard voices but could not make out any words in the noise made by the wheels. Actually it was quieter there than he feared.

He pushed the door open. Nobody was startled. Goremykin, the sentry, was the only one to stand up, while the others remained sitting. Kravtsov, the electric station operator, shifted his cigarette from one corner of his mouth to the other, slapped down a card on the table and said:

"Your card's beaten."

"Like hell it is, clubs are trumps," said Protasov, the car maintenance man, and laid a card on top of Kravtsov's.

Nizvetsky, the young electrician, rose to his feet, feeling ill at ease all at once.

All these men, with the exception of Goremykin, were high-class specialists and consequently the most difficult kind to manage. And Kravtsov, what was more, was a civilian.

"Looking for empty bottles, comrade commissar?" he asked, watching Danilov out of the corner of his eye. "You needn't trouble, the bottles have all flown away," he said with a wave of his hand in the direction of the window.

His eyelids were red, and his eyes were bleary.

Danilov sat down on a stool, and fell to thinking. The three specialists stopped talking and, looking at Danilov, also turned grave. Goremykin sneaked past behind Danilov's back out of the room, closing the door behind him as softly as he could. Danilov knew what to do about Goremykin. Here everything was clear. As for these three, he could also put them under arrest. Getting soaked, the bastards. He'd

noticed their running about and whispering in Vologda earlier
in the day.... Putting them under arrest was the easiest thing,
of course. But what then?

"Here, deal me a hand," Danilov said to Nizvetsky, who
looked quite badly worried now. "Come on, deal."

He played a keen, thoughtful game with his small, arrogant
mouth slightly open and showing the gold-capped tooth. He
won the hand and stood up.

"That's how this game should be played. Shall we call it a
day or go on with the fun till morning?"

Kravtsov and Protasov kept glumly silent.

"Oh no, we ought to get some sleep," Nizvetsky said
hesitantly.

"All right, let's go," Danilov told him.

Nizvetsky walked behind him through the carriages, in
nervous anticipation of a roasting. Danilov did not speak or
turn round once. He opened the doors, and Nizvetsky closed
them afterwards. The wheels thundered under the gangways
between the cars. Night had descended on the world, the
stars had all come out, it was not long till morning.

In the pharmacy car, Klava was trying her lampshade on a
shower spray, puffing sleepily with the effort.

"Look what she's up to," Danilov said to Nizvetsky.
"She's prettying up the place, and before you know it she'll
have it all pink and baby blue.... Listen, I'd like to have a
loudspeaker installed here. The wounded will come here to
have their dressings changed, and while waiting their turn
they'll listen to a broadcast. Will you do it?"

"Sure," Nizvetsky mumbled.

Danilov looked him over. The lad had a well-bred look, he
was turned out neatly and was evidently used to wearing
good clothes.

"What's the matter with you? Why were you deferred?"

"Piles," Nizvetsky replied, turning painfully red.

Danilov showed his surprise.

"How did you come by this old man's illness? Would you
like to be in the ranks?"

"I worked for six years on the Moscow-Vladivostok
train," Nizvetsky said with obvious agitation. "I might have
stayed on, but I asked to be transferred to a hospital train, to
do something at least...."

"And discipline on a hospital train, mind you, is as stiff as
in the ranks," Danilov told him. "Even stiffer. What is
permitted a front-line fighter, is not permitted us. Saints is
what we are expected to be. Angels, seraphs even. We are

the Brothers and Sisters of Mercy.... And there will be no
more vodka on this train hereafter, and you can take my
word for it," he said in a low, passionate voice, clenching his
fists.

* * *

The war was only in its second week, but it seemed like
years.

On the morning of June 22nd Danilov slept late and on
awakening became angry with his wife for not calling him
earlier. He had looked forward to spending this Sunday with
his son. He wanted the day to be a long one, and the boy and
himself to enjoy it to the full. His wife was sorry to waken
him and so had shortened such a rare and beautiful holiday
for them.

The plush-headed boy in his best white suit and blue socks
climbed into his parents' bed and straddled his Daddy's legs.
Sunlight lay on the freshly scrubbed yellow floor. Real
summer had only just begun, but the boy's cheeks and legs
were nicely tanned already.

"Daddy, are we going?"

He had promised his boy an outing. He had promised to get
up early and start off at once. And because of his wife he had
overslept. The poor kid had been on tenterhooks all morning.
His faith in his father had been shaken.

"Sure, we are, son. We'll just take a bite of something and
be off."

"Oh, must you brush your teeth?" the boy sighed, standing
beside his father. "You're not going to the office today."

While his wife made breakfast, Danilov went out into the
garden. They'd been living in town for over a year now, he
was the director of a trust, but his wife still could not get used
to buying their vegetables in a shop and raised her own. The
plot behind the house was not large enough for growing
potatoes and cabbages, and so his wife planted them
somewhere way out of town. She made periodical trips to
wherever it was by train to weed and water her precious
vegetables. Her hands were dark like a peasant woman's.
Danilov would remonstrate with her:

"It's just greed, you're willing to wear yourself to a frazzle
only so you don't have to part with an extra kopeck."

To which she would reply:

"And eat *bought* potatoes?"

On this particular morning, however, the sight of the green
beds was really pleasing. Danilov walked between them and

looked to see how the tomatoes were doing and how soon the lettuce could be picked, while his son squatted beside him and asked:

"Should we see if the radishes are already there?"

He remembered his son and himself in that moment as if it were a photograph of them: himself standing between the vegetable beds, the sunny, peaceful, smiling sky above, and his son squatting beside him and asking if they should not see whether the radishes were there already.

It was the last minute of the old life, with his son, with the Sunday leisure, with lazy thoughts about their outing and the pie they were going to have for dinner.

His wife rushed out of the house and screamed:

"Vanya, war has begun!"

He ran back to the house. The concluding words of the announcement coming over the radio left no room for any doubt. The radio fell silent. Danilov raised his head. Everything had become different. The sunlight. His home. His wife's face. That moment of peace and contemplation seemed years ago now. Everything was swept off by the whirl of his thoughts, racing on and away.

"Daddy, but we are going anyway, aren't we?" asked his son.

The boy was four years old.

"No," Danilov said, and his son began to cry....

That day, Danilov sorted out his papers, wrote a letter to his father, went to the post office and mailed the old man some money.

As he looked through a batch of old letters he came upon a crumpled envelope with the corner of a snapshot showing from it. He did not pull out the snapshot, and dropped the envelope without another look in the desk drawer.

What photos there were of his son he placed in his wallet.

In the night his wife cried, repressing her sobs so as not to disturb him. He pretended to be fast asleep.

She caught a slight movement he made, and half-raising herself in bed looked down into his face.

"You will get an exemption, won't you, Vanya?" she whispered.

He turned away. The question had been settled in the morning, during the radio announcement. He was going to the enlistment office first thing in the morning. And it was none of her business. She mattered least of all.

He was brought his call-up papers in the morning. All the better that way. People wouldn't say that he was pushing himself forward. He was drafted, and that was that.

At the enlistment office, Danilov was told to go and see Potapenko. This was a friend of his, a health-home director. Looking younger in uniform and with his hair cropped, Potapenko sat behind a desk that didn't have a thing on it, while a lot of civilians thronged around him. Although these men had only just come and although all the windows were wide open, one could hardly breathe for the dense smoke of their countless cigarettes.

"Aha, you've come," Potapenko said, offering Danilov a plump, warm hand. "Going to apply for exemption?"

"No."

"All right, wait a little."

It was not really necessary to keep Danilov waiting so long. Even the later arrivals were received first, but Danilov quite understood Potapenko's desire to show off. It tickled his vanity that Danilov was still in civvies and waiting to be received, while he, Potapenko, was already in uniform and handing out assignments and instructions. His effeminate, beautifully shaved face with a double chin glowed with pleasure. He drew his colourless eyebrows together to hide the glow, but it was no use. At last he called Danilov.

"Sit down," Potapenko said to him. "Were you commissar of a battalion?"

"I was."

"Good," Potapenko said, making a note in his pad. "You'll be the commissar of a hospital train. Hold it," Potapenko forestalled Danilov's objections. "I know all you're going to say. But you'll take on the hospital train all the same. The train has to be marshalled first. Do you know how it's done?"

"No. Do you?"

"No, I don't either. But it's not gods who bake the pots."

"Of course not," Danilov agreed.

"We have the instructions, here we are. You can read, so you'll see what's what. Take any people you want, we shan't quarrel over personnel, there's no time."

"Who is in command, or the head doctor, I suppose?"

"There isn't one yet," Potapenko replied. "But there will be, and in the meantime you go ahead and staff the train."

"Where is the train?"

Potapenko gave a burst of laughter.

"There is no train yet either, old chap. It's at the railway repair shop, not out yet. But you go ahead anyway."

"Very well," Danilov said, rising to his feet.

In the front door he all but collided with Grigoriev, the chairman of the local trade union committee, who was bringing in Danilov's exemption.

"File that scrap of paper somewhere," Danilov said to him. "And tell Merkulov to stay over at the office this evening. I'll be there to hand everything over to him."

But he could not make it that evening. It was only on the 26th that he was at last able to see Merkulov who had in the meantime been officially appointed director of the trust in Danilov's place.

All these three days Danilov had been busy trying to staff the train. He needed a large number of people: a general surgeon, a feldsher,* a surgical sister, trained nurses, ward nurses, male orderlies, soldiers, stokers, an electric power station operator, an electrician, train conductors, maintenance men, and what not. Danilov was not the only person rushing about town in search of personnel. No less than fifty hospital trains were being formed, and doctors, nurses, orderlies and train crews were as urgently wanted for each of them.

Danilov had his own way of sizing up people, which to many might appear rather strange.

For instance, when he had to make the choice between a self-confident city feldsher, a wit in the pink of health with a breezy manner, and a bashful, nondescript little woman with a nervous and sickly face and two years of village practice behind her—he chose the latter without a moment's hesitation.

And when he first saw Yulia Dmitrievna, the hawk-nosed, near-sighted surgical sister who looked like an ugly Red Indian, he was not startled at all. He realised right away that she was the very person he was looking for.

The male orderlies were picked from among the draftees, while the nurses were recommended by the Red Cross under whose auspices they had taken a course of training.

Danilov would enter a barracks where people sat dozing on their bundles and suitcases as if waiting for their train and yelled:

"Any feldshers here? Any pharmacists? Any stokers? Comrades, I repeat: any pharmacists here?"

Mostly there was no response. But in one barracks he did not draw a blank. A small woman with a boyish face that was

---

* Feldsher—a graduate from a three-year medical school, usually employed as an assistant doctor.— Tr.

pensively puckish and had a ready laugh in the corners of her mouth, stepped forward. She wore a blue cotton jersey, and had a boyish bob.

"Are you a pharmacist?" Danilov asked.

"No, I'm a games teacher," she replied.

"We don't want any games."

She laughed and said: "I know. I'll come as a ward nurse."

"Not you! Tougher girls are needed for that job."

Laughing gaily again, she quickly bent down, grabbed him under the knees and lifted him off the floor. For a second, to be sure, but lift him she did.

"Atta-girl! Not bad, not bad at all!"

She stood erect and her breathing was light.

"What's your name?" he asked.

"Lena Ogorodnikova."

The repair and maintenance men were the hardest to secure, and the ones he did find were snatched from under his very nose. The railway people refused to give up any of their maintenance workers. "You can do without," they told Danilov. "You'll come to us for repairs anyway."

The train itself had not been released from the repair shop yet. The head doctor who had to sign for it hadn't been appointed yet, and Dr. Suprugov refused to take on the responsibility.

"I'm only a small pebble on the beach, comrades," he said.

He was polite, quick to laugh at any joke, and was always handing round his cigarettes with tiresome generosity. One felt his nervousness, and it was apparent that the soul in this puny, civilian body was in torment.

Danilov went home every night to eat and sleep. His wife met him with a look of mute perplexity. He did not feel like telling her about anything. She could see that he already belonged body and soul to his new job. It had been the same with the state farm, and after that the trust. And now it was the hospital train. His heart was never in his home. Only his son existed for him there. In silence she served him his dinner and made his bed. Her face had become pinched in these last three days, and lost whatever comeliness it had ever had. At night, when they were in bed together, she lost her patience and began to nag him in a whisper:

"Merkulov has got his exemption, the chief accountant has got his, and even Grigoriev, even he...."

"So what of it?" he asked with feigned nonchalance, repressing his exasperation. "So they got it, good for them, what now?"

"You don't care for anyone. Not for me, not for little Vanya, not for anyone."

He turned away to the wall.

"That'll do. I want to sleep."

The new job was so absorbing that he hardly ever remembered the trust. On the 26th, with a couple of hours to spare, he went there to hand the business over to Merkulov. He turned down the familiar side street, and saw the black sign lettered in gold: "R.S.F.S.R. Trust Of Dairy State Farms". There was a crack in the bottom right corner of the signboard which had been there when Danilov himself first came here to take over from his predecessor. He went up the familiar staircase, and heard the abacusses clicking and the adding machines crackling in the accounts office. There was the door on the left covered with black leatherette. His door. His trust.

When he was finished with Merkulov, he went round the rooms and said goodbye to everyone. The old lady cashier shed a tear, and Danilov was flattered by her tears. Blowing her nose, she said:

"Our car has been requisitioned, have you heard? Merkulov's going to the state farm by train tomorrow, can you imagine it?"

Everyone was sorry Danilov was leaving, everyone but Merkulov who could not conceal his pleasure. It wasn't the thought of occupying the director's chair that pleased him, of course, for he was not that kind of person. It was simply the thrill of plunging into independent activity at last, the excitement of freedom attained.... Danilov did not know that he had hindered him so badly.

From the office Danilov went to see Potapenko whom he found in conversation with a little old man of sixty or so.

"Meet Doctor Belov," Potapenko said to Danilov. "He'll be in command of your train."

Danilov glanced at Dr. Belov and said to himself: What a sorry looking creature! He was slight, and had a thin little face. He had not had time to change into uniform and was in his ordinary civilian clothes. Oh Lord, what use could a poor chap like him be?

Aloud Danilov said to buck up the old man:

"I'm sure we'll make a go of it."

Dr. Belov had with him a small suitcase to which he had strapped a pair of felt boots and a kettle. He had just arrived from Leningrad, it appeared.

"Oh well, you know, there's nothing for it, let's fight," he said in a surprisingly vigorous, even martial voice.

"Together," said Potapenko, and glanced at Danilov with glee.

"Precisely," confirmed Dr. Belov.

Danilov invited the doctor to stay the night at his place. The old man trotted briskly at Danilov's side, swinging his raincoat which he carried on a dashingly curved arm. Danilov carried the suitcase with the felt boots and the kettle.

"Why did you bring your felt boots?" he asked. "Did you think our army didn't issue felt boots?"

"Now, you see, I have never served in the army, and the information I have been able to gather is most contradictory. Some say felt boots will be issued, and some say they won't. And one lady said that there won't be enough for such a huge army, and who will be entitled to them first? Not medicos, naturally. And so my wife packed these.... Just to be on the safe side, you see? They won't be in anybody's way, will they, if I push them under a seat, you know."

"No, of course, they won't," Danilov smiled.

At dinner, Dr. Belov ate and drank with a hearty appetite and chirped about the architecture of Leningrad, while Danilov watched him and wondered what on earth he was going to do with this old bird.

Early next morning Danilov went to make the final arrangements with Kravtsov, the rest of the maintenance workers having already been signed on, while Dr. Belov set off to take delivery of the train. Before going he had rung up the repair shop, the casualty clearing centre and the railway station, and announced to Danilov with a self-satisfied air:

"You'll find me at the railway station together with the train."

Danilov went to the engineering works as arranged the night before. The director told Danilov he would let him have Kravtsov if the man himself was willing to change to a hospital train. This untoward generosity did not delude Danilov: obviously, the director welcomed the opportunity to get rid of Kravtsov without a row. It was as obvious, therefore, that there was something wrong with Kravtsov. Danilov inquired at the trade union, where he was told rather evasively that Kravtsov was a highly qualified operator, his work could not be praised enough, but then—to err was human, wasn't it?

"Does he drink, or what?" Danilov demanded.

"Don't we all on occasion?"

Kravtsov's assistant was operating the diesel while Kravtsov himself was sitting on a packing case and drinking milk out of a bottle for his lunch. He had the lean, gaunt and stern face of an icon saint. The hot wind, raised by the diesel, tousled the upstanding grey hair above his forehead.

"Well, how about it? D'you want to work in our hospital train?" Danilov asked.

Kravtsov put his bottle down on the ground and wiped his lips with the back of his hand. He gave Danilov a stern, scrutinising look, and then said:

"*In* your train? *Under* the train I'd go as gladly! Get me out of this place, I refuse to stay here another day."

"How come? Had a quarrel?" Danilov asked sweetly.

"You know what, Comrade Commissar, let's talk straight. I'm not a youngster. You understand what I mean?"

"Quite."

"All the diesel men in town, as many as there are, were taught by me. And I won't have any Komsomol greenhorns ticking me off."

He stood up and pushed his small, greasy hands into the pockets of his wide, greasy trousers.

"In the wall newspaper it's always Kravtsov. At meetings it's Kravtsov again. If it's a reprimand from the director, Kravtsov is the one who gets it. I've no use for this self-criticism stuff. I tell you straight. All of them yelling that I'll get caught in the wheel when I'm drunk. Me, getting caught in the wheel!" Kravtsov gave a Mephistophelian smile. "You ask them: did we ever have an accident here, the smallest accident? Look here, would you say I'm tight just now?"

"Slightly," Danilov said cautiously.

Kravtsov shook his head.

"Not slightly but just right for the hour of the day. But in the lunch break they'll come here to sniff me and pass their remarks. Get me the hell out of here, Comrade Commissar, if my conditions suit you, of course."

They eyed each other squarely. Kravtsov's look was coldly self-confident, and so was Danilov's.

"I'm taking you on," Danilov said.

The matter with Kravtsov settled, Danilov went on to the railway station. A new, gleaming train stood on the farthest tracks near a long, grey wall. There were fifteen dark-green passenger coaches with red crosses painted on them, a freight car, and a small yellow refrigerator car. A soldier with a rifle stood guard.

Dr. Belov was in the staff car, walking up and down the corridor and rattling his keys. A huge bunch of them hung on his arm. The sun blazed into all the windows, and the car smelt of heated paint. Dr. Belov's face was wrinkled, perspiring, and blissful.

"Here we are—keys to all the doors and all the hearts," he declared, showing Danilov the bunch of keys.

"Is everything in order?" Danilov asked.

"I should say so!" replied Dr. Belov. "There was a whole commission there, you know, when I took delivery."

"And did you examine everything?"

"Oh.... Oh, yes."

Danilov gave him a hard look, and Dr. Belov dropped his eyes.

In fact, he had not examined anything. He was given this bunch of keys, he signed some paper, climbed into the staff car and, when the locomotive was hooked up, he rode off, happily playing with the thought that here he was travelling all by himself in seventeen cars! The train stopped before the grey wall. The locomotive whistled and went away, and Dr. Belov started walking up and down the corridor, anxiously awaiting Danilov, for whom he had already formed an attachment.

Danilov walked the length of the train. Everything really seemed to be in order. At least so it appeared to him. There were some things that baffled him, though. For instance, that zinc coated box with two partitions and a lid in the kitchen? There were water taps above the box, small shelves and hooks. Danilov tried to make out what it was for, then called in Sobol, the supplies manager, and putting their heads together they came to the conclusion that it was, obviously, a dishwasher.

The staff began to gather. The train was becoming tenanted. Lorries arrived with mattresses, linen, and medicines. Danilov and Sobol counted the stuff, looked it over and had it taken where it belonged. Yulia Dmitrievna, the surgical sister, with an avaricious glint in her eyes carried the packages containing bandages and cotton to the pharmacy car. It was then that the pharmacist spilled the iodine on the table. She and Yulia Dmitrievna put on white smocks and white kerchiefs on their heads, and after that one felt one dare not enter the pharmacy car without one's white robe. The stokers were testing the heating boilers in the kitchen,

stealing coal at the station for the purpose. The ward nurses
made the beds, singing as they did so and making eyes at
Bogeichuk, a very handsome sergeant. A group headed by
Sobol went to the supplies base, and on return the procession was headed by Lena Ogorodnikova—a slight girl
tripping lightly along with a 100 lb. bag of rice on her
shoulder.

Danilov ordered the rice, the condensed milk, the
chocolate and the butter to be stored separetely, under lock
and key. For supper that evening the staff was to have millet
porridge, he ordained.

* * *

The train started out for the front. It made slow progress
from one station to the next, and was side-tracked for hours
on end. It gave way to troop trains, carrying soldiers, tanks
and guns, and then also moved on unhurriedly and inelucta-
bly.

At the stops the hospital train was put on the farthest
tracks, away from the station bustle. People ran about the
platforms, saying goodbye, cursing, kissing, weeping, waving their handkerchiefs.... And when the hospital train rolled
past, so clean and handsome with the white curtains at
the windows and the red crosses painted on the dark-
green ground, they followed it in silence, with sombre
looks.

On the night, described at the beginning of this chapter, the
hospital train was approaching Pskov.

Danilov was returning from his tour of inspection, and was
walking through the nurses' car when a sudden jolt threw him
off balance and he struck his shoulder painfully against the
corner of an upper bunk. The wheels screeched, and the train
stopped.

"What's up?" A woman's voice asked loudly in the
darkness.

"What's up?" Danilov called into the darkness as he
opened the door and poked out his head.

A trainman came along, swinging his lantern.

"Red light," he explained, walking past. "The way is
closed."

A searchlight beam shot up into the sky again. Now that it
was really dark, the beam was blindingly bright. Soundlessly,
it streaked across the black sky, and slowly swung to right,
to left, searching and finding not what it was searching
for.

Chapter Two

LENA

Lena Ogorodnikova married her husband ten months before the outbreak of the war.

There was a local talent show at the suburban workers' township. Besides the singers, dancers and narrators, acrobats also had to demonstrate their skill, and the District Sports Council delegated Lena to the art review.

A lorry was provided to take people there. Lena climbed into this uninviting, dusty vehicle, and sat on the rear bench. A number of men she did not know, apparently representing some enterprise or other, came and sat on the side benches.

These comrades wore leather coats or raincoats, and carried briefcases. And Lena had on her blue cotton jersey, which she had taken in at the waist to better outline her figure. She sat all by herself, apart from the other passengers, and was jolted terribly. Her bobbed hair got into her eyes and tickled her face.

The men talked in loud voices and laughed. They did not take the slightest notice of Lena.

The heat was oppressive. A dark-mauve cloud was creeping up the sky from behind the horizon. It spread wider and wider, and without bothering to hide the sun suddenly burst with pouring rain. It was as if a wall of water had dropped from the sky. Lena's blue jersey, brief skirt, and bobbed hair were soaked through in a second. The rain streamed down her face and back. The men ducked under their leather coats or raincoats, and shouted something to Lena from the shelter. The driver had nothing to worry about in his closed cab. Lena was soaking and thinking: "What a coarse bunch!"

Suddenly one of the men rose to his feet. Holding his coat over his head and crouching, he slipped across to Lena and sat down beside her.

"This is what we'll do," he said, and covered her, head and all, with the skirt of his leather coat.

Lena found herself alone with him in the privacy of a narrow tent. She had to make herself as small as she could, to be all under cover. The rain drummed on the leather coat. She was so cold and wet that she did not feel the slightest embarrassment, only anger that rescue had come so late. Why couldn't the fool think of it sooner?

Her head was on a level with his chest. Looking down she saw only her clenched, wet knees with the wet skirt, as heavy and stiff as tarpaulin, stretched across them, and also a piece of the leather coat's tartan lining.

And suddenly she heard something knocking, slowly and loudly, just above her ear. It was a heart beating. His heart.

She listened, marvelling. Honestly, it didn't beat at first. Oh, naturally, it did beat, but merely as hearts usually beat, not thumping like this. And this hammering was not usual.

Why did his heart beat like that?

She terribly wanted to see his face. She had no idea what he was like. Maybe he was so ugly that his heart had better not beat at all. No, let it beat, no matter what he was like.

And his heart went on knocking.

Without stirring, she poked with her fingers and made a tiny slit between the skirts of the coat covering them. A little light seeped in and she glanced up into his face cautiously.

His face was shadowed, sombre and upset. And his very dark eyes were fastened on her, on Lena.

She quickly dropped her head, and did not lift it again. And now two hearts were knocking in the leather tent.

With her eyes closed, she listened to this raging storm in herself and in him.

She felt a hot whirl of shame, pride, amazement and joy mounting within her.

The rain stopped and he stood up.

"Here we are," he said with a quavering sort of smile. "We're almost there, I believe.... Oh, don't bother, stay as you are, you might catch cold," he added hastily, pulling the coat up over her shoulders.

But she felt sad sitting like that alone. She shook off the coat and began to wring out the hem of her skirt. The sun was hot again. The floor of the lorry was flooded with water. There was a smell of generously watered earth, of wet buckwheat, wet wormwood—the air was wonderful. And his face was wonderful. But the most wonderful thing of all was the rain, only why had it stopped so soon, why not go on pouring?

They had arrived. Blind to everything except to what was inside her, forgetting about the show, her part in it, and her bedraggled appearance, she climbed down from the lorry.

* * *

Until now Lena had not loved anyone in the world.

There had been no one to whom she could become attached. Life had swept her past people, past things, past homes. She never had her own family, or her own room. Even her name was changed several times. Her baptismal name was Valentina, and her mother called her Valya. But in the Children's Home there were six Valyas, and so to tell her from the rest they started calling her Tina. She tired of the name by the time she grew up, and re-named herself Lena.

She did not like to remember. When she was five or six she had her appendix out. She was in the children's ward in the city hospital. The anesthetic left her feeling wretched, she choked on her bitter saliva, there was no one there to wipe this saliva from her lips, and she was too ill to call anyone. The other children had their mothers sitting beside them. Lena's bed was behind a screen. "Stop yelling, you're not in pain," snapped the fat ward nurse when Lena moaned. She repressed her moans.

"Whose child is that?" someone asked on the other side of the screen.

"Nobody's." The nurse replied. "Just an orphanage kid."

Life with Mother had been bad. Mother was fond of drink. When there was any money in the house, she bought vodka and pickled cucumbers and invited her women friends who drank, sang, laughed, and told Mother what she must do.

"What you must do is sue the heel, and bring your suit in Moscow. Seeing he's such a heel he's got to be sued in Moscow, and that will fix him."

Lena had seen the heel twice. Both times she had her face washed, she was dressed with greater care, and taken to a small private shop in the market place. There was a huge brazier in front of the shop, right in the open, and in it pieces of mutton threaded on thin wooden sticks were sizzling and spluttering, making your mouth water. Inside the shop stood a table and on it there was a salt cellar, a pepper-box in the shape of a tiny barrel, and a plateful of spring onions cut into small pieces. The heel owned all this. He himself sliced the mutton, fried it, and swept the floor. Lena and her mother sat down at the table and ate the mutton, pulling the pieces off the sticks with their fingers. The fat trickled down Lena's arms all the way to her elbows, leaving greasy rivulets. The shop-owner sat at the table with them, and kept wiping his perspiring face with his grimy apron.

"You eat," he said to Lena, sighing sorrowfully. "Here, this will be more tender," and put a new stick on her plate, first feeling the mutton with his fingers. He was an elderly man, his moustache was a yellowish grey, and one of his legs was made of wood.

There was grease all over Mother's face, as if it were tear-stained.

"It breaks your heart to look at the poor mite," she was saying. "Some children are all dressed up, and some have gone without shoes all autumn and winter, and is she any worse than others?"

"You eat, this one's more tender," he muttered, piling Mother's plate. "But what can I do when I've a houseful of mouths to feed? And now my stepdaughter's come for a stay with her brood, and the tax this year is so ruinous, I really can't imagine what I'm to pay it from, from what profits.... The price of mutton has gone up, custom has dropped, I might as well become a bootblack."

"Then you shouldn't have led a woman on, you shouldn't have seduced her!" Mother said.

The shop-owner sighed mournfully and muttered under his nose:

"If you could give me proof, it would be quite a different story."

"Heavens above!" Mother cried, clutching the stick with the pieces of mutton on it to her breast.

Lena kept her eyes on the pepper-box as she listened to them. She turned for a last glance when she and her mother were leaving, but did not dare ask for it.

The shop-owner gave Mother some money. They went to the fish stalls, after that Mother bought some vodka, and that night her women friends came over again, they all drank and sang, and Mother, red all over, screamed:

"I'll give him proof, the hell, I'll show him how to lead an honest woman on, I'll show the son of a bitch, the dirty dog!"

"Sue him, sue him," yelled the women in chorus. "Let them get away with something once, and there's no telling what they'll get up to next!"

Mother worked as a scrap collector. Sometimes she vanished for two or even three days. Once she brought home a man. They had supper and went to bed. Lena was to sleep on two chairs pushed together. When she woke up in the morning, she went up to the bed and took a good look at their guest. He slept on the edge of the bed, and one fat arm hung down almost to the floor. It was roped with blue veins. The fingers were covered halfway with thick black hair. It was disgusting. Lena took a chip and hit the nasty arm across the blue veins. The arm went on sleeping.

Mother got up at noon, made a quick trip to the shop, and then she and her guest sat down to eat. Lena was given half a glass of beer and a piece of jellied fish. From their conversation she understood that her mother was going away. What luck! The beer made her giggle, and then she fell asleep in her chair. Next morning her mother took her to a strange street and pointed out a two-storied white building with the plaster peeling from the walls.

"This is where you must go," Lena was told. "Walk right in, just go straight in. You'll tell them you're an orphan, that you have no father, no mother, nobody in the world."

Mother baked a lot of pies, her women friends brought their own crockery and glasses, and there was a great feast. Mother, in her new silk blouse and with her hair dishevelled, jumped up to dance one minute, and the next flopped down on a chair, put her elbows on the table and, propping her face with her fisted hands, wailed:

"Oh, my fate, my love! And who will judge him? That one refuses what's his, and this one, must he pick up the leftovers or what? If only he, that heel, paid me the alimony I'm due, all right and proper, but no, the son of a gun tries to get off cheap with mutton, he takes me for a bloody fool. I'm not old, I'll have other children...."

"You will, Pasha, you will," shouted the guest, and again Mother got up and stamped about in her blue silk blouse which bellowed out on her back and looked as stiff as tree bark.

The yelling and the stamping tired Lena. She put on her torn knitted cap which she wore winter and summer, took her toys—an empty cold-cream tin and the handle of an awl, went out into the street and made straight for the white two-storied house with the peeling plaster.

Two big girls with cropped hair stood at the gate.

"I'm an orphan," Lena said to them. "I have no father, no mother, nobody in the world."

The girls looked at her gravely and silently. Lifting her face up to them, Lena repeated the words she had memorised.

"How old are you?" one of the big girls asked.

"Shall we call Anna Yakovlevna?" the other one asked her friend.

Lena peeped into the gate. She saw a playing ground with swings, and pretty green grass all around.

"I'm an orphan," she repeated cheerfully.

Anna Yakovlevna came, took Lena by the hand, and led her inside.

A lot of grownups surrounded Lena and all of them wanted to know where she lived and who told her to come here. They were big, and they sat her on a table to talk to her, but anyway she outwitted them all.

"No one told me," she replied, swinging her legs. "I don't live anywhere."

She guessed that they wanted to send her back home. And she wanted to stay here in this house with the swing and the pretty green grass.

"I want to live here," she told them frankly.

Everyone laughed, and a man wearing gold-rimmed glasses said:

"We must report her to the militia."

Still, she stayed the night in this house, sleeping on the cook's bed. The cook gave her a good scrubbing, and cut her hair short. The big children took turns giving her a swing all that evening and the next morning. There were no other young children in the home.

The cook said with indignation as she scrubbed Lena:

"I'd bash a mother like that on the head, I would! What did she do with the child to get her hair crawling with lice?"

The militiaman arrived. The man with the gold-rimmed glasses called Lena aside and whispered to her that the militiaman had to be told the whole truth or else he'd take her away to the militia.

"Let him," Lena replied. "Let him. I'm not afraid of the militia."

And she told the militiaman that she was an orphan and did not live anywhere.

"And what does your mother do?" he asked. "She collects rags," said Lena.

Everyone burst out laughing. But the long and short of it was that the mother who collected rags and had a little daughter named Valentina was never found: she had left town, and Lena was placed in a children's home for young orphans.

She lived there for a year. She had simple tastes and looked upon people with indulgence. She did not become attached to anyone, she did not demand anything, and forgave all. She accepted what people gave her with pleasure, but without gratitude.

Very quickly she became used to being taken care of, and it did not impress her in the least that people fed her, clothed her, taught her to read, washed her clothes, cooked food for her, and that there were women who stood before her clapping their hands and singing:

> *With our little baby feet*
> *We go pit-a-pat,*
> *With our little baby hands*
> *We go clap, clap, clap....*

They also sang the *Warsavienne* and the *Internationale.* Lena regarded singing as an unavoidable chore.

A year later the children's home was closed down and Lena was transferred to another one, in another town. The winters were longer and colder here, firewood instead of coal was burnt in the stoves, but for the rest everything was just the same.

She was growing up. She was not the little girl named Valya any more. All that was a long time ago. The girl she was now was called Tina. She had a place to live but no home. She had friends but no kin. She was treated well but without any tenderness. She was neither abused nor fondled.

Lena did everything that she was expected to do with great diligence, for she did not like to be scolded. When she was 7, a new director came to the children's home, he was a young man, a member of the Komsomol.

After hearing the song "With our little baby feet" he said:

"This goes out. I won't have you turning the children into idiots. They are almost morons already. What they need is physical culture."

Lena liked physical culture classes. She was the nimblest and strongest of the girls. It was pleasant to be praised all the time. And thereafter she endeavoured to do everything well so that people should praise her for it.

* * *

In the seventh form they studied the Constitution of the U.S.S.R.

The teacher would read a clause and then explain in a long-winded way that the clause was good and fair. Lena looked at the teacher and thought: why does he try so hard to explain something that's obvious to all?

She was already in her fifth children's home, she was a member of the Komsomol, she attended physical culture courses, and her name was now Lena. There the teacher went again, explaining the same thing only from the other end now.... He was proving to them that the Soviet state was the most just state in the world.... For Lena there were no other states in the world, except the Soviet state. She was a child of this state. It was her home, her world, her sky. To any person in this world she could say: comrade. She could accept bread from anyone, and she would share her bread with anyone. She could walk without fear into any institution, and so long as the conversation was formal and business-like, she spoke confidently, cleverly and wittily. But she was not accustomed to discussing her personal affairs with anyone, and if the conversation took this turn she immediately retired into her shell and became uncommunicable.

* * *

Twice she almost became more attached to people than she should.

When she finished the physical culture courses she was taken on as a games teacher at a school maintained by the railway and was given accommodation at a railway workers' hostel.

The secretary of the district Physical Culture Council was a girl by the name of Katya Gryaznova. Her very dark eyes were stupid and kind, and her cheeks were like hams. She did not go in for physical culture, and had grown into a lump of fat from sitting in the office all day. She admired Lena.

"How can you live in a hostel!" She would say. "With no one to cook for you and take care of you...."

She invited Lena to her place, and Lena went. Katya had a mother, and her mother had a small, three-room house, a cow, and a garden with lots of raspberry bushes. They had tea from a samovar in the garden under a bird-cherry tree. On Katya's bed lay about fifteen small cushions which her mother had embroidered with her own hands. These small cushions held the same fascination for Lena as the barrel-shaped pepper-box in the "heel's" eating shop.

"You really do live well," Lena said with a sigh.

"Come and live with us," Katya said. "We'll be just like two sisters. You'll pay as much as you can afford. We've a good cow, you'll put on flesh, because look at you—you're just skin and bones!"

"We'll be glad to have you, Lena dear," Katya's mother said too. "Katya has become very fond of you. And it isn't nice for young ladies to live in hostels. There are all kinds, you know."

Katya's mother was a quiet woman with a finely lined face and eyes that were as kind as her daughter's.

Lena accepted the invitation. A bed was put for her in Katya's room, and Katya with her own hands moved half of her cushions to this bed. Lena was given plenty of fresh milk to drink. Life became easy and comfortable. But this bliss came to an end all too soon.

Katya had a young man, a childhood friend. He worked as a book-keeper somewhere, and every evening he came over and sitting under the bird-cherry tree strummed his mandolin. Lena despised him for not being an athlete. She could not have told even what colour his eyes were.

Once, coming home from work, she found Katya in tears.

"What happened?" she asked with genuine concern.

"Nothing," Katya replied. She stemmed her tears and sat there in a huff, without looking at Lena

Lena heard Katya's mother muttering in the next room: "I don't know how to call it, repaying people like that for their kindness...."

"What's been going on here?" Lena asked.

"When people are decent to me, I have to be decent to them, and not do anything underhand," Katya's mother continued as she entered the room.

"What are you talking about?" Lena asked, never suspecting that all this had anything to do with her.

"We treated you like one of the family," Katya's mother said. "And you, look what you're doing, it's unthinkable, it's only in these modern times that young ladies have taken to doing such shameless things."

"I don't understand what you are talking about," Lena said. "I haven't done you any wrong."

"Don't try to make excuses, dear, don't try. In these matters it's always the woman's doing. A young man is no wiser than a calf, he goes whichever way he's tugged."

"You don't imagine that I have fallen in love with Katya's boy-friend, do you?" Lena asked in amazement, and then burst out laughing. "I swear I'm not in love with him!"

"Nobody is saying, Lena dear, that you're in love with him," Katya's mother replied. "But making him fall in love with you is wicked on your part, and you will forgive me, dishonourable."

Katya dropped her head on the table and sobbed.

"It's news to me," Lena said in a voice ringing with anger. "Bother him anyway, what the hell do I want him for?"

"Now, *that* we don't know.... An attractive young man who does not drink and earns a good salary...."

Lena went to the room where she and Katya slept, and lay down on the bed. She wanted to leave this house.

Katya came in, sat beside Lena and hugged her.

"Don't mind Mummy," she said. "I know you're not to blame. All men are heels, that's all."

Lena remembered the heel with the mutton, and laughed. Katya kissed her, priding in her own magnanimity. It was time for supper. Lena drank her fresh milk and said to herself: "I'll go away. I want none of this."

A few days later she received a love letter from Katya's boy-friend. She tore it up and went back to the hostel.

The second time happened about six months before she got married.

In the hostel, the first floor was occupied by men, and the second by women. Upstairs, on the women's floor, it was clean and tidy. In the common kitchen, the women cooked in spotless shiny saucepans and boiled their water in sky-blue kettles. The men boiled eggs and heated their shaving water in enamel mugs that were black with soot. They spat and threw their cigarette ends on the floor. Lena kept well away from them.

Once, as she was walking along the downstairs passage a man stopped her and asked in a deep baritone:

"Comrade, sorry to bother you, but do you happen to have a thermometer?"

"What thermometer?" Lena asked, pausing.

"An ordinary thermometer, you know," the baritone replied. "I feel I'm running a temperature, but I've nothing to take it with."

"Just a moment, I'll go and ask," Lena said, and went upstairs to her floor.

One of her room-mates did have a thermometer, and she went back to the men's floor with it.

The baritone was waiting for her trustingly on the same spot. He thanked her and asked her room number. A quarter of an hour later he knocked on her door.

"Thirty nine and four," he told her as if she were waiting to hear. "Here it is again, there's no getting rid of it, curse it."

"What is it?" asked Lena who had never been ill in her life, just that once with appendicitis.

"Malaria."

He stood shuffling his feet in the doorway, obviously reluctant to go. He had a long, thin, hawk-nosed and inspired face.

"And I've run out of quinine too," he said, throwing back his head with a martyred look, like Jesus saying: "Thy will be done." "Never mind," he swept caution away with a hopeless gesture. "I'll go to the chemist's and buy some. I'm used to going out with a temperature, however high it might be."

It was winter, and the frost was about 20 degrees below zero.

"Give me your prescription, I'll go," Lena told him.

"Oh no, why should you!"

"As you like."

"It costs a ruble twenty," he said, and gave her both the prescription and the money. His fingers were very thin, and as he dug for the money in his coin case he stuck out his little finger.

She brought him the quinine and gave him some hot sweet tea with lemon. She felt sorry for him.

They became friends. Every evening he came knocking on her door. When he had a malaria attack, she went down to his room and nursed him. He told her everything about himself. He was an engineer. This surprised her, for she never knew that engineers lived in hostels together with tram conductors.

"I had a beautiful flat, but I left it to my wife," he explained.

He had been married four times. All the four wives, he told Lena, left him. But it was a curious way of *leaving*: they kept the flat and everything in it, while he, the abandoned one, left his home without any luggage and took up his abode elsewhere, as a bachelor. Two of his wives had children.

"Wonderful little girls," he said with a sigh.

"But why couldn't you get along with any of them?" Lena asked.

For answer he began to whistle. He whistled beautifully, not at all like boys whistled in the street. When he had finished he told her: "This was from Tchaikovsky's Fourth Symphony." Then he asked Lena if she was fond of poetry, and read her Aseyev's poem: "No, you aren't my only darling, darlings never are like you...." The poem thrilled her, she had never heard anything like it, her acquaintance with poetry beginning and ending with the school reader. He

knew countless poems by heart, and was willing to recite
them at any hour of the day or night. They began to stay up
till late. It became a need with her to see him and listen to him
reciting poetry.... One night, they were in his room and he
was reading Pushkin's "Gypsies" to her. After reading the
concluding lines: "There's no defence from fatal passion and
no escape from destiny", he said in the same beautiful voice:
"I love you", and kissed her on the lips with his wet mouth
that stank of stale tobacco. She sprang up and gave him a
push that sent this malaria-ridden Casanova reeling against
the door and hitting his back against it.

"That was strongly put," he said after a silence.

She stood straight before him for a minute with her fists
clenched, then with light, swift steps she swept past and out
of the room with never a glance at him.

Upstairs, in her room, she rinsed out her mouth. No, it
wasn't clean enough. She brushed her teeth with tooth-
powder. Still, she had a taste left in her mouth as if she had
swallowed something nasty.

* * *

And here love came to her.

No one has ever known a love like this.

"Kiss me...." Who has ever been kissed like that? "Sleep,
little one. Is my arm too hard?" Who has ever been treated so
tenderly? "Kiss me...."

* * *

For the first time in her life she had her own home. It was
just one room, but heavens above! there were so many things
in it! A wardrobe with a mirror, an extension-table with fat
legs, a desk, a couch, and chairs! And in the kitchen there
was a dresser to keep their pots and pans in. And all this
belonged to her, and she belonged to Daniil, Danila, Danny,
Dan—to think that there could be such lovely names in the
world! For twenty years she had been "nobody's", and now
she gave herself into the hands of her legal owner with
elation.

She thought him rather elderly, for he was already 28. It
pleased her, however, that he was not very young, because it
made her appear more dignified too, she thought.

He enjoyed making her little gifts, for she accepted every
trifle with such raptures of delight. "I've never had shoes as

lovely as these," she would say, or: "I've never had such a beautiful dress." Touched by her gratitude, he said: "My darling, I'll give you dozens of them...."

Even ordinary chocolates she ate with such relish that it was a pleasure to watch her.

She wore a pinafore when she cooked their meals, and to look at her one would think that she had never known any other life but that of a happy housewife bustling about her own home.

Life turned out to be full of happiness and wonders. Love had transformed Lena: she had a different walk and posture, her voice had become deep and cooing, and her eyes, their colour enhanced, seemed to have a secret lurking in their languid depths. She glowed with jubilance, men turned to look at her in the street, and she glowed all the more.

This went on for ten months. Ten months—three hundred days and nights.

*   *   *

He was drafted at once.

It was a terrible day. Lena realised with a shock that it was not she who came first with him.

He moved about the room, collecting some of his things and answering her questions absently....

She did not feel hurt. Her feelings did not matter just then. What mattered was that she saw this new side of him for the first time.

A cause served by men came first with him, and now this cause was calling him. He had not gone yet, but he no longer belonged to her.

It could not be different. She covered her face with her hands. If it were, she would stop loving him.

No, she would not stop loving him, she could not do that, but her jubilance would be tarnished. She was a sportswoman, an amazon, a winner of competitions, she understood such things. One could jubilate only if one conquered a strong opponent. Was there much glory in conquering a faint heart? He had a strong heart. And she was proud of him.

She had to do something to make him see how well she understood everything. He must go away feeling pleased with her.

To begin with, she must conceal her despair from him. He was self-possessed: his manner was simple and calm. He made jokes. She could behave like that too.

She must also help him pack. What did she think she was doing, sitting there, twiddling her thumbs! The shirt he was putting into his knapsack had a button missing, she remembered.

"Wait, Dan, I'll pack it myself."

She re-packed the knapsack, first looking everything over and making the necessary repairs. She packed some food for him—a little, the way he wanted it. She reminded him to take his shaving things. Also shoe polish. And a shoe brush. She put some envelopes, letter paper, and boxes of matches in the knapsack.

He sat and watched her pack his things. This was as it should be: the husband sat smoking and relaxing while the wife got him ready to go to war.

When everything was ready, he drew her to him for the last caress. She laid his head on her breast and gazed into his face with a new feeling of infinite closeness and tenderness which wrung her heart.

She was his sister, she was his mother, as loving as the mistress she had been before this. She was everything in the world for him.

She saw him to the railway station, and did not weep at parting.

"What are you going to do with me gone?" he asked her.

"I haven't thought of anything yet," she replied with a diffident smile.

He looked at her with a flicker of alarm in his eyes.

"You won't think of anything too mad, will you?"

"I won't," she promised. "Not too mad."

"Little one, please, no heroics. A war has to be fought soberly."

"No heroics."

They kissed desperately for the last time, and after that no more could be said. He boarded the train. She turned and left the station, blind to the world.

She returned home. With unseeing eyes she looked at all those things in the room. They meant nothing to her without him there. How long would the war last? Two years, he said. Two years! When a minute lived without him was torture. She would die of longing. What was there to live by? Her very breath of life had gone, and she would simply suffocate....

She was sitting on the floor amid the open suitcases and scattered underwear. Her face was grey, and the light had gone from her eyes. Her lips were grey too. And now these lips smiled. She raised her eyes, and they were shining. Her fate was going to be the same as his.

She rose from the floor, took off the expensive dress in which she had gone to see him off, and put on a skirt and her old blue cotton jersey with a darn on the elbows. She'd give one key to the superintendent, and the other to Katya Gryaznova, asking her to keep an eye on the room. No use sitting here and moping. She must tidy everything up first—supposing he came back before she did? She put the room in order, left her paradise behind her, and went straight to the enlistment office.

* * *

Danilov liked Lena.

"She's tough," he said about her. "She can easily carry a hefty man to safety."

Lena liked Danilov too. Not Danilov so much as his name. Everyone called him Comrade Commissar, but she addressed him as comrade Danilov. It was nice pronouncing this name which reminded her of her husband's. Daniil, Danila, Danny, Dan....

Danilov meant to assign Lena to the pharmacy car, where he pictured her easily helping the wounded on to the dressing table. But Yulia Dmitrievna would not have her, and asked Dr. Belov to give her another nurse.

"Why? Don't you like her?" Dr. Belov inquired with his readiness to oblige everyone.

"No, I don't like her."

"Hm.... D'you know, I also thought her sort of, you know what I mean."

Yulia Dmitrievna pursed her thin, perfectly straight lips.

"Precisely."

"Somehow not quite so, eh?"

"Flippancy is written all over her face," said Yulia Dmitrievna through set teeth.

"Yes, yes, yes, flippancy.... Good! I'll think the matter over," Dr. Belov said with a regal nod.

And to Danilov he said:

"I wonder if we could put some other nurse into the pharmacy, what d'you say?"

"Why, do you think this one won't cope?"

"No, she won't cope. Sister and I watched her, and she won't cope, no. Takes everything too lightly. We want a steadier person there."

Danilov did not protest: after all, the medics knew better in such matters. He assigned Klava Mukhina to the pharmacy, and Lena was transferred to a Krieger car.

Dust kept gathering on the window panes and on the varnished shelves, and it took all of Lena's day to keep the place spick and span. She felt a little hurt, naturally, about being expelled from the pharmacy. It was the doing of that red-skinned witch, of course. Gosh, wasn't she ugly! Lena supposed that no man had ever loved her. Served her right. Why should she pick on Lena? All right, Lena's car would be the cleanest of all, just to spite the witch. And so she went about with a duster all day, polishing the window panes with crumpled newspaper as Katya's mother had always done, shaking out the blankets, and scrubbing away.... Where did the flies come from now? There had been no food in the car yet, no lived-in smell, and yet there were flies.... Two of them. Lena stalked them. She crept up to one fly and caught it, but the other one escaped and she could not find it. Klava had made lampshades from gauze bandages, gathering the stuff into pretty festoons. Lena felt envious: she did not know how to make these festoons. She must make friends with Klava and get her to teach her. But Klava spent all her waking hours in the pharmacy, and Lena did not want to meet Yulia Dmitrievna and kept away from the place.

...Her husband was always with her, he never left her for a minute. To be sure, she had such a lot to do that she could not talk to him all the time as before and calculate her every movement to appear attractive to him, but still she never forgot about his presence for a moment and addressed all her remarks to him. "Well, that's done, Dan," she would say absently, shaking up the pillows and admiring her work. "And now we'll scrub the floor once more," she said to Dan. And it was not until her hour of rest that she could completely withdraw into that sweet, thrilling world where they were alone, he and she, and their love.

But she had very little time left for withdrawal into this world. She was either wanted in the kitchen to peel potatoes, or else Doctor Suprugov was giving them a lecture on personal hygiene. In the mornings commissar Danilov collected the whole crew and read out the last war bulletin, after which he went on to tell them about the barbarity of the fascists, and to explain that our reverses were temporary, that ultimate victory would be won by the Red Army, and the Hitlerites would be routed.... Lena listened to Danilov and thought: "Why spout on and on, we know without you telling

us that we'll win in the end, Dan and I will, it can't be
otherwise, otherwise Dan will be killed and I will be killed,
and we'll never be happy again...." It did not worry her much
that the Germans were seizing one town after another. So
what if they did take another town? We'd recapture it
anyway. Only she wished we'd recapture them soon, so the
pre-war life would be resumed and Dan would come home.
She had not received a single letter from him, but she knew
that he was alive.

* * *

That night Lena slept so soundly that she did not hear
Danilov making his rounds nor the sudden jolt of the train.
She woke up when it was light. Just before awakening she
had had a lovely dream.

She lay in bed with her eyes closed, smiling and blissful,
and suddenly, without opening her eyes, she realised that it
was only a dream, that she was in a hospital train on the way
to collect the wounded, and that the train was not
moving—could they have arrived?

Poking her head out of the window she saw a track-
walker's cabin, a meadow, a forest where birds were already
singing, the pink sky in the east, such a lovely, dear sunrise
that you wanted to cry! And clouds like light pink feathers
spread all over the sky—she had never seen such a beautiful
sky....

"We've been side-tracked again. No hurry with us...."

She had awakened too early. Everyone was asleep. It was
two hours before reveille.... Maybe she ought to lie down
again and see if she didn't have another dream about
something nice....

But there was commissar Danilov, already up and about.
He emerged from the kitchen. Lena pulled on her skirt and
went outside in her bare feet. The air was fresh, and the birds
were singing louder and louder. A jasmine shrub was in
flower in the little front garden before the track-walker's
cabin, and Lena began to steal up to it with the intent of
pinching a twig.

"Hey, Ogorodnikova!" Lena heard Danilov's shout when
the coveted flowers were almost within grasp. "Get back at
once, we're starting now. You'll get left."

Lena pushed out her lower lip. What if the train did start?
An express, was it? Did he think she couldn't jump on? She
broke off a twig of jasmine, and cool dew sprayed her face.

The train did start. Danilov climbed up the steps. Lena purposely waited for it to pass her. From under the wheels a warm little breeze ran over her bare feet. When the end coach came level with her, she caught hold of the handrail, and easily jumped on to the step which came above her knees. She stood there for a minute delighting in her dexterity, her strength, and the breeze cooling her forehead and breast. "See, Dan, what a wife you have!" she said, grinning. She let him admire her a bit longer, and then went into the car.

Chapter Three

DR. BELOV

In Leningrad, the hospital train stopped at the Vitebsk marshalling yard. The locomotive was promised within half an hour, but two hours had passed and there was still no sign of it. Doctor Belov wandered about outside the staff car, muttering "How awful, how really awful...."

His mutterings were not about the delay at all. The thing was that he had sent a telegram to his wife saying that he would be passing through Leningrad and asking her to come to the station to see him. But he did not know which station. And so, naturally, she wasn't there to meet him. It was awful. What's more, she might be here somewhere, wandering over this burning hot ground, stumbling over the tracks in which it was enmeshed, looking for him. But there were dozens of trains, thousands of carriages. She'd never find him, because the locomotive might come any moment and they'd be off. He was in an agony of irresolution. He'd make up his mind to go and look for his wife amid the trains and actually start, but every time his courage failed him. The thought that the train might leave without him frightened him. He could catch up with it, of course. But what would Danilov say? The old doctor was a little afraid of Danilov.

And here Danilov himself came past and greeted Dr. Belov with a military salute. They had not seen each other that day. There had been a Party members' meeting in the morning called to elect a Party organiser. The meeting elected Yulia Dmitrievna. Danilov had also voted for her because there was no one else, and now he was assailed by doubts. For all her masculine mannerisms, Yulia Dmitrievna was a woman. And the Party organiser would be faced with the problem of Dr. Belov. Which was, put in so many words, to shape him into a responsible head of their hospital train. And that was too much of a task for a woman's weak hands....

As Danilov saluted Dr. Belov, he felt a twinge of pity for the old chap. The doctor was walking about in full uniform just where the sun was hottest. The breast pockets of his tunic stood out in cast-iron squares. What on earth had he stuffed in them? A shiny nose protruded from under the shiny vizor of his cap, and sweat trickled down both sides of this nose. He looked as hard-heated as an iron roof.

"Hot, isn't it?" Danilov said.

"Oh, terribly," replied Dr. Belov. "D'you know, you can feel even through the soles of your boots how hot the gravel is."

"Just look where they've put us!" he continued. "It's a veritable railway jungle. I'm an old Leningrader, but I don't know this part of town at all."

Danilov made no response: what did it matter where they stood? What mattered was that they were not getting a move on. He could not know the cause of Dr. Belov's distress. He did not know that his chief was on the verge of tears.

"Ivan Yegorovich, are you on good terms with your wife?" he asked.

"What do you mean?" Danilov asked, taken by surprise. "She's a wife, that's all there is to it."

"No, you see, what I wanted to ask you was this...." Dr. Belov faltered. "What I mean to say is that it does happen that after living together for thirty years a husband and wife are not real friends, doesn't it?"

Danilov averted his eyes.

"It does, of course...."

"And sometimes the opposite happens," said the doctor, and suddenly his face lit up with tenderness, pride, and bashful adoration. Danilov was completely baffled.

A very tall, grey-haired woman appeared from behind the train next to theirs, and came towards them carefully picking her way over the tracks. She wore a plain grey dress and a small black straw hat of ancient vintage.

"Sonia dearest," the doctor said faintly. "I was afraid you wouldn't come in time. Ivan Yegorovich, may I present you to my wife.... Sonia dearest, this is Ivan Yegorovich, I would be lost without him."

The woman looked into Danilov's face and held out her hand. On her left arm hung a huge net-bag, stretched to the utmost with packages.

"Come, dear, I'll show you my compartment," mumbled the old doctor, flustered by his happiness. "You came alone.... Here, give me your bag.... Yes, of course, you came alone.... You're always alone, always...."

"Igor's digging trenches, and Lalya could not get off from work," his wife said, walking behind him. "I've brought your mittens, Nikolai, you left your mittens behind."

Look at that young gallant, Danilov was thinking as he watched the old doctor smartly helping his wife up into the coach. The heavy shopping net had left a deep red welt on her arm. The arm was wrinkled, pale and skinny.

* * *

The ventilator hummed in the compartment.

Doctor Belov and his wife were sitting close together, and he held her hand. The packages taken from the net-bag lay on the table.

"Sonia dearest, have you noticed that everything is very much like that evening when we said goodbye, d'you remember? And do you remember me saying that perhaps we were sitting like that together for the last time? And here we are again, eh? Only ten days later, eh? D'you know what I think? I think that we'll be sitting like this many, many more times. And you, do you think that too?"

She kissed him on his wet, salty forehead, and said softly:

"I think so too. But just now, please give me some water. Cold water, and plenty of it."

He sprang up and clutched his head in despair:

"Forgive me, dearest! I've been thoughtless as usual! You're worn out, you've been wandering through this jungle, looking for me! Oh my God!... Here, here's water in the carafe, but it's tepid and nasty...."

There was a knock on the door. Fima, a plump, florid nurse with a pleated beret on her head, danced into the compartment with a tray. On the tray stood a coffee pot, a dish of biscuits, and a jug of fruit water in which floated a large chunk of ice. Another face peeped from behind Fima's shoulder. Everyone was curious to see the chief's wife.

Dr. Belov gave a peal of happy laughter.

"Sonia, dearest, that's Danilov for you! I assure you it's Danilov's doing! What a wonderful person! Fima, who sent this, Danilov?"

Fima replied primly as she poured the coffee out:

"Comrade Sobol has asked me to tell you that a pork chop will be ready in ten minutes."

"Don't drink the coffee yet, Sonia dearest. Eat the pork chop first. Of course it's Danilov's doing, and not Sobol's. Sobol, who's in charge of supplies, you know, feeds us nothing but millet porridge, can you imagine it, nothing, nothing but millet porridge…. I didn't even know we had any pork. It's Danilov deciding to show off, of course. What a wonderful person! Ah, what a person he is! Fima, bring in the pork chop, bring it in, bring it in…."

His wife wanted him to share the pork chop with her. It was too hot to eat sizzling, fat pork, she could not eat it all anyway, and he knew very well that she was a spare eater. He would not have any, but when she fed him from her fork he swallowed the pieces of pork delightedly. It was marvellous luck, really marvellous luck that she had found him!

"But how *did* you find me? I never would, I'm sure…. Darling, forgive me my silly questions. What I meant to say was…. Ah, yes! They're not going to make you dig trenches, are they?"

"No, they're not."

"Naturally, naturally, not with your health…."

"No one's going to make me dig trenches. I'll do it of my own free will." Her face quivered. "They're beating us so terribly, Nikolai…."

He looked at her with something like diffidence.

"They are, yes, but it's only temporary…."

"Oh, I know it is! I saw a man from Vilnius. Such horrors…. I don't want to talk about it. What else did you want to ask me about?"

"About Lalya and Igor."

"Lalya is working. She says that most probably they will also be sent to the trenches any day now. Igor left with the first party."

"Where?"

"To Pskov."

She was crying. He dropped her hand and stared at her in alarm. She never cried before. He used to be jealous of Igor. Their son was a failure—he was lazy and rude, and was always gadding about heaven knows where. It hurt Dr. Belov that his wife forgave the boy everything and pampered him at the expense of their daughter. He believed that he understood her now: she had known that the boy would have a special lot in life, the lot of a soldier, and that's why she always said: "Never mind, he'll finish school, do his military service, and the army will knock some sense into him." She had known that he was fated to go digging trenches with the first group, and that's why she coddled and spoilt him....

"Dearest, don't cry!" he beseeched her. "You mustn't weep over him as if he were already dead, darling girl of mine!"

"I'm not weeping over him. I'd go myself if it wasn't for my work. I'm crying because I can't bear to hear these communiqués."

Her work, of course. He hadn't asked her anything about her work.

"The same old routine. It makes you mad sometimes that people can want new teeth at a time like this. The other day one fool woman wanted me to change her two steel caps for gold, and brought her own gold too. I lost my temper and told her it was hardly the time for it. She took offence, and went to find another dentist. To hell with her."

"To hell with her," he repeated automatically.

They sat without speaking for a long time, gazing at each other with loving, tear-filled eyes. The coffee, forgotten, went cold. And the ice melted in the untouched jug of fruit water.

Someone knocked on the door again. It was Danilov. He begged their pardon for intruding, but he had to tell Dr. Belov that the locomotive was going to be hitched on any moment now.

"Oh? So soon?" Dr. Belov asked. "It means we're off, Sonia dearest...."

Danilov went out first, leaving the couple to kiss goodbye in privacy. A few minutes later he watched the doctor's wife walking away between the tracks—tall and slightly stooped, with grey hair showing from under her old-fashioned black hat. The puny doctor, looking manlier in uniform, walked beside her with mincing steps, seeing her to the station.

* * *

Dr. Belov had kept a diary before the war. In his heart of hearts he felt himself a writer. After all, there were doctor writers like Chekhov and Veresayev. Well, he wasn't a novelist perhaps, and had more of a flair for political writing, like—"Like Marat," his wife suggested, when he once shared these thoughts with her. Her taunt hurt him, and he did not tell her about the diary. He kept it a secret from his family, the children especially. He did not know that his wife and daughter, each on her furtive own, read every word he wrote when he was out.

The diary afforded him so much pleasure because in a literary rendering the smallest happening assumed importance, and sometimes even grandeur. If he had to write something not very nice about an acquaintance, he called him X., Y. or Z. and never gave his real name. He wanted to spare these people who came over of an evening for a game of *preference* the unpleasantness when, after his death, these notes would be discovered and published. Before leaving home, he put his note-books into a file, tied it with string and sealed the knot with sealing wax.

Holding the file with both hands as if it were an icon, he gave it into the keeping of his wife with the words: "Keep this safe, Sonia dearest, and open it only in the event of.... You understand."

After this meeting with his wife, the urge to write came over him again. He opened a thick new note-book, delightedly sniffed its oilcloth covers, drew a sigh and wrote down:

"July 2, 1941. Sonia came to see me."

The urge was instantly satisfied. The train was moving at a smart pace. It was nice and cool in the compartment, and the fan was buzzing overhead.... She had sat there in that corner. Was she still waiting for her tram or had she gone on? The doctor dropped his head on the table, resting his forehead against the cool oilcloth of the notebook, and sat like this, without stirring, for a long, long time.

* * *

On the morrow, having pulled himself together, he made the following entry:

'A strange character, NN is. I understand I. Danilov, I understand our nice though rather formidable surgical sister, I understand the overblown maiden in the pleated beret who looks after me and is happiest when I praise the way she has folded my napkin; I understand the drunkard Z, I understand everyone on this train, all except NN. And yet he is the person closest to me on this train, at least he ought to be the closest. After all, we belong to the same profession and might have talked for hours, but for some unknown reason I don't feel like conversing with him at all. He always offers me cigarettes and it's very polite, but that's all there is to it — mere politeness. I tried to draw him out on the subject of current events: his comments were word for word citations from the official newspaper reports. I tried to draw him out on the subject of medicine: he agreed with whatever nonsense I purposely said. I asked him about his family, and he told me that he was a bachelor and lived with his very old mother. He is a book lover, I believe, and is carrying with him quite a sizable library. I asked him to lend me a book, he promised, looking strangely embarrassed, but still hasn't given me anything to read. I wouldn't call him unsociable: he will start a conversation with people, but leaves them to do all the talking while he does not commit himself at all. I have noticed that I.D. does not like him either."

Dr. Belov dipped his pen into the inkpot and remembering how old novelists wrote of their personages added:

"There is something mysterious and repulsive in him."

Fainna, the head nurse, also found Dr. Suprugov mysterious. But not repulsive. Far from it. He attracted her, and mainly because he was a mystery.

"Doctor, what are you so silent about all the time?" she would ask him, pushing against him with a hot shoulder. "I want to know. Share your thoughts with me."

Fainna was an exuberant and curvaceous woman in full bloom, taller than Suprugov, and perhaps under different circumstances her attention would have flattered him. But at the moment he could not be bothered.

Suprugov was frightened. That was the whole mystery about him.

He was frightened sick.

He specialised in throat, ear and nose diseases—a quiet speciality. His patients were for the most part adenoidal children and deaf old men. In the latter case Suprugov would put on a grave mien and perform all that was required of him conscientiously, but because he knew that his patient would live for another twenty years with his deafness he did not feel the acute sympathy and the respect for another's suffering experienced by surgeons, children's specialists and country GP's. Nor was he accustomed to the sight of suffering and death. His patients did not suffer: they felt discomfort but not pain. And when they died it was from some other illness which had nothing to do with Suprugov. He was glad that he had such a clean job. As for himself, he ran to the doctor with every trifle. Once he had an abscess on his finger. He shuddered at the memory. It had been awful! His mother had been amazed by his moans. "Does it really hurt so terribly?" she had asked.

She was a carefree person. Of her seven children six had died, she had known much pain and grief in life, and yet until the age of almost seventy she had kept the light burning in her eyes, a light entirely lacking in her son. She had grown somewhat•flippant in her old age, developing a passion for cards and the circus and letting the house more or less run itself, but on the whole they got on splendidly.

Suprugov collected books, works of sculpture, porcelain, and Palekh lacquer. In his study he had a chest where he kept his Chinese porcelain and Venetian glass. Not that he was very much of a connoisseur of Chinese porcelain, Palekh lacquer or Verhaern's poetry, he simply liked pretty things and adorned his flat with them. He made a point of attending all the conferences to which he was invited, he saw all the new plays showing, called on his acquaintances, listened to the radio, read the newspaper and subscribed to medical journals, but what he liked best was sitting in his room in solitude, smoking and feasting his eyes on his collections.

"I wish you'd marry, Pavel dear," his mother would say, coming home well after midnight. "You're always alone, so alone!"

But he did not want to marry. Women were such a bother, really. Paying them compliments was as far as he permitted himself to go with them. One heard so much about unhappy marriages, divorces, and family troubles.... And what of venereal diseases? Heaven forbid. And then was he alone so much? Most of his time he spent with his colleagues, didn't he? Once upon a time, in his very early youth, he did get involved in this love business. He had two love affairs, and what happened? Both ended in terrible unpleasantness.... And that was experience enough, he wanted no more of it, thank you very much.

"I don't like you," his mother would say, shaking her head doubtfully.

Laughing he would kiss her soft cheek: poor Mummy, she was losing her grip. Was there ever a better son? He provided her with everything she needed, including circus tickets. And, mind you, he had made his own way in the world. His father had been a salesman in a shoe shop, and he, Pavel Suprugov, was a doctor, an intellectual, a connoisseur of art. It was generally said that Soviet power had flung open the doors.... Very true, but a man had to have his own wits about him too.

Suprugov was perfectly satisfied with his life.

Was he as satisfied with himself? He couldn't have given a straight answer to this question. But it was no, rather than yes. Something was not quite right with him, he lacked something, but he did not know what. He could never *order* anyone to do anything, he could only ask. Others ordered people and were obeyed with alacrity. How did one *order* others? And why was one obeyed? Why didn't he, Suprugov, ever dare to order anyone? And were he ever to dare, he would not be obeyed anyway, and people would only be surprised.... Why did others argue hotly while he was always prompted to agree though he didn't really think the same? He only dared to voice an objection when he was worked up to the extreme, and even then until someone cut him short.... Why did other people say the rudest things to one another without taking offence, while he was so painfully hurt by the smallest thing?

To spare himself these hurts he tried to be as polite as possible to people, always offering everyone a cigarette and a light, and promising to repay any favours done him a hundredfold.

Others behaved as if they owned the earth. And he hung about in the doorway like an uninvited guest. Why did he?

He could not understand it.

However, he tried not to brood on it. He was content with what he had: a sound profession, a solid position, a clean record, and these dear bagatelles which so adorned his existence. What more did a person want for happiness, he asked?

The war made a mess of everything from the outset. Everything was blown to hell—security, placidity and dignity. He was used to listening to life as to a violin played outside the walls of his citadel, and here it had suddenly changed to a big drum, beating right into his ear!

He was drafted. What, with his weak health? Well, if his health was weak he could serve on a hospital train. But he was not a surgeon! He did not know how to extract bullets and apply plaster casts! Never mind, others would do this for him, and he would take care of the wounded on the way to a base hospital, nursing them back to health. And there was no need for him to worry—in case of need he'd be taught how to extract bullets too....

But he did not want to be crippled! He was afraid of bombs! He was afraid of suffering!

"Go and fight, Pavel child, it's all right, everybody's got to fight," his mother mumbled as she packed his things. Her head was shaking. He had not told her how terrified he was. Just then he hated her. He hated everyone. Why did they all pretend they were not scared? They all knew as well as he did about the demolition bombs, about the explosive bullets, about mustard gas, and about the savage cruelty of the enemies. How dare they pretend that they were not scared? How could they laugh, discuss the trivialities of life, eat icecream, and go to the theatre when everything inside them was howling with fear!

It was like a conspiracy of make-believe. They pretended so artfully that even he was deluded into believing that they really were not scared. There was nothing for it but pretend too. And so he handed his cigarettes round with tiresome insistence, chatted about trifles, and tried not to betray himself. At night he could not sleep. The train was heading for the front. Suprugov chain-smoked, and his hair turned grey by the hour. Dr. Belov told him of interesting cases from his practice. Fainna made advances to him. Nizvetsky, the electrician, came to consult him about his piles. Suprugov responded to all of them with his usual courtesy, while the beast inside him, gone mad from fear, howled and howled without a stop.

*   *   *

Sobol, the supplies manager, was in an agony of irresolution: should he disclose the true state of affairs to Dr. Belov, or should he leave it to time to whitewash him, Sobol, and expose Danilov?

It was not Sobol's fault that the staff had to live on millet porridge and watery, meatless soup. Such were Danilov's instructions.

"Listen, Sobol," Danilov had said to him. "I want you to forget that you have a store of meat, butter, cocoa and other good things. Just forget it."

"Forget it for good? Or perhaps I may remember about it sometimes?"

"I'll tell you when the time comes to remember."

Their fourth day on the road, Dr. Belov shyly approached Danilov and said:

"All is not well with our diet, you know. People are grumbling. Perhaps we should put a bit of pressure on Sobol?"

"Sobol is pursuing the correct policy," Danilov replied. "We don't know what circumstances we might find ourselves in very soon, and where we'll get our next supplies, what kind and how much. And, mind you, we'll have the wounded to feed. I think Sobol is perfectly right."

"Oh yes, of course," Dr. Belov hastened to agree, embarrassed by the thought that Danilov might think him a selfish glutton. "Yes, of course, we can't know where and how, and Sobol is quite right...."

Everybody cursed Sobol, everybody starting from the housekeeper to whom Sobol measured out the millet each morning, and ending with Kravtsov. The latter did not deign to have it out with Sobol personally, and had Kostritsin tell Sobol that he'd give him a hiding if he didn't change his scoundrelly ways.

The thought of going to Dr. Belov and making a clean breast of it then suggested itself to Sobol. Kravtsov, he guessed, was not the sort who made vain threats. And Sobol yearned for Dr. Belov's protection. He tried to catch the older man's eye all the time and to run into him as often as he could. Dr. Belov took a humorous view of Sobol: it amused him that he was always counting something and doing mental arithmetic.

Gazing heavenwards, Sobol would mutter under his breath: "Sixty seven times one hundred and twenty makes eight thousand forty, that's grams or roughly eight kilos."

He never plucked the courage to make a clean breast of it to Dr. Belov, for there was no telling how Danilov would react. The commissar had cold eyes and a small hard mouth. He would not do Sobol any physical injury, of course, but who'd want to make an enemy of a character like Danilov? A schemer, if there ever was one.

And then he had a brainwave. Taking his chance while people were having dinner in the staff car, he took a tin of liver paste from the store-room, sliced off a large piece of butter and looted the sugar box. Whispering, he counted the lumps: "Forty-two. Too much." He counted off twelve lumps and put them back. Stuffing all this in his pocket, he went to find Kravtsov. The man was asleep on the top bunk of the crew compartment with a newspaper over his face. Only his thin little beard showed. Sukhoyedov lay asleep on the bunk below. There was no one else in sight.

Sobol gave Kravtsov a careful nudge.

"Comrade Kravtsov," he whispered when the man had pushed the newspaper off his face and glared at him sleepily.

"You've no call to be angry with me, it isn't my fault at all."

"What stuff are you pulling now?" Kravtsov asked, sitting up and looking at the delicacies which Sobol was laying out on his lap. "Oh, Good God, sugar for the babe to suck!"

But Sobol's humility moved Kravtsov, and he forgave him.

This put Sobol's mind at ease. It was rather pleasant to be considered an influential person. He now changed to a facetious tone with the nurses.

"Oh, noble knight, it was Fainna!" he exclaimed, encountering the head nurse in the corridor.

Danilov overheard him and asked:

"What is it supposed to mean?"

"I'm least to blame for this, I swear!" Sobol raised both hands. "It's Pushkin who wrote it."

* * *

The war was gathering momentum, the Germans were forging ahead to the heart of the country, their motorcycles tore over Russian roads, their planes flew over Russian towns.

"Have you noticed?" Dr. Belov said to Danilov. "Our people are laughing. And cracking jokes. As if nothing was wrong."

"Good for them," Danilov nodded. After a moment's thought he said: "It's good that they haven't lost their sense of humour, but it's bad that they don't realise the size of the calamity. We're too isolated on this train, you see."

Dr. Belov remembered how his darling Sonia had cried. A shadow crossed his face.

"Do you think this calamity is so enormous?"

"I don't *think* it," Danilov gave a mirthless chuckle. "It's there for all to see." He dropped the words slowly, biting his lips, and Dr. Belov could see how painful it was for him to say this. "It won't end soon. The end is nowhere in sight. It had only just begun...."

"Our people, you know, will go to the extreme of sacrifice," Dr. Belov said.

"What sacrifice? You make a sacrifice to someone, don't you? You can't make a sacrifice to yourself. By sacrifice you actually mean the natural function of a nation, your function, my function, the function of our girls here. For our people heroism is not a sacrifice but one of its everyday manifestations. In order for us to go on living as a Soviet state, a part of us will, possibly, have to die today. Supposing I am killed, or you, or Petrov, or Ivanov. Would you call it sacrifice? Offered to whom? To me, to you, to Petrov, or to Ivanov? I'm sorry if I'm not making myself very clear, but...."

"I understand you perfectly, and I'm inclined to agree with you," said Dr. Belov. "But heroism I shan't cede to you. You'll never convince me that heroism does not exist and is merely a function or some such thing. Heroism, you see, is the beautiful in man, the heights to which human spirit can soar, and it is not everyone who is capable of heroism, one must have a talent for it, you know."

"Talent is developed," Danilov said. "The world will gasp at the way it is going to develop in our people during this war. It's not God who breathes talent into a man, talent is built up by a person's upbringing, it's cultivated by the world he lives in, by his environment," he finished, sweeping the cramped and narrow compartment with a quick, angry look.

Dr. Belov shook his head. He disagreed. Danilov, he thought, was simplifying the question. According to him anyone could be shaped into a Hero of the Soviet Union.

And Danilov did say it: "In the Soviet Union, every single person can be shaped into a hero."

"We have a population of two hundred million, if I'm not mistaken," said Dr. Belov. "Are two hundred million heroes possible?"

"Quite possible."

"Two hundred million minus one," Dr. Belov said with a smile. "You can't make a hero out of an old sack like me."

"Two hundred million minus one," said Danilov. "Two hundred million minus Suprugov."

Both laughed. Their serious conversation ended in a joke.

* * *

After his wife's visit to the train, Dr. Belov was haunted by one thought, sleeping or waking.

He might worry all he wanted about his train, about the situation at the front, about Suprugov and Sobol, he might eat, sleep, make entries in his diary, chat, joke and fret, but all the time this one thought kept a tight hold on his mind and heart, squeezing painfully every now and again to make him feel it better, and NOT FORGET!

It was the thought of his son.

In the evenings, when he remained alone in his compartment, he took off his heavy uniform, pulled on a pair of stripped summer trousers and went to bed partly dressed (in case of an air-raid: with all those nurses there he couldn't jump out in his underwear, could he?).

He lay down on the wide, plush-upholstered berth, closed his eyes, and the same instant his son sat down beside him and they had a good, long talk.

(Once upon a time it was the other way about: his son lay in his cot, and he sat down beside him and told him to stop playing and go to sleep.)

"Igor dear, how did this rift between us come about, son?" the father now asked.

As a little boy he was wonderful.

When he was two he climbed on to the roof of the side wing, climbing up the ladder left there by the roofers. The children playing in the yard called Sonia. She looked out of the window and saw Igor sitting on the edge of the roof, dangling his legs. Sonia gave a gasp and fainted. A woman who lived next door went up to get him, and when he saw her coming he ran up the roof to the chimney. Still, she managed to grab hold of him, and then he howled and kicked her, because he did not want to come down to the ground.

The woman who rescued him told Sonia that she should give him a good spanking so he'd know better next time, but Sonia just kissed and kissed Igor, and when the doctor came home and heard the story, he also hugged and kissed the child. To think that he was only two....

A year later, the doctor was walking down Karpovka, where they lived at the time, with the two children. Igor walked between his father and Lalya, who was seven or eight, and each held him by a hand. Suddenly a dog jumped out from a gateway and started barking furiously at them. Lalya dropped Igor's hand and hid behind her father. Igor broke free from his father, ran to the dog and barked at it: whoof! whoof! And the dog turned tail in fright.

His mother still dressed him like a little girl, and that day he had on a pretty blue dress with a pinafore, and his hair was long and curly like a girl's.

He was a brave, wonderful boy.

Danilov said that courage was a cultivated quality. Maybe so, maybe so. But how could courage have been a cultivated quality in a child of two? No, this didn't make sense. Perhaps there were two kinds of courage—one a cultivated quality, and the other an inborn trait of character....

It didn't matter, really. Igor, his son, was born brave. And not only brave. He was a sensitive and altogether extraordinary child....

They had a woman in to do their washing once a week, and Igor thought that Laundry was the name of this woman, and that's what he called her: Auntie Laundry. He'd dance around her and jump to look into the tub which was so excitingly full of foam and soap bubbles!

Once Auntie Laundry brought her little daughter along. The girl who was three years older than Igor taught him how to play noughts and crosses and a game with pebbles. Igor adored this girl. He wanted to hug and kiss her all the time. Sonia was quite jealous.

"Whom do you love best, Mummy or Lida?" she asked him.

"Lida, of course," Igor replied.

And then Igor's toys began to disappear. Sonia had not the heart to disillusion the boy, and so she kept quiet about it at first. But then she felt she had to tell him.

"Lida is a bad girl, Igor darling. You love her so much, and she has stolen all your best toys."

Igor did not say a word to this. He went into the dining room, climbed on to the large sofa, and sat there alone for a long time. His look—Sonia later told her husband—was bewildered and sad.

At last, he crawled down from the sofa, went to his mother and said:

"Let's not count it as stealing, all right? Let's count it as if I gave her my toys. And let her come again."

Lida came.

Igor's mother heard him saying to her when they were alone in the room: "Take my toys if you like. Any ones you want. The whole lot. I don't need them."

Oh darling boy, darling boy....

When he was six, he stole some money from his mother.

He had beautiful pale-gold curls which his mother treasured and refused to cut. Igor begged her to cut off these locks because everyone teased him "Goldilocks". But Sonia, with a mother's vanity and selfishness, told him:

"Just don't take any notice, they don't understand a thing. We'll keep your hair long for one more year, only another year, shall we?"

One day Igor ran away and returned home with his hair shaved off and his scalp lavishly sprinkled with some cloyingly sweet scent.

"Who did this to you?" Sonia cried, staring at his face which had lost its prettiness and had coarsened at once.

She almost wept.

"The barber," Igor replied. "I gave him three roubles and he sprayed me with scent all over."

"But where did you get the three roubles?"

"I stole them from your bag."

"But why did you steal the money?" his mother asked, horrified. "You ought to have asked me and I'd have given it to you."

"No," he shook his head. "You wouldn't."

She did not say another word of reproach. She stroked his round, plushy head, mourning his curls, and kissed him, kissed him—a madly, foolishly loving mother....

His schoolteacher also spoilt him. Igor would come home and tell his mother boastfully:

"When everybody's doing a sum, I go around to see how each one goes about it."

"And you, don't you have to do the same sum?"

"I'd have done it already."

"But why does the teacher let you walk about the room?"

"Oh, because she likes me."

* * *

How did this gradual loss of affection for his son come about?

For some time the doctor had been aware of feeling irritated by this terrible pampering, and by the atmosphere of adulation which surrounded Igor in their home.

After working all day, Sonia would stay up till three in the morning drawing his diagrams for Igor because he was too lazy to do it himself and had to hand them in next day. Disgraceful.

It was an unheard of thing: the boy went to school when he felt like it. And more often than not he did not feel like it. He came home from the skating rink or the pictures after eleven, and it was too much of an effort to get up early next morning.... And his mother—disgusting, really!—would write a note to school saying that the boy had a bad headache.

What was she trying to make Igor into? A prince? Or a bum?

The doctor was sorry for Lalya. The girl was an excellent pupil, she was affectionate, gay, and beautifully good-natured. And she did not receive even half the loving lavished on Igor.

When her father came home she always met him in the hall, shouting joyfully: "Daddy's come!", cuddling up to him and cooing like a little dove.

And when Igor appeared for dinner, he'd sit sprawling at the table, tousled and sullen, retorting rudely when spoken to.

And Sonia turned a deaf ear to anything the doctor said on the subject.

He could not quarrel with her. Sonia would always be his darling Sonia. To him she was sacred, he could not insult her. But everything about Igor irritated him. The way he sat. The way he snapped at his mother. He was so unaffectionate, so cold, and his manner so supercilious....

Once, the doctor made his feelings obvious in Igor's presence.

They had boiled beef for dinner. Lalya liked bone marrow. And so did Igor. So he always was given all of it. This time, too.

"Couldn't we, as an exception, let Lalya have it today?" he said quietly.

Sonia pretended not to have heard. And Lalya (the dear child!) said cheerfully: "Oh why, Daddy! Let Igor have it, I'm old enough not to mind!" Igor raised his eyes from his plate and looked into his father's face with a reflective and cynical (yes, cynical!) curiosity. And then he calmly began to dig the marrow out of the bone. The doctor watched him, feeling hot and distressed.

After that incident Igor started avoiding his father. Evidently, he had drawn his own conclusions from it. After all, the boy was only fifteen.... And he, the father, had not sought him out to clear the matter up. Oh Lord, oh Lord. How silly, petty, and ridiculous. What a terrible misunderstanding....

When the family came to the station to see him off—the doctor remembered it now—Igor, who had first stood a little apart, suddenly came and stood close beside him. And when they were saying goodbye, Igor bent down to his father, looked him straight in the face and said in a crisp, firm voice: "Goodbye, Daddy." There was a new look in his eyes, a strangely piercing look. Was it goodbye? Forgiveness? Reconciliation? What did that look mean? That's when he ought to have drawn Igor close and said to him: "Igor, my darling boy, whatever there was between us has been crossed out forever, we're turning over a new leaf, and we shall write this chapter together, you and I...."

Igor, dearest, what happened between us is not true, and what is happening now is the real truth, and we are facing it together, you and I....

Chapter Four

YULIA DMITRIEVNA

"Nurse Smirnova has forgotten to insert the mandrin" Yulia Dmitrievna said to Fainna, the head nurse, and compressed her thin lips meaningfully.

Fainna was busy with her own thoughts and her preoccupation of the moment: she was winding a length of gauze round her head to make a becoming turban. Turning away from the looking glass to glance casually at the hypodermic syringe which Yulia Dmitrievna was solemnly demonstrating to her, as material evidence, she said:

"But what did you give it to her for?"

"She gave an injection to the electrician. He was in terrible pain from his piles, and Doctor Suprugov told her to give him an injection of morphia."

Fainna made a face: ugly diseases revolted her. Only two days ago she had thought Nizvetsky, the electrician, a rather attractive young man. And he had piles, of all the nastiest things! He simply stopped existing for Fainna.

"This train is truly an assemblage of fossils and cripples," Fainna said.

But Yulia Dmitrievna was not to be put off, and continued to develop her theme:

"A nurse who forgets to insert the mandrin into the hypodermic syringe will never be any good, I assure you."

Fainna finished constructing her headdress, made eyes at herself in the mirror, and then turned to Yulia Dmitrievna. The ugliness of the woman was a fresh shock every time. What a sight she was, poor thing!

"You take all these trifles too much to heart," she said to her kindly. "Save your nerves, we have a hard time ahead of us."

Yulia Dmitrievna raised her eyebrows. Actually, she had no eyebrows to raise: instead there were two slightly bulging red arches, sprouting the bristles of an old toothbrush.

"This is not a trifle. Don't you know that the needle might go rusty without the mandrin?"

"Oh, I do," Fainna replied, swept by a passion of womanly commiseration. "But don't take it to heart, dear. Honestly, it's not worth it."

The toothbrushes crawled still higher.

"And who will if I don't? It's my duty to take things to heart."

She's stark, raving mad, Fainna thought. The impulse passed, and she felt bored.

"I shall be obliged, Fainna Vasilievna, if you, for your part, will tick off Nurse Smirnova. If this goes on we shall not be able to trust her with a single instrument from the dressing station."

"All right, I'll tell her," Fainna's tone was irritable now.

She flounced out of the compartment, and Yulia Dmitrievna said to herself, correctly reading Fainna's intentions: "Gone to show herself off in the turban."

She remained all alone. She looked over her small gleaming kingdom with pleasure. There was everything there, and everything in its right place. Here were the instruments for bone surgery, and here—for tracheotomy. The sterile robes were in the wall cupboard, and the gauze swabs were in the sterilisers. It was a bit cramped for the three of them, but then everything was within easy reach. Complete satisfaction reigned in Yulia Dmitrievna's soul.

And what foresight! A hospital train was not required to perform any surgery, only to dress wounds. But, look, what a splendid assortment of instruments they had, nothing had been forgotten, and if need be they could perform any operation under the sun, even a trepanation of the skull. Ah yes, one could really work here. It would be a pleasure to work here! The commissar was a worthy comrade, and the doctors were such nice people, Doctor Suprugov especially.

Yulia Dmitrievna had a crush on Dr. Suprugov.

She always had a crush on someone. The moment she found herself in a new environment, she took a look about her and picked the object of her future affections, falling in love at once.

At the city hospital she was in love with Professor Skuderevsky with whom she had worked for fourteen years. She had watched him grow old, receive two Orders, start and finish a large treatise on the surgical treatment of malignant growths, fall ill with brucellosis and recover from it— and all the time she loved him.

She was untrue to the professor three or four times, falling in love with his young assistants. But old love is true love, as the saying goes, and she always went back to it, scolding herself for a feather-brained girl.

The professor knew nothing of this. Nor did the young assistants. Nobody suspected anything. Nobody regarded Yulia Dmitrievna as a woman. Professor Skuderevsky would have been astounded by the discovery that she was in love with him. Noone ever spoke to her on personal matters.

Just once, when the professor said to her:

"I'm glad you're not married."

(Noone told him, it was obvious).

Her heart seemed to stop beating.

(Although she knew that he was married, that he and his wife had just celebrated their silver wedding anniversary, and that he had grandchildren.)

"Why?" she quavered.

"I couldn't work with a married nurse," he told her. "A theatre sister must have nothing but work on her mind."

That night she walked home slowly along the dark and now deserted boulevard, going over this brief conversation again and again. She used to think that she had sacrificed her private life for suffering mankind. No, it wasn't that: it was for him, for Professor Skuderevsky, that she had denied herself wifehood and motherhood. This had a sadder and sweeter sound. It was a sacrifice made for him. Laid on the altar of her love....

At the Finnish front she had a crush on the brigade surgeon. But it was a brief campaign, and her love was as fleeting as a dream.

Here in the hospital train, her choice wavered for a time between Danilov, Dr. Belov and Suprugov.

Danilov was discarded first. "He's not refined enough," Yulia Dmitrievna decided.

Doctor Belov had features which gave him a kinship with the unforgettable Professor Skuderevsky: hair turning grey, bags under the eyes, a pleasant voice.

"No, in wartime one can have only formal relations with one's commander, there must be nothing else," she told herself.

This left Suprugov.

Her new passion did not interfere with her pattern of life. She worked tirelessly, slept like a top, and ate enough for four.

Were she asked: do you want to have a handsome, loving

husband on condition that you give up your work forever,
she would raise her eyebrows and answer: no!

Her work was her life, her soul, her hands. Work had given
her the place in life which Nature had denied her. To be
deprived of work was tantamount to being deprived of her
hands, of her soul, of her life.

She understood very well that love was not for her. She'd
look piteous and funny if her crushes became known. She
was proud. She did not betray her feelings. All these
feminine illusions of hers were hidden deep in the farthest
corner of her very healthy heart, and kept securely under
lock and key.

Yulia Dmitrievna's parents were ordinary people like any
other and their looks were ordinary too. By an inexplicable
trick of fate both their sons were remarkably handsome
boys, while their only and longed for daughter was
remarkably ugly. Yulia's mother wept and prayed the Lord
to take away some of the boys' handsomeness and give it to
the poor little girl, but with time she became reconciled. As
the years passed she even began to find a certain attractive-
ness in Yulia. The father often picked up the family
album and studied the faces of their relatives, both close and
distant, wondering which one of them could have handed
down such unfortunate features to his child. And finally he
did find the culprit. It was Yulia's great-grandfather, a Greek
who once owned a grocery store in Nizhni-Novgorod.

"I remember him," Yulia's father said. "He was wheeled
about in an invalid chair and was always playing solitaire. A
tray would be placed on his knees and he would lay out the
cards on it. He lived to be a hundred and four. A fine looking
old man he was."

"Really? And our Yulia looks like him?" asked the mother.
"She does, you know."

Yulia's mother nodded thoughtfully and said: "I didn't
know she had Greek blood in her."

This Greek blood lent the family grief an air of mystery
and exotic romance. No, Yulia was not pretty of course, but
there you had it—Greek blood!

Unfortunately one couldn't go and whisper into every
man's ear what the matter was. And men were so mean to
Yulia. Not one of them ever paid the slightest attention to
her, not one. They were much too hard to please. They didn't
realise what a treasure dear Yulia was.

Needless to say, the subject was taboo in the family. They
considered themselves civilised people. The father was a

feldsher. He liked to run down the young doctors whose patients, he claimed, trusted only himself. True enough, every evening women came knocking on his backdoor and he gave them pills and powders.

The two boys also chose medical careers: one was a pharmacist and the other a veterinary surgeon. Both were handsome like Greek gods. Their excessive popularity with women kept them too busy to go in for a higher education. When they had sowed their wild oats they married plain, jealous wives, fathered a brood of children, regretted their madly squandered youth, and envied their father his steady backdoor practice.

Of the whole family the mother alone had nothing to do with medicine. But she, too, learnt how to treat various illnesses. If patients came when her husband was out she would ask them what their complaint was and, judging by the symptoms, doled out either salol with belladonna (for a stomach-ache) or pyramidon (for a headache).

Yulia Dmitrievna had now been working as a theatre sister for twenty-two years.

She looked down on her family. She despised her father's backdoor practice. Her elder brothers, shiftless men with large families, were overawed by her.

They had weaknesses; they had made too many mistakes in the course of their lives; there were too many subjects on which they still lacked a clear-cut, sustained view although they had already drifted into middle age.

Not so Yulia Dmitrievna. She had no weaknesses (the ones under lock and key didn't count); she had not made a single mistake in all her life, and there was nothing on which she did not have a firm opinion.

The family recognised all this, and deferred to Yulia's superiority.

The mother ran the house. She dispensed the housekeeping money, she had the keys and the power over the pots and pans and the linen. The father sat at the head of the dinner table, he was the head of the family, and a porcelain door-plate with his name on it was nailed to the front door. But the real mistress of the house was Yulia. Because everything she did and said was right and virtuous. And virtue was sincerely revered in this family where each member had his own little sins.

In the hospital too, in the theatre rather, it was not Professor Skuderevsky at all who was boss—it was Yulia Dmitrievna once again. The staff knew it and a twitch of her eyebrows frightened them much more than the professor's fits of fury. When Yulia Dmitrievna came down with the 'flu, the professor refused to perform any serious operations until she was well again. This further confirmed the general opinion that Yulia Dmitrievna had less need of the professor than the professor had of her.

* * *

The door of the dressing station was pushed open roughly, and Suprugov came in.

"I believe we're arriving," he said. He was wild-eyed.

The train was running through the same country of woods and meadows. The sun was setting, the edge of the distant woods was illumined with a fiery glow, and the shadow cast by the train ran along the grass-grown embankment.

"Pskov is sixty kilometres to go," Suprugov said. "Have you noticed that we haven't stopped once since morning?"

He came to tell her this because she was the only person in whose eyes he saw human consideration and kindness. All the others disliked him, it was like a conspiracy, really. Fainna, it is true, was favourably inclined, but she was practising her feminine wiles on him, nothing else. Women had never excited him, and now they simply revolted him.

"They're taking us straight under the bombs," he said.

"I know nothing about this," Yulia Dmitrievna replied rather coldly.

"Take a good look at these trees," he said. "Maybe we're seeing them for the last time."

Tears rose to his eyes. Yulia Dmitrievna sighed. She had no fear of bombs. In the Finnish campaign she was a front-line nurse. It was nice to have him standing beside her and talking to her. Hers was a lover's sigh.

"Look! Look!" Suprugov cried. The forest parted, revealing a stretch of highway between its dark wings, in a cloud of dust. The highway was crowded with troops and slowly moving guns. Tarpaulin-covered lorries came in a thick stream. A man on horseback galloped along the side of the road, overtaking the vehicles. The picture flashed past, and vanished behind the wing of forest.

"They're retreating, and we're going where they're retreating from," said Suprugov.

"I can't see that it's a retreat," Yulia Dmitrievna objected. "How do you know that they're retreating? They may be simply shifting the troops. We can't know about such things."

"We do know," Suprugov raised his voice. "We do know that we're retreating, all the war communiqués say so, and yet you pretend that everything's fine. What are you pretending for? You don't know it yourself."

Why had he raised his voice? He had never dared raise his voice before. What made him so confident that he could speak to her like that?

"I do not believe that everything is fine, far from it," she replied calmly. "I simply said that they may be shifting the troops and not retreating. You've no proof that it's a retreat."

She compressed her lips into a stubborn line. There were certain points she would not cede. Not even in the name of love.

* * *

Black smoke flowed past the windows. The sun was still out, but it seemed that dusk had descended on the world. Breathing became difficult.

"It smells of fire," Danilov said. He and Dr. Belov were standing in the corridor of the staff coach. The highway here ran on a higher level than the train, and along it guns, lorries, and infantry were moving in a dense stream. Even Yulia Dmitrievna would have admitted now that it looked like retreat more than anything else. The troops were heading in the opposite direction to that of the hospital train.

"We're relinquishing Pskov," Danilov said quietly.

Doctor Belov breathed noisily as he looked out of the window and thought: has Igor left Pskov, has he left in time? It was a fantastic thought, of course, that he might find the boy amid this crowd of people. But supposing they did meet? How glad Sonia would be! He'd take Igor into the train as a male attendant. Danilov wouldn't let him play the fool, and in two or three months' time Igor would become meek as a lamb. And then, Dr. Belov would take him home to Sonia and say: "That's a man's upbringing for you...."

"We ought to close the windows before the soot has settled on everything," Doctor Belov said aloud. And to the head nurse who happened to be passing: "Fainna Vasilyevna, please have the windows closed."

It turned out that the ward nurses had already done so without waiting for orders, and Fainna had scolded them for it and ordered them to open all the windows again.

"It's silly," she replied to Dr. Belov with a shrug. "If they're closed all the panes will be smashed at the first blast."

She proceeded on her way. Doctor Belov and Danilov merely exchanged eloquent glances.

"What about the pharmacy car?" asked Dr. Belov.

"Can't be helped," Danilov replied grimly. The windows of the pharmacy car were hermetically sealed.

Further down the corridor Fainna ran into Sobol who greeted her with his usual: "Ah, noble knight, it was Fainna!" and stepped aside to let her pass. She swished her skirt against his knees and, without vouchsafing him a glance, went into her compartment. She detested Sobol for keeping her on a diet of millet porridge. Fainna had a particularly dashing and bellicose look that evening. Like Yulia Dmitrievna, she had also had her share of front-line experience in 1940. She knew what she'd be in for tomorrow, or perhaps this very night, or even this very hour. In the privacy of her compartment, she first took a look at herself in the mirror, then checked the contents of her first-aid bag, and after that sat down to rest up for the serious work ahead. She'd be damned if she didn't show every one of them that making gauze turbans wasn't all she was good for! She examined her hands with pride. They were a nurse's efficient hands with short, thick fingers, permanently stained with iodine and sublimate, and the nails were trimmed short.

"What d'you say, shall we have some supper?" Sobol asked, poking his head round the door.

"And what do *you* think?" Fainna demanded. "You'd be glad if you didn't have to feed us at all."

"Oh, I would," Sobol admitted. "This feeding business is such a bother. But seriously, is it all right to offer people supper just now? On the threshold, so to speak, of events."

"You make me sick," Fainna snapped at him. "This is the very time to give people a good square meal."

Danilov was standing behind Sobol.

"For supper, in addition to porridge, issue some beef, one tin for four people, and for tea issue some condensed milk in the same proportion," he ordered Sobol crisply.

Sobol was not really anticipating any events, he was simply baiting Fainna, and Danilov's order caught him unawares. The commissar was lifting the ban on the tinned beef and condensed milk, was he? This obviously meant that major events were expected. And Sobol started on his whispered calculations: "One tin for four…. Sixty seven divided by four, that's three over, so let's take sixty eight…."

"Thanks a lot, Comrade Commissar," Fainna said when Sobol was gone. "This millet porridge is enough to drive you crazy, you know."

"But what can we do? We're heading for the front, there's no knowing what food, if any, we'll be able to find there. I wanted to give you a word of warning: mind how you talk to Dr. Belov. The way you just talked to him won't do."

"And how did I talk to him?" Fainna asked in surprise.

"You told him: 'It's silly'. He gave you an order, and you told him it was silly."

"Heavens above! Did I mean *him*? I meant the ward nurses."

"Even if you don't agree with the orders he gives you, you must…."

A sudden jolt sent the tin cup clattering down to the floor from the small table, and the door would have slammed shut if Danilov had not held it with his shoulder.

"Oho!" Fainna said, and her eyes glittered. "Off we go!"

There was another jolt, harder than the first.

"I'm sorry, of course, Comrade Commissar," Fainna said. "I'm not a novice and I ought to know what discipline is. But remember that I am a woman first and foremost, and that I also have nerves…."

She paused to listen. She wanted to experience another jolt. *A la guerre comme à la guerre,* so what the hell!

* * *

They had supper.

The train crawled at a snail's pace, hardly moving at all sometimes. The highway along which the troops were retreating had again turned away from the railroad. What could be seen through the windows now were the suburbs of Pskov—timber cottages, vegetable plots and commons surrounded by wattle fences. Somebody's summer residence flashed past—four scorched walls with paneless windows and no roof. A village was burning brightly, and behind it a wheat field was smouldering, wreathed in clouds of dark smoke. The ground was welted with freshly dug ditches. There were hardly any people to be seen.

The jolting was incessant now. The continuous roar of a nearby barrage was distinctly audible above the rumbling of the train wheels.

Yulia Dmitrievna stood at the window of the dressing station. So this was the territory that was going to fall into enemy hands. Pskov. She had been to Pskov before. Their relatives lived there and as a girl she once stayed with them. There were no tramcars in those days, there probably were now, and a cabby took them to the house from the railway station. The lime trees were in bloom then, she remembered. And Pskov smelt of honey. It was late evening, the sky was tawny and warm, and the churchbells were ringing, slowly, majestically.... Her aunt always said: "We're Pskov people," with a peculiar intonation which seemed to imply that there were no finer folk in all of Russia than Pskovians. What was the town like now? Like that roofless dacha? Or that village, burning like a bonfire? The troops were leaving it, and there it stood, mutilated, smoking, with ditches dug all around it....

But Yulia Dmitrievna was not to see the town.

The train crawled for a long time over intersecting tracks between strings of freighters, the roar was deafening, and one could not see anything for the black smoke outside the windows. When the smoke parted for a minute, a patch of sky, a deep pink colour from the reflected fires, showed in the gap. The train came to a standstill.

"Klava," Yulia Dmitrievna called the ward nurse. "Go to the staff car and find out where Dr. Belov and the commissar are."

It worried her that she was standing there and doing nothing when it was perfectly obvious that there were people all about them needing help.

"Ask if they've any instructions for me."

"In a minute, Yulia Dmitrievna," Klava replied. "I'll run along the tracks, all right?"

"Don't you know that orders say none of us must leave the train? Go through the coaches."

Klava hurried off. The train which had been blocking the view from the dressing station window started off. Its sealed cars flickered past one after another. The train left town. There was one more train standing on the tracks beyond, but it did not block the view entirely, and Yulia Dmitrievna saw the tongues of a great fire leaping up into the ominously pink, smoky sky. The hospital train started moving forward. It came out into the glow of fires and stood there fearlessly

with its red crosses, alone and unprotected, while fires raged
to the left and right of it.

Klava came back.

"Well, what have they got to say?" Yulia Dmitrievna
asked.

"Dr. Belov said to tell you not to go away anywhere. The
commissar has gone to the clearing station for orders."

"Where does he think I could go?" Yulia Dmitrievna
enquired in a supercilious tone.

The train was on the move again. It was rolling into the
station. There were fires all around, and nobody tried to put
them out. People were dashing about frantically. Four men
stood on the edge of the platform: three civilians with bags,
and Commissar Danilov.

"They're surgeons," Klava told Yulia Dmitrievna, having
made another quick trip to the staff coach to find out. "The
clearing station has given us three surgeons, they'll operate
on the wounded here."

Surgeons! Yulia Dmitrievna's heart leapt in anticipation of
some real work. Therapy, indeed! What could therapy do?
From Yulia Dmitrievna's point of view therapy was not a
medical science, it was more like chiromancy. And now real
medical science had come to the hospital train in the person
of these three civilians with the bags. So operations were
going to be performed in the hospital train. Debridement of
the wounds.

Her mind worked quickly: three surgeons would want
three operating tables. One they had at the dressing station,
two they'd put in the scrubbing room. They had enough
instruments; enough gloves and coats. Who'd do the
assisting? Yulia Dmitrievna herself, naturally. Then Suprugov. No, he had weak nerves. It had better be Olga
Mikhailovna, the feldsher. And then Fainna Vasilievna.

"Klava, put the black-out blinds on the windows of the
scrubbing room, and switch on the light. Take those flounces
off the lamps. Wash the table with sublimate."

Crash! The window was blasted, and bits of glass flew into
the dressing station.

Klava made the sign of the cross. She had never done it
before, and suddenly she crossed herself now without really
knowing why.

Yulia Dmitrievna gave her a scathing look and said:

"I'll wash the table myself. Sweep up the broken glass, will
you."

Real work was beginning.

* * *

Fainna had been quite right: within half an hour not a window pane was left in the pharmacy car.

The ward nurses were told to sweep up the pieces. They were frightened. Two of the girls were crying from fear, and even more so from vexation that the Germans were ruining such a beautiful coach.

"And I tried so hard to keep it tidy!" Klava was saying brokenly as she collected the bits of glass into a metal dust-pan.

Iya, the fat girl, lost her nerve and bolted from the train. A shell hole behind the burning station building seemed to offer the safest shelter, and she stayed there overnight. She was not missed. She returned to the train the next day of her own free will: she was grimy with dust and soot, clots of earth were entangled in her hair, and her eyelashes were singed.

Danilov called a group together: medical personnel and soldiers. Nizvetsky, the electrician, came too.

"I'm coming with you," he said.

"And what about the lighting?" Danilov asked.

"Kravtsov will keep an eye on it. He knows what to do. And it's light now anyway...."

"No, we'll need artificial light today, there'll be operations."

"But Kravtsov...."

"Never mind Kravtsov. Kravtsov is a machine operator, and you're the electrician. So you'll have to stay behind."

"I, for one, am not staying behind, whatever you say," Fainna said. "I'm a field nurse, bombs and shells are nothing to me!"

Danilov could not help smiling at this boastfulness.

"Sorry, Fainna Vasilievna, I can't let you come," he told her. "Dr. Belov plans to use you in surgery."

"Oh hell, I never have any luck!" She handed her bag to Lena Ogorodnikova who stood on the platform with her hands behind her back and her boyish head tilted, and said: "Here, take my bag, girlie. Take it, you're a good girl, you've guts."

"Well then, doctor," Danilov said to Suprugov. "Let's get cracking."

Suprugov was hanging on to the handrail and it seemed he could never loosen his hold on it. He turned his dead face to Danilov. He was going to say something, when a bomb exploded on the tracks quite close, hitting both Danilov and Suprugov with a spray of coal dust.

Suprugov seemed to understand something.

"Finita!" he said, and let go of the handrail.

Later, retrospectively analysing his emotions, he defined them as a realisation, or so he imagined, that death was unavoidable. Also, or so he imagined, that it would be terrible. And he wanted it to be over and done with as soon as possible. Let there be nothing, nothing, nothing. Above all, let there be no fear any more. Peace, quiet, safety.... And for this, he had to get where it was most dangerous, quickly, quickly. "Here I am!" everything screamed in Suprugov when he stepped on the platform ominously illumined by the fires and hacked up by shells. "Here I am, hurry up and finish me off, I can't go on being afraid any more!"

Danilov took him by the hand, and Suprugov ran after him, his heavy boots thudding. It was very hot. The smoke made their eyes smart.... At the back of the station building, in a side street they came upon a soldier who was dragging his rifle along the ground, smearing the trail of blood he left behind him.

"Is it far to the hospital train?" the soldier asked. "They told me to go to the hospital train."

"It's over there, behind the hut, you'll see it," Danilov replied. "Can you make it or shall we carry you?"

"I'll make it," replied the soldier. "You'll need the stretchers yet."

Around the corner, a boy of fourteen or so lay on the ground. He was conscious, he did not moan, and watched the approaching group with stern, burning eyes.

"Stretcher, here," Danilov ordered, and Lena bent down and picked the boy up in her arms as though he were a baby. Suddenly he began to thrash about, tilted up his head and fainted.

"Don't grab if you don't know how," Sukhoyedov flared out at her. "Think you're playing dolls. Put him down on the stretcher, don't stand there gaping!"

Something screamed, mewed, and exploded quite near. A black cloud enveloped the hospital group. When it settled Danilov called out:

"Everybody whole?"

They were deafened and covered with soot, but otherwise they were all right.

Suprugov had a crazy smile on his soot-black face.

"Take the youngster to Yulia Dmitrievna," Danilov told

Sukhoyedov and Medvedev. "The rest, follow me! You'll catch up with us afterwards, and if you don't—pick up any wounded you find and take them to the train."

When they had started down the street again, Suprugov asked: "What was that, a shell or a mine?"

"A mine. Why?"

Suprugov coughed and spat out black saliva. The shoulder of his tunic was torn.

"Hey, have you been hit?" Danilov asked.

"Have I? Where? Oh, here? It's nothing, it doesn't hurt a bit. It just glanced off me. It's one of those small things, not worth talking about."

He felt drunk. He staggered from the sense of his own insane bravery.

* * *

Dr. Belov was walking up and down the train.

Currents of hot air raced through the empty coaches with the wide-open windows. A smoky, shifting light from outside lit everything up. Only this morning these coaches had seemed so cosy....

There was a ward nurse and a soldier in each coach. Frightened, and waiting, with nothing to do.

The staff car was deserted: everyone, except the people on duty, had gone off with Danilov.

Dr. Belov walked down the train thinking distractedly: "There's something I forgot to do ... there's something I forgot to do...." He just could not remember what.

He'd seen to everything, he believed. The surgeons had been installed in the pharmacy car, and they knew what to do. A group had been sent out to collect the wounded. Danilov was in charge, and he could be relied upon.... Ah, yes, food. People had to be given supper. And breakfast, too, next morning.

"Sister Smirnova, please have someone call Comrade Sobol, I'd like to speak to him."

Sobol did not keep him waiting. Dr. Belov glanced at him with a fleeting and involuntary curiosity: was he doing mental calculations or not? He was not. He looked strangely limp and shrunken, like a deflated baloon.

"Look here, supper must be prepared, for...." Dr. Belov thought for a moment, and said: "For a hundred and twenty people, yes, a hundred and twenty. A good supper."

"We've already had supper," Sobol mumbled.

"A good supper, you know," Dr. Belov repeated, ignoring the objection. "For the wounded, you know, who will begin to come in today. Not your orphanage gruel, you know, but something like semolina pudding with jam or something, and see that there's coffee, biscuits and butter, you know what I mean."

"Butter?" Sobol echoed like a sleep-walker.

"Yes. Fifty grams per person."

"Fifty grams, fifty times one hundred and twenty makes six thousand," Sobol began to whisper at once, staring at the ceiling. "That makes six kilos...."

And suddenly Dr. Belov remembered.

He had not done anything to try and find Igor. Obviously, he could have done something. Rung someone up. Put in an inquiry. Gone somewhere, asked someone.... Nonsense. Ring up whom, go where, ask whom? No, no. Something could have been done certainly. It's just that he did not know how to go about it. Sonia would have known what to do. He was slow-witted in such matters, he always had been slow-witted. Sonia would have found a way because she loved Igor. Real love always finds the way, real love can do anything. He did not love Igor enough, he always loved him too little, he was a useless, inept, bad father. He was fonder of Lalya. But was she so much better than Igor? Fancy hairdos, musical comedy, and flirting, was all she had on her mind. She was a cuddly little thing, that's all. She cuddled up to him and he gave her the money to go to the musical comedy, and when Igor once asked him for some money he needed, he had refused. A miserable thirty roubles, too.... Oh my darling boy, forgive me! Take everything, take my old, waning life, only please live! Please be found! Please don't go away so suddenly, son....

*   *   *

When Yulia Dmitrievna was leaving home to serve in the army, her two brothers with their wives and children, and all their relatives came to see her off. Pies were baked and icecream was made as for a birthday party. Yulia Dmitrievna herself pushed the tables together and covered them with their best white tablecloths.

And here she was again shifting tables about and covering them with white linen.

The first wounded arrived: the soldier who had been sent

on by Danilov. He put his rifle in a corner, and surveyed the
pharmacy car matter-of-factly.

"Which table do I lie down on?" he asked.

One could see right away that he was a smart chap who'd
had such experiences before.

"Any one you like," Yulia Dmitrievna told him graciously.
"Just take your things off first. What is it, your leg? Klava,
rip his boot open."

Yulia Dmitrievna stood holding a sterile coat for the
professor, waiting for him to finish scrubbing his hands.
These white, slightly puffed hands were exactly like
Professor Skuderevsky's. The curtains in the scrubbing room
had been drawn, and blinding white lamps were burning over
the tables. It hadn't occurred to anybody how absurd it was
to drape the windows in order to hide this light, when the
whole train was illumined by the fires outside.

Klava finished ripping the soldier's boot, and turned away
in horror.

"What's the matter with you?" The soldier asked, screwing
up his face with disdain. "Not used to it yet? Why, it's just a
scratch, if you want to know, even the bone is intact."

Yulia Dmitrievna helped the professor into a white coat,
poured some alcohol into his crimson palms, and handed him
his gloves. The handsome old professor who looked like an
actor, looked puzzled to see her pleased face.

But it only took him a couple of minutes to understand her.
She was performing a rite. He did not have to ask her for
anything, she needed no prompting. She handed him
everything he needed before he knew he'd be wanting that
very thing next.

The soldier endured the cleaning of his wound stoically,
without a moan, and only puffed noisily now and again. Yulia
Dmitrievna adored such patients. She hated people who
screamed. She was so engrossed in her work that she no
longer heard the noise outside. The only thing that worried
her was the heat. It was unbearably stuffy in the coach, and
the ventilator hardly helped. She picked up a gauze swab
with a pair of tweezers and mopped the patient's perspiring
face.

"Thanks, Mother," he said.

The boy with the shattered shin was brought in. He was
unconscious. He had beautiful muscles: he must have played
football and cycled.... At a glance Yulia Dmitrievna saw that
his leg would have to be amputated, she saw it before the
professor did.

"Damn the nazi swine," Fainna said, looking at the boy.

He jerked his chin and gritted his teeth.... The professor asked Yulia Dmitrievna:

"Can you give the anesthetic?"

Heavens, could *she* give the anesthetic! If the whole truth be told, she could perform the amputation. She did not undertake to do it only because she did not have the formal right.

She placed an ether cone on the boy's face. Fainna, when she heard the sound of the saw cutting through the bone, walked away to the window and cried.

Dr. Belov came in.

"Am I needed?" he asked.

Yulia Dmitrievna gave him a swift glare. He came up timidly, craning his neck, and peering at the boy.... A woman was lying on the operating table in the scrubbing room.

"The boy is to go into coach number eleven," Dr. Belov said to Nurse Smirnova who had accompanied him. "And the woman...."

"No need," said Olga Mikhailovna who had been assisting the surgeon at the second table. She took the mask off the woman's face. It was a broad, Slav face with high cheekbones. Slender black eyebrows. A beautiful mouth. A line of brown freckles on the nose.

"It was too late," said the surgeon.

Suddenly, the surgeon was flung against the other table, on top of the boy, the boy was thrown down on the floor, and everyone fell down, everyone but Yulia Dmitrievna who was hurled to the door of the dressing room and held her feet by clutching at the towel rail. Bits of white paint dropped from the walls and ceiling. A piece of the split door-frame jabbed Yulia Dmitrievna on the side of her head.

"This was very near somewhere," said Dr. Belov.

"Very," confirmed Yulia Dmitrievna, picking up the boy. "I should say it was a direct hit."

* * *

Privates Kostritsin and Medvedev rushed in from opposite ends of the coach, shouting:

"Coach 14 is on fire! Where's the chief?"

Dr. Belov was already running along the platform to the burning coach as fast as his legs could carry him.

The coach was burning hotly—dry wood, dry paint. Thank God there were no wounded in that coach yet. Were the personnel all right? Oh, they were, they were: there was Nadya, bent over and spitting.... She had blood on her coat.

"Nadya, what is it, are you wounded?"

"Heavens, no. I bruised my mouth against a shelf."

"And is Kostritsin all right?"

"Sure, he's gone to fetch you...."

There was Kostritsin now, running to the burning coach with a pail of water. Nothing much could be done with a pail here.... And there was Medvedev coming behind him. And Kravtsov and Nizvetsky approaching from the other end of the train. They shuffled as though their kneecaps were smashed.

"Quickly, boys, come quickly!" Dr. Belov shouted.

Nizvetsky broke into a trot. Kravtsov did not hurry a step, and shuffled on with his hands thrust deep into his trouser pockets.

"Bring water, boys," Dr. Belov ordered in a flurry of excitement. "Call everyone, we're going to put out the fire."

"What water, where is it?" Kravtsov asked carelessly.

"Why, there's water in the tanks. There's water in the locomotive...."

"That's chicken feed, not water," Kravtsov said, and suddenly yelled: "Hey you, unhitch that coach! The fools, the generator's next door, and they just stand there pop-eyed!" He grabbed hold of a greaser who was walking past, and begged him: "You're a specialist, help us. This here coach has got to be unhitched."

"Let go of me! Hundreds of coaches have perished, and you think I'll bother with this trash?" the greaser shook Kravtsov off.

"You've got to, precious," Kravtsov said grimly. "There are the wounded here and the generator there, so there's no other way but to unhitch."

"You tell your mother to unhitch trains under fire," the man said.

"And I'm telling *you*!" Kravtsov snarled and hit the man on the jaw. Dr. Belov was speechless. The greaser kicked Kravtsov in the stomach, and received another slog. He swore foully, and went off to unhitch the coach. The conductor of the train appeared from somewhere: judging by the dirt on him he must have been hiding in a shell hole. The burning coach was moved off, and men started putting the fire out with water from the tender.

All this while Yulia Dmitrievna stood beside the operating table and handed instruments and swabs to the professor. She prepared the wounded for their operations. Gave the anesthetic.... The bombardment of the town continued all through the night, and all through the night the wounded kept arriving. Some were brought on stretchers, some in lorries, and some made their own way to the train. Towards morning the professor begged off.

"I'm done up," he said, ripping the strings of his coat, too exasperated to bother with the knots. "I can't take any more. It's the fifth day that I...."

Fainna took him to the staff car where he could get some sleep. She told Yulia Dmitrievna that she'd also take a little time out and change. The sight of blood was already turning her stomach, and her underwear was soaked with sweat.

"I give up too," said the second surgeon, a small, dark man with a sallow face. Olga Mikhailovna curled up on the sofa right there in the scrubbing room, muttering in a childish voice: "I'll be up in a minute, I'll be up in a minute," and instantly falling fast asleep.

Only the third surgeon remained—he was a young man, taller than Danilov, with cropped flaxen hair and a beaked nose.

"Shall we?" he said inquiringly, looking at Yulia Dmitrievna.

"Shall we!" she replied with readiness and went over to his table.

The two of them worked in silence. The coach shook from the shelling, but they worked on without pausing to wonder how long it was till morning, how soon the bombardment would end, and when they would get some sleep. The surgeon whistled softly as he worked, a beautiful tune. Yulia Dmitrievna liked it.

Olga Mikhailovna woke up about two hours later, and rushed off to rouse the others. The first to return was Fainna, looking as fresh as a daisy, and next came the old professor.

"You're still up, I see," he said contritely to Yulia Dmitrievna, and started scrubbing up.

Yulia Dmitrievna made no reply for she was busy counting the swabs which the young surgeon had taken out of the patient's wound, and merely indicated to Fainna with a twitch of her brows that she should help the professor into his coat.

The wounded kept arriving all morning. There were hardly any spare cots. Breakfast was made for three hundred

people, and Dr. Belov gave Sobol orders to have dinner for
five hundred. The ward nurses did not empty their pails into
the nearest shell hole any more, and simply dashed the blood
on to the tracks.

At noon, Danilov came into the staff car and asked Dr.
Belov: "What do you say, are we full?"

"I'm afraid we are," Dr. Belov replied. "We're full up here
too. We're bedding the wounded down on the floor, and we
might get a terrible roasting for it, you know."

They went through the train together. The coaches were
packed and smelt of medicines and sweat, and there were
flies. There were many lightly wounded people. They had
made their own way to the train and had remained there to
have a chance to get out of the town. Civilians for the most
part. One woman, wounded in the shoulder-blade, had
brought her four children along, and Fainna had stuffed them
all into her compartment. All this was against the rules and
regulations, but that night there was no remembering
regulations — only their common Russian adversity which
had to be coped with by common effort.

Dr. Belov peered into each cot for the umpteenth time on
the off chance that he might find Igor there. No, Igor wasn't
there.

"Ivan Yegorovich, you should lie down and have some
sleep," he said to Danilov. "You've been carrying the
wounded all night, you know."

The doctor himself had not had a wink of sleep, he had
rushed about all night, accommodating the wounded and
putting out the fire, and had not had anything to eat or drink
except for that glass of vodka given him by Kravtsov. But he
had the feeling that he had done nothing, that he alone had
idled through the night, and he felt that drinking that
wretched glass of vodka was a heinous crime, a gross
violation of army and human ethics. If only Danilov never
found out about it....

"I've an idea," Danilov said. "There are some abandoned
trains here with valuable goods, and they're going to be set
on fire. We might easily pull one out."

"How do you mean?"

"With our locomotive. Hitch it on. I've already spoken to
the station commandant about it, and he'd be only too
glad."

Danilov expected Dr. Belov to be glad too, but the older
man was slow to respond and just looked at him with his tired
eyes.

"I'm sorry, Ivan Yegorovich," he spoke at last, "but I'm afraid we can't decide this question so rashly. You see, I'm a doctor in the first place who is answerable for the lives of his patients. If this additional load will adversely affect the movement of our train, I shall be compelled to object...."

He spoke very mildly, but there was something in his tiredly blinking eyes which told Danilov that Dr. Belov had fully assumed command. Danilov flushed, it was on the tip of his tongue to say: "You're not only a doctor, you're a Soviet citizen, and it's your duty to salvage state property!" but the doctor forestalled him by saying:

"The loss of property can be made up, you know. Our freight is the most valuable of all, isn't it?"

Yulia Dmitrievna was walking towards them, as erect and dignified as ever, but less red-faced than usual. A trickle of blood had dried on her temple.

Dr. Belov saluted her. She nodded graciously, and walked on her way.

"Now this is perhaps the most valuable asset we have on our train," he said, his eyes on her departing figure.

"And who found her, I'd like to know?" Danilov said to himself. "It's I who found her! You only arrived when all the groundwork had been done, and now you're throwing your weight about!"

He pulled himself together: it was wartime, and this was his commanding officer. And so he did not say anything.

* * *

Suprugov returned to the train together with Danilov.

He, too, had walked about the town all night, bandaging wounds under shell fire. Actually, he was too frail for that kind of work. It was his nervous tension that kept him going. He did not start when a shell burst nearby. He seemed to see himself from the side that night, from a madly high flight. Also from up there he saw with relief that here was a surgeon returning safely from the field of battle where he had been in constant danger of being killed or crippled. The tunic of this selfless, brave surgeon was torn on the shoulder where a shell fragment had grazed him. He was dead tired, he was covered with soot, the cuffs of his sleeves and the knees of his trousers were saturated with blood, his feet were blistered.... But he pulled himself up by the handrail smartly, and walked into the staff car. Fima, the kitchen girl, recoiled from him in horror.

"I want hot water and a clean white coat," he flung the order at her. "And see that you wash this one today."

Fima looked at him with devoted eyes, and dashed off to fetch the hot water.

"Smirnova!" Suprugov called out from his compartment to the nurse running past his door. "Tell the housekeeper I want my breakfast."

He was in the act of pulling off his tunic. Sister Smirnova paused in the doorway and saw a Negro's black head and hands crusted with blood. She swung round sharply, and raced to the kitchen.

"Aha, how they're running to do my bidding, are they?" Suprugov said to his gratified self.

He went to wash flaunting his naked torso and his dangling braces. Fima tiptoed behind him, bearing a jug of hot water.

"Pour," he ordered, holding out his cupped hands.

*　*　*

The hospital train—scorched, sooty, with smashed window panes—was returning from the front. The charred coach was attached to the rear. Green lights went on at its approach, and other trains gave it the right of way.

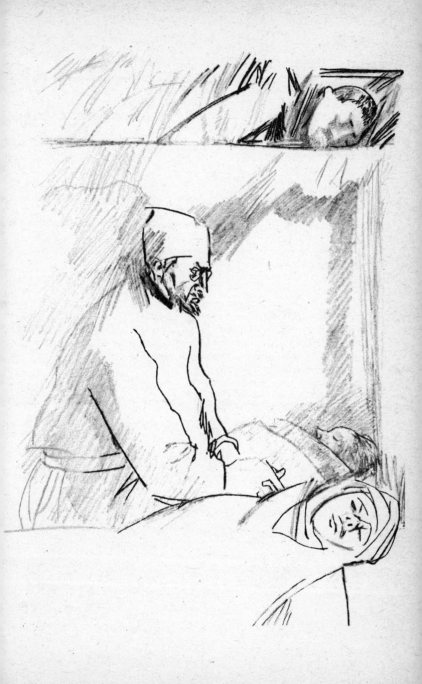

PART TWO

Chapter Five

WESTWARD-BOUND

Recalling their first trips, it amazed them that they did not understand the simplest things then. For instance, why did they bother to drape the windows when the train stood uncamouflaged at an open platform, visible from afar to the German bombers? Why did they think the train the safest place, and the people who ventured abroad to collect the wounded the bravest of the brave, defying certain death? Actually, there was much less danger of being killed out in the open. But they understood this much later, when their train made no more trips to the front. And when they did understand, they made fun of their silliness.

"Can you imagine it," Suprugov said to Yulia Dmitrievna with whom he was more talkative than with the others. "I believed it was sheer madness for us to leave the security of the train, and yet it was the only sensible thing we could do...."

This endless chewing of the cud exasperated Fainna, but she kept her silence because she had her cap set for Suprugov.

She now shared a compartment with Yulia Dmitrievna. It was really Olga Mikhailovna she should have lived with, for the head nurse and the feldsher had practically the same functions. Olga Mikhailovna worked in the coaches carrying the gravely wounded, and Fainna in the ones with the up-patients, but they had almost identical duties. And so by all accounts they ought to be sharing a compartment, but the two women did not get on. Olga Mikhailovna, a modest, unsophisticated and straightforward person, took a dislike to Fainna whom she regarded as a loose woman. She kept finding fault with her, and did not forgive her the slightest lapse. At the morning ten-minute conferences she never missed her chance to take a dig at Fainna. They were trifling lapses really: once, two of her charges were seen strolling up and down the train in violation of the doctor's orders; another time, a patient who had been put on a strict diet was caught eating cabbage pies bought, what's more, at one of the stops and therefore of dubious origin. Olga Mikhailovna's voice shrilled when she recounted all these outrageous goings-on, and Fainna turned purple from anger and breathed stertorously but said nothing in self-defence because she had not a leg to stand on: those two patients did really go wandering all over the train, and the lieutenant from coach 5 did gorge himself on cabbage pies and was sick afterwards. And Fainna was answerable for all this.

It was all very well for Olga Mikhailovna, she only had a hundred and ten wounded in her Krieger coaches, and most of them with amputated limbs. They just lay there, the poor things, in their cradles, and thought their own sad thoughts. Olga Mikhailovna could be quite sure that none of them would break the rules and go loitering about the other coaches, or jump out at a stop in their underwear to buy cabbage pies and homebrew....

Whereas she, Fainna, had close on three hundred people to watch on every trip east. The after-lunch hours when the various cures began—massage, local baths, electrisation and whatnot—could drive anyone crazy. The ward nurses and sisters were all run off their feet, and Fainna more than anyone else. She didn't have three hundred pairs of eyes to see that none of them ate anything they shouldn't! They weren't physical wrecks, good heavens above! They were big, tough men who had suffered damage in battle and who wanted to live every minute of their lives. At first, when their wounds hurt very badly, they groaned and moaned, unmanned by the thought of possible disablement; but once they became a little better they immediately started spinning jolly yarns, cracking jokes, flirting with the nurses, singing songs, letting the doctor's orders go hang, and raring to go into battle again right there and then. If Fainna tried telling them that homebrew was bad for them, they'd just laugh and say: "What, homebrew? That's a good one! Give us a tumblerful each, and we'll be as good as new!" What could she reply to this? They were right, it did make them as good as new....

Russians were made that way and Fainna, being a Russian woman, understood it. Listening to Olga Mikhailovna's accusations, she was thinking: "You don't know life, my dear. You still see all this as a series of touching pictures: the wounded man whispering: 'Sister, sister dear! Water!' And you bending over him, an angel of mercy.... Oh no, angel, you might get a glass flung at your pretty face, because they're a hot-tempered lot, they're high-strung, they'd met death face to face; and if one of them does that to you, you must just wipe your face, keep your mouth shut, fetch another lot of the medicine and coax him into taking it. That's what you're a Sister of Mercy for. And while you're cajoling him, your other wounded will go wandering about the train."

Fainna did not voice these thoughts out loud. There were the general rules and the local regulations, they had their head doctor and their commissar, while she, Fainna, was small fry, so who wanted to hear her suggested amendments to the rules?

Quite unexpectedly, she found an ally in Yulia Dmitrievna. "Olga Mikhailovna will never be much use," she once said.

"Why not?" Fainna asked eagerly.

"Because she lives in trifles. Trifles occupy all her thoughts. She has no time to think about anything really important."

"But you, Yulia Dmitrievna, forgive me for saying so, but you also live in trifles," Fainna said.

"I have to, because in surgery overlooking the smallest of trifles may result in grave consequences for the patient. But at the same time a medic must have the courage and ability to overlook a harmless trifle. Olga Mikhailovna is conscientious, no more. With time she'll develop into a middling physician. She'll treat 'flu and the itch well, I imagine. She's no use for science, just for everyday medical practice."

"And I?" Fainna asked.

Yulia Dmitrievna surveyed her critically, from her permed hair to her down-at-heel stylish shoes.

"You might be. One feels you have scope. You could make good in science provided you didn't let yourself get too diverted from your work."

Fainna sighed and hugged Yulia Dmitrievna. She wanted to kiss her, but thought better of it.

"You're so terribly right," she said.

When the nurses had to double up in order to make room for the office, it seemed the natural thing for Yulia Dmitrievna to move in with Fainna who was sincerely glad to have her.

* * *

Their hospital train made no more trips to the front line. Special "flying trains" made up of just a few coaches were instituted for the purpose. Trains of a more sophisticated type evacuated the wounded from the front-line hospitals to the nearest regular hospitals. And hospital trains proper transported the wounded into the deep rear, often a distance of many thousands of kilometres from the field of battle.

The train described in this story was typical for this last category. It was too unwieldy, too vulnerable and too expensive to be used for front-line trips. This was a mobile hospital, comfortable and elegant. And after the first two trips to Pskov and Tikhvin, it was not sent to the front any more.

The change was welcomed by some of the staff, mainly by civilians who found it a great nervous strain to work under fire and maintain their composure. Others took the change indifferently.

But there were those among the staff who were disappointed, aggrieved and almost hurt by this transfer to the deep rear.

Nizvetsky was aggrieved. Yulia Dmitrievna was disappointed. And Fainna was hurt.

Danilov was in two minds about the transfer. On the one hand, he had already come to love his train and became more and more attached to it with every day. Deep down he was glad that this beauty of a train was now safe from enemy bombs. But, on the other hand, he resented being so far from the front and doing such a small job. Sometimes, like Sukhoyedov, he had the creeping thought that he had been cheated, and then he became irritable, mentally cursed Potapenko for assigning him to this train, and put the young nurses in a dither with his scowl. With an effort he took himself in hand, his irritability passed, but a little later it came over him again.

The Germans had already been driven back from Moscow. Leningrad had survived its first terrible winter, and spring had come. Danilov waited tensely to see how events would develop in the summer. The Germans had launched a new offensive and were forging ahead to the Kuban and the Caucasus. A sense of his own wretched helplessness added fuel to his furious anger. But, sobering, he told himself: "Keep your shirt on. You think they won't manage without you?"

Still, he wrote to his superiors asking to be relieved for combat duty. No reply. Then he wrote a personal letter to Potapenko, and again there was no reply. Finally, he wrote to the Central Committee of the Party.

* * *

The coach which had been on fire in Pskov was repaired in Kirov.

The railway had refused to take on the work for lack of manpower. It was suggested that the coach should be dumped on the scrap heap as no one in his right senses would want to get involved in such a hopeless job. The transport workshops were now staffed with inexperienced boys and girls replacing the regular workers who had gone to the front.

Danilov talked the matter over with his people and they agreed to undertake the repairwork. Protasov, the lazy and smug old car-maintenance man, was appointed team leader. Kravtsov proved to be good at any job—he was an expert fitter, welder and glazier. The two men argued all day, shouting themselves hoarse, each defending his techniques and his superiority. But in the evenings they vanished together, and came back a little drunk and glowing with mutual tenderness. Sukhoyedov, Medvedev, Kostritsin, Nizvetsky, Bogeichuk, Goremykin, all the men, excluding the doctors, took a hand in repairing the coach, and Danilov himself—remembering the lessons taught him by his father—became Kravtsov's self-appointed apprentice. The girls tidied up after the workers, painted the coach, and generally made a nuisance of themselves. It was April, the weather was fair, and in a mere six days the job was done.

Danilov was delighted. He derived the most satisfaction not from the sight of the rehabilitated coach, but rather from the knowledge that they had lost none of the property entrusted to them, and had not let the enemy profit by anything that belonged to them. It made him all the happier to see that this feeling was shared by others on the train, and that the people looked at the repaired coach with a new, possessive sort of pride. Even Protasov's puffy, unshaven face beamed with pleasure when, standing on the platform with his legs planted wide apart and his belly thrust forward, he surveyed his handiwork.

A meeting was held to celebrate. Kravtsov came wearing a good suit and a necktie. A lot of nice things were said about him. And Danilov could not believe his own eyes—where was the man's Mephistophelean sneer? The old drunkard blushed like a maiden from these compliments.... But next morning, he was once again the hard-boiled devil with a haggard face and bleary eyes.

Danilov had his hands full, and something always demanded his urgent attention, taking his mind off his harrassing thoughts.

Much still wanted doing to put the hospital train on a higher level of efficiency. Danilov went into everything himself, and listened to what the staff were saying. Sobol was perpetually engaged in mental calculations, and Danilov started doing some calculating of his own. He worked out that on the average they spent ten days a month actually transporting the wounded, and the rest of the time the train either stood idle or ran without a load. The people lazed about, staring out of the windows and chewing the rag because there was no work for them to do.

Yulia Dmitrievna made the best of the off days to promote political education. It was splendid, of course, but, after all, Party and Komsomol studies was not what all these men and women had been assembled here for....

At one station, they stood for several hours alongside another hospital train, and curiosity drew everyone to the windows. They saw two nurses doing some sewing, laughing and chatting. Three men wearing uniform trousers and singlets, and no tunics, were playing billiards in the staff coach. "The devils," thought Danilov, "they had the wits to take down the partition between the compartments to make room for the billiard table!" A team of repair workers walked briskly between the two trains: several young boys and two girls in men's greasy overalls. "These poor kids have to repair our coaches, and those strong oxen chase billiard balls twenty days out of thirty.... And I'm a good one too, standing here and watching them at it...."

He pursued this thought further: "If we had the ability to make that burnt coach as good as new, surely we could handle the current repairs ourselves? We have masters of different skills among us, so surely we could learn to do the work these kids are doing for us! If every hospital train did its own repairs it would be a great help to transport in general, and we'd be helping ourselves too because we wouldn't have to wait our turn for weeks. We wouldn't have to stand idle for days on end, and consequently would make more trips. It's a simple business, no need to put it off."

And Danilov did not put it off. Having secured the approval of Dr. Belov, he called a general meeting and set forth his idea. And quite unexpectedly he encountered resistance.

"Comrades, the offhand manner in which this question has been posed evokes my doubts," said Dr. Suprugov. "Shall we not be putting our people under too much of a strain? It's no secret, comrades, that when we are carrying a load our people are tried far beyond all human strength. Can't they ever rest? And when else if not when we're travelling empty? No, comrades, this is not a question to be decided lightly."

Danilov stared at him, his mouth open in surprise. This meek character who always agreed with everybody was openly opposing him, Danilov? How come? What was happening anyway? Suprugov spoke softly but very distinctly. People were listening to him. Dr. Belov had begun to fidget in his chair and was scribbling something in his writing pad. And there was Iya, the fat nurse, dropping her chin into her hand and looking terribly sorry for herself, now that she knew that she was being tried beyond all human strength....

Had Danilov taken more notice of Suprugov he would have long marked the change in him. But he was not interested in Suprugov and missed the change which came after Pskov. It was after Pskov that Suprugov suddenly felt that he was a somebody, not just a run of the mill nose-ear-and-throat doctor, but a Surgeon-Major, an active participant in historic battles and, if you looked at it quite objectively without any false modesty—a heroic participant. It hurt him that the people about him did not seem to be impressed. Kravtsov had been publicly praised for a paltry thing, repairing some pipes or other, while not a word had been said about Suprugov's exemplary behaviour in the streets of Pskov.

And he wanted to draw attention to his merits, to give people to understand that he pulled some weight here, and that his opinion had to be heeded. This desire was so overpowering that it outweighed his usual prudence. He asked for the floor with his heart literally in his throat, the way it is with a poor swimmer on the point of diving from a high board—he wants to make the dive, but he's afraid of drowning....

For a second, terrified by the angry look flashed at him by Danilov, Suprugov thought that he had already drowned. With nervous desperation he kicked out, and surfaced.

"Please do not take me wrong," he said. "The only thing I'm afraid of is that the over-exertion might harmfully affect the efficiency of the staff in nursing the wounded defenders of our Motherland."

He had surfaced, he had surfaced! Dr. Belov nodded approvingly, and Yulia Dmitrievna assumed a pensive look which made her face all the more unattractive.

Danilov kept silent. He wanted to hear what everyone else had to say first. Suprugov's objection was like a stone thrown into a pond—it was bound to start circles on the water. And here they were.

Protasov spoke next. "Note this well: the proposal has been made at our general meeting. Had the question of repairs been in accordance with the regulations it would not have been raised at a meeting, an order would have been issued, and that would have been that. The regulations don't say that the staff should go climbing all over the coaches all the time without a moment's rest. It's the business of the railway. I'm an old railwayman, so you can take my word for it."

Still Danilov kept silent.

"Comrades, we have to obey discipline without arguing," Goremykin said resentfully. "If my commander tells me to lie down under the train, I have to lie down without discussing the order. If my commander tells me to paint the toilets, I'll paint those toilets, even if it isn't said in any rules and regulations that a soldier must paint toilets. Our job is to obey orders."

Sukhoyedov stood up.

"Comrade Commissar!" he began in the gasping voice of an asthmatic. "Allow me to say that you posed the question correctly, in the Bolshevik way, in a statesmanlike manner. I shall ignore the arguments of Comrade Goremykin and Comrade Protasov, as politically immature. We cannot heed them when the situation is what it is at the front and the proposal is in the interest of the entire country."

"You fat lazy bum," Kravtsov suddenly spoke up, looking at Protasov with loathing. "If you've the talent to do something over and above what's in the regulations, why not do it, who's got to do it if it's not me or you? All you want is to sleep and swill vodka, you useless devil...."

Protasov turned away and winced as though each word struck him across his face.

Danilov rose to his feet.

"Comrades," he said in a low voice, his glance flitting over Suprugov's face. "You did not quite understand me. I never suggested including the medical personnel in this repair work. What I propose is to form a permanent team from among our specialists. And if any of the medical personnel give what assistance they can when we travel empty, surely it won't make you nurse the wounded less efficiently, comrades? Will it?"

He asked the question in a gentle, considerate tone, knowing perfectly well what the response would be. The girls all shouted: "Of course not! Of course not!" Yulia Dmitrievna drew herself up proudly, and Dr. Belov stopped fidgeting and settled down in his chair with satisfaction and relief. The problem was solved at once, easily and unanimously.

Thereafter Danilov began to watch Dr. Suprugov more closely. But he did not notice anything unusual—Suprugov's manner was cautious and ingratiating as before. It puzzled Danilov why he had spoken up at the meeting the other day, and it was a long time before the answer suggested itself: Suprugov had wanted to make himself popular with the personnel.

Once, Danilov came upon him in the nurses' coach telling some old jokes at which his listeners laughed readily. It occurred to Danilov that he ought to arrange a theatre outing for the girls or something, and it was then that it dawned on him that Suprugov was trying to find favour with the personnel. Oh well, let him. Let him give people a laugh, it was better than sitting in his compartment like a brooding owl.

Another time, however, Suprugov made him very angry. They were in Kirov again, going empty. The stop was not long, and when the order was given to start it was discovered that there was not a single ward nurse on board. Suprugov had, on his own bat, given them permission to go to the pictures. The train's departure had to be delayed for three hours. Danilov wanted Dr. Belov to give Suprugov a written reprimand in an order, but this the kind old soul refused to do.

"He wanted them to have a bit of fun, you know," he said placatingly. "They're at an age when it's a need like air to breathe—pictures, you know, and dances, and operetta.... Dr. Suprugov may not have known that we'd be starting so soon. We ought to have warned him, don't you think?"

Danilov did not insist, but from Dr. Belov's compartment he went straight to Suprugov's and told him:

"Doctor, if you ever let anyone off again without Dr. Belov's or my permission, you'll be transferred to another unit with a lot of unpleasantness. I guarantee both—the transfer and the unpleasantness. Clear enough?"

He turned round sharply and left. Suprugov had raised his eyes from the book he was reading to hear Danilov out, and watched him go with a slow, ponderous look.

* * *

Doctor Belov received news of Igor.

A letter came from Leningrad, the only one in all that time. It was dated September 5, and reached Dr. Belov on New Year's Day. Sonia wrote that the outlook was not too heartening, but begged him not to worry about them as an excellent air-raid shelter had been fitted up in their apartment house. She wanted to know who looked after his clothes and how his stones were behaving. (Heavens, she meant his renal stones to which he hadn't given a thought since he was mobilised!)

"A letter came from Igor yesterday," Sonia wrote. "He left Pskov with a tank unit, and won't come home until the Germans have been routed. The letter did not surprise me, what did surprise me was my attitude to it. Three months ago I would have gone insane with worry if Igor had stayed out the whole night, and now I didn't even cry."

Lalya added a few lines to say that Mother was working and bearing up bravely, and that she herself was also working but not at the public library any more; she was now a registry clerk at a hospital. Lalya approved Igor's decision, only she was sorry he did not come home to say goodbye.

There were no more letters after that.

When the first alarming news of the blockade and the beginning hunger in Leningrad came through, Dr. Belov went to pieces. Food stuck in his throat, he felt hungry but could not eat. Danilov came to the rescue.

"Didn't your family leave Leningrad?" he asked.

"No, they didn't, you know," Dr. Belov murmured. "We somehow just didn't think of doing this."

"We might arrange a parcel," Danilov said.

There was nothing he could not do. By some devious ways, through the librarian at a Party school with whom Danilov was acquainted and whose daughter was married to a pilot, a parcel containing rusks, flour, lard, and all sorts of good things was sent off to beleaguered Leningrad, to Sonia's address. Dr. Belov did not know whether the parcel had reached his family or not. It was better to think that it had. The day it was sent off he felt as if he had just fed his darling Sonia and Lalya to repletion with rusks and lard, and he rejoiced in the knowledge that they were so full. He saved up the sugar, biscuits and other delicacies which occasionally came from Sobol, and waited for an opportune moment to ask Danilov to arrange the despatch of one more parcel.

Many days had passed since then. No letters came from Leningrad. The hospital train had already received two lots of mail in the course of those months, but there was nothing in it for Dr. Belov.

He was an optimist by nature. He worried, of course, but not too much. The situation in Leningrad had eased somewhat, evacuation had been resumed, and he had seen one such train with his own eyes.... It was terrible, terrible.

People in a state of extreme emaciation, suffering from starvation diarrhea. Children shrivelled like old men.... But Sonia and Lalya had food. Danilov had sent them a parcel. They could not have starvation diarrhea. Their letters were still on the way, that's all.

But possibly they had left Leningrad even before the blockade. Sonia was always so efficient.... And perhaps they were living in peace and safety somewhere beyond the Urals. And Lalya was as buxom and apple-cheeked as ever.... Letters would come from them soon. A whole stack of letters. There would be letters from Igor, too, among them. Sonia had sent him his father's address, and he was certain to write. After all, the rift between them wasn't forever.... Igor was a clever boy. He'd grow up and understand that he mustn't wound his father's soul like that. Sonia would make peace between them.

Oh, how he longed for the day to come when all the four of them would sit round the table in their small dining room, and the lamp under the old lampshade with some of the beads missing would shed its light on their beloved faces! But will that day ever come?

Yes, it will, asserted Danilov's calm, imposing figure. It doesn't stand to question! one read in Yulia Dmitrievna's superciliously raised eyebrows and haughty composure. Why, of course, it will! said Lena's sweet, puckishly carefree face.

And only Suprugov's manner did not inspire confidence: who knows, maybe it will and maybe it won't....

* * *

When Danilov was asked what school he went to he invariably replied: primary school.

It was quite true. He was born into a peasant family, went to the primary school where all the children were taught was reading, writing, arithmetic and scripture, and never left the village until he was eighteen. All these subjects were taught by one teacher.

And at the same time it was not true, because he studied continually after the Revolution. He was taught by the Komsomol, by the Party, and the Red Army. He was taught in special schools, courses and circles. The courses sometimes lasted ten or fifteen days, while study at the circles stretched into years.

He had more work than he could cope with, one would think, he had no time left for study, and yet he was always learning something, and actually knew quite a lot.

He was a practising agronomist, a practising veterinary surgeon, a practising architect, and had experience as a carpenter, fitter, blacksmith, bookkeeper and tradesman.

When he worked in the village he read books on agriculture. In the hospital train he took up books on medicine. He wanted to get to the bottom of this medical business. Dr. Belov gave him his Pirogov to read. Danilov opened the thick volume with deference and a lurking fear that the celebrated surgeon had written the book in too special a language for a layman like himself to understand. To his amazement, the book was written simply, and throbbed with passion and urgency. He discovered that as far back as 1854, during the defense of Sebastopol, people had pondered the very same problem which worried Danilov now, in 1942: the transportation of the wounded from the front to the rear.

Needless to say a big stride had been made in the ninety years. Danilov wished Pirogov could see the Krieger coaches, the pharmacy car, and the modern assortment of instruments. Still, much more wanted doing, much more that was new and worthwhile. And, as usual, Danilov's hands itched to get down to the work.

* * *

Suddenly the coaches which he had liked so much looked drab and unattractive, even the Kriegers. He could not at once understand what was wrong, and then he knew: it was the bed linen.

After transferring the wounded from the train to the hospital, all the cots were stripped and the linen sent to the town's laundry. The laundry was short-handed, the women workers could not cope and did a pretty poor job. And very often some torn, drab sheets were slipped in with the good ones that had gone into the wash.

"But why is everything so snow-white in your pharmacy car?" Danilov asked Yulia Dmitrievna.

"Because Klava does the washing herself," Yulia Dmitrievna replied. "I wouldn't put on a badly laundered coat or hand one to the surgeon, would I?"

"And do you think the wounded don't mind lying down on badly laundered sheets?"

"I've been thinking about this," Yulia Dmitrievna said, ignoring the sarcasm. "It would be much better if all the washing were done here."

"If you've been thinking about it, why didn't you say anything?" Danilov said reproachfully. "You've got to speak up, you know."

"Very well. I'll tell you what I think of our train. I think it could be greatly improved. We need a laundry, and what we need even more is a disinfection chamber for the blankets, flannel dressing gowns and so forth."

Danilov nodded. Yes, a disinfection chamber was essential for their hospital train.... He had often watched the delivery of blankets and dressing gowns from the disinfection station. Lorries brought them as far as the railway station, and from there people carried armfuls of them over the tracks, often crawling under the trains that blocked the way on either side. Sometimes the blankets arrived smeared with grease and coal dust, and there was no one to blame. Moreover, Sobol and Bogeichuk were always complaining about the difficulty of securing a lorry, and if Sobol wasn't so resourceful they'd never get hold of one.

One day Sobol said to Danilov: "Believe it or not, but the thought of our slops really breaks my heart."

"What slops?" Danilov was puzzled.

"Great heavens, what slops! Kitchen slops, of course."

Sobol said this in a swooning voice, and closed his eyes. Danilov looked at him with new interest.

Garbage, vegetable peel, slops and greasy dishwater were emptied in bucketfuls down the embankment every day.

"What do you propose?"

"Oh, I don't know," Sobol said coyly, expecting to be given a sympathetic hearing. "We might fatten a pig or two."

"Where will we keep them? We're on wheels, you know."

"Well, obviously we'd carry them with us."

Danilov thought over Sobol's proposal, approved of it whole-heartedly and persuaded Dr. Belov to agree, arguing that fresh meat would make a very welcome addition to their patients' diet.

A corner was partitioned off in the luggage van where it adjoined the refrigerator car, and two piglets were installed there. Danilov put Kostritsin, an elderly soldier who had farming experience, in charge of the animals.

"There you are, Comrade Commissar," Sobol said happily to Danilov. "Next thing we'll start a poultry farm."

And they did. Twenty hens and a rooster were bought and installed in a cage, devised by Sobol, that was attached under the carriage. Dr. Belov took a look at them and said:

"They won't survive. They have to walk on ground."

"Sure, every chicken walks on ground, but let them show their worth and lay eggs in these conditions too," Sobol replied.

Later, cupping the first warm egg in the palm of his hand, he confessed to Danilov that he had very much doubted that the hens would lay eggs on a moving train.

"And now I think, the movement of the train should actually help!"

* * *

On those long days when the train, having delivered the wounded to the hospital, went back for the next lot, a multitude of petty, humdrum cares overwhelmed everybody, and life began to seem bleak and monotonous. It was difficult to imagine that guns were roaring somewhere and blood was shed. And that this very coach, gleaming with white paint inside and dark-green outside, had burned like a torch at Pskov and they had put out the fire....

But when the hour of loading approached, everything changed. Sobol would not have dared to bother the commissar with any piglets at that hour, nor could he bother about such things himself.... Everyone, or almost everyone, was roused to a heightened sense of responsibility, self-discipline, and personal involvement in that tremendous, terrible and awesome thing which had ordered them to gather together in this hospital train and live, as they were living, for months or years until the day of victory.

And now War invaded the coaches where every wrinkle on the cots had been smoothed out by loving hands, entering noisily, with loud talk and moans, with a clatter of crutches. Smoke started curling ceilingward from a dozen cigarettes at once. Blankets were crumpled, and pillows were stood up on end. The reek of pus, sweat, and men's breath drowned out the smell of disinfectants.... The train was starting East with a full load.

Chapter Six

EASTWARD-BOUND

Lena did her work dutifully. She swept and cleaned the coach, dressed and undressed the wounded, helped with the bandaging, brought them their meals, and read the newspaper aloud, stumbling a little over the names of foreign towns.

The wounded loved her. The older men called her "daughter" and stroked her bobbed hair. And the younger ones said wistfully: "What a wife to have!"

She patiently cleaned up after them and coaxed them to eat their oatmeal porridge at the sight of which they generally flew into a rage.

"Honestly, you amaze me," she would say. "You're no better than children. It's the most nourishing food, if you want to know. You wait while I go and ask the diet nurse how many calories there are in oatmeal."

"Go on, go and tell your diet nurse to eat these calories herself," they'd shout back. "We're not horses to be fed oats!"

When they were taken down from the train at their destination they shook her hand long and heartily, and gazing at her with affection said:

"C'mon, give us your address, nursie, I'm going to write to you, I'll never forget you."

"No, I won't give you my address," she replied. "You'll write and I won't answer, I hate writing letters."

Yet she often wrote letters, and always to the same address and to the same field post.

She wrote and wrote and dropped her letters not into a mailbox, it seemed, but into a bottomless well. There was not a whisper of an echo from that well. The mail was delivered to the hospital train only once every three or four months when it arrived at its "port of hail". There were letters in envelopes, or just a page folded into a triangle with the address written on it, there were picture postcards and military postcards with red stars on them.

When the mail came, Lena went about with a glowing look, for she seemed to hear his voice, a manly voice quavering with tenderness, right there, close beside her.

...The weather was dry and hot. The windows were open, and black dust settled on the white curtains, bedsheets, bandages and smocks. The ward nurses had double the work to do now, what with shaking out the curtains and bedding every few hours, washing the floor, and wiping the tables, windowframes and walls with a damp cloth.... The wounded suffered from the heat, and refused food.

They had just been taken on board for the long journey east, to the Urals. There were twelve patients in Lena's Krieger car. They were difficult to please, they smoked, refused to drink boiled water and wanted tap water with ice. Number 17, who had his left leg amputated at the knee, did not smoke or clamour for anything, and this was even worse. He did not eat and did not sleep. His face, which looked dark-bronze against the white pillow, had become pinched and a squeamish grimace was frozen on it.

Olga Mikhailovna bent close to him and spoke gently like a mother: "Why don't you eat? You don't like the food?"

"The food is good. Thank you very much," he replied through set teeth.

"Perhaps you'd like something else? A boiled egg? A cheese cake? A dumpling with fresh strawberries? Just name it, and we'll have it made for you."

"Thank you. I do not want anything."

Olga Mikhailovna had another 109 gravely wounded men waiting. A hundred and nine case histories, hundreds of prescriptions, hundreds of complaints from the wounded—about the heat, the oatmeal porridge, the cruelty of the nurses who refused to give them tap water with ice, and hundreds of complaints from the nurses about the wounded making a mess of the place, dodging their medicine, and demanding that the door be left open so there'd be a draught.... Olga Mikhailovna read the case history of Number 17 to the end, and told him:

"You're a sailor, Comrade Glushkov, you've got to take a grip on yourself."

"I *was* a sailor," he said.

Lena could not take her eyes off him: the bronzed face with the white forehead and black eyes made her think of her husband.

"Lena, straighten the lieutenant's pillow, will you," Olga Mikhailovna ordered her, and went over to the next patient.

Lena lifted the pillow, and looked deep into the resentful, suffering black eyes.

"Are you Lena?" he asked.

"Yes," she replied.

He looked at her, and his glance softened.

"My sister's called Lena too," he said, and fell silent.

Another patient called her. She went about handing bedpans to the wounded, coaxing them to drink boiled water, wiping things clean with a wet cloth, and straightening pillows and sheets. At one of the stops, she ran to the station at their request and bought them a pailful of raspberries. A captain, a corpulent, cheerful man with his torso encased in a plastercast, cracked funny jokes as he divided up the raspberries and handed Lena a bowl filled to the brim.

At dinnertime she went up to Glushkov again.

"Eat," she told him. "This has been specially ordered for you. It's mutton with tomatoes. And for supper you're to have some cheese cakes. Come on, eat!"

"I am eating," he said vexedly, and put a slice of tomato into his mouth. "Stay awhile, don't run away, you keep going away all the time. I'll eat if you stay."

"All right," she said, and sat down beside his cot.

"But you're not eating, you're only pretending," she said after a while. "You must eat."

"To live?"

"Why, of course. To live."

"I lied to you about my sister," he said. "She's not my sister. We were going to get married. She'll marry somebody else now.... Oh, I don't give a damn. I couldn't care less.... Look, eat this extra-special mutton if you like. I don't want it."

"How d'you know she'll marry somebody else?" Lena said.

"It makes no difference to me what she does.... I'm not going home." He gritted his teeth. "A cripple, how repulsive! Appearing before her with a wooden leg ... damn the Fritzies. I'll send for my mother, wherever I may be. We'll live in some other town. Mother will come with me anywhere. Mothers, they'll go with you always...."

"I don't see anything repulsive at all," Lena said, staring fixedly before her. "I don't understand how it can be repulsive. For your mother and for anyone else you're as

dear without one leg as you were with two. And if you want
to know your trouble is the smallest ever. You're as able-
bodied and handsome as you were, you're young, you can
get educated in any profession you wish, you'll marry, and
there's your whole life ahead of you. And you won't have a
wooden leg either, you'll have a good artificial limb made for
you, you'll be able to wear smart shoes and no one will notice
anything...."

He closed his eyes and lay still. And she went away to the
other end of the coach because all of a sudden she terribly
wanted to stroke his cropped head. To put her hand on his
forehead, so very, very white above the line of sunburn. Oh,
Dan....

The long, hot day was coming to an end at last. The
evening bustle was over—serving supper, administering
treatment, straightening the beds for the last time before
sleep. Olga Mikhailovna gave her patients a last look, and put
out the lights, leaving only the lamp on the duty nurse's small
table. Lena slowly paced the thick rug. The car with the
partitions removed was spacious and cosy with its chaiselon-
gues and little tables, and it would be quite like a proper
hospital ward if it were not for that second tier of cots. There
were ten cots on the right, and ten on the left: five standing
on the floor and five suspended above them on each side.
And on each pillow lay a man's head with cropped hair and a
sunburnt face.... The lamp under its blue lampshade shed a
pale light on these dark faces, closed eyes, and lips
compressed in sleep. Glushkov alone was awake. Every time
Lena walked past him she saw his glittering eyes.

She wanted to talk to him, but she was afraid. Why had she
been on the verge of caressing this white forehead above the
bronze line of sunburn?

"I feel sorry for him," she told herself. "I want to comfort
him. Like a sister.... He looks like Dan. I'll come up to him
and caress him. A little, only a very little. There's nothing
wrong with it if it's only a very little.... But I'm not in love
with him, am I? No, not at all: if he's taken off and put in
hospital tomorrow I won't care."

She meant it.

"I'll come up to him. He has black eyes. He spoke so
nicely to me. I'll comfort him and he'll comfort me."

"I'll go and talk to him. I'll get him to talk to take his mind
off things. I'll even place my hand on his forehead.... As
though I were his sister, that's how I'll place my hand on his
forehead."

She went up to his cot. He was asleep. His face was haggard, but he breathed softly, like a child.

Lena stood for a while, watching the even rise and fall of his chest under the shirt. "I'm so glad he has fallen asleep," she forced herself to think, while disappointment and even hurt stirred in some hidden recess of her mind.

Suddenly he gave a sob—a drawn-out, moaning sob. He must have cried himself to sleep, and went on crying in his sleep. He had been crying, and she had not noticed.

Summer nights are short, and light was already breaking.

"I'm not going to caress anyone except my one and only love, the only one for the rest of my life. He is my husband, I saw him off to war, and he went, trusting me. Trust me, Dan, trust me, darling. I want only you. It's my brother who sleeps here, a brother, one of the thousands I have.... But, Dan, tell me, why must there be all this— these wounds and suffering, these cots, these bedpans, and this terrible longing when life was so wonderful, so full of happiness...."

"Nurse!" someone called from the other end of the car.

"Coming," Lena called back, and hurried with her light step to answer the summons.

* * *

A man named Kramin had cot Number 18, above Glushkov.

This was a puny little man with a completely bald, shiny scalp, a dry, sardonic face and sharp features. His horn-rimmed round glasses made his features seem all the sharper. With his glasses on he looked like an owl.

His spine was injured and both legs were paralysed. The agony he was suffering had desiccated his body, and it weighed no more than a child's. He was doomed to crutches for the remainder of his life. Every now and then he would throw back his blanket and, thrusting out his lower lip, examine his skinny, yellow, flaccid legs.

When he was brought into the train, he immediately asked for books, and the more the better.

Lena fetched everything she could find in the train's meagre library: Pushkin's *Yevgeny Onegin* printed in a separate slender volume, a collection of Jack London's stories, a solitary number of the magazine "Propagandist" brought out some time in 1939, and a book that could not be immediately identified because the first and last pages had been ripped off and used as cigarette paper.

"Lovely," said Kramin.

He finished the lot before the day was out. He read lying on his back and holding the book low over his face. His head jerked right and left from the extraordinary speed of his reading. He seemed to be pecking at the book, as a hungry hen pecks at seeds.

When the personnel made ready to receive a new lot of wounded, a book was placed on each of the bedside tables—such was the custom. Kramin gobbled up all the reading matter there was in his coach. He became the talk of the train—a man whom it took an hour to finish a book that would have lasted anyone else the whole trip! Danilov, Dr. Belov and the nurses all brought him whatever literature they had.

With the same speed and absorbing interest Kramin raced through Pirogov, the satirical magazine *Crocodile*, and the novel *Keys of Happiness* from Fainna's private stock of love stories.

When he had nothing to read, he removed his glasses, crossed his arms behind his head, evidently taking delight in the knowledge that his arms and hands at least were his to use as he pleased, and joined in the conversation.

He was not a chatty person, and just put an occasional word into the general talk.

He found everything lovely.

"Lovely porridge!" he would say, handing Lena an empty bowl and laughing with his very light, almost colourless eyes.

"Lovely novel," he told Fainna as he returned to her the *Keys of Happiness*.

"You really think so? Honest?" Fainna was so glad that a clever man had praised the book which none of the personnel took seriously.

"Naturally," replied Kramin.

He had no dressings to change—he was spared that anyway. Sometimes he asked for a morphine injection, very quietly and politely, and was readily obliged. Ahead of him were long months of hospital treatment, before he could hope to walk with the help of crutches.

Here is his story. Before the war Kramin was the legal adviser of one of the largest and most important factories in Leningrad. Among his friends he enjoyed the reputation of a book-lover, theatre fan and sybarite. He led an easy and pleasant life. His wife was a beautiful woman.

The rumour that Kramin had declined his draft exemption, had enlisted and was taking a junior lieutenants' course of training, was so amazing that his friends refused to believe it. But they had to when one of them ran into Kramin on Nevsky Prospekt wearing uniform.

He received his commission with one of the first lots of graduates, and with the platoon under his command carried out small reconnaissance assignments for about a month. His performance was sound, but his commanding officers hesitated to place too much reliance in him, put off by the frailty of his physique.

Leningrad's grim days of trial began. The Germans seized Gatchina, Pushkin, and Krasnoye Selo. With his platoon Kramin went on reconnaissance to these magic places where he used to take a dacha for the summer. He had packed off his wife to the deep rear in summer, in good time.

The battalion commander summoned him one day and said, without looking Kramin in the eyes:

"You shall have to hand over your platoon to Lt. Nikolayev."

"May I know why?" Kramin asked.

"Because your platoon is to be despatched to Nevskaya Dubrovka."

Dubrovka, on the left bank of the Neva, was a strip of territory one and a half kilometres long and seven hundred metres wide, which our troops had recaptured from the Germans and which they were set on holding and enlarging. The Germans kept this strip of land and the crossing to it over the river under constant artillery and machine-gun fire.

"Lovely," said Kramin. "But why must I hand my platoon over to Nikolayev?"

The battalion commander stared fixedly at Kramin's belt buckle.

"This has been agreed with the regimental commander," he said. In those early days of war, a conversation like this between a senior officer and a junior one was still possible. Scowling and evidently losing his temper, the battalion commander faced Kramin squarely at last, and said with brutal straightforwardness: "Men of sturdier stuff are needed for Dubrovka. These glasses of yours, your lovely, lovely, and everything.... You're a flighty sort of person...."

Kramin turned pale.

"Comrade Battalion Commander," he said. "Allow me to point out that for over a month I have been making my soldiers accustomed to the thought that very soon, it might be required of us to all die together. Together, you understand? And now they will go, and I will stay behind. It's impossible. It's tantamount to your slapping my face in front of the whole formation."

Emotion made his voice thin and piercing. The battalion commander was an old soldier. He understood.

"Very well," he agreed, albeit rather reluctantly. "You shall go with your platoon."

On a dark, moonless, rainy night Kramin and his platoon got across the Neva. Nineteen of his men were killed by German shells.

Kramin left the right bank of the Neva as a platoon commander, and landed on the left bank as a company commander: the commanders of two other platoons were killed during the crossing, their depleted ranks merged with Kramin's, and a company was formed.

Kramin crawled along a trench almost filled in with corpses into the heart of the territory, recaptured from the enemy. German tracer rockets burst over Dubrovka, and German machine-guns spurted fire along the trench. The whole of next day Kramin and his men lay low in the trenches under hurricane fire. Towards evening he received orders to lead the company into attack as soon as it grew dark.

Crawling from one trench to the next, he roused his men. The rain went on pouring, and Dubrovka was pelted by water and fire.

They went into attack, took prisoners, and it was on the way back that Kramin received the wound in the back which crippled him for life. Two of his men, a Russian and an Uzbek, carried him along that same trench, almost filled in with corpses, to the bank where there was a first-aid station installed under a sheltering cliff. He was unconscious when they got him to the other side of the river. He stayed in a front-line hospital for a time, and was then moved to Leningrad.

Here his military career ended.

The window panes in the hospital had been blasted in the air-raids, and were now boarded up. It was too dark to read. He was alone with his pain, day and night. Kramin refused to reconcile himself to this state, and sent notes to all the acquaintances he could remember asking them for a *roll* of paper (that's precisely how he wanted it) and a ruler.

When he had what he needed he began to write. Holding the ruler across the paper, he would write just above it, and when he came to the end of the line, he would move the ruler down a little. The result was quite neat and legible.

He wrote ironical letters to his wife and his friends, and made parodies of the poems broadcast over the radio.

He was a gourmet, and all the poems sounded bad to him.

His parodies were clever and he derived much amusement from them. The air-raids did not worry him, for after Dubrovka they did not seem frightening at all. He endured his pain. The cold was very trying: the wounded lay in bed in their uniform tunics, fur hats, and all but their mittens. Kramin would prefer to be in his underwear. But he was not allowed.

He knew that people around him were dying from starvation. He endured it just as he endured the pain in his spine. He melted away like a burning candle, and wrote funny epistles.

The wife of a friend brought him a truly generous gift: several baked potatoes, a glassful of honey, and some vegetable oil poured into an empty scent bottle. This woman whom he knew for a flippant fashion plate, came to visit him in a dirty shawl covering her head and shoulders and a man's down-at-heel felt boots on her feet. She looked twice her age. He was moved. He kissed her hand, and afterwards wrote her a sincere, warm letter with none of his usual clowning.

* * *

He did not feel like writing on the train, and preferred to read and talk.

The patients in his coach were a self-controlled lot. The nurses were attentive and polite—apparently ruled by someone's very strong hand.

The loveliest of all was that simple-hearted, jolly young woman with the frizzed hair who was so happy when he praised her trashy novel.

The thought that he was going somewhere pleased him. He loved travel and had travelled a lot. Once, he even tried to get a job on an ice-breaker going on an Arctic expedition. But he happened to fall in love just then, he was busy courting and marrying his wife, and the Arctic had to be shelved.

He'd never go to the Arctic now, of course.

Never mind.

He was going somewhere anyway, through the window he could see familiar peaceful landscapes, he was reading all the books he knew over again, he had done all he could in the time allotted him, all that fate had granted him to do. Good.

The wounded were not supposed to be told the itinerary of the train. The experience of the first few trips had taught the personnel to use this crafty tactics. Just let somebody say that the train was going via Moscow, for example, and immediately scores of people would claim to be Muscovites and demand to be landed there. Everybody wanted to go to his home town for treatment. The wounded made terrible scenes, and escapes were attempted by some. And so, to put an end to this, it was decided to keep the itinerary a secret.

But there was no deceiving Kramin. He knew the railroads too well. On the third day of the journey, he beckoned to Danilov to come closer, and said to him in a confidential whisper:

"Comrade Commissar, we are going via Sverdlovsk."

"Oh no, you're wrong," Danilov replied.

"Please do me a favour, my wife is in Sverdlovsk," said Kramin. "Please let her know that I shall be passing through. I very much want to see her. Here's the address. If it isn't too much trouble, of course. I shall be extremely grateful."

"But you're wrong, I tell you," Danilov persisted, but he took the bit of paper with the address on it and sent a telegram to Kramin's wife.

* * *

And then there was Kolya.

In his case history he was titled Nikolai Nikolayevich, but everyone called him Kolya and treated him like a youngster.

Kolya was eighteen, he joined up as a volunteer, distinguished himself in the battle at Vyazma, was wounded, recovered, went back to the front again, distinguished himself in the battle for Orel, was wounded, and was now on his way to the deep rear to get properly mended.

He already had two Orders and was due for a third. He spoke of these decorations with artless jubilation, never doubting that everyone shared in his delight and felt kindly disposed towards him.

"Oh you, Kolya, Kolya boy," said the corpulent captain in a plaster cast. "By the end of the war you'll have a full set of all the Orders there are, and in the meantime take a crack at these raspberries."

Kolya ate the raspberries and licked his fingers clean. Kramin gave him some of his sugar, because the daily ration was not enough for the boy.

He could never tell an articulate story of the feats he had performed. He ran, he fired. He crawled, he fired. He sat, he fired. He had but a vague notion of tactics. All he understood well was his immediate function, and he performed it well, judging by his accounts and his decorations.

The corpulent captain listened to him attentively and said: "Seems you had a good commander, because like hell you would have distinguished yourself, fellow, if you didn't have a good commander."

Kolya hailed from Voronezh Region where he finished seven-year school three years before and worked on a collective farm as foreman of a youth team. Kramin asked him what made him enlist in the army without waiting to be drafted, and Kolya replied:

"Why, because they want to break up the collective farms and give the land away to the exploiter class."

He stated this matter-of-factly, without emotion, as one says a dog is mad when it has rabies.

According to Kolya, Germans were not frightening, nothing to be afraid of.

"They wanted to throw a scare into us with what? With motorbikes. Three hundred men would straddle motorbikes and tear down the road. Three or maybe four hundred.... They'd come straight at you raising a lot of noise and smoke.... Some fellows, the weaker ones, lost their nerve. But what's so frightening about them, they're just motorbikes? Before the war I dreamed of buying one."

"And now? You dream no more?" asked the captain.

"Oh, now! Now I'll get myself a motorbike for free."

He had an unblemished child's face which did not yet know the touch of a razor. Of all the men in that coach he was the only one who was ashamed of appearing in his nakedness, in his infirmity, before the nurses. His blue eyes would rest with a pensive dismay on Lena.

He was shy, yet he couldn't help talking about himself and he talked never fearing that the older men might laugh at him.

"The most awful moment was when I was wounded the first time. I went sick with fear, thought I'd die."

"Fear of death, was it?"

"No, not that. I was sorry to die before I'd seen anything in life. Before I'd seen any damned thing," he repeated, looking straight ahead defiantly and sternly.

He had been wounded with an explosive bullet in both legs. He began to develop gangrene when he was in the front-line hospital, but his powerful constitution came to the aid of medicine, and the process was stopped. Kolya thought he was perfectly well now. Supported by a nurse he walked on his own two feet to have his dressings changed, and liked to sit in a chaise longue with his big boyish hands resting on his knees. His pose, however, bespoke unchildish confidence and dignity. His whole figure and his thick-lipped, blue-eyed open face seemed to say: "I've done a bit, and I'll do more, never worry."

Dr. Belov liked to come into this coach and listen to Kolya's stories. No, Igor was not like him, not at all. Igor had a different face, and a different disposition. "Igor is a hothouse plant, and Kolya is simple, innocent and fresh like a wild flower," he was thinking. But then Igor was only a youngster like Kolya, even younger, and the doctor enjoyed watching him.

*   *   *

Danilov, wearing a doctor's white coat stretched clumsily over his enormous shoulders, sat beside Glushkov's cot and related the latest news. And then, standing in the middle of the coach, he traced a map of the Crimea on the rug with the toe of his boot. The Germans were fighting for a foothold on the peninsula.

"It's hard to say, of course, how things will work out," he said, "but one thing is sure, the Germans will break more than one of their teeth against Sebastopol."

"Ah yes, history will certainly award Sebastopol a second Order," said the captain in a plaster cast.

The talk turned to Moscow and Leningrad and the fabulous resistance they had put up.

Danilov kept addressing Glushkov, as though inviting him to join in the conversation.

Glushkov did at last unclench his teeth to mutter: "Sure, our towns are putting up a damned good defence."

"The Germans are fizzling out, and that's a fact," said the captain.

"I'm waiting to see where they'll trip up," said a handsome Georgian who had a head wound and lay in one of the suspended cots. "I've been poking my finger at the map with my eyes closed to guess where we'd start driving them back." He spoke with a soft accent, and chuckled at his fortune-telling attempt.

"A map is no good for that," said the captain. "Now, in Penza I once tried my luck with a fortune-teller, and it's amazing what she read in her cards, all came true too!"

Everyone there burst out laughing. Before leaving the coach to continue with his usual after-breakfast round to tell people the latest news, Danilov placed his hand firmly on Glushkov's shoulder and said for him alone to bear:

"Chin up, Lieutenant. Chin up. You've got to eat, you've got to sleep, you've got to live."

Glushkov raised distrustful eyes.

"It's fun living with two legs," he said loudly.

"Naturally two legs are more fun than one," Danilov replied. "Nobody will deny that. But just think how many men got killed in that scrape you were in, and you're alive. Excellent artificial legs are made nowadays, your amputation is first class, walking will be easy. So you can consider yourself lucky."

"Better be dead than live as a cripple," Glushkov said glumly.

"That's not true," Kramin suddenly interposed in a calm, clear voice. He removed his glasses, breathed on the lenses and polished them carefully with a corner of his bedsheet. "The commissar is right: what happened to you was a rare piece of luck. You were prepared to die" (he examined the lenses against the light) "...and remained alive. In other words, you were granted a second life. Try to think of a gift as valuable as this."

He fell silent. Everyone waited for him to go on and did not break the silence.

Finally the captain asked Kramin:

"I'd like to follow your thought to the end, so tell me: do you consider yourself lucky too?"

"Certainly," replied Kramin.

* * *

Danilov left the coach. The conversation had tired the wounded, and a hush fell on the coach.

Suddenly Glushkov spoke up with brusque animosity, addressing Kramin in the cot above him:

"Here you were asking Kolya why he joined up as a volunteer. Why did you?"

Kramin hung his head down over the edge of the cot and peered at Glushkov.

"I can see that you're not a very young man and not very well suited for fighting," Glushkov said with a challenge.

"Yours is some kind of learned profession, it shows right away.... So why did you join up? To show off?"

"I am a wealthy man, you see. And I went to war to defend ·my wealth," Kramin replied, picking up his book again.

* * *

As Lena walked past Glushkov's cot she noticed that he was weeping. His back and his head shuddered not in time with the jolting of the train, but with a rhythm all their own. His shoulders rose and fell convulsively.

"Sasha," she whispered, bending low over him. "Sasha, what's the matter?"

He dug his head deeper into the pillow, ashamed of his tears yet glad, too, that someone had come to comfort and pity him.... She was stroking his cropped head with both hands.

"It's all right, Sasha, it's all right...."

He turned his hot, wet face to her.

"They think I'm a coward!"

"Bless you, Sasha, nobody thinks that, what nonsense, come now, come...."

"And it's not that at all. The sea is my life, and I'll never go back to the sea, can't you understand it?"

"Quiet, Sasha, quiet. Here, drink some water. It's all right, it's all right...."

He took a gulp of water.

"Dammit, letting myself go to pieces like that...." he said.

"It's just nerves. You'll get fit again, you'll relax, and start a new life. This will pass...."

He tried but could not control his tears and, turning away to the wall, pulled the blanket over his head.

The commissar said he was lucky and could get along with one leg. That paralysed chap in the cot above said he'd been granted a second life. And none of them understood what it meant never to go out to sea again.

He closed his eyes and saw a tall wave rising before him quite palpably: on one side it was dark-green and smooth as glass, and on the other it was ruffled with small, live wrinkles; the crest seethed and curled.... It gave out a beautiful coolness, a smell of salt, a feeling of the great open seas which took a sailor's breath away....

The doctor, the feldsher and the nurse were making their daily, tiresome round.... Glushkov gritted his teeth at the same old hateful consolations.

"I don't like this, my dear chap," Dr. Belov said to the captain and felt his plaster cast. Pus had oozed through again.

"Sorry, doctor," the captain replied. "But I feel perfectly fit."

"We might have to cut a window in the plaster," the doctor said worriedly.

The tall wave was receding into the great blue freedom of the ocean, playing with the breeze and sparkling in the sun, utterly indifferent to men's battles and tears.

*　*　*

Sergeant Nifonov never joined in the conversation about him, and confined himself to such essential utterings as "yes", "no", "water, please". However, when he saw anyone new he inevitably asked:

"You don't happen to know a man called Beryoza, Semyon Beryoza, a machine-gunner?"

He named Beryoza's regiment. But no one knew Beryoza—neither the other wounded, nor the doctors, nor the nurses. Was this Beryoza a relative or a friend, they asked? Nifonov did not vouchsafe a reply and, closing his eyes, feigned sleep.

He'd like to know whether Beryoza was alive. It would be good to hear that he was. And then to find out where he was just now....

But what was the sense of wasting breath on empty talk? There was nothing to talk about before the main question had been decided. And it was on this question that Nifonov would have liked to consult Semyon Beryoza.

They had known each other for a brief ten minutes, but Nifonov felt that he had never had a closer friend than Beryoza.

In a foxhole to the right of Nifonov on that cursed field where the hot dust clogged your throat, there was this young chap from another company. With the corner of his eye Nifonov saw only the chap's shoulder, forage cap and flushed ear, and the shoulder shuddered in time with his rattling machine-gun. When a lull came, the chap turned his head and looked at Nifonov with prominent pale-blue, daredevil eyes.

"Stranger friend, give me a pinch of your tobacco!" he said.

His face was grimy with dust. He took a pinch of tobacco

from Nifonov's pouch, rolled a cigarette, nodded his thanks and lit up, gripping the cigarette angrily between his hard lips.

Nifonov was pretty sure they would not leave this field unscathed, but he did not say it to the chap. He rolled a cigarette for himself and said:

"Here, let me light it from yours."

They introduced themselves then. A shell burst just behind the coppice.

"Damn," Beryoza said softly.

The Germans retreated, and their artillery got busy again. Beryoza stared before him without blinking or starting at the explosions, and his stern face seemed made of cast iron. Nifonov liked the idea of Beryoza's shoulder so close to him. It was a hard, strong, reliable shoulder. He thought how wonderful it was to have a real friend, male friendship was a good thing ... and thought no more, he *was* no more, for a long, long time.

He remembered an argument once overheard as in a dream. It was in the hospital. Two surgeons were arguing, thinking that he was unconscious and could not understand. One of the surgeons said that they'd have to amputate both his arms and both legs. The other insisted on the left leg only. They argued for a long time. And Nifonov did not care. The real Nifonov was dead, and the Nifonov they were talking about was someone else, a stranger, not a real person, of no use in this life, so let them amputate anything they liked. Even his head.

He listened to the surgeons' voices through a faint ringing in his ears, then something cloyingly sweet and suffocating poured into his nostrils and his mouth instead of air, he drew a meek sigh and fell fast asleep for what seemed an eternity....

He woke up. The pain must have wakened him. He could not locate the pain. It was everywhere. Especially in his left leg, in the crushed shin. He moaned feebly like a child—the real Nifonov could never have moaned like that. The pain was so awful that tears poured down his cheeks. The real Nifonov never cried. The old nurse sitting by his bedside rose to her feet and said:

"Well, thank God, he's come to. Have a good cry, son, have a good cry, it'll do you good."

She went away. Another woman came up, wiped his lips for him and patted him on the head as if he were a kid.

The surgeons came and went. They did not argue any

more, and talked in muted voices. The old nurse returned and gave him a glucose infusion.

"Where does it hurt, son?" she asked.

"My leg."

"Which one?"

"The left leg."

"Oh dear," sighed the old nurse.

Nifonov no longer possessed a left leg, but he only discovered it on the following day.

Surely a thing like that could never have happened to the real Nifonov—he wouldn't have felt pain in a leg that wasn't there.

The surgeons and the entire staff were very proud that they had managed to save Nifonov's right leg and both arms.

The old nurse told Nifonov: "Dr. Cheremnykh, he staked everything—your life and his good name. 'I refuse to turn this handsome young fellow into a stump,' he said. And so he took the risk and won. God helps the brave, you know. We'll get you back into shape, never worry." And added with a boastful wink: "Your operation will be described in all the medical journals!"

Nifonov hardly listened: what did he care about Dr. Cheremnykh's success? This weak, pain-racked body, encased in plaster, swathed in bandages and unable to lift a finger, was not Nifonov anyway.

Nifonov was a worker who knew his job and commanded respect. And this useless person could not even turn over on his side, and the nurse had to do it for him. His sacrum had gone numb from lying on his back, and a rubber ring had been placed under him. He could not do anything, he did not want anything, he did not care what happened to him, it made no difference to him whether he lived or died....

The same old nurse told him that a friend of his had carried him to safety from the battlefield. He was wounded too, people said, but still he hauled Nifonov all the way to the first-aid station. "That would be Semyon Beryoza," Nifonov thought, and asked:

"Is he alive?"

"Now that's something I couldn't know, son," the old nurse replied.

* * *

Some time later Nifonov was told that he was going to be moved to another town, to another hospital. He had his clothes put on, he was laid on stretchers and carried outside.

The fresh hot air and the glare made him gasp and blinded him. The wind tore at his cap, and Nifonov caught at it just in time....

"Mind the plaster cast!" shouted the nurse.

Nifonov looked at his hand in wonder. So it had begun to work, had it? So the doctors weren't lying when they told him he'd be able to move about soon and would be as strong as ever? So he was the real Nifonov after all, was he?

The air made him dizzy, there was a ringing in his ears, he yawned and fell into a doze.

This was to be the last time he dozed off like that, the last fit of overpowering weakness.

Once in the train Nifonov woke up for good. He did not feel like sleeping any more. He was hungry. He felt he was the old, real Nifonov, with his former strength ripening under the plaster casts and bandages.

He lay staring at the ceiling. The ceiling was made from narrow strips of wood, neatly fitted together. It was low overhead. It gleamed with paint, and it was very, very white, scrubbed beautifully clean.

The suspended cot swung gently with the jolting motion of the train, but nothing could lull Nifonov any longer. What was the use of his returning strength when one of his legs was gone and the other would be useless anyway— that much he had gathered from the surgeons' obscure talk. What was he supposed to do with his former strength, he'd like to know?

He visualised the machine tools, rows of machine tools in the factory workshop, and himself walking between them, delighting in the smoothness and efficiency with which the work was running.

Reporters visited the factory and then wrote the funniest things in the newspaper, such as, for instance, the approximate number of miles Nifonov covered in a day, operating his machine tools.

He made good money, he had a good record and a good name: his father and grandfather had both worked at the same factory. He did not choose his trade, he inherited it like the little house where he was born and where his parents died.

He had a wife.... His friends teased him: this marriage was sure made in heaven, they said. His wife was the chairman of the factory's trade union committee. She came home late, looked at her husband with tired kind eyes, and asked him absently: "What was I going to tell you?"

He warmed up the supper for her and poured out the tea. He made fun of her grandness, spared her as much housework as he could, and sincerely respected her. They had two daughters who sort of grew up by themselves: in winter they went to school, and in summer to a Young Pioneer camp.

God, how all of them would cry when they found out that he had no legs. Women would come to his wife's office and pity her with simple-hearted outspokenness.... Never mind that, it was a small worry. People survived bigger misfortune. It wasn't his legs that were uppermost in his mind, nor the thought of his wife and daughters shedding a few tears.

The thing was what was he going to be when he emerged from his plaster casts, what was to be his place in life? Neither his wife nor his daughters, nor even a wise book could give him the answer. He had to decide this question himself.

"Comrade Commissar," he called Danilov who happened to be walking past.

Danilov came up to his cot.

"Comrade Commissar," Nifonov repeated haltingly. "You wouldn't remember a man named Semyon Beryoza among your patients, would you? A machine-gunner?"

Danilov thought for a moment. "No, I don't remember the name. A relative of yours?"

"No, just a friend," Nifonov replied.

He felt that Semyon Beryoza was the only person who could advise him.

What he had in mind was this.

In the old happy days Nifonov had a small passion of which he was almost ashamed. This passion was playing the accordion. The accordion belonged to his older brother who had been killed in the First World War, and Nifonov had learnt to play it. He loved music and had a good ear. As a matter of fact he was one of the first musicians who ventured to play Chopin's waltzes on this instrument.

Before he married he readily played at birthday parties and weddings. His wife thought it common. Still, she permitted him to play in the amateur concerts staged at their club.

With the years he appeared less and less often in public. He was past his youth which excused many things; he was a sedate man now, he was a specialist whose work was written about in the papers, and his wife held a conspicuous position at the factory. He himself began to feel that there was something improper in his passion for the accordion. And he only played it at home when he was all by himself.

And now as he lay in bed he thought about it and for the life of him could not see anything improper about it. It was just Olga's high and mighty ways. So what if she was the chairman of the factory's trade union organisation? More power to her, but he, he'd play the accordion, and that was that.

He pictured himself slowly coming on stage with his artificial leg and his crutches. The audience would be hushed and perhaps awed by his crutches.... He would sit down on the chair and a boy, his pupil, would hand him the accordion.

Perhaps his real vocation was playing the accordion and not adjusting those machine tools? Who could tell.

"Well, Olga, that's how it is," he would say to his wife. "You'll have to live with an accordion player."

But what if the doctors were wrong? What if he never recovered the use of his hands? Horrible thought. Lord, what happiness it was to be able to use your hands and play the accordion, he never even suspected what happiness it was....

There was no denying it, starting a new life at forty after years of a settled, secure existence, would daunt any man. If he could only talk it over with a good friend, with a brave, resolute man without any prejudices....

"Nurse, please come here. Was there ever a man named Semyon Beryoza on your train? A machine-gunner he was."

* * *

During their stop at Sverdlovsk, a beautiful young woman asked to see Dr. Belov and handed him a paper from the clearance centre endorsing the transfer of Lt. Kramin to a local hospital.

"Is he badly crippled?" she asked. "I am his wife."

"He will have to use crutches, you see," replied Dr. Belov. "But as regards mental activity, his faculties are unimpaired. This is unquestionable." And, moved by a desire to say something more comforting to the young lady, he added: "And, d'you know, his self-control is quite remarkable."

"Really?" said the lady. "That's good."

She stood very straight with her head held high, and spoke in a low, well-controlled voice. There was an elusive resemblance to Kramin in her beautiful face. He must have taught her a great deal, thought the doctor.

He went with the lady to coach number 11. Kramin was carried out on a stretcher. The lady's poise as she stood beside the doctor was admirable.... The hot sun lit up Kramin's yellow skull and thin yellow neck, and caught a glint in his spectacles. The lady made a sudden step forward, and bent over the stretcher.

Kramin pushed her away gently and, squinting in the sun, said:

"Hello, Inna love, hello." He kissed her strong yet delicate hand. "Let me say goodbye to the doctor...."

There is much more that he will teach her, Dr. Belov was thinking as he watched the lady walk down the platform beside the stretcher, saying something to her husband with her beautiful head inclined, devotedly and humbly.

Chapter Seven

LETTERS

On the way back from Omsk, the hospital train became jammed in the traffic moving westward. Trains carrying tanks, planes, guns and fuel got the green light while the hospital train made slow progress, obliged to give the right of way all the time to the next half-a-mile-long military freight train. In Perm, for instance, they were side-tracked for eight days.

The slow progress and the enforced idleness unnerved people, leaving them free to brood about home, their loved ones, and hunger for news....

Dr. Belov suffered the worst torments of all.

It was almost a year since that one letter from his wife, dated September 5, had been written. A second food parcel had been sent to Leningrad from Omsk, and still there was no reply.

Of course there ought to be letters, but they were in the mailbox at V. And there was no knowing when the train would be routed via V. next time.

Danilov decided to send someone to V. to collect the mail. There'd be any number of volunteers, for many of the staff came from the town and it was a rare chance to visit home. Danilov would have gladly gone himself. But it was Lena he chose.

"Make it snappy," he told her. "You'll find out at headquarters where we've gone. Don't rely on passenger trains, freights will get you to us much quicker. Hop it from train to train, but I don't have to teach you, do I?"

He gave her a small parcel neatly tied with string, behind which was tucked a piece of paper with an address on it.

"Here, give this to my wife. I've a growing son at home, he needs it," Danilov put on a frown to hide the smile that betrayed the weakness he had for his son. "Take a look at him and see if he's all right. My wife's letters don't tell me much."

Carrying a bagful of letters and calling addresses, Lena got on the first freight train going in the direction of V. And now the days of waiting dragged even slower for everyone in the hospital train.

Olga Mikhailovna suggested a berry and mushroom picking trip to the woods so jam could be made for the wounded and a store of dried mushrooms put in. The nurses thought it a wonderful idea, and a party set off with buckets. Yulia Dmitrievna wondered rather anxiously if Suprugov would come too, and her heart leapt when he asked her:

"Will you permit me to join you?"

It was *her* he asked, and not Olga Mikhailovna or Fainna!

She felt embarrassed at first when they set out side by side. She was not used to walking with a man she was in love with in full sight of everyone. Luckily, Fainna and several ward nurses came with them. Fainna took control of the conversation right away. She threw back her head with the becoming yellow kerchief tied loosely round it, and laughed boisterously, although nothing really funny had been said. Yulia Dmitrievna watched her in silence, thinking that she herself had never laughed so loudly. Nor could she ever talk such silly nonsense: everything she said sounded serious and instructive, which was probably what frightened the men away from her…. Ah yes, men were attracted to women like Fainna, vivid and noisy women who never thought twice about saying things with a double meaning, and who laughed, throwing back the head and inflating the throat. "Oh well, since I can't I can't," Yulia Dmitrievna decided reasonably. But she was sorry that Fainna had come with them….

Once in the woods, the younger girls left the three of them alone—Yulia Dmitrievna, Fainna and Suprugov. Fainna was the first to find some mushrooms, and called Suprugov to come and help her pick them. He was in no hurry to go: sitting on the grass, he leaned back against a pine and lit a cigarette, taking amusement, it seemed, in Fainna's enticing calls. To Yulia Dmitrievna he appeared extraordinarily attractive at that moment. He caught her glance and said with a smile:

"A cheerful young lady, isn't she?"

Her spirits soared at once: he was not enchanted by Fainna at all, he was mocking her, and she had been afraid that Fainna would charm him away.... No, evidently he did really prefer Yulia Dmitrievna to all the other women there.

Fainna, however, was not going to give up so easily. She came and dragged him away, tucking her arm in his and pushing him on with a shoulder and even with a knee.... Yulia Dmitrievna walked behind them, chuckling softly. Fainna's presence did not irk her any longer, and on the contrary it provided a pretext for her closer comradely intimacy with Suprugov, for an exchange of looks and smiles whose meaning only the two of them could understand....

Unfortunately, the pleasant outing did not last long: the mushrooms grew in abundance, and the pails were filled to the brim much too soon. The party would have started back if it had not been for Fainna declaring that the air in the forest being so salubrious it was stupid returning to the stuffiness of the train before they had to. She lay down on the soft grass in the huge dark shadow cast by the trees and presaging the approach of dusk, and assumed what she thought was the most seductive pose. Yulia Dmitrievna and Suprugov sat down primly beside her.

"Doctor, tell me, were you always so lifeless?" Fainna asked, with closed eyes.

"Why lifeless?" Suprugov asked, exchanging a look with Yulia Dmitrievna, and pretending not to understand. "I have always felt a sufficiency of life in me."

"Your feelings are deceiving you," Fainna drawled.

Since he made no comeback, she went at him again:

"Were you ever in love?"

"What a question," Suprugov shrugged.

"You are a rare phenomenon," Fainna said. "A forty-year-old bachelor is a rarity in our days. Everyone is married nowadays, everyone to a man. Even boys of 20 are all married, or getting married, or are engaged to some girl. Are you?"

"But I am not a boy of 20," Suprugov joked.

"Oh no, I won't let you get away with that!" Fainna screamed, turning a neat somersault to come face to face with him. "Answer me!"

Yulia Dmitrievna listened, gazing into the sky. It was beautiful at this hour, neither blue, nor gold, and diffused with a gentle, serene light.

"All is well," Yulia Dmitrievna thought as she smiled at the sky, at the conversation beside her, and the vague, radiant hope arising timidly in her heart. "All is very well."

When they returned to the train, Fainna said to her: "He's a downright moron."

* * *

Lena was striding along the street of the town she knew so well. Pity the trams weren't running, something had happened to the tracks. She'd have reached headquarters by now and received Dan's letters. Rather absently she noted the scarcity of men in the streets, practically all the passers-by were women. It was different at the railway stations: there one saw only men in uniform, and hardly a woman among them.

She came to the avenue lined with spreading, unruffled elms, and slowed down. When she crossed the avenue she would see a house in the side street, a grey three-storied house, the second from the corner, the abode of her brief happiness.... There it was, just as she had left it a year ago. A bit shabbier perhaps, and the front door no longer seemed so grand, it actually looked lower and narrower. No, she wouldn't go in now, she'd come here afterwards with Dan's letters.

At headquarters she was given a whole stack of letters and some two dozen parcels. They were small parcels, and Lena swept them into her bag. She flicked through the envelopes quickly: there was no letter addressed to her.

Sitting down on a bench in the dusty mail room, she went through the envelopes once more, one by one. There was a letter for Danilov from his wife, and another one in a large envelope with the stamp of the Central Committee of the Party on it. There was a letter for Dr. Belov from Leningrad. Here was one for Nadya, one more, and yet another one, all from her boyfriend most probably.... And no less than thirty letters for Bogeichuk. There were letters for all of them, for every single person on the train except herself.

She threw the letters into the bag with the parcels, heaved it on her back, and went home.

Probably his letters were waiting for her there. He had changed his mind for some reason and decided to write to their home address. She would ask the neighbours or the house superintendent.

She ran lightly up the stairs to the third floor without stooping under the weight of the bag or getting winded.

The door was locked. Dan had his own latch-key, it was a defective key and never worked at the first try. Lena always heard him fumbling with the key, and loving the sound of its impatient scraping did not hasten to open the door for him.

The neighbours had no letters for her. They had nothing— no firewood, no kerosene, no soap, no thread. The old women who were at home surrounded Lena, and enumerated for her the things they did not have. The younger women were either in the army or away at work. Lena disentangled herself from the old women, and went downstairs to the superintendent's room.

There were no letters for her. She collected the key to her room and slowly walked up the stairs. All at once she felt dead tired. She had hardly had any sleep these last three days and had not undressed once.

Nothing had been touched in her room since she left it. Everything was covered with a thick layer of dust, and the white window curtains had turned yellow.

A half-smoked cigarette lay in the ashtray—Dan's cigarette.

Lena took off her boots, lay down on the sofa and tried to relax as she had once been taught, loosening all her muscles and giving her whole body a rest. The absence of letters puzzled but did not alarm her. Dan was alive, she knew. The room smelt of his cigarette.... It's the people who had some chink in their lives who died: death stole into that chink and got them. There was no chink in Dan for death to steal into. His life was wonderfully complete, nothing could cut it short.

Dan dead? Rubbish. Anyone else might die but not Dan.

Closing her eyes she kissed him goodnight and fell asleep.

She awoke about two hours later, feeling rested and active, and started putting the room in order. She took down the dirty curtains, dusted the furniture and scrubbed the floor. The half-smoked cigarette she left in the ashtray.

The old woman who lived next door was in the kitchen, frying something on an electric cooker, and when Lena walked in she quickly pulled out the plug.

"Electricity's been limited, we're not allowed to use cookers, irons or anything," she grumbled, and carried the cooker with the smoking pan on it to her room.

Lena treated her to some liver paste and tea with sugar. The old woman liked a sweet with her tea, but her grandson had eaten all the sweets she had, she told Lena plaintively.

"The civilians have it tough," Lena told herself. "We're much better off."

She took a cold bath, and luxuriated in the feel of the soft bathrobe she put on afterwards. She was an entirely different person in this bathrobe, she was once more the Lena men stopped to ogle in the street. Standing before the tall looking glass she smiled at herself. "That's the girl," she said to her reflection, lifting an eyebrow. "We can be any kind we choose, it's up to us!" Suddenly a thought struck her: Katya Gryaznova might have her letters. She flung away the bathrobe at once, and got back into uniform.

She did not stop to reason why Dan should have addressed the letters to Katya whom he disliked and called a smug fool, but Lena was sure that the letters had to be somewhere, and she'd find them if she tried hard enough.

When Katya opened the door and saw Lena, she burst into a storm of sobs. Her husband, that young man with the mandolin, had been killed. Katya had received the notification two months ago.

"Oh, you can't imagine how he loved me!" Katya sobbed. "He literally carried me about in his arms!"

Lena remembered the love letter she received from him, and doubted that this weedy chap could have lifted his big fat wife at all, it was the other way about more likely.... Katya's grief, though, was genuine and demonstrative. She recounted for Lena in minutest detail how she was called to the enlistment office, how she was invited to sit down and prepared for the shock, and how she understood everything and went faint, and how they gave her a glass of water, and how she could not get over it till this day and would never get over it ever.... Tears poured in streams down her kind, plump face.

"Dan doesn't write," Lena told her.

"There's grief everywhere, everywhere," Katya's mother rustled in the next room. "It does not miss a single home, it visits everyone...."

They had no letters for Lena, of course.

* * *

Later that evening Lena went to the address given her by Danilov.

The house was on the outskirts which had begun to be built up just before the war. You had to enter from the yard, and the gates were locked. It had grown dark while she wandered about looking for the house. There was a dimly lighted window on the groundfloor, and she knocked.

The window opened outward in the village way. The curtain was pulled aside, and a very plain woman poked out her head.

"I've brought a parcel from Ivan Yegorovich," Lena told her.

"Oh, heavens," the woman said in a fluster.

She let Lena into the gate, and then took her through a dark kitchen into her room. A desk lamp was burning beside a sewing machine. All the chairs and the sofa were buried under huge bundles of cotton wool and pieces of khaki cloth. A boy of five or so lay curled up in a quaint, uncomfortable way in the corner of the sofa, with his head pillowed on a bundle of cotton wool, and was fast asleep.

"Please sit down," the woman said in a low, halting voice. "You're from the hospital train, are you?"

Having seated Lena she remained standing before her, nervously pulling out the threaded needle stuck in the lapel of her blouse, and pushing it back in again.

"How is he?" she asked. "Is he well?"

"He's all right."

"You don't know, out there, when the end will come? Did he say anything?"

"The end of what?" Lena asked.

"Of the war. Everyone's sick of it, you know."

Lena looked at her in dismay. That's not how she pictured Danilov's wife at all.

"How can we know?" she said. "He sent you this parcel, here you are."

"Sugar again," said Danilov's wife, taking the parcel. "He shouldn't do it, he's denying himself, and Vanya has enough to eat. You tell him that we have enough to eat, we're out of the woods now, tell him not to worry, he has cares enough.... He's fallen asleep," she said, intercepting Lena's glance at the child. "I was too busy to put him to bed, so he fell asleep where he was playing. I'm working, you see. Making padded jackets for the army. I don't want to put him in the day nursery, the food isn't very good there, so I take work home. Still, they've given me a worker's ration card.... I'll just go and get the samovar going."

Lena tried to decline the tea.

"No, I won't take no for an answer," Danilov's wife protested. "Here you brought a parcel from Ivan Yegorovich, how can I let you go without even a cup of tea! No, it's not done."

As she chipped the kindling in the kitchen she went on speaking, peeping round the door every now and again:

"We make do now, but when the ration cards were first started I didn't know how Vanya and I would survive, and I felt quite lost, you know. Habit means an awful lot: before the war, you see, we were used to very good food.... Naturally I didn't write Ivan Yegorovich about it, there was nothing he could do to help, he sent me the certificate that we're his dependents, and what more could he do? He saw how it was for himself when he came home for a visit.... Well, my kitchen garden saw us through at first: I'd sell some potatoes and buy milk, and now that I have a worker's ration card, things are not bad at all. And then I have relatives in the country, they sometimes bring me some cream, which is very kind of them, and I make butter for Vanya from this cream. Merkulov, the present director of the trust, helps too: he sent me some firewood in the spring, and has promised to send more.... You tell him that we're doing well, tell him not to worry...."

"Why don't you write and tell him so yourself?"

"Oh, I'm not much of a writer," Danilova said. "And I've no time, there's all this work."

The kitchen table at which they drank tea and ate boiled potatoes heated up over a fire of chips was covered with a clean oilcloth. Every single thing in this house was very clean, but it could not be otherwise in Danilov's house, Lena thought. The sugar she had brought was served in a pretty bowl. As for butter, there was none.

"I haven't been getting any cream for a long time," Danilova said apologetically. "And we haven't bought anything against our August card yet."

"The civilians certainly have it tough," Lena said to herself for the second time that day.

"I teach Vanya to do his share of the work too," Danilova continued. "Anything might happen, God forbid, and if he and I are left to fend for ourselves he's got to know how to do any job...."

Lena marvelled more and more: to think that Danilov hadn't even told his wife that the train had been transferred to the rear!

"We don't go to the front any more," she said. "We're in the rear all the time. So don't be afraid."

"Well, you never know," Danilova sighed. "It's wartime. It might be bombed anywhere."

She grew pensive, and the expression on her tired face said that she was prepared to take any blow fate might deal her, lying down.

As Lena walked home she wondered about the Danilovs. "How can they live together? How can he live with her? And how does she live with him? What do they talk about? It must be terribly dull for them.... How different it is with Dan and me!"

She delivered all the other messages she had in the course of the next morning, and started back for the hospital train whose whereabouts she was told at headquarters.

* * *

The hospital train was side-tracked at Z., a junction. The station was crowded with trains—all of them troop trains, all of them entitled to priority.

It was suffocating in the coaches.

Dr. Belov walked the length of the train along the platform. The dry coal dust crunched under his feet with a nasty sound.... A cock was crowing in the cage under the crew car where the poultry were kept. A crowd of soldiers and children had gathered to look. A porter had abandoned his hand-cart to peer under the train. And a little girl was skipping and shouting: "When the train's moving their tails go flutter-flutter!"

Kostritsin was also there. His face was grim. The soldiers were laughing, and one of them said:

"That roster fellow never loses heart, he crows even under a train!"

"They've a soldier to look after the chickens," another one said, nibbling pumpkin seeds and spitting out the husks.

Dr. Belov came up closer.

"You see what's going on?" Kostritsin asked.

"Oh well, it isn't so terrible really," said Dr. Belov.

"One day I'll throw myself under the train on account of these cracks," Kostritsin said sullenly.

"Oh, nonsense. Come to my compartment, we'll talk it over," Dr. Belov told him.

He walked on down the platform. Dr. Suprugov was taking a sunbath on the roof of coach 8. He was wearing a skullcap and shorts. Fima stood in the window of the kitchen plucking a chicken, and the fat on her bare arms quivered with every motion. The electrical potato peeler was rattling away, and Sobol's voice sounded above the noise:

"Why do you make it as many portions as before with Ogorodnikova away? That's minus one portion. And then Nizvetsky has colitis, so that's minus one more portion...."

Dr. Belov said to himself: "Our train, I must say, does present a picture of life in all its fullness." He recalled their first trip. The burning coach, and the blasted windows.... And now they had hens laying eggs under one of the coaches. Little by little the train had become a home, a household.... "Oh well, it's the natural course of things...."

His thoughts were sluggish, he was compelling himself to concentrate on his surroundings. Alarm had been gnawing at him ever since Lena had gone off for the mail. The arguments from which he had drawn comfort only recently seemed infantile now. He had persuaded himself that all was well, and found solace in his silly daydreams. Even if his parcel had reached them, how long would it last them? A month at best, with the strictest economy.... He'd know how they were within the next few days. He would hold in his hands an envelope addressed in Sonia's hand. He knew her handwriting, he knew every letter and every smallest flourish.... Yes, but why one envelope? There'd be a stack of envelopes. Oh, all right, let it be one, just one, so long as he knew that they were alive....

That day in early July last year was just as hot when their train arrived at Vitebsk Station in Leningrad. There were as many trains on the other tracks then. No, they were fewer. And suddenly Sonia had appeared from behind one of them in her dear grey dress....

He asked Danilov when Lena was expected back, and Danilov replied: in eight days or so.

Eight days? Well, let's say ten to be on the safe side. With a blue pencil he drew ten squares in his notebook, and at the end of the day he crossed one out with a red pencil.

*   *   *

Danilov spent the whole morning at the commandant's office trying to get his train despatched, and they did start off in the early afternoon. It seemed they would never clear the station, they stuck at every semaphore, but at long last the going became a little easier.

Then a telegram was received, urgently ordering the train to R. and suddenly they were racing full speed ahead, roaring past big stations where people signalled them along with their little flags, and followed them out of sight with their eyes.

In the evening Dr. Belov took out his note-book to cross out yet another blue square, the seventh. There was a knock on the door, and when the doctor called out "Come in", Kostritsin entered the compartment—a big, clumsy grey-haired soldier who stood before his superior at attention.

"Sit down, do," said Dr. Belov. "Let's just have a chat, shall we? Do sit down, please do."

Kostritsin obeyed.

"Now then, what is your complaint?" asked the doctor.

Kostritsin coughed into his fist, and said: "You're not very young yourself, sir, you must see the spot I'm in. I'm the laughing stock of all and sundry."

"It's fantastic, of course, keeping the chickens, I mean," said Dr. Belov. "But fresh eggs are very good for the wounded, you know. Very good indeed."

The train slowed down as it approached a station, but a whistle was sounded and it was on the move once more.

Kostritsin tried again.

"It wasn't to tend chickens that I volunteered for the army," he said. "I thought a hospital train was a soldierly business too. And here I am, for no reason or fault of mine...." "I was told that you were an expert on farming," Dr. Belov gave him a dose of innocent flattery.

Kostritsin nodded.

"Sure, I've been used to tending animals since I was a kid. At home everybody kept them. Personally I kept a goat. But it's one thing at home, and quite another here. I've nothing against the pigs, they're in the luggage van, nobody can see you there. But these blasted chickens, they're there in full view!"

"Ah, Kostritsin, it's such trifles really," the doctor said with a sigh. "One day we'll eat the lot of them, served with white sauce...."

Kostritsin was not listening.

"They have to stretch their legs sometimes, don't they? Living things feel miserable in cages.... So I let them out wherever I can. And they stretch their legs. They go wandering off from the train, quite a distance too.... I beg our girls to tend them a bit, but they're young girls, they dream of princes and lieutenants all the time, and they won't stoop to tending chickens. And when you come to think of it what's so difficult about tending chickens? They've already become trained: when the engine gives a whistle they all rush back to the cage. It's not the work I mind, it's the cracks...."

"Stop," said the doctor.

For the last minute or so he had been listening not to Kostritsin but to the commotion somewhere down the coach—running feet, slamming doors, voices raised in exclamation.

Kostritsin rose to his feet.

"Shall I go and find out?"

"Yes, do."

He came back beaming: "The mail has arrived."

Dr. Belov blinked nervously and rose. Danilov, also smiling happilly, appeared in the door.

"Here's a letter for you from Leningrad, doctor."

"Thank you, thank you," Dr. Belov mumbled, taking the envelope in his shaking hands.

* * *

The letter which Danilov received from the Central Committee of the Party was brief, polite, and cool. For all its politeness, the gist of it was: stay put, comrade, and mind you do your job properly.

Clear enough.

Flushing slightly from the implied ticking off, Danilov folded the letter neatly and tucked it behind his Party card in his breast pocket.

The second letter was from his wife. He glanced through it quickly. They were well. Their relatives and friends sent their regards—and there followed a list of them. He would find out everything from Lena, she'd make more sense. What a girl, the train had stopped but for five minutes, yet she had managed to catch it.... Good for her!

He wanted to hear what news the personnel had received, to see what mood everyone was in. He went out into the corridor and saw Yulia Dmitrievna, Fainna and Suprugov standing by the window. Fainna was clutching Suprugov by the shoulder and talking breathlessly. Suprugov had a languid air.

"A misfortune has befallen me," he said with dignity when Danilov approached. "My dear mother has passed away."

Danilov did not know what one said to a person one disliked in such cases. But he had to say something, if only to be polite.

"How old was she?" he asked at last.

"Seventy-eight," replied Suprugov.

"Yes, that's quite an age," Danilov said with sympathy.

What else was there to say? An old woman, unremark-able in any way, had lived a long, long life and died a natural death....

He went on to Dr. Belov's compartment, to hear what news he'd had from home.

Dr. Belov was sitting on the berth, exactly where he sat when his wife came to see him. Danilov was shocked by the change in the doctor: he had left him ten minutes ago looking hale and flushed with excitement, and now he saw before him a shrivelled, broken old man with an ashen, wan face.

He read the letter that lay on the table.

Dr. Belov looked at Danilov dully. Danilov sat down beside him and did not speak. Suddenly the old doctor began to breathe noisily, his eyes filled with tears, and his hands groped helplessly over his knees and the upholstery of the berth.

"You cannot imagine," he whispered, "You cannot imagine...."

He wanted to tell Danilov that he could not imagine what an angel Sonia had been, what an angel Lalya had been, and what they had meant to him. But his strength failed him, he could not speak. His shoulders shook, and covering his face with his hands he burst out crying. He sobbed and moaned, his tears trickled down his fingers and wrists into his sleeves, he caught his tears with his shaking lips, swallowed them and chocked over them.

Still Danilov did not speak, and just sat there, erect and pale, with glittering eyes. Then he went out into the corridor and called Fainna. She brought some bromide and luminal. The two of them made the doctor take the sedative, and stayed with him until he fell asleep. They went out together, and Fainna cried.

"I'd give anything to comfort him," she said.

"And I," said Danilov, "I'd like to kill with my own hands one, if only one of those beasts who are doing this to us."

That night at R. they took on a load of wounded. Dr. Belov was not wakened. Danilov said that the head doctor was unwell, and signed for the wounded together with Suprugov.

In the morning he went to Dr. Belov's compartment and reported that a patient in coach number 6 who was suffering from a slight wound in the foot and shell shock, was being unmanageably difficult. He called for the doctor every five minutes, demanded a bath, gave no peace to the other patients there, and simply could not be calmed. Perhaps Dr. Belov could go and see him himself....

The only thing that penetrated from what Danilov said was that he, Dr. Belov, had to go somewhere. He put on his white coat, and shuffled after Danilov.

With faltering steps he went from one coach to the next, peering into the faces of the wounded with a curious urgency. Fainna and Smirnova came with him on his rounds. Nurse Smirnova handed him the case notes of the patient before him, and he read them through with tense concentration. Now and again the notes appeared insufficiently conclusive, and then he read the whole case history.

He was afraid that he might read what wasn't there, and do something wrong. He was afraid that he would forever lose the faculty to think, read, and treat patients. The world had withdrawn from him with its sounds, smells, and tangibility. It was only natural: was it conceivable that the world would remain the same now that Sonia and Lalya were no longer in it?

But as he went through the coaches, awareness of his surroundings gradually returned to him. The words written in the case notes and spoken by people reached him less slowly now and evoked the response they should evoke. His attention could now be focused on familiar objects, and these objects were acquiring their former properties. Voices no longer came from somewhere across the world, they sounded close and each had its identity. The plaster casts and bandages gave out their own peculiar, unpleasant smell. The stethoscope transmitted familiar murmurs. This patient here had to be transferred to the special coach because he was apparently developing pneumonia in his right lung.

The world wanted to live on as before in spite of the fact that Sonia and Lalya were no longer in this world. It was incredible and horrible, but he could not do anything about it. He himself was living. He wanted to see that petulant patient Danilov had told him about.

This turned out to be a strong man of thirty or so with curly hair and ruddy cheeks. He lay stripped to the waist on his rumpled bedclothes. His body was pink, and his shoulders sloped effeminately. "Ivan Mironovich Lutokhin," the doctor read on the case-sheet above the cot.

"What is your complaint?" he asked.

"The heat," Lutokhin said.

"I can't stand this heat. At the hospital I was given baths all the time, and it was the only thing that refreshed me."

He began to moan, loudly and theatrically, throwing back his head and rolling his eyes.

"Now, now," said Fainna. "It can't hurt all that much."

"I'm suffocating," moaned Lutokhin.

Dr. Belov read his case history. He had been wounded and shell-shocked slightly. He had had no fits in the last two weeks. The wound was healing satisfactorily. Baths put him in a better mood, it was noted.

"We have no bath on the train," Dr. Belov told him. "A shower, yes. And we can make you a local bath."

"What the hell do I want your shower for?" Lutokhin screamed, and cursed obscenely. "I want to sit in a bathtub and sit there, damn and blast you all to hell!"

He moaned louder than ever. "Oh shut up, will you," someone called down from an upper cot. "Comrade doctor, don't bother with him, he's just putting on an act."

Doctor Belov told the nurse to take Lutokhin's temperature, and the thermometer showed 37.1.

"You see now?" Lutokhin said with malicious glee.

The examination showed a lightly hightened blood pressure, a weakened reaction to light, and the impure breathing of a habitual smoker.

"His appetite is good, and his stool is normal," said Fainna.

"I assure you there is no cause for alarm," Dr. Belov told Lutokhin. "You have to bear up for the remaining few days of the journey. Once in hospital you will be given baths again, and the heat will be easier to endure."

Lutokhin jumped up and cursed violently.

"Easy, easy, there are ladies present," the doctor said, and turned to go.

"Hey, where are you off to?" Lutokhin yelled. "Tell them to give me a shower!"

"A shower for this patient," Dr. Belov told the nurses, and his order was taken down.

"A real pain in the neck," Fainna muttered.

The shower was ready and waiting for him in about twenty minutes, no more. But when nurse Smirnova came to fetch Lutokhin she found him asleep.

"The moment you left he stopped fussing and fell asleep," the patient in the nearest cot told her. "He'll be all the better for it if you make less of a song and dance about him."

Lutokhin slept with his face buried in the pillow. Nurse

Smirnova saw a bit of his ruddy cheek and a cherry-red earlobe.

"Let him sleep," she said, and went away.

This was at about eleven in the morning. Just before lunch Faïnna burst into Dr. Belov's compartment to tell him that Lutokhin was dead.

He had died from a haemorrhage of the brain.

Until now they had had no deaths in the train, if one did not count that woman in Pskov with a stomach wound who had died on the operating table. But she was dying when they brought her in.

Lutokhin's death came as a terrible shock. It left everybody with a feeling of guilt, although no one was really to blame. It was one of those cases which science cannot yet foresee or prevent. Shell-shock does sometimes have such unpredictable after-effects. Death will lurk in the patient's body, hiding and scheming, and suddenly it will grip him by the throat and triumphantly show its fangs....

"He ought to have remained in the hospital, evidently," Dr. Belov was thinking in an agony of guilt. "Perhaps the train has jostled the brain resulting in instant death. But who could have foreseen it? He'd had no fits for two weeks, and he gave the impression of a healthy person. But perhaps I am to blame," he tried to remember how he examined the patient in all the details. "I allowed myself to be deceived by superficial indications which seemed favourable, and I missed something very important, some unfavourable signs, and failed to take the necessary measures.... Yes, I did not take due notice of his poor reaction to light. I took note of it, I remember very well that I did, but I did not do anything about it."

He realised that he could not have taken any radical measures, that it was a rare case, insidious and difficult, and only a genius could have perhaps prevented death in a flash of inspiration or by divine guidance.... But just the same this death weighed heavily on his conscience.

"He probably had a wife and children," he was thinking. "A wife and children.... And they have now been bereaved because an old, useless doctor failed to notice the reaction of the pupils. I have suffered a terrible loss, but why should others suffer from it? Why should Lutokhin's wife and children? It's monstrous. If this were punishable by law, I should give myself up and say: judge me, I failed to save a human life because of my personal tragedy. It is because of me that private Lutokhin, Ivan Mironovich, has died.... They say that I am not to blame, that it was simply one of those unfortunate cases. Oh if only I could believe that, what a relief it would be!"

On the table under glass lay the letter he had received from an old friend and card partner informing him that Sonia and Lalya had been killed in Leningrad in one of the first air-raids in September 1941.

Chapter Eight

MEMORIES

In the autumn of 1942 the German armies reached Stalingrad. The battle which for five months was to hold the attention of the world began.

At first there was fear of the Germans breaking through to the Volga. Then hope was born that this would not happen. And then came confidence that Stalingrad was the threshold which the Germans could never cross and from which the Red Army would start driving the enemy back, liberating Soviet territory, seized by the aggressors.

When they travelled without a load Danilov gathered the personnel together twice a day now, in the morning and in the evening, to discuss the war news. They talked about Stalingrad mainly, as everything else seemed of secondary importance in comparison. In coaches where room permitted Danilov installed notice-boards on which newspaper clippings were tacked. Stalingrad held sway over the minds and hearts, the word came to symbolise hope, promise of a new day, the dawn of victory.

The men who were fit for combat duty were recalled from the hospital train and put in the ranks. Danilov was not recalled. He always remembered the letter he had received from the Central Committee and stayed "put".

The younger of the ward nurses joined up as volunteers, and many of them received rifle and machine-gun training right there in the train.

It did not surprise Danilov that Lena Ogorodnikova had joined up, but he gave a whistle of amazement when he saw the signature of the fat Iya on one of the applications. Why, only a year ago she had crouched all night in a shell-hole, paralysed with fear!

He liked to hear what people were talking about on the train. He had more need of listening than talking now.

He would come up to a group, sit down, clumsily roll himself a cigarette (he had taken up smoking lately), listen to the talk for a minute or two in silence, and be on his way.

"He's fed up with everything," Sukhoyedov said. "He's tired of us and of our conversations. Just look at him, he's a young man, he wants scope for his energy."

"And who isn't fed up?" the others asked.

But they were wrong. Danilov found them more interesting now than before.

Yulia Dmitrievna had unravelled some knitting, and as she wound the wool into balls said to Suprugov:

"We have stopped them at any rate. Remember Pskov. Our resistance there was quite different in character. Do you remember? We saw our troops retreating with our own eyes.... Ah yes, you were the first to draw my attention to it.... And now one feels that this battle will be won by us. Apparently, that's as far as they will come. I can well imagine what's going on in the streets there and in the houses...."

She sounded sorry that she was not there—in the streets and houses of Stalingrad.

* * *

One day early in the winter the hospital train got stuck in the traffic jam on Moscow's circuit railway and chances were that it would stay there for all of 24 hours. They were travelling westward without a load.

Danilov gave the staff permission to go to the pictures, and came along too.

They went to a small transport workers' club hung with red bunting from which the inscribed slogans had been almost completely washed off by the autumn rains. The spectators were mostly schoolboys. They were a demanding, noisy audience: every ten minutes or so when the projection went awry they raised a terrible row, whistling, stamping their feet and yelling.

First there were war news, and then a wartime film. The leading man was a young chap, as pretty as a picture, and his girl-friend matched him in looks. They performed a series of heroic feats, and then the girl fell into the hands of the nazis and was tortured to death. The nazis on the screen were too obviously fake, but the feats, the hatred for the nazis, and the beautiful girl dying for her motherland—all this was happening today, it was their life, and everyone was moved by the film. Towards the end, the shouts of the boys at the fumbling booth-man reached a climax.

It was snowing when the people emerged from the club. Large flakes slowly drifted down on the tracks. The young ward nurses walked in clusters, hotly discussing the film. Most of them had been crying. Yulia Dmitrievna and Fainna walked past Danilov, and then Sobol caught up with them and, exclaiming in a high-pitched voice: "Ah, noble knight, it was Fainna!", crooked his arm in hers.

Danilov fell behind everyone, and walked at a leisurely pace, his hands thrust deep into the pockets of his greatcoat, and his face tilted to catch the snowflakes.

Take any film, any book, there was always love in the story. Was it really so essential for every single person in real life? He, for one, had lived without love, and he hadn't lived badly at all. He had his days full without this love business....

He had loved a woman once, but it was a vain dream, so he had mastered his feelings and thereafter done without love.

He had been as young as that chap on the screen, only not as good-looking and grownup.

Youth was a wonderful thing, really. A joy to recall. You felt a bit ashamed of yourself, a bit sorry, but still it was a joy. Oh well, he was not answerable for the actions of the lad he was twenty-five years ago.

He already had three false teeth and his hair was turning grey on the temples. It was six or seven years now since he had last taken her photograph out of the envelope....

That lad had made a mess of things. He had no luck. But Danilov was grateful to him for these awkward, bitter-sweet memories.

* * *

When he was fifteen, a Komsomol cell was organised in the village where he lived.

A skinny young chap wearing huge boots arrived from town with the mail cart. He assembled all the boys and girls in the schoolhouse, gave them a long, passionate talk, and then started putting down the names of those who wanted to join the Young Communist League.

Danilov joined not so much from conviction as from a desire to spite the mothers. The mothers had gathered in the passage outside and were ordering their children home, some shouting, and some hissing: "Mishka! Tanya! Come out this minute, you hear me?" Danilov was proud that his mother was not among them.

"I've joined up," he told his mother when he returned home.

And his mother said: "You might at least have put on your new shirt for going to the meeting. That city man didn't think much of you, I'm afraid."

Thereafter his mother never meddled in his affairs, nor did his father (except once). They believed that their own honest life was a good example for their son, and that he would never disgrace himself or his parents whatever road he chose to follow.

They were a hard-working family, they talked little, never raising their voices, and were good to people in general. It was their way of life. Danilov never once saw his parents drinking, quarrelling or idling. His father owned a small smithy. He was a devout man, but even if it were Easter Sunday he would not refuse to shoe a horse; he would put on his black apron and go to his smithy.

"God does not mind people working," he would say.

He was a good carpenter, metal worker, harness maker, he could weave a fishing net, and was one of the best mowers in the district. Before the Revolution, the landlord would hire him for the mowing; and now, in his old age, he would put on a white shirt, shave his cheeks, whet his scythe, and go to the state farm to offer his services for the hay-making. He was an artist in this business, and liked to be admired.

Danilov had lived a good half of his life apart from his parents, and saw them very rarely. But the inherited passion for work, and the desire to do this work so well that respectable people should praise him for it, remained always alive in him. His father's precious legacy....

His mother taught him how to cook, darn socks and launder his clothes. "It will come in useful in the army," she always said.

She sometimes caressed him when he was a baby, and then she stopped doing it. He could not remember her kissing him, he did not hold a wake when she died, but he would revere her memory for as long as he lived.

And then came the Revolution. With it came new words and new concepts. He became a member of the Y.C.L. But his life was little changed because the village was so far removed from town—it was all of ninety versts to the nearest railway station.

The Komsomol cell received books by post. The boys read them, but did not understand much of what they read. And there was noone to help them. That skinny chap, who had now grown a moustache, came down occasionally, and gave talks that elucidated some things for them, but not all. On Sundays the Komsomol members—there were four of them—put on clean shirts and went to church. They did not go there to pray, but just to see people. There was nowhere else. Once Danilov was a best man at a church wedding, and held the crown over the groom's head during the marriage ceremony. The groom was also a member of the Komsomol, but he got married in church because his bride would not agree to a registry-office wedding for anything in the world.

All this was changed when the old schoolteacher retired, and a new one arrived in her place.

The new one was called Fainna. A very young teacher she was—hardly over twenty-years-old. She was beautiful, and wore her thick, long hair in braid pinned into a crown high on her head.

"What kind of Komsomols are you?" she demanded of the Komsomol members. "I'd have taken your membership cards away from you long ago."

She requested the village Soviet to build a club house next to the school, and when the Soviet declined her request she went off to the district centre and came back with a written order in support of her demand. She also brought back two packing cases of books, and in the evenings gave readings in the school.

At first only the pupils came to listen, but little by little curiosity brought the adults and even very old people to the schoolhouse. They liked the way she read. They had never heard anything like it before. She began reading in a low voice, bending low over the table where a paraffin lamp was draped over her shoulders. Her tone was level and even casual at first. But soon the story gripped her. A flush suffused her face, and her young eyes shone. She raised her voice, or dropped it to almost a whisper, she shrugged off her shawl, kneeled on the chair, and propped up her glowing cheeks with both hands. When the listeners sighed in sorrow over the misfortunes of the strangers they were hearing about, she, too, would shed a tear, the glistening drops falling from her eyelashes on to the open page before her.

Danilov had never known before that a person could be so interesting, and beautiful. And he could not tear his eyes away from her. He wanted to be like her too. But he realised that it was not easy to achieve. Look how she read, she did not stumble over a single word! And she spoke for different people in different voices. The funny passages were all the funnier for her rendering, and the sad ones were so sad that you wanted to cry.... But why not? She was older than Danilov, she was terribly literate, she'd learnt things which he couldn't have learnt yet at his age. And what was she? An ordinary person like himself. Her felt boots were patched, and her shawl was exactly like his mother's. She had studied much, and that's what learning had made her! He would study, too, and become like her.

"And her step was slow and stately, like a swan's 'twas smooth and gliding," Fainna read in a purring, sing-song voice. "When she spoke, her speech was gentle, like a sweetly ringing brook.... In her hair she wore a crescent, on her brow a shining star...." And, enraptured, he was thinking: "You yourself are a Princess Swan.... My sweetly ringing brook, my shining star...."

Fainna told the Komsomol members to take a stack of books each and carry them round the houses, urging people to take up reading. Next, she announced that they were going to start a drama circle, and they began rehearsing a play. Its purport was revolutionary, but the scene was set in the old world with counts and princes in it. Few boys and many girls had joined the circle. The girls refused to play male parts, and to show them an example Fainna took upon herself the role of the old prince, a despot and villain who cruelly abused the serfs he owned. A magnificent grey beard was made for her from oakum, but at the last moment Fainna thought it a pity to make herself so ugly, and instead painted on a small trim beard and moustaches with burnt cork. As a result the old prince looked much younger than his own daughter, a tearful widow who wanted to take the veil, and was also more feminine and charming than all the young countesses and princesses there. The spectators liked the old prince best, and applauded him with an enthusiastic stamping of their feet in spite of all his villainy.

The play was a great success. The drama circle grew. The parents, seeing that their sons and daughters benefited from the company of the schoolteacher, reading books and suchlike, actually urged them to go over to her place in the evenings. They went when the day's work was done. Danilov alone could not wait till evening, and his first waking thought was to find some pretext to call at the school. Once or twice he came in the middle of a lesson, and was strictly and quite sharply reprimanded by Fainna. But he could not survive an hour without seeing her. Work became a bother: it could wait while he went to see what she was doing, to hear what she was saying....

When she had to go to the district centre for a few days, he suffered agonies of longing, and counted the hours. And when he saw her the world glowed for him with warmth and light, and everything took on a new meaning, strength and beauty. The songs sounded differently, and every word acquired depth. "Ivan is in love with the teacher," the boys teased, but he didn't care.

A lot they understood! He simply respected her and wanted to be like her. How could he be in love with her? She was not of this world, she was unattainable.... Had someone said to him that she was just an ordinary young teacher, one of many in the country, he would have gone for that person's throat.

* * *

He turned seventeen. He was a big lad, a head taller than Fainna, with broad shoulders and strong arms. The skin on his face was white and soft, and a pale downy growth appeared on his upper lip.

For some time now the strength he felt in his body had irked and burdened him. His mood changed unpredictably from sullen brooding to fits of coltish merriment. And his mother, without preamble, told him that it was time he married. Her strength was failing, she told him, she felt she did not have much longer to live (she was suffering from some woman's disease because of which she'd no more children after Ivan). She wanted him to bring a good daughter-in-law into the house to take over her cares, nurse her through her last days and close her eyes. A daughter-in-law to whom she could leave her home with an easy mind.

Ivan was too young to marry just yet, of course. He might wait a year or two. But it would do no harm to start looking for the right girl now....

He interrupted her with unwonted rudeness to ask with an angry smile: "Who are you hinting at, I wonder?"

He knew, of course. It was Dusya Kasatkina, the miller's daughter. She was supposed to be eating her heart out for him, so everybody teased. But what did he care if she was?

Why on earth should he marry her in two or ten years from now?

His mother took offence at the rudeness of his interruption and also at the word "hinting" which carried an insulting connotation.

"Hinting is not my way, Ivan, I'm thankful to say. And I want you to know that she refused two suitors because of you. She's a quiet, hard-working girl."

He picked up his hat and made for the door.

"Where are you off to? To that teacher?" his mother cried sharply, and when the door had banged shut behind him she sighed bitterly: "Ah, what a to-do!"

And he was hastening to the school. Early winter dusk had descended on the village. The windows in the schoolhouse were strangely dark, although usually the lamp in the big classroom was already burning at this hour. Had she gone away? His heart sank....

A group of boys and girls were coming from the school. They told him there would be no rehearsal and no reading that evening because the teacher was ill in bed. He heard them out, and continued on his way. To her. They shouted something after him, but he was not listening. His lips were twitching.

He went up the porch steps, trampled with snow, walked the length of the dark corridor past the empty classrooms and, without knocking, pulled open the familiar door.

Fainna lay fully dressed on the bed with her face to the wall. She sprang up in fright.

"Who is it?"

"It's me."

"Vanya Danilov? Didn't you hear? There isn't going to be a rehearsal."

"I know. I just dropped in."

Did he? Didn't he come here to say to her: "I don't want to marry. I don't want anyone in the world but you. I want to be with you. Let me be with you always!" And here he was, standing tongue-tied in the doorway. If she ordered him out, he would burst into tears.

She must have guessed how he felt, and said:

"You gave me a fright. I was asleep, and had some sort of dream...." She stretched languidly with a little moan of pleasure. "Light the lamp, will you? It's on the table. And the matchbox is on the shelf. Take off your hat, for heavens sake. There's no teaching you manners.... Yokels, that's what you are."

He took off his hat and lit the lamp, feeling a miserable, clumsy lout of no possible interest for her, and yet the thought of leaving was farthest from his mind.

Fainna sat up in bed and started pinning up her hair into a bun. Holding the combs in her teeth, she wound the braid on her hand as if it were a snake. Her arms, bared to the elbow, were rounded and strong. She had funny stockings on her feet, they were striped red and blue, and a tiny pink toe showed through a hole in one stocking.

"Stop staring at me," she said drowsily. "What did you come here for, to stare at me? Sit down, you're in the light."

He sat down. She pushed her feet into her old felt boots and, huddling in her shawl, sat down at the table beside him.

"I'm not really ill, you know," she said pensively. "I received a letter today saying that my grandmother has died. You know, I'd only seen her about three times in my life and didn't love this grandmother a bit, and still the news distressed me, I don't know why. I've no close relatives left now, just second and third cousins.... And I don't want to know them. They're shopkeepers. Do you know, Vanya, a person doesn't have to keep a shop to be a shopkeeper. They're like that. They hate us, communists. And my grandmother couldn't stand us either. So why am I weeping over her, silly me?" She laughed and wiped a tear away with a corner of her shawl. "My father was a good man, the only one, he was a teacher, the whites killed him. It's three years since I'm alone." Tears began to rain down her face, and she rose from her chair. "I've lost control today. We'll have some tea. I'll give you a book, you can look at the pictures. It will be jollier than looking at me."

She placed a thick book on the table before him, and went out to make tea. He sat there without daring to stir and surveyed her room.

He had been here before, but always with a crowd and only for a minute, and standing behind the others, which invariably happened for some reason, he could not see a thing. He was in the room all by himself now, and nothing blocked his view.

It was a small room with timber walls, a narrow bed covered with a flimsy flannelette blanket, with a book shelf on the wall above the table, and a wash-stand in the corner. All these objects were shabby and featureless, but for Danilov they were alive with an infinitely dear, significant life. Within these walls *she* breathed, here she slept, there she washed her hands and face, and sitting at the

table she went over her pupils' exercise-books. And all those
books on the shelf had been leafed through and read by her.
The few things which obviously belonged to her *alone* and
initiated Danilov into her private world intrigued him and
touched him most. There was that photograph on the wall in
a polished wooden frame with bronze corners showing a lean
middle-aged man wearing a Russian shirt under his jacket — this must be her father, although there was no likeness.
And here was a thimble, her thimble. He wondered what she
kept in that little box painted with golden roses? Thread,
hairpins, ribbons? Her grey shawl was draped over the back
of her chair, and there hung the pink blouse she put on on
holidays.... Dear things, lovable and singular, like she was
herself.

Hearing her approaching steps, he quickly opened the
book before him. It was the "Niva" for 1912. There was a
picture of a huge iceberg and a small steamer, and the
caption: "S.S. TITANIC SUNK".

Fainna came in with the tea kettle.

"Oh, look how far you've gone! Do you know about the
'Titanic' disaster?"

She told him about the "Titanic", gave him tea, and then
wept a little over her grandmother again. He sat there
spellbound, looking and listening raptly, and stayed on until
she told him straight that it was time for him to leave.

It was the middle of the night. There was not a light in any
of the windows, not a sound save the drip of the melting ice
somewhere. He turned back to look: the light was on in her
room.

What did she do when she was alone? He walked back to
the window and took a careful peep. She was sitting at the
table, deep in thought, her face resting in her hands. What
was she thinking about? Now she rose to her feet, drew the
white curtains together, and blew out the lamp, plunging the
room in darkness....

He went home, taking the longest way through the
deserted streets to think about her.

He started coming over every evening.

His presence did not seem to bother her. She would give
him a book to read, and carry on with whatever she was
doing: correcting exercise-books, reading, or darning her
stockings. Sometimes she went out, and he stayed on like a
sentry.

If someone had asked him why he came, he would have
replied: "Because I like it."

If someone had asked him if he wanted to kiss her, he would have been appalled. Why, he had never even shaken her hand!

One evening he did not find her at home. The old watchwoman told him that the teacher had gone to the bathhouse, and would soon be back. He went into her room, lit the lamp, took down the "Niva" and settled down to wait.

She returned looking gay and flushed, and when she came closer to him he caught a smell of warmth and cleanliness. A towel was wound round her head turban-fashion.

"Oh, you here already?" she said. She undid the towel, shook her head, and her heavy, wet hair tumbled over her shoulders and down her back.

"Comb it out for me, Vanya," she said, and handed him a comb.

Obediently he began to comb out the heavy, cool strands. He would take a strand in his hands, and the moistness and the heaviness were communicated to his hands. His fingers became entangled in her fine, silky hair. And he could not understand why his fingers trembled so.

He stood behind her, facing the mirror, and in it he saw her face, smiling happily and mischievously.... He dropped the comb, put his arms round her, and tilting back her head kissed her hard on the mouth. And she kissed him back, she did! But she freed herself at once, and said with an angry chuckle:

"Little boys should behave!"

He could not remember rushing out into the street. He had left his hat behind, and he walked home hatless, feeling utterly lost and confused. A little boy, she had called him. Of course he was a kid, a whelp, a fool, a cheeky lout, how did he ever dare? But then why did she make a fool of him? Why did she make him comb out her hair? She did it on purpose. Why did she kiss him back? She did, he could still feel her soft lips moving so tenderly, so tenderly under his.... She had answered his kiss only so she could laugh at him afterwards. No, no. Her eyes were shining, and she did kiss him, she did kiss him!

"Are you drunk or what?" his mother asked him in a dry, mournful tone.

He did not answer, and quickly climbed up into his plank bed. He sat there without taking his clothes off, hugging his knees, his hot head dropped low. He fell asleep like that when it was almost dawn. But even in sleep he saw her shining eyes and felt the tender movement of her soft lips under his.

In the morning, a school pupil brought him his hat.

He trembled as though this was a message from Fainna and not simply his old hat.

He wanted to run to her, but repressed the impulse. How would he come in? What would he say? She would laugh at him, and what was he supposed to do, look at pictures in the book? He did not want to keep silent and look at any more pictures, he wanted to kiss her, he wanted to be always with her, close to her, in her room.

He'd see her in the club that evening and tell her so, if his courage did not fail him.

They were opening the club that evening. Danilov came late because he still could not find the words in which to tell her.... All the Komsomol members came early to put up the curtain on the stage and nail the posters on the walls, and he didn't go for fear of running into her.

The gala meeting was on when he entered the hall. Fainna was one of the presidium sitting between the chairman of the village Soviet and a stranger in city clothes who was there to represent the Gubernia Executive Committee. There were speeches and applause.

Danilov clapped his hands without registering a word of what was being said. He saw Fainna's proud and easy manner, he saw her in whispered conversation with the city man, he saw how beautiful she looked—and he was blind to everything else about him. He tried to catch her glance, but she did not look at him once. There was dancing after the meeting. The middle of the floor was cleared, the accordion player gave the opening chord and couples were waltzing away.... Danilov almost worked up the courage to go up to Fainna, but he saw her dancing with the newcomer.

Danilov was no good at waltzing. He flattened himself against the wall and followed the pink blouse with his eyes. He felt a mounting alarm, and longing.

Was she cutting him off forever, for good? Could nothing be done to remedy matters? She left the hall on the arm of the newcomer from town. Should Danilov follow her? His pride, his modesty told him: don't go. He hesitated for a few minutes.... And when he dashed out to look for her, he discovered that she had left the club.

What, left in full view of all these people with that bloke in city clothes? Where did they go? He saw red, and clenched his fists. Where look for them? He ran out into the frosty, starlit night: there was not a soul about, the entire community was in the club. He ran to the school.

He stopped dead in his tracks: there was a light in her window, she had gone home. His fury subsided for a second, quelled by the memory of the peace and happiness which this lighted window had always meant to him. "My darling is tired, she came home, and will now go to bed...." He came close to the window.

Fainna stood against the wall. Her tilted face and her lips, parted as in fear, looked strange and unfamiliar to him.... The newcomer from town was sitting on the bed, smoking and saying something. Now he got up, walked to the window, reached out a hand and drew the curtain across. The light dimmed, as the wick in the lamp was turned down.

The light had dimmed.

Danilov wept. Hot tears trickled down his cheeks. He did not feel them. A fat icicle hung close to his hand. He broke it off and, running back a step, threw it at the window with all his might. There was the sound of broken glass and a scream—Fainna's scream. Danilov turned and ran.

He ran and wept. Everything was over. Goodbye, love, goodbye Fainna, goodbye sweet dream!

* * *

The city man was no fool, he did not report the incident. On the morrow it became known that the schoolteacher had slipped on the ice on her way home from the club and cut her cheek; she was not badly hurt but she'd probably carry the scar always. The village women gushed and gasped, fearing that her good looks would be ruined. They were genuinely fond of the teacher.

"For heavens' sake go away somewhere, Vanya," his mother begged him.

He had nowhere to go.

A tree-felling job was offering, he took it and spent more than a month in the forest. He tried to stifle his heartache with sheer exhaustion. He drove himself into such a state of weariness that he fell asleep wherever he dropped at night. "God, you're a fiend for work, Ivan!" the other men marvelled. And then the Komsomol cell sent for him: the Gubernia Komsomol Committee had given the cell one vacancy in the Gubernia Party School, and it was decided that Danilov should have it. He saw Fainna's efforts behind this.

Just before leaving the village he went to see her. He was
quite determined in his mind that everything was over, and so
he thought it was all right to call and say goodbye. It was late
evening when he walked into her room. She was sitting at the
table, working on a stack of exercise-books. Surely she had
recognised his footsteps before he reached her door? But she
did not start up, she looked him straight in the face, and her
hand holding the pen lay serenely on the open page. She gave
him a calm, cold look. He came up closer for a better look,
and saw a small, star-shaped pink scar on her cheekbone—he
had marked her for life. She did not ask him anything, and he
did not utter a word. He stood before her for a moment, then
turned on his heel and walked out of the room.

He left the village on the following day.

* * *

He had the sound mind of a peasant son who had grown up
in a straightlaced family. He was young and in love, his heart
lay open for passion. Dreams, hot sunlight, and women's
voices excited him, but his clean mind swept aside the cheap
temptations that were offered.

The set where Danilov found himself was dominated by
chaps who preached that love and marriage should be
taken lightly. Rashly, indiscriminately, these youths
attempted to shatter the old moral code. They began by
raising their puerile hand against the people's holy of
holies — the home and hearth. They made ridicule of such
notions as "bride", "chastity" and "marital fidelity". Decent
girls were dubbed prudes. There were some who followed
the lead of these youngsters because they were well-read,
smart and glib-tongued, and also because many young men
with no life experience had become light-headed from all this
freedom, the poems and songs, and the infinity of the vistas
opening before them.

Danilov observed how freely some boys treated the girls
and how free the girls were with the boys, he saw the ease
with which marriages were made and broken, and did not like
what he saw. All this was alien to his nature. He listened
when the young people talked about the "laws of nature" and
the fuss made over an act that was no more important than
drinking a glass of water, and did not argue with them
because he had not the words as yet for driving his point
home with these wiseacres, but to himself he said: "No, this
does not suit me."

"I will marry, of course," he sometimes thought. "But I'll wait a bit: I have more learning to do, I must grow up, and shape into a worthwhile person. For another thing, I want to marry a girl who will be a friend and an honest wife to me, like Mother was to Father. But what if *she* suddenly changes her mind and calls me?" He went hot all over from this crazy thought, just thinking of Fainna gave him wings and fired his imagination.

But the thought became ever more hopeless, it visited him more and more rarely, and then stopped coming altogether.

He kept it at bay by sheer strength of will.

What a fool he was at first. God what a fool, longing, repenting and hoping.... He asked his mother to write him whether the schoolteacher still ran their circle, and if she had married anyone. His mother wrote regularly. Though disapproving of her son's infatuation she pitied him, and till the day she died she wrote him everything she knew about Fainna: she was well, she taught school, ran the drama circle, and remained unmarried, for who was there to marry in their village? And then she wrote that Fainna had been elected to the Gubernia Executive Council and was moving to town. People were sorry to see her go, and were collecting money to buy her a present to remember them by.... Danilov lost sleep. He actually went to the Gubernia Executive Council to find out where she was, but his audacity frightened him and both times he went away without asking.

And then he received a letter from his mother saying that the schoolteacher once came from town to give a lecture, called at the house afterwards, said that she was now married, asked where Vanya was and sent him her best regards.

That was when he *ordered* himself to stop thinking about her. It was difficult but not impossible, for by that time the poignancy of the separation had become less acute and he was becoming used to the idea that she was not for him. The smell of her hair was growing fainter in his memory, and everything had the unreality of a dream seen long, long ago. The main thing, however, was that he had finished the Party School and was to serve in the Red Army. He thought a great deal about the new and responsible life ahead of him, and prepared himself for it.

Still, her image did rise before him now and again, and he was as overwhelmed by the incandescent wonder of her as before.... The curve of her neck, her laughing eyes, her wet hair clinging to her cheeks and her shoulders—"Comb it out for me, Vanya...." But time passed. He was growing up, and working. And the vision now came to him very, very seldom. Well, it was all for the best.

* * *

He served in the army for two years. While in the army he read a great number of political books and joined the Party. When he returned to his home village after he was demobilised he was elected to the Volost Executive Committee and appointed its vice-chairman. In later years he was to gain a wide range of experience in Party, Soviet and economic work.

He had long lost sight of Fainna. She had gone to live in the East somewhere with her husband, and that was all he knew. Danilov was married now, he had another woman for a life partner.

He did marry the miller's daughter Dusya, after all. He did not marry her because his mother had willed it: it simply came about soon after his demobilisation and appointment to the volost. He knew that he ought to marry. He was holding a conspicuous position, and he wanted to command respect and be safe from any *nonsense* distracting him from his work which was the most important thing in his life.

Once he came to the village to see how his father was doing, and happened across Dusya who was taking water from the well. She blushed profusely when she saw Danilov. He said how-d'you-do, and stopped to exchange a few words with her. She was already twenty-four, like himself. She was not particularly pretty, but she was young and healthy. Her small blue eyes gazed at him with such timid adoration, that he felt touched. "She'd probably make a good wife," he thought.

He called at the miller's home that evening, and a week later came to the village again, this time to take Dusya away with him. She brought her trousseau trunk along, in which the neatly packed linen, underwear and dresses had long been waiting to have the folds shaken out. Danilov took her straight to the registry office in town. The ceremony over, she went to her new home and got down to her housewifely chores at once—she made dinner, washed the windows, and aired her mothball smelling trousseau out in the yard. And Danilov went to his office where he had some urgent matters to attend to.

And that's how they lived: he worked, sat at meetings, and

travelled about the district on business, and she ran the house. He never felt for his wife anything even remotely resembling what he had felt for Fainna. He did not once desire her as powerfully and tenderly as he desired Fainna. He never once hurried home because he could not wait to see Dusya. When his friends came over, he was the host who welcomed and entertained his guests, while Dusya served the food. He liked the house to be spick and span, and he liked to have a hot meal waiting for him whenever he came home. Dusya tried to please him, and though his salary was not very large she budgeted it so carefully that it sufficed for plentiful food, good clothes, and entertainment.

His conscience worried him sometimes when he noticed her daily grind. Resenting her for causing him this worry he said:

"Why must you do the washing yourself, toiling all day like a drudge? Take it to the laundry."

"They'll ruin all my linen there," she replied, thinking meanwhile: "A wash this size would cost such a pretty penny, I'd run short long before pay day, and what would I do then, I'd like to know."

In the beginning he would occasionally say to her:

"You've got to study. You don't know a thing. You definitely must study."

But he knew very well that she had no time for study, bogged down as she was in her housework. And she knew it too.

At the same time it angered him if a dish was overdone, if he discovered dust behind a heavy piece of furniture, or if the clean shirt she laid out for him was missing a button. And she spent her entire life watching out for dust and missing buttons. He also demanded that she should always be turned out well. She must never go out of doors wearing any old clothes and with her hair carelessly done—he simply would not stand for it.

He stopped talking about her education, deciding that she was simply made that way: she loved keeping house, and that was all she cared about.

She should be very happy, he thought. A woman who had secured the husband she wanted to secure could not help being happy. His infrequent caresses pleased her, he noticed, and this further confirmed his assumption that she was very happy.

The town's institutions and enterprises gave parties for their staffs on big holidays, like the anniversary of the

October Revolution and May Day. Danilov always took his
wife along. She had her hair curled at the hairdresser's,
dressed up, and scented herself with eau de cologne. He
would find her a comfortable chair, and drift away to engage
in conversation with people whose company he enjoyed. It
never once occurred to him that she might be finding it dull.
Other men brought their wives, and he brought his. She was
well dressed. She was treated with the courtesy due the wife
of the boss. And so, everything was fine.

Now his son—that was an entirely different matter. His
son was himself, Danilov. His flesh, his soul, his potent and
imperishable energy and strength. He gave the boy his own
name, too, Ivan. It was decent of his wife to bear him a son.

She did bear him, of course, but the boy belonged to him,
to Danilov. The whole of the child belonged to the father,
even his funny, fluffy reddish eyelashes which he had singed
the other day over the stove. What were a mother's duties
anyway? To give the boy his bath and his dinner. While he,
the father, was creating a world in which his son would have
plenty of scope for a good life.

And so as to give the sons a chance to walk through life
along a radiant and smooth road, they, the fathers, were
willing to pave this road with their own bodies. That's how it
was!

* * *

A snowstorm started up in the night, and the wet snow
pelted the window of his compartment.

The train was going in circles round Moscow. It would
suddenly make a spurt and fly past blue lights and
streetlamps amid a screaming of whistles, or as suddenly it
would stop in the darkness, with no telling where they were,
and scream in alarm into the snowstorm.

They always had to circle like that until one of Moscow's
railway stations could receive them.

Oh well, if they must circle they must. Everything was
going in circles, and so was he. He would close the circle of
his life honestly. The main thing was to do it honestly. Isn't
that so, Sonia dearest?

Those whistles tore at his heart.

A large snowflake alighten on the black window. When he
was a little boy he had a book in which there was a picture of
differently shaped snowflakes drawn on a black ground. A
pretty snowflake like that had now alighted on his window.

He remembered the book, the picture, and the inkblot on the margin of the page. His sister gave the inkblot a pair of arms and legs, and Mother was very angry: such silliness for a big girl! His sister was grownup, she was a university student then.

His sister was dead. Mother had died earlier.

Everyone was dead.

Doctor Belov pulled the thick curtains across the window, and switched on the light. On the table stood a cup of tea that had gone cold. There was always some kind of food on his table. The nurses kept slipping in things, though he begged them not to do it.

But today he had been left in peace. The nurses had been away somewhere, and he had spent the entire evening alone. As a rule there was always someone there. It was Danilov's doing, in all likelihood, it was he who kept sending people to his compartment on various pretexts.

He was a dear man, Ivan Yegorovich, but surely he didn't think that talking with people could take his mind off Sonia and Lalya for a minute?

His friend, Alexander Ivanovich, wrote that the house lay in ruins. It was not just Sonia and Lalya who perished, but also all their things, their frocks, the little table at which Sonia always worked, and Lalya's school exercise books which he had treasured. Letters, diaries, everything had perished.

All that remained was recollections.

They could not be put in writing. There was once a little girl, she went to school, and was a very good pupil. The pages of her exercise books were covered with a clear, beautiful writing. And the teachers wrote "excellent" in red ink. The girl grew up. The father collected her exercise books and put them away so that in her old age she could remember her schooldays from them. The Germans dropped a bomb on their house, the house collapsed, and there was no girl, no exercise books.

There was nothing.

Could this be put in writing?

It was a small table, covered with a white oilcloth. On it stood a pharmacist's scales, a large glass jar with gypsum and a white porcelain bowl in which Sonia mixed the gypsum into a paste. That little table with the scales, the jar and the bowl, had stood in the room for almost thirty years. Sonia had a short blue robe to work in. It was very old, all the buttons were different, and one of them was actually a trouser button. How write this down? It would sound terribly silly: what did a trouser button have to do with it?

He was going out of his mind. But did it matter? Sonia had been a friend, his truest and most beloved friend. They had been together for thirty years. And never quarrelled. Oh, how wonderful she was when he or the children were ill! She never left their bedside, night after night....

His memory stubbornly clutched at trifles, as though it wanted to collect them all together without mislaying the smallest thing.

Now he recalled how he and Sonia drove home from the church after the wedding. They could not afford a carriage, and so they had taken an ordinary cab. Sonia wore a white dress with a high lace collar, she had a gold locket worn on a thin gold chain. She had removed her veil before leaving the church. "It's silly wearing it in the street," she had said. "People stare."

There were her initials on the locket: S.K. It ought to be S.B. now, he said. "I shan't have them altered, because it's my mother's locket," she replied.

Or now he remembered the year 1919. He was sent to the country to fight the typhus epidemic. He stayed there for four months, contracted the disease, and when he got better he was sent home to recuperate. He brought Sonia a gift of flour and butter (everyone said he should and that was why he bought some), and felt very proud of himself for being such a good provider. Life was very hard at home: for lack of firewood the small iron stove was fed old magazine collections. There was no electricity, and the sewer was choked. The slops had to be carried out into the backyard, and they lived on the fourth floor. Sonia would never let him help, and carried the slops herself. Once he rebelled: he was not an infant or a cripple. Look how fat he had grown after his typhus, he was strong as an ox! He grabbed the slop-pail and stomped out. It was dark on the staircase, someone had spilled the slops over the steps earlier that morning so by this time a crust of ice had formed. He slipped, fell down, and his pail went clattering down, spilling the contents as it went. He could not find it in the darkness. A door clicked upstairs, and Sonia appeared on the landing with a candle. She came down the stairs unhurriedly and said: "Well, of course." She found the pail and started wiping the steps dry with a cloth, while he stood there holding the candle.

Dearest, I never could do anything for you....

She could not devote much time to housekeeping because

she was working. And in consequence, mishaps occurred sometimes. Once, she set some dough for pies—it being Lalya's birthday and her girl friends invited for dinner—and became so engrossed in somebody's teeth that she forgot all about it. The dough rose, pushed off the lid, and oozed all over the kitchen table and down to the floor. "Oh, small matter," Sonia said. She bought some dough at the bakery, and the pies were ready when the guests arrived.

He wanted her to be well-dressed, but was helpless again. She took charge of all the money he earned, and spent it on food, on the children, on him, while she herself went about in her old dresses. This made him very sad, for he heard that women thought clothes terribly important and believed that she must be suffering because she had no finery. And so once he kept back some money from his pay and decided to buy her a present. He wanted to give her a silk dress, but discovered that it cost more than he had kept back. He went looking for something cheaper then. This was his first venture into the world of female frippery, and he went dizzy from all the buttons, handbags, hankies and things displayed at the shops for ladies. At last he bought his wife a pair of gloves. They were wonderful kid gloves with embroidered cuffs (the salesman told him they were very fashionable). The gloves seemed very tiny, he was afraid they'd be too small for Sonia. But she laughed indulgently and tried them on. They were many sizes too large, and only seemed small because the fingers had been folded that way. He was terribly put out. Sonia forbade him to buy her any more presents, and eventually gave the gloves to someone for a birthday gift....

For thirty years he had dreamed of taking her on a pleasure cruise down the Volga. He'd take his leave at the same time as she did, he'd book a good cabin, and give her a chance to rest from her dentistry, from the children and from keeping house, let her sleep her fill and put on weight, because she was so very, very thin, poor thing. He wanted to be her knight, to forestall her every wish, to make her feel how much he loved her, how gladly he'd do anything in the world for her peace and happiness. At home, his attempts at knightliness fell flat. The children wanted constant attention. Sonia was busy all the time, and when he tried to make himself useful, she always said: "Never mind, Nikolai, let *me*." And in spite of his efforts she always did everything herself, and he was just a nuisance getting in her way. It was she who obtained the firewood, she who kept their flat in good repair....

He said to her every spring: "Now *this* summer I shall take you on a voyage down the Volga, come what may!"

But nearer summer it became obvious that the most sensible thing, the cheapest and the simplest, was to rent a dacha in Pargolovo or in Tarkhovka. Igor was allergic to some food, and she could not leave him. Or else, he himself needed a new winter coat, and so they could not afford the cruise.

What with one thing and another, she had never given him a chance to be her knight.

But maybe she did not even know how much he loved her? He could never express his feelings well. He was ridiculous, and he knew it. People often laughed at him, and quite rightly too. And she had always been so tender and so full of concern for him....

Clutching his now white head in his hands, he thought in an agony of despair how terrible it was that it was not he, a man called to fight in the war, who had died for everything that they had loved together, but they—civilian women, such sweet and meek women, such....

"My darlings, my saints, where did I fail you, my precious girls...."

Chapter Nine

YULIA DMITRIEVNA

One of the central newspapers published a big article
signed by Surgeon Lieutenant Suprugov about the work of
the medical personnel on a hospital train. It was written with
modesty and no mention of names. It told about the staff
undertaking the maintenance of the coaches, the laundering
of the bed linen, and the poultry and pig farm housed in
special premises on the train. The feeding of the wounded
was superbly organised—they had fresh meat, newly laid
eggs, spring onions grown in boxes, jam made from
strawberries picked in the woods and also mushrooms,
gathered and dried, ready for use.

The article cited the laudatory comments of officials who
had visited the train, and ended with the following words:
"We intend to do much more for better transportation of the
wounded defenders of our Motherland."

The train staff were greatly impressed by this article, it
was read by everyone and warmly discussed.

Suprugov went about with a self-consciously beaming
look.

"What is your opinion of this article?" Dr. Belov asked
Danilov when he had read it through.

"Oh well, it's a good idea," Danilov replied. "Of course we
have to exchange experience. Our undertakings will be of
benefit to the state only if they are practised on a
countrywide scale. Suprugov did a good thing to write about
it. He shouldn't have lied, though, about the spring onions—
we're only planning to grow them."

"But, Ivan Yegorovich," Dr. Belov said, flushing. "How
can he say we, we, we, all the time? What have *we* got to do
with it? Suprugov and I never helped with the organisational
matters at all! It's you, you alone who managed everything,
and your name has not even been mentioned!"

"Oh, it doesn't matter," Danilov said.

"You don't think he left it out intentionally?" Dr. Belov
asked, blinking nervously.

"No, I don't think so."

Danilov was perfectly certain that it had been done intentionally. He refused to admit even to himself that he cared. To hell with it, he wasn't doing his job with an eye to newspaper notoriety, was he? And yet, the mean little thought kept gnawing at him: here you have stayed awake nights, planning and organising things, and there were those other people who worked on these plans with you and put their hearts into the effort, and not a word has been said about any of you. Anyone reading the article would give all the credit to the doctors, only to them....

All he said to Suprugov was: "You've put us in a fix, Doctor: we'll have to start growing the spring onions double-quick now."

Yulia Dmitrievna liked the article more than did anyone else on the staff. It was beautifully written! And how considerate of him to mention the model efficiency of the dressing station....

Her crush on Suprugov was developing into something she had never experienced before.

He was the first man to seek her company. In the beginning he did it because Danilov bullied him, Fainna frightened him with her aggressive flirting, and all the others cold-shouldered him when he finished telling one of his funny stories to which they had been willing enough to listen and laugh. He felt more confident in the presence of Yulia Dmitrievna who was invariably well-disposed and understanding (he appreciated it but never suspected the reason behind it). They became friends, and suddenly, after his mother died, it occurred to him that, perhaps, he should marry her.

Marriage? Well, it had its attractive sides.

Housekeeping for one thing. Say what you may, it was nice when there was a woman in the house. No need to worry about his meals and about keeping the place clean. Laundry too. All those socks, handkerchiefs and things.... A man could live a civilised life. No eating in canteens. It wasn't dignified for a doctor to eat in canteens, and the food was tasteless there besides.

He thought of his flat. His lacquer boxes and dippers. The pink Venetian glass goblets with their rainbow tints. Hired servants were sure to pilfer his treasures. And his heart ached at the thought.

By and large a man should marry.

On the other hand, however, both literature and life abounded in instances of emotional inconstancy. Were there so many lasting unions in the world? Practically every family had its own drama.

He was not afraid that he himself might prove wanting. He would be an ideal husband no matter whom he married. (Provided, of course, his wife was willing to consider his habits and demands.) He was a stay-at-home, he did not drink, he was not interested in sex. The question was: would his wife remain as steadily keen as he was on a quiet life? What if she wanted to have people in every night? The expense, the bother, the cigarette stubs.... Or supposing she fell in love with somebody. Or suspected him of infidelity. A woman's jealousy was almost always groundless, but still.... Or supposing she wanted to have children. Children always made a mess and smashed things.

Yulia Dmitrievna would probably want children. Motherhood couldn't be more unbecoming to any woman he knew, and the picture made him smirk nastily. Oh well, there were lots of plain women who passed muster when they were all dressed up.... No, he'd rather not picture her all dressed up.

But then she obviously liked him. She was a very sensible woman and a good manager. She would worship him....

Would she, though?

Seeing that she was an old maid she should be eternally grateful to him for marrying her, and seeing that....

But something told Suprugov that if Yulia Dmitrievna became his wife she would immediately make demands on him which he would not find it easy to meet.

"She'll want me to be public-spirited," he was adding up the odds. "It's easy enough to become reputed for a public-spirited person, and I wouldn't mind being so reputed as it gives you a position in society and weight. But the thing is that she would expect me to be sincerely interested, and I'd have to pretend that I was and devote my whole life to it. She'll want a child and she'll have one whatever arguments I might adduce. To be sure she would be a good support for me in life because she has such a remarkably strong, masculine character, but isn't it a bit too strong and too masculine? She might well squash me completely with her powerful will. She won't fall in love with anyone because she is incapable of falling in love, but what if she reduces me to a messenger boy, a servant? There *will* be order in the house, but it will be *her* order, and I'll have no choice but to observe it implicitly. It's charming when a wife genuflects, as it were, before her husband, eager to forestall his wishes. Is it possible to picture

Yulia Dmitrievna in that attitude? Of course not, and my having any say in the house is simply out of the question...."

And still, he could not help wanting to nestle under the wing of this straight, strong woman in whom he divined his protectress. In all fairness to Suprugov it must be said that her unloveliness was not what made him hesitate. Naturally he saw how unattractive she was, but he also saw the respect and all but timidity with which everyone treated her, and it flattered him that this proud and imperious woman who was reckoned with by everybody was "booked" by him, that she gladly conversed with him and clearly enjoyed his company. No serious women had ever taken an interest in him before.

To Yulia Dmitrievna he could say anything he wished about himself, and the profound attention with which she heard him out raised him in his own estimation. He believed that her attention was inspired by his exceptional personality, and because she was the first to discern and appreciate his peerlessness boosted her worth enormously in his eyes.

He told her about his wretched childhood, and about his student years when he worked nights loading barges, which was what had ruined his health. He told her how he was appreciated eventually, how he built up a practice and a cosy little nest, and how his Mamma (who was he to judge her?) neglected him, flitted from the cosy little nest every night and gambled away the money earned by him. As a matter of fact he was always lonely, very lonely....

"I hope that my loneliness will not be everlasting," he said to her one day. "I am almost certain that it will end soon."

She trembled inwardly from this empty phrase.

And another time when it occurred to him to describe his flat to her in detail and actually sketch the layout, she wondered if she was not fated, perhaps, to live in this flat?

She could hide her feelings from anyone in the world, but not Fainna. By reading some signs and clues, Fainna saw that an *affaire de coeur* was afoot, and gave it her whole-hearted support. She was mad at Suprugov for resisting her appeal and would not have allowed any other woman to get in her way, but non-interference in Yulia Dmitrievna's romance was an act of such humaneness that Fainna, who loved a pose, immediately assumed the role of Guardian Angel in this nascent love affair. When Suprugov came to their compartment in the evenings she always found something to do elsewhere in order to give Yulia Dmitrievna a chance to be alone with him. True, the door was always left open. Both of them saw to this, and Yulia Dmitrievna was even more particular than Suprugov, for she treasured her reputation of a chaste maiden.

* * *

"I was in love twice," Suprugov told her, "but I have never known real happiness."

He was a student when he fell in love for the first time. It was the beginning of the NEP period—a cold, hungry winter. Zinochka wore sandals with wooden soles. The leather straps were wont to tear at the buckle, and if this happened in the street Zinochka would hop on one foot into the nearest gateway and there secure the strap with a safety pin.

Suprugov wore frayed trousers, and had his meals at the students' canteen. He and Zinochka saw each other at the small parties given by their mutual friends. No food to speak of was served but fun was had by all. Suprugov was young and he had a good time. They danced and sang the song: "The young Marquise before him now dropped her lovely eyes."

He and Zinochka went to the cinema and saw Vera Kholodnaya in "Forget the Hearth" and Ivan Moszhoukhin in "Jubilant Satan". When the lights were dimmed, he took Zinochka's hand tenderly, and held it. He was in love according to all the rules, and her admiration of Moszhoukhin made him jealous.

In the summer they took their walks in the cemetery. It was a wealthy cemetery, and well kept. There were flower-beds and trim lawns, and among them stood white marble angels in graceful attitudes, with one foot behind the other. It was in the shade of their slightly dusty wings that Suprugov permitted himself to kiss Zinochka. Everything would have been very nice, had not Zinochka spoiled it all by suddenly turning petulant and really immodest. She was not a doll, she told him, she was a flesh-and-blood woman and wanted to be treated as such. If he did not care for her enough, they'd best part.

Suprugov reasoned with her, saying that no good would come of their affair and they should wait until they were better settled in life. But Zinochka was adamant. He had to obey her whim. A woman's caresses did give him minutes of happiness. But every time he walked home after their love-making, he had the feeling that he was doing the wrongest thing. His frayed trousers used to be an embarrassment, and now they seemed a disgrace.

Zinochka insisted that they should go to the registry office. He went for fear of being called a cad if he didn't. But in his heart of hearts he thought it most untimely.

Though married, they continued to live apart: she—in a very small room with her father and mother, and he—in an even smaller room with his mother. Zinochka's father and mother flatly refused to have Suprugov in his frayed trousers moving into their eleven-square-metre room with the fire-breathing iron stove in the middle. Suprugov's mother, a carefree, generous woman, would readily share their six-and-a-half square metres with Zinochka, but here Suprugov was adamant. No, thank you very much. He could not allow it. He had to study somewhere. Tears and rows left him unmoved. And Zinochka had to accept defeat.

And that's how they lived—neither as husband and wife nor as lovers, it was awful, no romance in it, nothing but inconvenience and humiliation. It was all Zinochka's fault. He had warned her.

And then, out of a clear blue sky, Zinochka announced that she was going to have a baby. She couldn't have thought of anything more killing.

At the news he felt a real, chilling horror.

A baby?! His parents-in-law would immediately rid themselves of Zinochka, and he'd be landed with her and the baby in their six-and-a-half metre room. They were callously selfish. They didn't give a hang for Suprugov's future. The baby screaming from morning till night, the mess, the diapers, they'd drive him crazy!

And the expenses? He'd have to drop his studies and become a village feldsher.

He decided to stand firm. Zinochka must have an abortion, and that was that. It was her own fault, after all. And it was nothing to raise the roof about. Thousands of women had abortions....

But here Zinochka's mother put her foot down. She said: enough! You have wrecked Zinochka's life, and I won't let you make a physical wreck of her too.

Oh, how she had shouted at him! She had actually called him a rotter. On hearing this Zinochka began to shout too, and then Zinochka's father shouted the two women down. Mother and daughter wept in each other's arms and kissed.

Suprugov kept silent, and his knees shook. Zinochka's mother told him: "Go away, I do not want to see you ever again." He went.

But Zinochka did get rid of the baby anyway, and came running back to him. She had lost both weight and looks. He had already divorced her. After that scene in her house he had gone straight to the registry office and obtained a divorce. He went there in a state of righteous indignation. Dragging him into the mess and then abusing him! No, he'd had enough!

However, he was to fall in love once more. One read in old novels that love made the world go round, and there might be some truth in it.

She was a patient of his.... Ah, her pretty nose, and her tiny ears were sweet to remember.... She was even bolder and braver than Zinochka, but at the same time all her ways were so seductively enchanting.

Their affair was brief and tempestuous. She worshipped him. Never a day passed without her giving him a present. They were charming gifts, all antique things, he treasured them till this day. So far so good, but then it transpired that she expected return gifts from him. She was a very greedy woman. Her husband was making a pile, while Suprugov had an old mother to support and had only just begun to live decently.... He was against love sold for money or gifts on principle.

To cut a long story short, she began bypassing caustic remarks and then made scenes. He realised that a rupture was unavoidable. And, indeed, they parted shortly afterwards. It was a pity, for his was a beautiful love, but perhaps love was only good in novels while in real life these vehement passions gave a man far fewer sweet moments to remember than bitter ones....

Both love affairs sounded quite elegant in Suprugov's rendering, and in them he made a sad and noble figure. Yulia Dmitrievna, who *needed* him to be unhappy and noble, listened with bated breath.

The secrets of a man's intimate life were revealed to her for the first time. Also, a twinge of jealousy touched her honest heart, and this had never happened before. She was jealous of those two women he had been attached to in the past. She had never felt jealous when she was in love with Professor Skuderevsky, and now she did. Because Professor Skuderevsky had been an *illusion*, and Suprugov, to her joy and anguish, was gradually becoming a *hope*.

* * *

New people appeared in the hospital train.

Danilov had been looking for a carpenter to do various small jobs, such as making stretcher sections, headrests, and light contrivances for therapeutic exercises. What's more, Danilov dreamed of providing each cot in the Krieger cars with a small hanging chest in which the patient could keep his cigarettes, books and things, and which could be slid forward and back, as desired. He had designed this contraption himself. And in the ordinary sleepers he'd like to install tables with pull-out drawers between the berths.

"I wish heaven sent me a carpenter," Danilov would sigh.

And heaven did send him one at Ivanovo Station. The man's name was Bogushev, but everyone called him Uncle Sasha.

He had been a train attendant, and his family had lived in Luga. The family consisted of his mother, his wife, his widowed sister, two daughters, and a young niece. He called them "my six women" for short. When the Germans approached Luga, Uncle Sasha arranged to have his six women taken on board the train of evacuees where he was to service the head coach. He could not put them in this coach, and his old friend, also a train attendant and a good chap, took them into his tail coach. The Germans dropped bombs on the train. The two end coaches were destroyed and not a soul survived. Uncle Sasha helped to pull the bodies out from under the wreckage, and identified all his six women. He also saw the body of his old friend, the good chap who had taken them in. Uncle Sasha fell ill.

He stayed in the mental hospital in Ivanovo for nearly eighteen months, and was then discharged. It was there, in Ivanovo, that Danilov picked him up.

Uncle Sasha set up a tiny joiner's bench in the end car, and got down to work. He had a jolly disposition, he got on well with people, and had a light touch. Danilov was pleased with him. To begin with he made several devices for exercising the toes and the fingers. After that Danilov told him to make some exhibits for the display mounted by the Evacuation Centre and timed for the forthcoming conference of military surgeons.

A hospital train was not entitled to a carpenter, and so Uncle Sasha was formally taken on as the pharmacy-car attendant.

Apparently, he had gotten over his tragedy while in the mental hospital, for he never spoke of the past, and no one ever saw him crying or mourning. But he had to be doing something all the time; if he had nothing to do he grew restless and his hands began to shake. When he was on duty in the boiler room, he sat and knitted socks, an art he had learnt at the mental hospital.

He sang. He must have had a pleasant tenor once. His high notes were still powerful, and when he took them he strained his whole body and blood rushed into his small face, adorned with drooping grey moustaches. Putting one foot forward, he would strike a smashing chord on the guitar and chuckle, as if to say: "Nor bad oh!"

He sang only old Russian songs and ballads like the one about Prince Oleg which wound on forever.

Danilov once said to Uncle Sasha: "It would be a good idea if you sang for the wounded."

"Oh, yes," Uncle Sasha responded readily. "The Army always gave me a good reception at the railway stations. I was a success even with the big shots. A Lieutenant-General once gave me a hundred cigarettes for a song."

When supper was being served to the patients, Uncle Sasha put on a white robe on top of his padded jacket, combed out his moustaches, took his guitar and went on a tour of the coaches.

It is hard to say wherein lay the secret of his success, but his success was invariable. He would place a stool in the middle of the coach, sit down and begin with "There's My Campfire In the Gloaming."

He sang sorrowfully, nodding his head in sympathy with the lovers in the song, and nobody thought it funny. When he moved on to the next coach, the wounded begged him for more:

"Uncle Sasha, give us another song," they shouted. "Hey, don't let him go, make him sing some more!"

To some songs he gave a political commentary as he went along. For instance, when he sang:

> The great man fell to brooding then,
> His arms crossed on his chest.
> Before him lay a sea of flames,
> Ahead, he saw his end,

he stopped to say: "Hitler didn't learn a lesson from this in good time." And, striking a passionate chord, went on:

> *Man is a toy in fortune's hands,*
> *And in its fickle way*
> *It carries him aloft one day*
> *Or throws him down a chasm....*

And from all the cots the wounded shouted: "Bravo, Uncle Sasha, good old Uncle Sasha!"

Danilov thought it high time the staff bestirred itself to set up a local talent group, and blamed Nurse Smirnova, the Komsomol organiser, for the procrastination.

"It's your immediate duty, and it has been pointed out to you often enough," he stormed. "You're the Young Communist League, damn it all! Uncle Sasha is old and ill, yet look how much pleasure he gives to people!"

The group was formed forthwith. Actually the staff had more need of it than the patients, and all they wanted was someone to start the ball rolling. Everyone, it seemed, was longing to sing and dance. Nizvetsky put his name down, Fainna did too, and even old Sukhoyedov who played the balalaika. Danilov bought several balalaikas and mandolins, and the girls started taking lessons from Sukhoyedov and Uncle Sasha.

To everyone's surprise, Iya, the fat nurse, turned out to be a gifted compère. Admittedly, her sense of humour was not too fine-edged, but she was full of fun and had a talent for repartee which in olden times distinguished the clowns at country fairs and made them so popular with the children and soldiers.

Even Danilov was impressed by her quick and informal exchanges with the audience, and noted in amazement: "That's a clever wench!"

* * *

The Germans had been routed at Stalingrad, and were now being driven off the Russian soil. The fighting was fierce, and the medical service had its hands full.

The Red Army pressed the enemy back to the West, liberating one occupied region after another.

And a river of such appalling human grief, homelessness, orphanhood and despair burst forth from these regions to spread over the Soviet land that people who first encountered it were literally dazed.

At a railway station in the steppes where only charred chimney stacks survived and where a shack had been hastily knocked together to house the railway service, Kostritsin found a stranded girl of thirteen or so, and brought her into the train.

She had fair hair, as fine and soft as silk, grey eyes, and a starved look.

"Here you are," Kostritsin said to Danilov. "Here's a natural peasant girl who knows more about chickens than I do. Because, whatever you say, there's no such rule in any army in the world as to make able-bodied soldiers tend chickens."

"How old are you?" Danilov asked the girl.

"Seventeen."

"Where are you from?"

"Petryayevo. But it's not there any more."

"Shelled badly, was it?"

"Burnt down," the girl said in a low voice.

As she answered she gave Danilov a quick once-over with her full grey eyes, and also took in Yulia Dmitrievna who stood beside him. She spoke in a hurried, panting voice as though she had been stopped in the middle of a fast run.

"Have you any papers?" Danilov asked.

"Sure."

The girl withdrew from inside the front of her dress a carefully folded sheet of paper on which the ink had run, as though from tears. The paper certified that in 1941 Vaska Burenko had passed from the 5th to the 6th form of the seven-year school in Sagaidak, Ukraine, with such and such marks. They were all excellent marks.

"This is not a document," Danilov said.

"What is it then?" Vaska demanded.

"It doesn't say what you're doing here, such a long way from the Ukraine."

"I came here, that's all. We were running away from the Germans, but they got here too," Vaska explained.

"Have you any relatives?" Yulia Dmitrievna asked.

"Sure. My Granny. Only she's not here, she's in Likharevo, it's right across the ravine, no more than six kilometres to go."

"But why did you leave your granny?" Yulia Dmitrievna asked again.

"Because she lives with friends and I didn't want to be a drag on them. Their house has been burnt down, they live in a dugout."

"And your father and mother?"

"Mum's dead. And don't know where Dad is now. He's at the front. We've had no news of him."

Vaska said this lightly, and only the twitch of her fair eyebrows betrayed her sorrow.

"I'll take you on," Danilov told her, "on one condition — no more lying. You're not seventeen."

"Cross my heart I am, may my eyes bust if I'm lying," Vaska said quickly.

"What age did you give the Germans when they were herding girls off to Germany?" Danilov demanded. He already knew something about the practices in the enemy-occupied regions.

"Thirteen," Vaska replied.

Danilov and Yulia Dmitrievna laughed.

"That's more like it," Danilov said. "What's your name again?"

"Vaska."

"Very well then."

Vaska's earthly possessions comprised a checkered shawl tied into a small bundle, and the clothes she stood in: battered boots, a cotton dress and, over it, a man's huge and very old coat.

"What's in that bundle?" Yulia Dmitrievna asked. "Perhaps you'll leave it here?"

"Oh no!" Vaska clutched the bundle to her chest.

What was going to happen to her now? Would they give her something to eat first, or start teaching her how to nurse the wounded right away? Neither, it seemed. Yulia Dmitrievna took her to an ordinary box car, where two young pigs were grunting in a corner behind a partition. They looked nice and clean, and well fed. Even now they were chewing something between grunts. "Golly, how clean!" Vaska marvelled. "Not smelly at all." Yulia Dmitrievna pushed open a low door, and Vaska found herself in a large compartment with lots of washtubs and washing boards hanging from big nails in the walls. Metal tables ran along two walls and against the third wall stood a queer-looking contraption, like a large chest painted green and sprouting funny thin pipes. A huge thermometer was fixed to the side of this thing. A man in white stood watching the thermometer thoughtfully with his hands behind his back. Must be a doctor, Vaska thought.

And then Yulia Dmitrievna said to him: "Sukhoyedov, when you're finished with the dressing gowns, call a ward nurse and tell her to process this new girl." And to Vaska she said: "Sit here and wait, my dear."

Yulia Dmitrievna went away, and Vaska sat down on a stool to wait. The place was hot and had a sickeningly sour smell.

The train lurched, Vaska swayed and started slipping down from her stool, but at the last moment she clutched at the metal table and held on.

"We're off, it seems," she thought.

A pile of blue flannelette blankets lay on this table. Sukhoyedov counted them. "Nineteen," he said and looked at Vaska commiseratingly. It was time to start a conversation with him, she decided.

"Uncle, what are you going to do with them?" she asked.

"I'm going to stuff them in there, that's all," he replied, studying the girl before him and thinking: "What are we going to do with this infant?"

"What for?" she persisted.

"To steam them."

"What for?"

"To kill the germs."

"Do they die?"

"Not a one escapes."

After a silence she asked again: "Uncle, what am I sitting here for?"

"To wait your turn."

"To do what?"

"Look at that shrimp talking!" Sukhoyedov thought with grudging approval, but his voice sounded surly when he answered her:

"I'll take the dressing gowns out in twenty minutes, and you're to go in next."

"Go in where?"

"Where! In there, of course. Into the disinfection chamber," Sukhoyedov said, and started twirling the knobs on the green monster.

"How hot is it inside?" Vaska asked.

"A hundred and four degrees."

Neither spoke for several minutes.

"Uncle, supposing I refuse to go in?"

"Nobody's going to ask you. We've all of us gone through this business, everyone from doctor to stoker."

Vaska nodded.

"Oh shucks, if they've all done it, it won't kill me either," she decided, and now she couldn't wait to get into that green contraption to see what it was like inside.

Sukhoyedov took pity on the girl, and said: "Don't be afraid, lass."

"But I'm not afraid, Uncle!"

Vaska was given an old white coat and a piece of gauze to tie round her head.

The coat was much too long. Vaska cut it short and hemmed it. Next, she sewed the missing tapes on the neck and the cuffs. Loving the turban Nurse Fainna arranged the gauze into, Vaska tried to copy it, but Yulia Dmitrievna would have none of it. "This won't do," she told Vaska. "Tie it decently."

Vaska was too young to be a ward nurse, and so she was assigned to Uncle Sasha as an assistant.

She fell in love with the pharmacy car at first sight. The walls were so white, just like in their white-washed cottage which the Germans had burned down. And everything here was so clean and beautiful!

Her place was in the furnace compartment really, and here, too, it was clean and very warm, which was wonderful seeing how cold and raw it was outside that early spring.

"Ours are no ordinary passengers, they're precious passengers," Uncle Sasha lectured her. "Those men have lost their health defending you and me, they're weak from loss of blood, and they want plenty of warmth. Our job is to keep them warm, but we've no coal to squander either. So you've got to regulate the heat: open the furnace door a ways and close the ash-pit, or again open the ash-pit and close the furnace door. You've got to learn to find your own way out of any difficulties that might arise. Our daily allowance of coal is pretty stiff, but when it gets real cold we can't do with less than six or seven buckets. So your job and mine is to provide the necessary quantity of coal."

Uncle Sasha had worked out his own routine of procuring the coal: on arrival at a station he would simply pick up a bucket and go pillaging. If the station guards caught him red-handed and took him to the commandant's office, Danilov was notified and came to bail him out.

After charging the furnace with coal, Vaska usually went out into the corridor and stood at the window, waiting to see inside the wash room. When people came in or out she got a glimpse of this white paradise with its potted palm, glittering gadgets on the walls, and mirrored door into the dressing station proper. The patients waiting for their dressings to be

changed sat on the folding chairs or on the couch covered
with a snow-white sheet. The radio was playing soft music.
Everything in that paradise was so cleverly arranged, so nice,
and so unlike the ugliness that had surrounded Vaska in their
enemy-occupied village.

The wounded all wore the same dark blue flannel dressing
gowns. Even the rowdiest behaved well here, they did not
smoke, and sat decorously leafing through magazines.
Vaska believed they were afraid of Yulia Dmitrievna, that's
why.

Yulia Dmitrievna came to the dressing station at 6 a.m. and
left it at 11 p.m. Vaska once tried to keep count of the
wounded she attended to in a day. There were forty six
before lunch, and after that she got mixed up and lost count.
The changing of dressings began immediately after breakfast
and went on till 9 p.m.

Sometimes the two doors opened simultaneously and then
Vaska saw Yulia Dmitrievna, broad-beamed in a coat that
was whiter than snow, her face all the redder for the white
kerchief framing it, and red hands raised to the level of her
face as if in threat. Or again she saw Yulia Dmitrievna bent
over the table, engaged in some wise and mysterious rite.

Vaska stood at her observation post so quietly that even
the bad-tempered Nurse Smirnova did not chase her away.

After 9 p.m. there was no one left in the coach except
Yulia Dmitrievna and Klava (lucky Klava!). A metallic jangle
and clatter came from within. Klava kept running for hot
water, and every time the door swung open Vaska caught a
whiff of something sour and biting. At long last Yulia
Dmitrievna was through, and only Klava remained to scrub
and wash the whole car clean. She let Vaska come into the
wash room and the smaller room where the wounded
exercised their limbs. Vaska was also allowed to walk up and
down the corridor, treading on the soft runner on the floor.
But the pharmacy door was forever locked, nor was she
allowed into the dressing station.

Klava was usually too tired to answer Vaska's questions,
and Vaska went quietly about the car, peeping at her
reflection in the mirrored door and stroking the hard, shiny
palm leaves.

At about 3 in the morning Klava tottered off to bed, and
Vaska remained mistress of this magic kingdom. True, Klava
always locked up the dressing station and took the key away,
but the wash room was exciting enough. Vaska would lie
down on the couch, look at the pictures in the magazines, and

marvel that here she was reclining on the coveted couch
under the palm, and reading magazines! Anyone seeing her
like this would gasp: Look at that beautiful girl lying there
on the couch, what a wonderful life that beautiful girl must
have!

Vaska's hearing was as sharp as a hare's, and when she
heard a door clicking shut somewhere, she jumped up,
straightened the sheet on the couch, and dashed to the
furnace room. But her hearing played her false one night.
Uncle Sasha came to take a look at the furnace and caught
Vaska sleeping on the couch. He had a time waking her, and
when she did open her eyes at last he began to shout at her in
a muffled voice and stamp his feet in anger.

"What are you up to? Just look at her! The wounded sit on
this here couch, and she sprawls on it in her padded jacket,
spreading germs all round her. What if Comrade Danilov
catches you at it? There'll be hell to pay! See you never do
this again, or else!"

He did not tell on Vaska, but thereafter he came to check
every time she was on night duty. And just to be on the safe
side, Vaska kept clear of the couch.

* * *

Danilov was not called a commissar now but a political
officer and deputy commander. He had been promoted to
Captain, Suprugov to Senior Lieutenant, and Dr. Belov to
Surgeon Major. Many of the women also put on shoulder
pieces with little stars denoting their rank.

Vaska, standing by the window, held a mental conversation with herself. "I, too, will wear shoulder pieces one day.
I'm going to be a surgical sister like Yulia Dmitrievna. I'll be
as good as she is too. And if I feel like it I'll study for a
surgeon and show them all...."

Yulia Dmitrievna noticed that Vaska was always hanging
about near the wash room, and she also noted that the girl
had intelligent eyes.

Late one evening she found Vaska kneeling in front of the
open furnace door, trying to wedge a small tin into the
burning coals.

"You'll burn your fingers, Vaska," Yulia Dmitrievna
warned her. "What's that you're doing anyway?"

"I'm making some joiner's glue for Uncle Sasha."

"Mind it doesn't burn."

"It won't. I'm minding it."

The hot light from the furnace gave Vaska's face a rosy transparency and laid a streak of gold on her hair. "She's still such a child," Yulia Dmitrievna thought, and awkwardly stroked Vaska's hair where it fell over her forehead.

"You should brush it back," she said, as though ashamed of her impulsive caress. "D'you think you could dress a patient after he's had his bandages changed?"

"I could."

"It has to be done with care so as not to cause the patient any pain, and also with speed because there are others waiting."

"I could with speed too."

"We'll see," said Yulia Dmitrievna.

She stopped in the doorway to glance back at Vaska. The girl was crouching low, and the tip of her blond plait had fallen into the coal box.

One day, on their journey West when the personnel had no work to do, Yulia Dmitrievna called Vaska to the dressing station.

"I'll try to teach you. Klava will give you a white coat."

And now Vaska was at last admitted to this holy of holies.

Yulia Dmitrievna, placing her hands solemnly on a round metal container that gleamed like looking-glass, told Vaska:

"This is a barrow."

"This is a barrow," Vaska repeated.

"In it I keep my sterile dressing material. We sterilise it here, in this steriliser."

"Sterile ... steriliser," Vaska breathed out, while her glance flitted after Yulia Dmitrievna's fingers.

"Repeat what I said."

"This is a barrow," Vaska said, placing both hands on the gleaming container.

"Don't touch it," Yulia Dmitrievna told her. "Don't touch anything with your hands unnecessarily. Hands collect and carry infection."

Vaska thought with fleeting resentment: "Seems all right for *you* to touch things," and stored away this bit about infection in her mind.

"Enough for now," Yulia Dmitrievna said, terminating the lesson. "You can go."

And to Danilov she said: "That's a very intelligent girl."

"Really?" Danilov sounded doubtful.

He had a reverent regard for the dressing station and its

instruments, and found it hard to believe that young Vaska
was capable of handling such delicate tools.

"Why did you suddenly decide to take on a pupil?"
Suprugov asked Yulia Dmitrievna. "And such a child,
too."

"She is very keen," replied Yulia Dmitrievna. "She'll make
a good nurse, given proper training."

"But, heavens above, you have so little spare time!"
Suprugov protested.

"We must teach the young," Yulia Dmitrievna replied in
her no-nonsense tone.

A few days later, Vaska dropped a hypodermic syringe on
the floor, and it was smashed to bits. Yulia Dmitrievna gave
her a glare and expelled her from the dressing station. That
evening, while conversing with Suprugov, she kept thinking
of Vaska and wondering what the poor girl was doing at that
moment. She pictured her squatting dejectedly in front of the
open furnace door, with the tip of her plait in the coal box. A
streak of gold lay on her hair....

"She will not come back, I presume...."

But next morning Vaska came for her lesson as if nothing
had happened the day before.

Chapter Ten

DR. BELOV

A year passed.

"How very strange," Dr. Belov wrote in his diary, "that an
Order should have been given not to I.Y. (Danilov) but to me
who has not distinguished himself in any way and has been
nothing but a resident physician all these years, insufficiently
observant sometimes and lacking foresight (let us recall the
tragic death of L.). I am at a loss, and I told I.Y. that I'd do
everything in my power to see justice done. But I.Y. finds
that it would not be very tactful of me to do anything about it.
Needless to say he tried to convince me that I did earn that
Order, but then I.Y. is a very, very well-meaning person, of
course.

"I think he is losing weight. He devotes so much time and
effort to improving the organisation of the train and to
keeping people in a workmanlike mood, that it makes me
quite ashamed of my idleness.

"Now Z., on the contrary, is looking fine. He has even
begun to develop a paunch. He looks disappointed because

he has not been awarded anything. I am sorry, but I think he deserves an Order as little as I do. He said to me: 'You must admit, doctor, that we wouldn't have been noticed so soon if it hadn't been for my article.'

"That is perfectly true. I reminded him that his speech at the conference of military surgeons must have also played a role of importance. He spoke for a full forty minutes and the chairman never stopped him once, although speaking time was very strictly scheduled. People listened attentively, they applauded him again and again, and laughed encouragingly. He began rather shyly, but gained in confidence as he went on, and ended his speech with wit and eloquence that evoked a storm of applause. In the interval we were surrounded by a crowd of delegates. Col. Voronkov, the head of the Evacuation Centre, shook our hands and expressed the wish to be personally entrusted with the album describing our improvements to take along with him to Moscow and submit it to the head office.

"However, I could not help noticing that in this speech, just as in his article, Z. never mentioned I.Y. and kept saying 'we' this and 'we' that. I pointed it out to him, and he replied: 'Stressing the merits of one person would belittle the merits of the staff as a whole. I thought it would be unfair to the staff.'

"We all of us keep harping on fairness....

"I wanted to take the floor and correct Z's ommission as tactfully as possible by telling the Conference that it was I.Y. who was really responsible for initiating and inspiring all our improvements. But the next speakers dwelt on avitaminosis and the means of curing it, and it was quite impossible to bring up the subject of our sterilisers and pig farm again. Besides, I'm a very poor speaker, I'd rather write than speak. However, I did pen a report about I.Y. and handed it to the Colonel.

"I cannot shake off the unpleasant thought that Z. is purposely trying to nullify the part played by I.Y."

Dr. Belov had again taken up his diary, and had almost filled his thick note-book. Like Uncle Sasha he had to keep busy all the time. When he had nothing to do he felt that he was going to pieces. His head began to shake, and heart-rending memories haunted him again.

He tried to take a hand in everything, wrote about the useful practices introduced in their hospital train, rushed about the coaches, and drove his memories away.... But wherever he was and whatever he was doing, the two dear faces were with him, the two precious images, forever alive....

And also a third face, the hazy image of his son.

There was no letter, no rumour, no sign confirming that he existed.

Was he dead?

Someone advised Dr. Belov to write to a certain address in Moscow for information. He did write, but there was no answer yet.

Igor was dead, of course. What was he like when he died? How old was he exactly, how did he look?

"We travel about the liberated regions of the Ukraine," he wrote in his diary. "Sometimes we come quite close to the front. The Germans have lost the advantage they had over us in the air at the beginning of the war, and we hardly fear their air-raids now. We have not become accustomed yet to the spectacle of the appalling devastation which our towns and villages have suffered at their hands, and the spectacle affects us painfully. But here I have fully appreciated the wisdom of the old saying that 'two in distress makes sorrow less'. There is such a sea of suffering and grief left behind by the Germans, that I (crossed out)... that for me (crossed out). I do not mean, of course, that it makes my own personal loss any easier to bear, or that it comforts me at all, but .... (crossed out).

"The railway stations lie in ruins here, and there are no water towers in most places. Sometimes we have to fetch the water we need in pails from the river or the well. Everybody goes for water then, including the commissioned and the non-commissioned officers. We fill all our boilers, tanks, tubs and buckets, but we still have to use the water very sparingly because we cannot know where and when we shall be able to replenish the supply next. Near Brateshki Station our people picked up a cistern with four holes in it made by shell fragments. The railwaymen wanted to know what good that 'metal scrap' was to a hospital train? In order to squeeze the thing into the luggage van, Bogushev and Protasov had to remove the doorframes and put them back afterwards. I.Y. says that the first chance he gets he will have the holes soldered, and we'll be the richer for a water container with a capacity of two thousand litres! Kravtsov has suggested that a rubber hose should be run from the cistern to the cooking pots in the kitchen, which is next to the luggage van.

"I cannot stop marvelling at our people, at their endurance, industriousness and inexhaustible enthusiasm. I cannot stop marvelling at them, envying them, and wanting to be like them."

* * *

The train, travelling without a load, made a stop at K. to have the kitchen pots tinned. The stopover was expected to last five days.

"I should like to go to Leningrad for two or three days," Dr. Belov said to Danilov.

"Whatever for?" Danilov asked.

Dr. Belov did not respond at once, and stood looking away.

"I have to go, you know," he said. "I trust my absence will not affect...."

"No, it won't," Danilov said. "Go ahead, if you must...."

He arranged for Dr. Belov to travel in comfort. He had a word with the chief conductor of a train which was taking the evacuees back to Leningrad, and the man let the old doctor have his bunk in the service car.

There was an iron stove which the crew kept going, and the car was nice and warm. Dr. Belov would not eat the bully beef he had unless the men had some too, and shrank from the thought of usurping someone else's bed. Reluctantly, he succumbed to everyone's persuasions at last, and lay down on the chief conductor's bunk.

He discovered, somewhat to his surprise, that railwaymen knew all about his hospital train.

"There was an article in our paper about it," the chief conductor told him. "It said that your train was an example to others, that it was always so neat and tidy, that the coaches were washed both inside and out, and the windows were polished. Remember when you were in Vologda and were shifted to the front track? Well, that was because a general had arrived, a big railway chief, and so the stationmaster ordered your handsome train to be placed right before the station windows...."

Dr. Belov made an effort to remember. To be sure, the train was shifted to the front track that time in Vologda, and a general came aboard and wrote something laudatory in the visitors' book.... He must not forget to tell Danilov about it.

Inactivity was especially irksome that day. He could not sleep. He tried to read the novel he found on the table, but the tragedy of the lovers in the story left him unmoved. The

chief conductor brought that day's *Pravda*,   and Dr. Belov
read it through from the first word to the last. He even read
what was showing at the theatres in Moscow: the opera "Ivan
Susanin" at the Bolshoi, and the drama "Tsar Fyodor" at the
Arts Theatre. Everything was back in place. Life went on.
And it was broad daylight.

The train was approaching Leningrad, but he tried not to
think about it, not to brood on what he would find there, nor
why he was going at all. He shouldn't have gone. He was
indulging in fantasies again. Grief had not broken him of the
habit.

Hundreds of times he imagined himself arriving in
Leningrad....

He dreamed about it in his sleep too. Sonia and Lalya were
always alive in his dreams. The house was intact, they came
out to meet him, talking and laughing.... Alexander
Ivanovich had got it all wrong because he was so very old and
so busy. In another dream there was no house, only a handful
of ashes. Sonia and Lalya stood beside it, both alive, and told
him this handful of ashes was their house.

The worst thing about such dreams was the awakening.

Of course he did not hope to see Sonia and Lalya alive.
Such mistakes just did not occur. And the letter was from his
kind, old friend, who attended the funeral himself.

In his waking hours he wove a different daydream in which
he met Igor by chance in Leningrad.

...The boy has not been killed. Dr. Belov arrives in
Leningrad and walks home from the railway station. He goes
down Nevsky Prospekt, turns on to Liteiny and then to
Pestel Street. He walks past Mikhailovsky Castle across the
Field of Mars, past Suvorov's monument, and over Kirov
Bridge to Petrogradskaya Storona. There is the Mosque now.
(Sonia used to say that the minarets made her think of
serpents' heads. She also said that the side wings of Kazan
Cathedral seemed to carry it aloft over the earth. Sometimes,
exasperated with her household cares and chores, she would
say: "Lord, I'm sick and tired of the lot of you!" and go out
alone to look at the Mosque, at Kazan Cathedral and the
Neva. She would come back footsore and humble, and would
ask contritely: "Were you all right without me?" and start
making the tea.)

...And now he is walking down his own street, and from
afar he sees his house lying in ruins. And there, from the
opposite direction, comes Igor in uniform. He is thin, tall and
slightly round-shouldered. He is a bit pigeon-toed. No, he

was taught to keep his toes straight in the army. And he does keep them straight now.

They walk towards one another. "Daddy!" Igor cries and throws himself on his father's neck. "Daddy, it's really you! I didn't recognise you in uniform...." And both weep from happiness.

No, Igor won't weep, nor will he throw himself on his father's neck. He will say: "Hello, Dad," and shake hands. And his father will gulp down the tears choking him even now. He stands beside his son, and they look at the ruins of their home. It's growing dark. "Come, let us go," Igor says. They walk side by side. They go to Alexander Ivanovich's place, and they will ask him to put them up for the night. Polina Alexeyevna, the old lady whom Dr. Belov treated when she had an inflammation of the liver, opens the door and gasps in amazement: "Heavens above, it's you, Doctor! And Igor is with us, you know. He has just arrived. Igor, come here, Igor!" No, that's all wrong. How could there be two of Igor? He had already found Igor, he was there with him, they came in together to ask Alexander Ivanovich to put them up for the night, didn't they?

His daydreams became tangled together. His thoughts were muddled. Polina Alexeyevna had died of starvation in Leningrad during the blockade. And such chance encounters only happened on the stage, never in real life.

What did happen in real life then? Or didn't anything? Wasn't there anything left in the world save grief?

He fell asleep at last, and slept until evening. The light was on in the coach, but none of the crew was there. The train was not moving. Dr. Belov sat on the bunk wondering whom he might ask how much longer it was till Leningrad. And just then the chief conductor came in and announced:

"We're in Leningrad!"

*　*　*

The stopover at K. was to last longer than expected.

There was no urgent work on the train, and so Danilov let part of the staff take a few hours off.

The girls polished their boots, prettied themselves up, and hurried off to town to take a stroll about the streets, see what civilian life was like, and maybe take in a film.

Vaska and Iya went to a beauty parlour. The place was stuffy and had a cloyingly sweet smell. An ancient cloakroom attendant who looked very much like Dr. Belov told them they must leave their overcoats with him. Obediently they gave their army coats into his keeping, and sat down primely to wait their turn.

The beauty parlour lived its own, terribly exciting life that was not like any other. Two women sat facing each other across a small table in the corner. The one who had on a doctor's white coat was doing something to the fingers of the other woman with a pair of small snippers.

"What is she doing to her?" Vaska asked.

"Silly fool," hissed Iya. "She's manicuring her nails."

Women, some young others elderly, sat in armchairs facing tall mirrors which reflected their uniformly resigned faces. All had towels wound round their necks. Hairdressers, some young others elderly, bustled round these women. Scissors clicked, and tufts of dark and light hair went flying. A meek-looking brunette who sat in the end armchair had her eyelashes and eyebrows smeared thickly with black paint. Her hairdresser blew on the hot tongs in her hand and started winding the brunette's hair on them. Smoke poured from the brunette's head. She blinked her smeared eyes cautiously, and endured everything.

The next room, however, was a real torture chamber. There was a woman there sitting in an armchair, and she was attached to the wall by forty or more wires that stretched from her head. She could not move her head, and only rolled her eyes.

"And what are they doing to her?" whispered Vaska with morbid curiosity.

"Giving her a perm," replied Iya.

The hairdresser came up to the wired woman and began to plug things in and out of her head, much like Nizvetsky did at his panel.

The woman facing the manicurist now stood up and waved her hands, and Vaska was fascinated by her bright pink nails that gleamed like lozenges.

The brunette stood up too, and Vaska was stunned by her beauty. Her hair was arranged in small, tight sausages; her eyelashes were black and curling upwards; and there was no describing the loveliness of her eyebrows—they ran from the bridge of her nose to her temples and were so smooth and neat as people simply didn't have in real life.

Vaska was devoured by envy. She had to have that same beauty.

"Next please," one of the hairdressers invited.

Iya sat in one of the armchairs facing the tall mirrors, while

Vaska said she'd have a manicure. The water in the bowl was awfully hot, and the manicurist, struggling with Vaska's neglected nails, cut too deep into the cuticle twice, and though her fingers hurt and bled Vaska did not bat an eye. Others endured this torture, and she would endure it too.

She looked lovingly at her bright pink nails. Everybody would say: "Doesn't this girl have lovely fingernails! Oh look, look, what lovely fingernails!"

Now she sat in the armchair to have her hair waved.

"Do you want a permanent wave?" the hairdresser asked her.

Vaska wanted to say: yes, please, but Iya interfered.

"No, there's no time for a perm. We must be back home in an hour. Have a hot wave instead."

"A hot wave, please," Vaska whispered.

The hairdresser put her heart into the job. There was something endearing in these girls wearing army uniform. The hairdressers plied them with questions: what they were, where they were from, and where they had been. Conversation became general. Everybody joined in—the other clients, the manicurist, and even the ancient cloakroom attendant. All but the wired woman who watched them from the other room like a spider.

"D'you want your eyebrows done?" the beautician asked Vaska, and before she had finished nodding her agreement her eyebrows were almost completely shaved off.

"Ouch!" cried Vaska. "Not too thin?"

"You like them wide? We'll make them a bit wider then."

Too soon all this delicious fuss was over.

"The eyebrows are guaranteed to stay dark for six months," the beautician said, admiring her handiwork. "They won't wash off or get bleached in the sun, nothing will happen to them, dearie, don't worry. I hope you enjoy wearing them."

After paying up, Vaska and Iya put on their army coats and left the beauty parlour with the sincere good wishes of everyone there.

When they returned to the train they found Danilov walking up and down the platform.

"What's that?" he asked, looking at Vaska.

A pair of thick black eyebrows ran from the bridge of her nose to her temples, giving her pale, freckled and childish face a sinister, tragic, old look.

"You went to the beauty parlour, did you?" Danilov asked,

glaring at the ringlets which showed from under the girls'
side-caps and catching the smell of hairdressers' scent. "The
curls never mind. But this has to come off."

Vaska stood before him at attention.

"Comrade Political Officer," she reported, "they will not
wash or get bleached in the sun, no matter what."

"I'll wash them off you myself," Danilov said. "Just see if
I don't."

"Oh no, you won't!" Vaska said saucily.

*   *   *

That day an article about the hospital train appeared in the
local paper.

Danilov read it with interest. In this article, too, a great
deal was unnecessarily embellished and a great deal left
unsaid.

He read it through a second time, and chuckled softly.
Why, he had almost missed the most interesting part of all!
The article was not so much about the train as about Dr.
Suprugov: "Dr. Suprugov has described the enthusiasm with
which the staff installed the cistern in the luggage van,
readily shouldering the unwieldy and immensely heavy
load...." "Dr. Suprugov says that...." "Dr. Suprugov has
shown us that...."

It was Suprugov, Suprugov, Suprugov all the time! He
showed, he told, he inspired! The tricky son of a gun.
Danilov laughed heartily, sprawling on his berth.

Yulia Dmitrievna walked in.

"What's the joke?" she asked.

Danilov held the paper out to her.

"I've read it," she said. "I didn't notice anything to laugh
about in it."

She liked the article. The repeated mention of Suprugov's
name gave her a secret thrill.

*   *   *

The chief conductor asked Dr. Belov not to leave the train
till morning. Obediently, Dr. Belov sat and waited, speaking
with no one.

A young train attendant brought an armful of firewood, lit
the stove and boiled a kettle of water. A cup of tea was
poured for Dr. Belov, and he drank it. A boy carrying a chess
box followed the train attendant like a shadow and whined:

"Come on, Mishka, let's have a game!"

"Haven't I beaten you times enough? Hankering for more?" the chap called Mishka replied.

"I know where I went wrong last time. I'll play a different debut now."

At last he wore down Mishka's resistance, and they had a game which Mishka won before the other chap knew what hit him.

"Oh, to hell with you, you're always losing, it's no fun playing with you," Mishka said, and both settled down to sleep on some packing cases.

The night passed.

In the morning, Dr. Belov said goodbye to the chief conductor and started on his walk home.

From Nevsky Prospekt he turned down Liteiny, then down Pestel Street. He walked past Mikhailovsky Castle, past Suvorov's monument, over Kirov Bridge to Petrogradskaya Storona, taking the route he had come to love in his daydreams.

Were he asked how Nevsky looked now or what he saw on Liteiny, he could not have answered. He had noticed nothing. He even missed the Mosque.

It grew lighter as he neared his house.

Here it was. Why, it looked the same as before! Ah yes, he remembered someone telling him that houses were camouflaged with plywood so that the damage should not show and the streets should have a normal appearance. The house was actually painted on plywood. And it had a normal appearance. It did not exist, really. One could not go inside.

Dr. Belov stepped back into the middle of the street the better to see his house painted on plywood. There, in the middle of the street, he felt faint and collapsed. He came to in the yardkeeper's room. He was lying on a large trunk. The yardkeeper was standing over him and saying:

"Pity the doctor's dear wife can't see what a smart young man he looks now, bless him."

The woman obviously knew him, but he could not place her and said so.

"Heavens, I'm Auntie Laundry's sister, surely you remember?"

He did remember Auntie Laundry, but he did not believe he had ever seen her sister. She went on speaking. The import of what she was saying did not reach him at first, and when it did he sprang up, and his legs buckled under him. Igor was here a month ago. He sat in this very room and asked Auntie Laundry's sister to tell him how his mother and Lalya had died. He did not cry and didn't say anything, he only asked questions. He asked if they knew where his father was. They did not have his address. Then Igor wrote a note and left it with them, in case his father came back. He also told them that he was going to leave more notes for his father with all the acquaintances he could find in Leningrad.

"Where is the note?" Dr. Belov asked.

The other sister, Auntie Laundry, had put it away, she was on night shift, but would soon be home. She did come at last, after a hundred years it seemed, but come she did. She had aged terribly, but at least she was alive and still able to work. Her daughter Lydia was working too, but she was married now and expecting a baby.... It took the woman another hundred years to find the note. Lydia had wanted to read it, and had stuck it somewhere afterwards.

At last Dr. Belov held the note in his hands.

"Father, where are you, are you alive? I want you to be alive," he read. There followed a few more words and five numerals—the number of his field post, his son's address, a soldier's address where he could be reached on *this* earth. I am alive, Igor darling! You and I are alive. We shall meet when we have finished our job. Would you like that? I am alive, my darling boy, I am alive!

Chapter Eleven

LENA

Everybody on the train was engaged in some kind of study.

The nurses were studying surgical instruments and surgical dressing techniques under Yulia Dmitrievna's guidance. The ward nurses had lectures given them by the doctors. Nurse Fainna was doing a month's practice at a regular hospital where she specialised in physical therapy, and Nurse Smirnova was taking a course in therapeutic physical training.

Fima, the kitchen help, had been away to a cookery school and, coming back with an excellent certificate, had been appointed cook in place of the woman they had had whose meals never pleased the patients.

Lena was attracted by the light and pretty devices they had for therapeutic exercises, and quickly learnt their simple enough application from Nurse Smirnova. The wounded derived more benefit from these exercises under Lena's supervision because, being a physical culture instructor, she knew such secrets and potentialities of the human body of which Nurse Smirnova was entirely ignorant.

"Ogorodnikova has become much more serious," Yulia Dmitrievna remarked one day.

Lena hid a smile, knowing that she had not changed a whit.

None of the nurses had a way with patients like she had. If a patient was quite unmanageable, he was transferred to Lena's coach. She would know how to mollify him.

"Lena, do tell us how you make them behave like lambs," the nurses were always begging her.

"I really don't know. They just do."

To take the patients' minds off the pain they were suffering she talked to them, asking them about their homes, families, schooldays. There were any number of things a person liked to be asked about. If a patient had a spell of weeping she stroked his head, kissed him and comforted him. If he threw a tantrum, she did not lose her temper and instead tried to carry out his whims, joking meanwhile and finally making him laugh too.

Lena was given the rank of junior sergeant. She put on the sergeant's shoulder pieces with the same smiling satisfaction with which she once pinned on the badge of winner at an athletic mete.

Iya, the fat nurse, said to Lena with regret: "Do you know, love, you're ageing."

Lena looked at her face critically in her palette-shaped mirror. There really were wrinkles at the corners of her eyes, but why on earth? And there was no colour in her face, but that was from lack of fresh air and exercise. After all, she had been used to daily training since a little girl.

Never mind. The war would be over soon, she'd get back into shape, she'd take on a group of children to train, she'd win prizes at competitions again, and love Dan, love Dan, love Dan!

There were still no letters from him. This stupid misunderstanding made her separation from him all the harder to bear. All kinds of misunderstandings were apt to happen in wartime.

But the end was in sight. The Germans had been driven off our territory and were now getting a beating in Poland. The hospital train went across the border to collect the wounded nowadays. Damn the Germans, why didn't they hurry up and surrender! No, let them first get a lot more of what was coming to them for wrecking her life.

There came a day when she almost believed that Dan was dead. Why did she? Because the weather was foul, raining without letup for four days, they had to have the light on all day, and everyone was feeling low. And to top everything Nadya received news that her fiancé was killed. She was going to visit him, and while she was planning the trip he got drafted for combat duty and killed during a forced crossing of some wretched little river which wasn't even on the map. His friends wrote and told Nadya. As Lena comforted her, she suddenly thought: what if Dan, too? But it was a momentary weakness. No, death could not triumph over them.

The war would be over soon, and they'd be together again. Lena now looked in the mirror more and more often, and one day saw that she was really losing her looks, losing her looks at twenty-five! She was furious, she was beside herself with anger, she was outraged, and everything in her screamed in protest.

I'm losing my looks because I live without happiness. It's bad enough to live without happiness, but I am stifling my longing for happiness, I stamp on it with my feet every day, tramping it in as deep down as I can.... I can't go on like this. Comrades, hurry, please! Hurry and finish off the nazis, otherwise I'll wilt without happiness, I'll wilt for good and very soon too!

Why doesn't someone fall in love with me? Oh, let someone! Anyone! It doesn't matter who. Even if it's only Nizvetsky. He is ill, poor thing. Never mind. I don't want him ill or well. Let him fall in love with me, that's all I want of him.

She began to seek him out, and took care to stand or sit where he could see her face. She joked, laughed, narrowed her eyes seductively, doing all this for him, so he should fall in love with her. She did not address him directly, but spoke to the others there. He watched her with a puzzled and woebegone look, raising his eyebrows unbecomingly and wrinkling his sallow forehead, while she thought with calculating coolness: "Come on, get a move on, fall in love with me."

And he did fall in love with her promptly enough. He started walking through her coach on every pretext he could find. But she never so much as turned her head. So you want to see me, do you? Good. Keep wanting, because I don't want you at all.

* * *

On Yulia Dmitrievna's request Vaska was transferred to Coach 6 to be a ward nurse.

One night when Vaska was on duty an emergency occurred there: a patient who'd had an arm amputated suddenly started bleeding at the stump. Vaska, making the rounds of the cots, noticed a dark spot on the man's pillow and, taking a closer look, guessed that it was blood. The man was fast asleep. She ran to the next coach and asked the girl on duty there to call Nurse Fainna. Picking up a clean bedsheet Vaska hurried back to the patient who still slept like a log.

"Uncle," she whispered frantically into his ear, afraid of waking and alarming the other wounded. "Uncle, oh Uncle, please wake up!"

"What's the matter?" the man started up.

"Quiet, Uncle, don't be scared, you're bleeding," Vaska told him.

She made a tourniquet out of the bedsheet above the stump and twisted it, pushing a knee against the cot and gritting her teeth with the effort.

"Uncle, help me a bit with your hand," she whispered, puffing hard.

"Here, let me twist it. There now. Still bleeding?" the patient asked.

"A bit. Twist some more, Uncle." When the nurses and Dr. Belov arrived, the haemorrhage had stopped, the bedding had been changed, and Vaska was eating a sweet given her by her patient.

"I'll post up an order about you, you know," Dr. Belov said to Vaska. "Good girl."

"I only did as Yulia Dmitrievna told me," Vaska said, shifting the sweet to one side of her mouth.

* * *

They were travelling without a load along the Southern Railway.

"That's my home over there," Vaska told Lena, standing with her at the window.

It was early winter. Luxuriant snow lay on the boundless Ukrainian fields and cloaked the remains of the burnt down houses and the mountains of scrap at the railway stations. Vaska stood hugging herself, with one hand supporting her chin, in the age-long sorrowful attitude of old peasant women.

"You'll see three young oaks in a minute, but it's still quite a way from there," she said. "First there'll be Sagaidak. Even if the station's not there any more I'll know it anyway because I went to school there. And our kolkhoz is a little further on, down Yereski way...."

Lena was called away, and Vaska remained at the window. The three oaks flashed past. Vaska sprang away from the window, grabbed her coat and shawl, and dashed out of the coach to the small open platform.

She expected the train to stop at Sagaidak, but on it sped past the snow-drifted shacks built on the site of the station. Yereski was next. They were sure to stop there because she had heard Kravtsov saying to Protasov: "We'll buy some in Yereski."

Blast the snow for burying everything under, all the familiar landmarks! No, not all. There was that young poplar tree, grown into a big chap in these three years, but still she did recognise it! Holding on to the cold handrail, Vaska stood on the lowest step. A snowdrift flashed past. She screamed, and jumped.

She lay there until all the coaches had rumbled past. Then she clambered to her feet, brushed off the snow, straightened her shawl, and ran along the embankment, peering for signs of the road to her village in the blanketing of snow.

It had suddenly occurred to her that their kin at the village might have news of her Dad, and that's why she jumped from the train. Maybe Dad had written them asking where Vaska and Granny were, and they wouldn't know.

For another thing, she'd love to tell her relatives how she had stopped that wounded man's bleeding.

She was missed at once. Sukhoyedov saw someone falling off the train five kilometres or so past Sagaidak, and it was soon established that that someone was Vaska.

"She told me her home was near here," Lena said.

"You get involved with dumb kids, and there you are," Danilov said vexedly. And Yulia Dmitrievna was thinking: "Poor child, I only hope she hasn't killed herself."

The stop at Yereski lasted two hours. Departure was intentionally delayed by Danilov who hoped that Vaska would come back. And she did, when the time he gave her was almost up. She smelt of apples and snow.

"Well? Been home?" he asked her.

"Oh yes!" she replied, beaming.

And he had not the heart to scold her.

"Is everything all right at home?"

"It's not too bad, they live in a dugout, but it's not too bad," Vaska was off and away, unwinding her shawl as she chattered. "They gave me some apples. A letter came from Dad, he sent his regards, he was with the partisans...."

* * *

Lena watched Nizvetsky's flounderings with dispassionate interest.

He'd make up his mind to stay away from her coach and would give it a miss for a while, and next thing he'd start running there and back all day. He would not look at her at all, and then she would again intercept his bewildered, sorrowful gaze. By and large, everything was going just the way she wanted it. Completely unmoved, she carried on with her duties and her own inner life.

She was the first to finish tidying up her coach after the wounded had been taken off to hospital. Her duty done, she went back to her compartment and did some mending on a slip and a pair of stockings which she kept in her small trunk. This done, she wrote another letter to Dan. Writing was very difficult, for all the love words had already been committed to paper and uttered hundreds of times. Only the passion in her heart remained unexpressed, but she did not know how to put it into words.

Lena kicked off her shoes, lay down on her bunk and opened the book she had taken from the train's small library. It was a volume of Lermontov's poetry. She read:

> *They loved each other tenderly and long....*

and then:

> *Came death. They met upon the other shore,*
> *But did not recognise each other any more....*

They just didn't love each other, that's all.

The three old men—Sukhoyedov, Kostritsin and Protasov, were holding a surly conversation on the other side of the partition. They were sitting on the bunk, three in a row, as village men sit on the earthen bank built round a cottage, and on the bunk across from them lay Nizvetsky who was very ill. His face was the colour of parchment, his eyes were sunken and the eye-sockets were almost black.

"It's the same with me," Protasov rippled on. "My joints are swollen something terrible, my fingers are all knotty,

see? And take a look at my veins. Just look. Can a man live
with such veins, I ask you?"

"Why not?" said Sukhoyedov. "You can live with such
veins too. It's called sclerosis, an old man's illness, it is.
Drink iodine in milk instead of vodka, and you'll live to be a
hundred, working too."

"Not me," sighed Protasov. "I've done my stint, and as
soon as things come back to normal after the war I'll retire,
and that will be that."

"You can talk," said Kostritsin. "Your sons are safe and
sound, you can lie back and enjoy your old age. But mine's
come back without an arm, and his wife has four kids, so try
and raise them all."

Nizvetsky gave a low moan.

"No, there's nothing meaner than illness," Kostritsin
observed. "It's the bitchiest thing, illness is, worse than a
bomb...."

Lena was telling her fortune. Closing her eyes she would
open her book at random and poke a finger at a line.

> *Your dreams to know we don't aspire,*
> *You're here before us to admire....*

This had nothing to do with her. She tried again.

> *Oh, to forget!*
> *God did not grant forgetfulness,*
> *Nor would forgetfulness accept....*

It was all wrong. Not what she needed at all.

* * *

The train arrived at B. Lena went to the station to mail her
letter and stretch her legs.

She still wrote to the address Dan sent her soon after the
outbreak of the war.

The station had been destroyed by bombing. The surviving
skeletons of buildings had no roofs or windows. The place
was so desolate and grim! There was a drizzle and grey slush
underfoot, more like late autumn than winter.

Lena walked with her hands thrust into her coat pockets
and her hat pushed far back on her head.

A troop train rolled in. Soldiers poured out of the box cars
and flooded the platform.

"Coming with us, pretty?" shouted a chap with a broad, ruddy face as he dashed past Lena. She smiled at him. He gave her a big, white-toothed grin, and ran on.

"Dan!"

He was walking in a stream of uniforms and did not hear her. She had recognised him from afar and called out. It was a wonder she knew him. She had never seen him wearing an army coat and hat before. His face looked darker and more rugged. His walk was exactly like that of the other hundreds of men about him. And yet she had recognised him the moment she saw him.

"Dan, oh Danny...."

She was laughing weakly from happiness.

He came to her and she stretched out her arms. He took her right hand and shook it. There were people all around, she was shy to kiss him in public.... Heavens, has she become estranged from him after all? She took his head in her hands and kissed him.

"You here?" he said.

"Yes, oh yes," she replied breathlessly, gazing radiantly into his eyes. "You're alive."

"I am, and I'm very lucky to be alive, considering the spots in which I've been.... You're a sergeant, I see," he indicated her shoulder pieces with a nod. "Look at that!"

"That's my train over there," Lena said.

"Really? And we're off to Warsaw. We're going to recapture Warsaw. How are things with you in general? You look thinner...."

"Danny, I don't want to talk, I only want to look and listen.... Look at me. Why didn't you write?"

"Who didn't? I did write. My letters went astray most likely," he fell silent, and looked at her worriedly. "Fancy us meeting like this."

"You're alive!" she said, and gently stroked his face. He moved away slightly.

"Don't, Lena...."

She didn't notice anything. Happiness made her blind.

"I'm laughing, and do you know why I'm laughing? I don't, either.... Look, darling, everybody's running, can your train be starting already?"

"Yes, in a minute," he muttered, and strode to the train with Lena walking beside him. "Pity I didn't have the time to fill a kettle with hot water. We have a stove in the car, but it would be simpler filling it here...."

"I've just dropped a letter to you in the mailbox," she said, her gaze fastened on his face. "I'd have better given it to you. Do you get my letters?"

"No," he said. "That is, of course I do. But just now I don't even know where you could address them...."

They stopped before Dan's box car. Two officers stood in the open door, smoking and watching them.

"I love you!" Lena said in a loud voice, threw her arms round Dan's neck and reached up to kiss him.

"Lena, I don't want to deceive you," he said, taking her by the elbows and giving them a small, apologetic squeeze. "Forgive me. It simply happened, you know. I'm married."

She was gazing at him raptly. She didn't understand. Who was deceiving whom? Forgive him what? He was married? Of course he was married, he was married to *her*!

"It simply happened," he was saying in a low voice. "Such is fate, apparently," he smiled awkwardly. "I met one woman. Don't blame me, Lena dear, these things happen in spite of ourselves, you know.... The war parts you with some people and brings you together with others.... You take the room of course, and all the things in it," he added hurriedly with a fastidious grimace.

What things? Why take the room? Did he think he was going to be killed?

"Forgive me," he said, dropping his eyes, unable to hold her glance.

Suddenly she understood. Her shoulders drooped.

"I thought a great deal about it," he said haltingly. "How did it come about.... I don't know. Maybe because we didn't give ourselves time and came together too soon.... Everything happened too suddenly.... We were swept off our feet. And when we were parted, the infatuation passed...."

"It didn't with me," she said with ashen lips.

He did not catch the words but guessed their meaning from the look in her eyes and the movement of her head.

"You managed to keep it safe...."

She turned, and walked away from him.

Her walk was not her own: it was a slow, heavy trudge.

She was so sorely laden that she could barely drag herself along. The love that once gave her beauty, strength and joy, now bore down on her shoulders like a heavy cross. And she was to carry this cross until she found the strength to cast it down.

Chapter Twelve

DANILOV

Danilov wasn't much of a nature lover. Rather, he did not give nature much thought. He grew up among woods and meadows and never noticed how beautiful they were. When he looked at a lush, flowering meadow he thought: "The hay will be good this year." And when he saw a forest, he thought: "What a lot of building timber!" What interested him was people, their doings and their relationships.

But on the way to Warsaw even he was impressed by the beauty of the wooden landscape. Firs and only firs grew on either side of the railroad. The trees were perfectly matched in stature, spread and luxuriance, like a picked regiment. And everything was immersed in the downy, unblemished whiteness of new snow. Cushions of snow lay on the wide branches, while between the twigs the snow was caught in fluffy little balls. "A scene out of a fairytale," Danilov thought, standing on the open platform, and squinting from the dazzle of the silvery whiteness sailing past—silent and majestic, bathed in the radiance of its virginal loveliness. The setting sun scattered pink spangles on the snow, and then changed them from pink to raspberry-red. And as the sunset glow faded away, soft blue shadows like a blessing of peace entered the forest....

The train stopped. It was stopped by a small company of Russian and Polish soldiers under the command of a young junior lieutenant. Snow clung knee-high to the men's felt boots and lay on their shoulders and hats. They had emerged from the depths of this fairytale forest.

They were on their way to wipe out the bands with which the forests round Warsaw were teeming, and wanted a lift.

"It's a domestic matter," the young lieutenant said. "The Germans have bolted with their heavy guns, and the bands have only machine-guns. The last band in Chervonny Bor was wiped out only yesterday."

The soldiers were accommodated in the staff car and given tea. They got off soon.

Late that evening the train took on its load of wounded from a hospital housed in a four-storied building standing solitarily in the forest. There were no outbuildings or later additions to adulterate the arrogant beauty of the architecture.

Ambulances bringing the wounded drove out of the forest without dimming their headlamps. The transfer was accom-

plished quickly and efficiently, the whole operation taking no
more than three hours. The wounded were all recent cases,
coming practically from the field of battle.

"Do you know, there are two women in Coach 6," Dr.
Belov said to Danilov when the train moved off. "Officers,
both of them. One's had a leg amputated at the hip. I'm
awfully sorry, you know, that we had to place them in a day
coach, but there's no room at all in the Krieger cars."

The number of gravely wounded men was especially large
this trip, and the Krieger cars were full up.

Making his rounds next morning, Danilov stopped to see
the two women officers. They had the end compartment in
Coach 6, and on Dr. Belov's orders the entrance had been
curtained off with a bedsheet. Danilov moved it aside
cautiously. Both women were asleep. One of them was lying
face down, with her face buried in the pillow, and her bobbed
blond hair bounced a little at the jolts. The other woman had
pulled the bedsheet up to her eyes. Her forehead was lined,
her hair was grey with a few pitch-black strands in it, and her
eyelids were big and very dark. These closed eyelids spoke
of such utter weariness and despair, that Danilov tiptoed
away and said in a whisper to Vaska, who was on duty that
night.

"You've two women here, let them sleep, don't disturb
them. Look in often, but don't bother them. Because I know
you nurses, you start thrusting thermometers at people
before daylight...."

Vaska went in awe of Danilov, and so she went to find
Nurse Smirnova at once and said to her:

"Comrade Danilov has been, he told us not to disturb the
two women and let them sleep...."

However, Nurse Smirnova and Fainna, run off their feet
as they were, had no intention to bother with the two sleeping
women. The trip certainly promised to be a difficult one for
all.

There were so many things to do that busy morning that
none of the medical staff, except Suprugov, appeared for
lunch at the usual hour.

"I believe in regular meals," he liked to say. "Keeping
regular hours in everything is an earnest of efficiency."

He divested himself of his white coat, washed his hands,
and settled down with relish at the small table on which lunch
was already waiting in dishes covered with gleaming starched
napkins. Sobol joined him.

"Where is everyone, can you tell me?" he asked. "Lunch is

going cold, I simply have not the facilities for warming the dishes up ten times."

"They'll come, don't worry," Suprugov said, lifting a napkin. "Oh, what do I see!"

"Ah yes," Sobol said with a deep sigh. "When we carry a trainful of wounded we eat as we'd have been lucky to eat back in good old 1940."

Their conversation was interrupted by a loud and tactless banging on the door. It was Nurse Smirnova.

"Doctor," she said in a strange voice. "Come quick to Coach 6."

"What's up?" Suprugov asked.

He had a piece of roast pork on his fork, nicely smeared with mustard and crowned with a ring of onion.

"That wounded woman is in labour."

Suprugov did not seem to understand.

"How come?"

"How all babies come," Nurse Smirnova replied rudely, maddened by the worshipful immobility with which he held the fork with the roast pork speared on it before his eyes. Lord, how she'd love to knock his plate away from under his nose. She was young and hot-tempered, and her feelings were reflected in her sombre grey eyes.

"The jolting's brought it on," she explained. "It's the woman without a leg."

Suprugov popped the pork into his mouth, and followed it with a bit of bread. The mustard brought tears to his eyes.

"Just a minute," he said when he had finished chewing. "In her case history there isn't a word about pregnancy, is there?"

"No, not a word."

"Is Nurse Fainna with her?"

"No, she's in Coach 9 with the patient who has fits. They're all there."

"And Olga Mikhailovna?"

"She's in one of the Krieger cars, changing dressings."

Suprugov sat and thought. It was always like that: whenever there was an emergency everybody was busy elsewhere. And what had this to do with him? He was not an obstetrician. Ear, throat and nose were his province. He wasn't obliged to act as a midwife.

"Why the panic?" he demanded. "If anyone should know how to help in such cases, you should, being a woman!"

The thrust went home, he was pleased to see. Nurse Smirnova turned purple, and her frank eyes reflected her longing to strike him dead on the spot. He rose to his feet and told her:

"Go along, I'll come in a minute."

When he arrived in Coach 6, having washed his hands and donned his white coat, he found Olga Mikhailovna and Yulia Dmitrievna already in control. Apparently, they had been called by young Vaska. Suprugov glanced at the woman in labour with squeamish curiosity. Her big body with the mountainous belly was writhing in convulsions under the sheet. Her grey head with black strands surviving here and there tossed on the pillow.

"Scream, dear, scream," Olga Mikhailovna coaxed her in a quick, affectionate patter. "No need to feel ashamed of screaming, it's quite all right, you'll feel better for it."

The woman did not scream. The stain of sweat around her head spread over the pillow. Her bitten lips were swollen. She suppressed her wailing moans, and her eyes in their dark hollows stared wildly from her feverish face.

"Scream properly, dear, if only once," Olga Mikhailovna went on wheedling.

Yulia Dmitrievna saw Suprugov in the corridor, and came out to speak to him.

"You're not wanted here at all," she said with a maidenly blush. "We'll manage without you."

He looked at her, and a playful thought suggested itself to him. There was definitely something behind all this—the eyes dropped self-consciously, the quick and clumsy movement she made on seeing him. Oh, so that's how it was! As a matter of fact he had been suspecting something of the sort.

Awfully amusing, dammit.

"What does surprise me is that her case history makes no mention of pregnancy," Suprugov said officiously.

"But even if it did, we could not have prevented this happening," Yulia Dmitrievna objected.

"It's a crime!" Suprugov said. "Evacuating a woman in her condition is a crime."

"You are forgetting that she could not be left so near the front. The baby is premature. She had two more months to go."

Yulia Dmitrievna had already mastered her embarrassment and spoke in her usual confident tone, though she still avoided Suprugov's eyes.

Dr. Belov came running. The shell-shock case in Coach 9 was over his fit, and now he hastened to help the suffering woman. To think of it, to think that it should be that poor woman with a leg amputated almost at the hip....

"Tell me, how is she?" Dr. Belov looked beseechingly from Yulia Dmitrievna to Suprugov.

"Not too bad. She has a healthy constitution. If she could make a proper effort, things would go much faster. But she can't because she has only one leg, you see," Yulia Dmitrievna replied.

Suprugov merely put on a sad mien and sighed. Dr. Belov, however, was touched by his sympathy and gushed with gratitude.

"I'm so glad you're here, doctor, it's so good of you! How is her heart?"

Suprugov hesitated, and Yulia Dmitrievna rushed to the rescue.

"I am watching her heart. Everything is well. She'd have been delivered already if she had been able to get a foothold with both legs."

From behind the curtain came a scream, startling all the men in the coach. The grey-haired woman had lost control, and screamed.

* * *

The premature baby was a weak little boy.

Dr. Belov telegraphed to M. from the first station they came to requesting an ambulance to be provided for the mother and child.

When all this upset was recounted to Danilov he listened with his mind elsewhere. He was preoccupied with the shell-shock case in Coach 9. The man's illness irritated Danilov, as did everything else that did not conform to pattern and was difficult to explain. He had already become accustomed to wounds, infection, gangrene, and the destruction wrought in the human body by metal and those invisible creatures called microbes. But the man he had struggled with for a good two hours that morning had not been wounded. A shell had burst and the blast had knocked him off his feet. He did not even hurt himself badly when he fell. He did not lose a drop of blood. He only passed out, and came to very quickly. And then he started having these fits. He seemed possessed by the devil who threw him head down on the floor, arched his body as in tetanus, and made him foam madly at the mouth. The man was not an epileptic, his nervous system was in order, and his parents and grandparents were all healthy people. Danilov could not understand it, and thought the doctors' explanations inconsistent and too hazy. Had he read about a case like this in a book he would not have believed it, and decided that something was wrong somewhere. But here he had watched the fit with his own eyes. He had himself spoken to the man, held his head and had actually felt the evil strength that dashed his body so mightily against the bed that four hefty men could hardly hold him down. The fit was unquestionably a fact, but such things should not be, just as there should not be anything obscure, senseless and wicked to torture man....

Danilov returned to the staff car at the end of the day. He refused dinner. He felt tired and uneasy, and was not hungry. He rolled a cigarette, and as he smoked it his mind cleared and his uneasiness passed. Science would eventually learn how to cure this horrible illness, just as it had found a way to defeat tuberculosis, syphilis and gangrene. And, come to think of it, the predicament of that shell-shocked man wasn't the worst yet. If he were offered to change places with that one-legged woman who'd just given birth to a premature baby, he'd think twice about accepting. Remembering that poor woman made him want to go and see her.

She lay under several blankets. It was warm in the coach, but she was feverish. The baby was not with her, the nurses were looking after it.

"How do you feel?" Danilov asked.

Her face was in the shadow of the upper bunk, and her eyes glittered in the darkness. The light had not been put on yet.

"Well enough."

She had a cracked, husky voice. Danilov sat on the edge of the blonde woman's bunk. She was busily rolling a cigarette and with her thin, ungroomed fingers picked up every grain of tobacco that fell on her blanket.

"Don't you mind people smoking here?" he asked the grey-haired woman. "Might be bad for you...."

"I'm making it for *her*," the blonde said with a shade of exasperation. "She smokes all day and makes me roll the cigarettes for her. Here," she said angrily, giving the cigarette to her friend.

"I'll smoke it later," the grey-haired woman said, putting the cigarette on the table, while the blonde immediately started rolling her another one. Evidently the grey-haired woman had a bad chill because she now pulled up her blankets higher still.

"What are you, a doctor?" she asked, peering into his face with her glittering eyes.

He told her what he was.

"Have you been here long?" she asked.

"Since the first days of war."

"And what were you before the war?"

He had meant to ask her a few questions, and here she was interrogating *him*. So much the better, he didn't have to start a conversation. Briefly he told her about himself, and then asked:

"And what do you do?"

"Me?" She did not reply at once, and when she did her tone was brusque: "I worked in a government office."

"And your husband?"

"He was killed at the front."

She did not want to talk about herself. And he felt snubbed.

"It will be hard on you, all on your own and with the baby too," he said with brutal straightforwardness.

He came here to comfort her, to cheer her up and tell her that even without a leg and with a baby on her hands she'd make out all right. And she snubbed him. He told her everything about himself readily enough, and when he asked her a question she became unapproachable at once, putting up a wall between them. Don't pry, her brusque tone implied, mind your own business.

"Have you any relatives?"

"I have."

"They'll help."

She gave a harsh laugh.

"They will if I come begging."

Her laugh told him that she would not come begging. He pictured her leaving the nursing home with the baby. She could never wear an artificial limb, and was sentenced to crutches for life. Someone would have to carry the baby for her, she couldn't do it herself. He pictured all this clearly, but what he felt was not pity. The pity which brought him here in the first place changed to respect, respect for this woman and the struggle ahead of her. Pity was too shallow a feeling for a plight like hers.

He wanted to ask her where her home was, had she other children, and was she a Party member. But she said in a hollow, suddenly tired voice:

"If you'll be so kind, please call a nurse for me."

Clearly, she did not want to continue with the conversation. He took his leave of her. And as he left he heard her say to the blonde woman:

"Now I'll have a smoke! A good long smoke!"

He had a dream about her that night. He saw this big, grey-haired, unapproachable woman walking down the street with crutches, and someone was carrying her baby for her. Even in the dream he did not recognise her.

He only recognised her the next morning at the M. railway station. Two orderlies carried her and the baby out of the train on a stretcher. Danilov was watching from a window. The woman clutched the bundled up baby protectively to her breast, and the face she turned to her child was stark with pain. Now, in the bright, winter-morning light Danilov recognised this face, and through the mask laid on it by age and by suffering, through all the shadows, crenelations and pouches, he saw the one and only beloved face with the white star-shaped scar on the cheekbone.... "Ah, noble knight, it was Fainna!" someone shouted into his ear in Sobol's voice. The stretcher disappeared into the ambulance. The ambulance moved off, and so did the train. Danilov still stood at the window. He did not understand anything yet, he only recognised her. "Ah, noble knight, it was Fainna!" Sobol's voice trumpeted into his ear. "Ah, noble knight, it was Fainna!" rumbled the wheels as their speed and fury mounted.

And so they had met.

They met and he did not recognise her, and sat with her like a stranger. And he spoke to her through the wall she had put up before her.

But she, she had recognised him at once. The more he thought about it, the more certain he was that her recognition had been instant. That's why she had peered at him so intently and asked him what he was before the war. She wanted to know what the pupil who had left an indelible mark on her face had become.

She would not tell him anything about herself. She would not reveal her identity to him.

How relieved and even glad she sounded when she said: "Now I'll have a smoke! A good long smoke!"

A burning match would light up her face, and that was why she did not smoke in his presence. And she sent him packing before he recognised her.

She was afraid he would know her, guess who she was from some familiar note in her voice.

He had not known her, he had not guessed.

But how could he have?

Nearly a quarter of a century had passed. This forbidding, grey-haired woman had as little in common with the Fainna of old as Danilov had with the lad for whose actions he was not answerable.

That lad with a bit of fluff on his upper lip and Fainna, laughing and shaking out her wet hair, were precious images, left behind on the threshold of life.

There was none of that desire, that tenderness in him now. A quarter of a century.... How many days and nights, how many thoughts and actions! And his hair had turned grey on the temples too. That lad, surely he wouldn't feel homesick? And Danilov did, you see.

Chapter Thirteen

ON THE EVE OF PEACE

Fainna had long noticed that Nizvetsky was in love with Lena. These things never escaped her. And Lena's spiteful, coolly mocking face made her furious.

"What does she think she is! She thinks she has the right to toy with men just because she's young and pretty!"

One evening, on her way from the pharmacy car, Fainna collided with Nizvetsky who was fixing the wiring in one of the day coaches.

"Oh, it's you," she said, hitting him with the door.

He stepped aside silently. He always stepped aside humbly to give way to anyone coming down the corridor.

"There was something I wanted to ask you, comrade Nizvetsky.... Let me see now.... Oh yes, could you fix my table lamp for me?"

"Of course."

"Tonight? Right now?"

"If you like," Nizvetsky replied in his quiet, despondent voice. "I'll just check the wiring here."

Fainna had not planned this, and had invited Nizvetsky impulsively and quite to her own surprise. She entered her compartment humming a song, and immediately started making preparations for tea, putting some biscuits in a pretty dish and setting out the jam she had.

Nizvetsky appeared half an hour later with a length of wire in his hands and the woebegone look of a man who despaired of ever knowing the joys of life.

"Oh, the lamp?" Fainna said. "It's been broken for ages, and I stuffed it under the berth somewhere. Let's have some tea first, I'm simply dying for some tea!"

(She couldn't tell him that the lamp was in perfect order, could she?)

Nizvetsky felt wretchedly shy. The compartment was very clean. The embroidered slip covers on the blue pillows were snow-white. In front of the mirror stood a family of elephants ranging in size from a tiny baby elephant to a huge animal. Nizvetsky counted thirteen of them. He sat on the edge of the berth, conscious of his grimy work clothes. Had he known, he'd have worn his good suit.

"Maybe I'd better drop in some other time?" he mumbled.

"Oh heavens, no!" Fainna protested, putting some jam on his plate and hers. "Sit still, don't jump up like that, you're in my way!"

Nizvetsky left Fainna with a faint ringing in his ears, a full stomach, and a heart touched by the womanly concern lavished on him with such generosity.

"She's nice," he thought, remembering her jam, her good-natured chatter, and her peals of laughter. The thought that she might be flirting with him never entered his head, and he was simply grateful to her. The crew coach seemed stuffy and uninviting after Fainna's compartment which smelt deliciously of perfume and vanilla. Walking past Lena's bunk he gave it a fleeting glance. She wasn't there. She was probably in her Krieger car, but he did not feel like going there just then.

He had not fixed Fainna's lamp. He only remembered the purpose of his visit when it was time to leave, but Fainna said it was too late, she was sleepy, and would he mind coming tomorrow night. The lamp really had to be fixed, she was quite helpless without it....

* * *

The last battles were being fought on the approaches to Berlin. It was the middle of April 1945. The hospital train was sent to Omsk for a complete overhaul.

Dr. Belov received an order by telegraph granting leave to many members of the staff. He emerged from his compartment with his face wrinkled up in a happy smile and the telegram held in an upraised hand.

"This concerns you also," he said to Yulia Dmitrievna, who was the first person he encountered. "But, mind you,

you'll all have to do a little dance first. Everyone who has been named in this telegram."

In the same breath, however, he read the telegram out loud, foregoing the dance-for-good-news ceremony. Among others, leave was granted to Suprugov, Yulia Dmitrievna, Kravtsov and Lena Ogorodnikova.

It quite distressed Dr. Belov that not all of them were overjoyed.

"How can we both leave, Yulia Dmitrievna and myself?" Klava wanted to know. "Who's going to look after the dressing station with us gone?"

Lena refused the leave granted her, saying that she did not feel like going anywhere, and asking Dr. Belov to give it to Nadya instead. And he thought she'd welcome it more than anyone else. She had such a strained, tired look, and lately she had looked quite unwell....

On hearing the news, Yulia Dmitrievna turned supernaturally red, then suddenly went pale and, compressing her lips, assumed a grimly preoccupied look.

This leave had to decide her fate. She was to travel together with Suprugov.

Didn't he describe his flat to her? He even sketched a plan of it for her. She had put it away, and sometimes took it out and feasted her eyes on it.... Didn't he say "goodnight" to her so tenderly that time, kissing her hand....

And when he heard that they were both getting leave, didn't he say: "We shall travel together, of course?"

A mad hope took possession of her for the first time in her life.

This is how it would be:

(She wasn't very young, of course, she would be 44 soon, but thanks to her good health she looked much younger, she didn't have a single grey hair and hardly any wrinkles. But then he was not a youngster either. She was not beautiful, but wasn't the world full of not beautiful women who were loved and made love to? Why, she knew one very plain woman who was married four times, and a very handsome doctor almost committed suicide because she turned him down. He was actually on the point of doing it, and his friends barely managed to talk him out of it.)

This is how it would be: they would arrive together at their home town, and he would tell her.... No, he would tell her on the train, everything had to be settled before they arrived. He would say to her: "I can't do without you, dear. Be my wife." Perhaps he would add: "my comrade" or "my companion for life", or something like that. But maybe he would not add anything because all these notions were blended in that beautiful, eternal and thrilling word "wife". How lucky were the women who were somebody's wives. Or had been somebody's wives! How splendid was the life of women who had children....

Children.... Timidly she ran her hands over her breasts and her stomach. She would have healthy, lusty children. She was made for motherhood. She knew it.

He would propose on the train, and they'd go straight to his flat from the railway station. He would take her to his home.... It would feel a bit strange to her, she'd have to get used to it, settle in and make friends with the neighbours, but there you were! The wife's home was wherever her husband's home was.

She would take him to meet her parents the same day. They would walk in arm in arm—a loving couple. Oh, wouldn't Daddy and Mummy be pleased! They had probably quite given hope of her ever getting married, and there she'd walk in on her husband's arm....

At moments her certainty was so overpowering that she came close to sending off a telegram at once. "ARRIVING ON LEAVE WITH HUSBAND LOVE YULIA."

At other moments it seemed a hopeless dream, and she lost faith. She suddenly felt so deflated that it made her physically ill. "It cannot be," she told herself. "Nothing like that can happen to me."

And then she would see Suprugov, hear the special, meaningful inflections in his voice, catch his glance, which was also special and meaningful, his smile that was meant for her alone, and once again her spirits soared....

She was so tired of this alternation of hopefulness and despair that at times she could hardly repress her impulse to go and ask him point-blank: yes or no?

Her woman's pride, and the shame of doing such a thing held her back. And there was one other feeling, stronger than even pride or shame—fear of being left without any hope at all.

She could not forfeit her dream. This was her first real bid for marriage. The first and the last. She was 44. Soon she would be old. And life was slipping away. If she lost Suprugov, she would lose her last hope of marriage, motherhood, and that normal life which millions of women lived without appreciating it.

*   *   *

"How very, very unfair that leave hasn't been granted to you as well, Ivan Yegorovich," Suprugov said to Danilov in his most courteous manner.

It was an extremely gratifying thought that Danilov had not qualified for the privilege while he, Suprugov, had. He was quite certain now that he would receive an Order. The train was praised everywhere, the newspapers published articles about it, a scale model of it was to be displayed at the all-Union exhibition, and it was all thanks to him. It was he who first wrote about their train and brought notice to their effort. It was a pity that Danilov would be similarly decorated, of course. Oh well, naturally, being the political officer. But on the other hand, Danilov had been shelved in this matter of leave....

Danilov could not bother to explain to Suprugov that he did not wish to go on leave before the war was over, and that the list of nominees had been drawn up by Dr. Belov and himself.

"In a fortnight or so I'll be going to V. on Party matters," Danilov said.

He was thinking about Kravtsov at the moment. He'd have to let the man go first and wait for his return before he went himself. One of them had to stay and keep an eye on the repair work. This could not be trusted to Dr. Belov, Sobol or Protasov.

"What about the generator? Will you get it repaired in the time you have?" he had asked Kravtsov.

"I thought you'd known me long enough not to ask that," Kravtsov had replied.

"And will you be back as agreed?"

"Look, enough is enough. I'm sick of all this fun and games. It's high time I was given leave. I'm a civilian employee and not a convict sentenced to hard labour, after all."

Danilov gave Kravtsov a big send-off. Before the assembled staff Kravtsov was officially thanked for his good services and presented with a suit length and a watch with an engraved inscription.

Back at his post Kravtsov said to the men: "I'll be bringing gifts home. The suit length I'll give to my old woman, and my old watch to my son — it's better than any new ones there are."

* * *

Vaska and Iya were to study at a nurses' training school and were also getting ready to leave. Danilov called the two girls to the staff car and made a small parting speech:

"You know what kind of gossip is spread about nurses by all sorts of irresponsible characters. Don't mind the gossip, just ignore it, but make sure you're above suspicion in your behaviour. The way you dress, walk and talk must be modest and proper. See that your behaviour is an example to others. And see that there's no more of this muck," he finished, pointing at Vaska's eyebrows.

"I can't help it," Vaska retorted. "They're guaranteed to stay black for six months."

"That guarantee's run into more than a year, I seem to think," Danilov said.

"But what can I do?" Vaska wailed. "Shall I hang myself, or what? I tried sublimate and kerosene and everything, there's simply no washing them off!"

She was lying, of course. In the course of that year she went to the beauty parlour twice to have her eyebrows done.

Danilov told Sobol to provide them generously for the journey, and the two happily excited girls, carrying large medicine boxes in lieu of suitcases, got on to a freight train destined for Leningrad.

Yulia Dmitrievna and Suprugov left two days later.

"My very dear, I wish you the best, the best of everything!" Fainna said to Yulia Dmitrievna at parting. "You can't even imagine how much I wish it!"

With a big, radiant smile she flung her arms out jubilantly, hugged Yulia Dmitrievna and kissed her. Shrinking with embarrassment, Yulia Dmitrievna gave her a hard-lipped peck.

She and Suprugov were travelling first-class express, and the journey was to take thirty-six hours.

Had her mind been in less of a turmoil she would have found the compartment shockingly dirty, shabby and musty after her spick and span pharmacy car. The plush upholstered berths were saturated with dust, the light bulbs were dim, and the luggage nets torn. The remaining feathers were oozing from the limp pillow brought her by the car attendant. But for all her neatness and fastidiousness, she simply did not care this time.

They left in the evening. Suprugov started making ready for bed at once and, after exchanging a few casual remarks with Yulia Dmitrievna, went to sleep. She went to bed too, but sleep would not come. Never before had she been in such close proximity to the man she loved. Only a small table stood between them. There were other passengers asleep on the top berths—officers, judging by the boots standing on the floor. She lay awake on her back, shuddering with the jolts of the train, and thinking. There were so many males in the country—young men, old men, men who were ill and men who were well, and yet not one of them wanted to share his male life, his male world with her. Suprugov lay with his back to her, she saw the nape of his head with the neatly trimmed hair, she saw his arm in the striped pyjama sleeve resting on top of the blanket, and realised that he was infinitely remote from her, that all her expectations were a fantasy, a mirage, a frustrated woman's nonsense. The realisation was so painful that she wanted to cry, it would ease the pain, but she never cried.

He got up in the morning just as if nothing had happened, just as if he did not know that she had spent a sleepless night because of him. When she went to make her morning toilet he offered her his eau-de-cologne, and then made sandwiches for her, treating her with such courtesy and regard that her heart leapt again. The officers watched them from their top berths, smoking their strong tobacco, and Yulia Dmitrievna enjoyed being watched. Still, she was very glad when a young lieutenant-colonel came and took the two officers away to play cards in his compartment, and she was left tête-à-tête with Suprugov.

He seemed embarrassed. On the pretext of it being stuffy in the compartment, he opened the door into the corridor. "Isn't he a perfect gentleman! He's afraid of compromising me," Yulia Dmitrievna was thinking.

"Is the train making good time?" she asked, to fill in the awkward pause.

"Oh yes, we'll be there at six sharp tomorrow morning," he said and, glancing at his watch, added: "Another eighteen hours to go."

And she thought: "Another eighteen hours of waiting." She wanted the train to be late, she wanted it to go on and on, so that she might remain with him and with her hopes for a long, long time.

"Shall we have something to eat?" he asked.

She did not feel like eating, but she said: "Yes, let's." He unpacked their luncheon box again, and again made the sandwiches for both of them, doing it lovingly and competently. She munched her sandwich and thought: "We'll go on eating and eating all day, then the officers will come back, then it will be night, and before we know it we'll have arrived, and everything will be finished."

"Shall we have a nap?" Suprugov said, his hunger appeased. "Where else if not on a train journey can a person catch up on his sleep, don't you agree?"

He quickly curled up on the berth and went to sleep, or perhaps feigned sleep, while she sat at the small table and said goodbye to her hopes, to her first and last realistic dream.

Her red hands with the stained nails were so ugly! Feathers oozed from the pillow and her skirt was covered with fluff. The cursed prosiness of an old maid's life for which nobody had any use.... Those officers had probably watched Suprugov's attentions to her with a snicker. Oh God, what a fool she was, what a fool, it served her right....

Passengers walking past the open door glanced into their compartment, and she tried to put on a calm, unconcerned look for fear that they might read the suffering on her face. But the passengers who glanced into the open door thought the woman officer had a very tired face, and that's all they thought.

In the morning, Yulia Dmitrievna and Suprugov said goodbye at the railway station.

"Are you taking a tram?" he asked.

"No, I'll walk. It's very near."

"Shall I call a porter for you?"

"No, I'll manage."

She spoke in a firm, imperious voice, and looking at her he was thinking:

"That woman has miscalculated. But she's putting on quite a good front."

"Goodbye," she was the first to say it, but suddenly her voice broke and a sob sounded in it.

"Au revoir, my dear, not goodbye," he corrected her gently. "Till we meet very soon in our hospital train."

He kissed her hand. She pulled it away quickly and clumsily, and started walking quickly away—a broad, unwieldy figure, carrying a heavy suitcase.

She was remembering how that morning, after their early breakfast, he took stock of their remaining provisions, divided them between them with meticulous care, and transferred so many tins and so many packages to her suitcase. There was something so horribly humiliating in the

way he counted those tins and cut the bacon that a lump of
bitterness rose in her throat at the memory....

She was crossing the busy thoroughfare when a piercing
shriek rang out behind her: "Yulia Dmitrievna! I say, Yulia
Dmitrievna!" She turned round and saw Vaska rushing
straight at her. The child was in uniform and had freshly
blackened eyebrows running from the bridge of her little
nose to her temples.

"Vaska? What is the matter, Vaska?" Yulia Dmitrievna
asked with a preoccupied frown.

"Oh, thank God, Yulia Dmitrievna! I've been coming here
to meet your train every morning! Golly, what luck that I
didn't miss you!" Vaska cried with passionate relief, and
prattled on in breathless haste: "We've been attending
classes since the day before yesterday, Iya and I, and
everybody marvels at us because we're so well-mannered
and know such a lot, me especially, cross my heart!"

"Where is Iya?" Yulia Dmitrievna asked.

"At the hostel. She's still asleep. We went to the pictures
last night, the whole class went, and did Iya and I cry! Here,
let me carry your suitcase for you," she said, deftly snatching
the suitcase away from Yulia Dmitrievna.

"Come with me, Vaska," Yulia Dmitrievna said, feeling
less broken in the girl's presence. "Come home with me."

She walked on without listening to Vaska's chatter. They
came to a clean, quiet street lined with elms in one of the
town's oldest and most sedate streets. Each of these elms,
each of these cobblestones was familiar to Yulia Dmitrievna
since childhood.

"How far is it to your place?" Vaska asked.

"It's just around the corner now."

On the street corner stood a woman with a milk can, gazing
about her in perplexity.

"Where does the doctor live?" she asked.

Yulia Dmitrievna smiled. The woman with the milk can
looking for the doctor was a sort of prelude to home, sweet
home.

A heavy bolt was shot back, the door flew open, and her
mother flung up her senile arms, bared by the slipping
sleeves of her housecoat.

"Darling! Darling! I saw you from the window and I said:
here comes our heroine, here comes our own beautiful
darling! Can you imagine, Professor Skuderevsky has been
asking about you only yesterday! Mitya, Mitya, come here,
our darling child has arrived. Our Yulia has come home!"

* * *

One of the first things Kravtsov heard from his old woman on arriving home was that Sergei, their son, was appointed assistant operator of the very same diesel which he himself had operated before the war. The boy was only seventeen, and his mother was bursting with pride.

"What's so extraordinary about it?" Kravtsov said. "I started working with motors when I was fifteen."

He shaved, put on his Sunday suit, and went to the factory. He met the new shop superintendent—a woman, if you please—and spoke to her with an air of superiority and condescension.

A woman! What could women know about electricity....

After that he went to look at his diesel. Sergei was busy, he gave his father a big smile and shouted: "I won't be a minute, wait for me!" Kravtsov sat on the window-sill and watched his son manipulating the machine. He was a short lad, and his rubber boots were too high for him....

"It's the same here as in the railway workshops. With us away it's the women and children who have to man production," he was thinking.

He had a chat with the operator, an old friend and a man of substance, treated him to some honey-flavoured Ukrainian tobacco, and invited him over to his place after work.

The shift was soon over, and Kravtsov went home with his son. The boy wanted to hear where his father had been, and Kravtsov told him about Kiev, Brest, Leninabad and Tbilisi. "Oh well, that's just geography," he dismissed the subject, as he would much rather talk about the hospital train.

"The political officer and I do everything between the two of us, just every damn thing. He gets an idea, he's a brainy chap, and I carry it through. And routine work, too, who does that, I ask you? Who put the electricity into the luggage van? I did. Who keeps the radio working—me again. And when the heating pipes need repairing, it's my job too. Why, they can't even tin a tea kettle without me, honest to God!"

It was very gratifying to be able to talk to his son about everything and to know that his son would understand.

"Take the sun-lamp treatment. I had to change the whole system to 110V."

In the meantime his old woman had been round all the neighbours, borrowing vodka rations wherever she could. It was considered indecent not to set out drinks when a man came home on leave from the war, and when it was someone like her old man a dry welcome would be downright insulting.

Kravtsov noted the array of vodka and beer bottles on the table with satisfaction, and said to his old woman in a kindly tone:

"Not a bad show, eh, Mother? You're a wonder worker. But, I say, where are the guests?"

They arrived soon enough: a married couple, relatives of the Kravtsovs, and several old friends with the operator who was Sergei's boss among them. The party was decorously gay, with no yelling. People often touched glasses and said pleasant things to one another. But all their flattering attention and geniality was focused on Kravtsov. Every arriving guest had to be told about Kiev, Dvinsk, Brest, and the wound inflicted on our land by the Germans. Kravtsov would hasten through his account, and go back to his pet subject of the hospital train.

"It was sure tough. They'd give us heavy engine oil. The piston rings got clogged and you can guess how much more often they had to be dismantled and cleaned."

"Why sure," his old friends responded, tossing off their vodka with dignity. "Sure thing.... With heavy oil, naturally...."

"How is Sergei doing? He's not a disgrace to his father, is he?" Kravtsov asked the operator in everybody's hearing.

The operator said that Sergei was doing well. And then Kravtsov took out his watch and gave it to his son with the following injunction:

"Remember this, son: don't come near the motor unless you're sober. A motor's got to be loved, and then it will love you too. If you love it, it will greet you the moment you open the door, because you're someone who has earned its respect. But if you treat it any old how, it will go and mangle you, chew you up and spit out a lump of flesh.... Just think what a machine it is too—it took two flat cars to bring the fly-wheel alone! Slowly and lovingly does it, son," Kravtsov rumbled on, losing the thread of his thought and fumbling to recapture it. "Work in general calls for culture and a beautiful performance.... And electricity, mind you, is the most progressive, the most scientific business of all...."

He spoke at great length, feeling a fresh upsurge of eloquence with every glassful. The guests had all gone home, but he still held forth, preaching to his son.... Awakening next morning on his own stove bed, he started up in fear that he was late for his shift. And then he remembered that he

wasn't working at the factory any more and was home on
leave from the hospital train. His mind clearing a little, he
began to wonder who could have hauled him up to the stove
bed and whèn. The old woman was squatting on the floor,
polishing his boots.

"Where's Sergei?" he asked her.

"Gone to work."

He threw off the quilt and sat up, resting his bare feet on the
warm bricks of the stove.

"Good. Give me a drink, mother, to set me right," he said
sternly.

*   *   *

Everything was settled between Fainna and Nizvetsky.

Nizvetsky had no idea how it happened at all. He came
over in the evenings to have tea with Fainna, she laughed,
chatted, bustled about the compartment, now brushing
against him with a shoulder, now touching him with a knee.
She was eager to know everything about his family, and
wondered if it was true that there were many Chinese in
Vladivostok. She was sincerely concerned about his illness
and assured him that he did not necessarily have to have an
operation. He must consult a homeopath first, she insisted,
because homeopaths, she heard, sometimes performed
veritable miracles in cases like his.

He did fix her table lamp at long last. As it turned out only
the bulb needed changing, and Fainna, in her innocence, had
imagined that the lamp itself was broken.

She told him that he was terribly attractive and lots of
women must be crazy about him. He was surprised to hear
this, but a good look at himself in the mirror convinced him
that he was really not bad looking, rather sallow perhaps, but
this would pass when he was cured of his illness, and on the
whole Fainna had something there....

He felt more and more reluctant to leave her compartment
where he basked in affection and flattery to go back to the
crew car. An hour without her was more than he could
endure now. He never gave a thought to Lena any more....
And then one night, with Yulia Dmitrievna gone on leave and
Danilov away on business, he did not leave Fainna as usual,
and stayed with her till daybreak.

"One thing I can't understand is what made you fall in love
with me?" he asked her in blissful humility.

She held him in her arms as tenderly as a baby.

"You silly goose, you silly goose," she said with tears in her eyes.

But he wanted her to tell him in so many words.

"Well, because you are modest," she enumerated his merits rapturously. "Because you are so polite, so cultured, and so, so wonderful...."

She honestly believed that these qualities of his had captivated her from the first. She even fancied that their meeting in this hospital train had something mystic and preordained about it, and that it was to find her happiness, that she had to go through the war, through dangers and labours....

"I beg only one thing of you," she whispered hotly into his ear. "Always remember that I love you, always! These flighty young girls will make a play for any man, just for the fun of it, and I, only I will be a real wife to you, a real friend. Dearest, it's awful, I feel I'm going to be a madly jealous wife...."

* * *

Fima, who had long since been promoted from kitchen help to cook, once came to see Danilov and addressed him very formally:

"Comrade Political Officer, we, the kitchen staff, kindly request you to take a personal interest in our future."

"How d'you mean? Marry you off, or what?" Danilov asked. Fima giggled politely at the joke.

"We learnt a lot working here, we're professionals now, and after the war we'd like to be employed in our new capacity," she explained. "You'd be surprised, but Olya and Katya are quite capable of working as cooks in a canteen, I know because I taught them myself, you see. And as for me," Fima blushed slightly, "as for me, Ivan Yegorovich, I'd like to be the chef or the head waiter in some posh restaurant."

"That's a good idea," Danilov said. "I'll try to help. In any case I'll give you a good character, whatever else."

"That's all very well, Ivan Yegorovich, but besides giving us a good character couldn't you apply officially for a post for us, or something like that...."

"I'll see what I can do."

When Fima left, he thought her request over, and saw that she was quite right. It really was up to him to see that his staff were settled in peacetime life as they deserved.

There were people who had no need of his help. The doctors, for instance, Yulia Dmitrievna, Lena Ogorodnikova and some others.

But what about Nurse Smirnova and Klava Mukhina? Hadn't they earned the right to work in some large, model hospital?

Sobol would continue in his present capacity, but on a larger scale. Vaska.... Vaska would be at home anywhere at a state farm, a hospital, any place under the sun. Let Yulia Dmitrievna teach this bright kid. She had no children of her own, she might welcome the idea....

It would be wonderful if they could all keep in touch after the war. Fellow travellers became inseparable friends after only a four-day journey together, and they had been travelling for four years, not days, and were not just fellow travellers but fellow workers.

He always thought the kitchen girls had their brains askew like their starched caps, and never suspected that what they whispered about in the evenings was their future, and the experience with which they would re-enter peacetime life.

And what about himself? He'd find something to apply his energy and experience to. There'd be a lot for everyone to do. But before anything else, he must reorganise his family life. It wasn't right the way he lived with his wife before.

* * *

He would see his son soon.

He was going to see him in a few minutes.

Danilov strode home along the street that was as wide as a waste plot, the way new streets were on the outskirts.

A mottled cow plodded along slowly. An old woman shuffled behind it even slower, leaning on her switch as if it were a staff. A man in an old, greasy jacket overtook Danilov, his heels rapping merrily on the wooden pavement, and glanced back at him over his shoulder. Danilov was a stranger in this neighbourhood.

On one side of the narrow wooden pavement the earth was dug up for potato plots. It might have been a village and not a town. The boards had rotted in many places, and the houses had a neglected look.

His house would be like that too, of course. The trust could hardly have done a major repair job on it this past year. And Dusya could hardly bother with repairs either.

She had lived without him all these years, all on her own.

An honest, self-forgetful, modest life. He had no doubt of her fidelity, whereas he rarely gave her a thought and hardly ever wrote.

Some children were playing in front of the neighbours' gate. His son was not there among them. Whose children were they? He thought he had seen that dark, gypsy-type girl before. But all these children had grown so big, there was no recognising any of them.

Here was his gate.

It was closed. But he knew the secret: all he had to do was squeeze his hand through between the planks and push back the wooden bar. He did that, and entered the yard.

There was no one there. Danilov stood looking about him. There were neat patches of dug up and harrowed earth with new grass sprouting round them. Neat walks. The porch. And a padlock on the front door.

Why was it locked?

He felt strangely disappointed. It was natural for the door to be locked, of course, since he had not notified his wife of his arrival. Still, it made him sad.

He was wondering what to do. Before the war Dusya used to hide the key under the porch in case he came home when she was out. He went down the shallow steps and groped under the porch. He had forgotten that once familiar sensation of mossy dampness.... The key lay where Dusya always left it, in a cleft between two bricks.

The hiding place was like an old friend and seemed to welcome Danilov home.

He unlocked the front door and entered the house.

In the small kitchen everything was as before: the same table, the aloe on the window sill, and the dough-trough covered with a raw-linen dish towel. It was darker in the rooms than outside, and he recognised the various objects one by one.

On the dining table covered with a bright oilcloth stood a glass jar with sugar. Bits of eggshell lay on a saucer. The oilcloth was worn through on the corners, and when he went off to war it was brand new. There were ink spots on it. Why ink spots? But, of course, his son wrote in ink now. He was a big boy and wrote in ink.

Danilov closed his eyes. When he opened them they were moist.

He gulped down the sweet and heavy lump that rose in his throat and laughed with the tears still in his eyes: his son was a big boy now, and wrote in ink!

He went into the bedroom. Nothing had changed here either, but it wasn't as sparklingly clean and pretty as his wife usually kept it. Instead of a white bedspread, the bed was covered with a rough grey blanket. On the table beside the sewing machine lay a partly darned child's sock, stretched over a wooden spoon.

A tricycle stood in the corner. One pedal was missing. There was no sense repairing it. His son was a big boy, he needed a bicycle now.

Danilov went outside, sat down on a porch step and lit a cigarette. He sat there, smoking and thinking. Nobody disturbed him, nothing distracted him. He thought about Dusya, his wife, with gratitude and something approaching tenderness. A star winked faintly in the gentle sky. And a coolness rose from the ground.... He heard his wife's voice out in the street, scolding angrily and running short of breath:

"If you were a good boy you'd tell him: Uncle, don't teach me any silly nonsense, I have no use for a sling, and you'd better go and work, Uncle, instead of teaching bad things to little boys...."

Danilov did not go out to meet them. He remained sitting on the porch, hugging his knees.

His son entered the yard first. Dusya came behind him with a heavy sack on her back.

His son saw a stranger sitting on the porch step and slowed down, stopping altogether half-way to him.

"Daddy?" he asked haltingly, and laughed.

He was tall and skinny, he was sunburnt, and missing his front teeth.

Dusya gasped. She dropped her sack on the ground and sank down on it as though she had no strength to walk on.

Danilov rose to his feet, hugged the boy and kissed him on the top of his cropped head. Then he went to his wife.

"Get up," he told her.

She got up. He took the sack and carried it into the kitchen. His wife followed him in. With shaking hands she took off her head kerchief and smoothed her hair.

Danilov switched on the light. The bright light illumined the happy face of his son and the aged face of his wife.

Danilov said to her, tenderly, remorsefully, and wearily:

"Well, tell me how you lived all these years...."

1945

VALYA

1.

Before the war Valya and Lucy lived in a new house, built the year Lucy was born.

It was a grey building with large windows. Each window was divided into many equal square parts, like a pie.

The balconies were long and grey, and they made the house look like a chest of drawers with the drawers pulled out.

Next door was a large catering complex where you could eat, take dinners home or buy ready-to-cook stuff, and the building was also new. The first floor ran the whole length of the building, and the ground floor only halfway—the rest of the space was stuck with round stone pillars that supported a stone porch roof. Children, playing out in the street, would run in here and shout: "Aha!", "Hurrah!" or "Yoohoo!" delighting in the strange and booming reverberations their voices set off amid the stone pillars.

The pavement in front of the house was covered all over with chalked hopscotch figures.

The street flowed into a large thoroughfare. There was a tramline there, and the long, jingling cars passed the crossing in red streaks. The thoroughfare was noisy and crowded, while the street where Valya and Lucy lived was quiet, and no one got in your way when you played hopscotch.

2.

You entered the house from the courtyard, not the street.

The courtyard, not a very large one, was asphalted and when people walked across it their steps made a sharp, clacking sound.

Windows looked down on the courtyard from all four sides. They were different colours when the lights were on—some orange, some white, and some green.

When the war started they glowed no more—it was blackout. Everyone went to the shop and bought special blinds made of black paper. But it was simpler not to put the light on at all, since it was the season of white nights. Women sat at the dark open windows, their faces gleaming in the pale dusk. The square of tawny sky over the courtyard was cooling off after the day's heat.

On Sundays, in the old days, people would set out their gramophones on the window sills and play foxtrots and songs, making a jumble of sounds. The gramophones fell silent in the war. A black radio loudspeaker was now installed in the courtyard, under the archway.

The loudspeaker, blaring loud enough to be heard in all the flats, read war communiqués, made speeches, sang, and shouted slogans. It wailed terribly to warn people to go and hide in the basement. And even in those rare moments when it was silent for a while, after talking, singing and wailing without respite, its restless heart went on knocking loudly and heavily.

It was knocking like that, not speaking, that very hot day when Valya and Lucy left the courtyard in a hurry with their mother.

The yardkeeper stood at the gate with a gas-mask bag slung over her shoulder.

"Where's the train leaving from?" she asked them.

"Vitebsky Station," their mother answered without stopping.

The red cars came jingling to the tram stop. The small signboards telling where they were going had been removed from the cars (so spies couldn't use the information for their own ends). No. 19 came to the stop. Mother did not know if it went to Vitebsky Railway Station, and so she asked everybody, but no one knew either. "You'll get there," a man said at last from the top step, but it was too late — the tram started moving and Mother was afraid to jump on with Lucy in her arms. "Oh heavens, we'll be late now," she kept saying. No. 9 came to the stop next, that was the tram they wanted, so they got on feeling quite safe.

The shop windows were screened with plywood. A newspaper was pasted on one of the screens, and on another a verse was written in black paint. Valya read the title, it was: "To Leningraders".

A fat silver sausage hung in the sky.

Sandbags were piled up round a monument.

Some men in civilian clothes were walking down the middle of the street, and with them there was an officer in uniform.

There was a long queue at the lemonade stand.

A small dog was running along, behind it came a young girl

clutching the leash and a shopping net with a cabbage in it as if it were a ball.

All this sailed past in the midday heat—screens, verses, the silver sausage, the small dog, sandbags, lemonade, men in uniform and civvies.

Valya had been to Vitebsky Station before. It was from here she went to Young Pioneer Camp in Detskoye Selo the summer before, and it was here the train brought them when they returned home. The sunburnt boys and girls had marched down the platform with a drum and bunches of flowers, and their parents had been there to meet them. Valya now ran along the familiar platform holding Lucy by the hand, with their mother holding her by her other hand. They were jostled and pushed by the milling crowd. It had never been so terribly hot ever before. They ran the length of the platform and down some steps to where the ground was red-hot and criss-crossed by gleaming rails. They crawled under freight cars and tank cars, and for a second were in the shade which felt beautifully cool. There was a hot smell of metal, there were black oily puddles on the ground, and black mountains of coal.

They crawled from under a tank car and saw a huge crowd of people. There were no platforms here, no lemonade stands or anything—just a crowd of people, and towering over the crowd a whole chain of box cars. Wilted branches, with their lifeless leaves curled up, hung from the roofs. A man stood on one of the roofs and shouted familiar words about the fascist aggressors. The words were clearly heard one minute, but the next a gust of hot wind would carry them away into another direction. Mother dashed from one car to another muttering all the time: "Where is he? Oh, where is he?"

And suddenly they heard Daddy's voice.

"Nyura, I say, Nyura!"

He was in uniform. And it made him look thinner and shorter.

"I was afraid you'd be late," he said.

"I went to fetch the children," Mother replied.

She took off her head kerchief and fanned her face with it. When she had got her breath back, she burst out crying, and Daddy comforted her.

They weren't late at all, the locomotive had not even been hitched up yet. There it was, that big black steam engine, chugging busily back and forth a little way off, moving its levers energetically. It was approaching now: everyone faced about to watch it, and talk ceased. But once again it moved away big-heartedly, blowing vividly white, plump clouds of smoke into the blue sky. Lucy watched it from Father's arms and shouted: "Toot-toot!" Some people nearby were singing in chorus: "Let noble fury seethe and swell...." An icecream woman was selling choc-ice sticks.

"We want some," Father told her.

But she didn't hear him, she had just sold some icecream to someone else and was busy counting the change, digging for it into the pocket of her white jacket. Valya terribly wanted icecream, her throat was simply parched. What if the woman sold everything out and there was none left for them? No, their turn came at last, and the woman gave them four icecreams. Mother, her face tear-stained, also had one.

"We never had a picture taken all together," she said.

"Take the children away if there's a chance," Father told her, watching Lucy licking her icecream.

The people nearby were singing: "A patriotic war is on, a people's holy war!"

Suddenly the box cars swayed and jangled: the engine crept up unnoticed, and hitched on. Mother began to sob. People were kissing goodbye all about them. An accordion blared out so loudly, as though it were screaming. Father kissed Lucy and set her down on the ground. He kissed Valya: she caught the familiar tobacco smell, but her lips were sticky and numb from the icecream, and she said with her numb lips:

"Goodbye, daddy darling."

The man on the roof was shouting quickly now, in a hurry to say all he had to say. The volunteers clambered up into the cars.

The box cars moved off, and rolled away on their tall wheels: the wide-open doors showed faces, uniforms, forage caps. The crowd swept after it, but could you follow a train far? It went faster and faster, the cars flickered past, you could not make out the faces any longer, all you saw through the trembling rainbow of tears was a dark, breaking strip.

Valya rubbed her eyes, and wiped the rainbow away.

The end car disappeared, leaving an emptiness of rails and sleepers.

They went home.

3.

Aunt Dusya came and told their mother:

"The first thing you must do, Nyura, is make some knapsacks."

Before Aunt Dusya came, Mother had tried to do a hundred things at once: she'd wash some clothes and start ironing them, but before she'd ironed the lot she'd start mending things. Then she'd drop her mending, and start making over her dresses for Valya and Lucy.

"At least they'll have something to wear," she told her neighbours. "We'll look no worse than others. They've grown out of everything, you know."

She didn't go to the factory any more.

When Aunt Dusya came the room was in a mess, what with the wash, the mending, and the bits and pieces of cloth strewn all over the place.

"Once you've made the knapsacks everything will become clear," she said. "You'll know exactly what to take and what to leave behind."

Mother took her advice, left the dress she was making unfinished, and began cutting some brown stuff into knapsacks under the supervision of Aunt Dusya who stood over her, screwing up one eye against the smoke rising from the cigarette stuck, as usual, in the corner of her mouth.

"Take all your warm things, whatever else," she was saying. "Overcoats, felt boots, everything you have. The temperature drops to thirty degrees below zero and more where you're going."

"Surely you're not going to stay here?" Mother asked.

"I have no family, and someone's got to stay, everything can't stop just like that," Aunt Dusya replied. "We're going to put out diagonal and possibly cloth for army greatcoats."

"I'm scared to death of these air-raid alarms," Mother said. "When the wailing starts, I become quite demented."

"And I can't stand queues," said Aunt Dusya. "They make me so sick that I'd rather not eat than stand in a queue. But it's all right now, I gave my ration cards to Klava and her daughter will get my ration for me when she gets hers."

When Aunt Dusya left, Mother settled down at her sewing machine and made two knapsacks. A big one for herself, and a tiny one for Lucy. Though a baby, Lucy also had to carry her share from that day on.

Valya had an old knapsack which she had taken to the Young Pioneer Camp.

Mother was proud of the result—the knapsacks were neat and the seams were good and strong.

"And your hands are left free to carry other luggage," she said. "Knapsacks are really most convenient."

When talking with her school friends, Valya repeated this: "Knapsacks are really most convenient."

She didn't expect her neck to hurt from carrying this sack. When they went to summer camp their rucksacks travelled in a lorry, while the boys and girls walked along, free of any load, and picked the daisies that grew at the roadside.

4.

The weight made itself felt after the first few steps. But Valya did not say anything.

Nor did her mother, although she was carrying the heaviest things — a basket in one hand, a shopping bag and a milk-can in the other, and the knapsack making a huge hump on her back. She stooped under the weight, and the strain on her arms made them seem very long.

Only Lucy was running and skipping merrily, because all she had in her knapsack were socks and hankies, a piece of soap, a comb and a small towel for the road, and a tin water mug. That's all.

The yardkeeper stood at the gate, and they said goodbye.

"Good luck to you," she said. "All the best. Come back soon."

"Goodbye, Auntie Olga."

It was early morning. The sun shone mildly on one side of the street. The asphalt must have just been flushed, and there were puddles of water.

Lucy was wearing her new dress with a flounce. And Valya—her new dress with a belt and a bow. Their mother had taken them to the hairdresser's the day before to have their hair trimmed. It was nice to set off on a journey looking so smart.

Valya and her mother had tidied their room before leaving. They brushed the crumbs off the table after breakfast, washed the crockery and put it away in the dresser. Newspapers were spread over the couch so it shouldn't collect dust. Mother had already draped the lampshade in an old bed sheet the night before. Tucking it in, she had wept. Buying that lampshade was a sweet memory, it was like an orange, such a cheerful reddish yellow, and all they needed now was a new tablecloth and then the room would look really pretty,— and instead, look what had befallen people!

5.

And here they were sitting on their luggage outside Moskovskaya Station.

From the railway station, down Ligovka, all the way to the square women and children were sitting on their bags, waiting to be evacuated.

Somewhere quite near the steam engines were screaming, and theirs was the voice of hope.

Auntie Dusya collected all her group together, counted them over and grumbled:

"How they love their old junk! Weren't you told you could take sixteen kilos and no suitcases? And look what you've brought!"

"You told us yourself to take all our overcoats and felt boots, so what are we supposed to do now—throw them away right here?" the women screamed.

"And what about the things we left at home? How do we know they'll be there when we come back?"

"There'll be three cars for the lot of you. You'll squeeze your luggage in, and yourselves you'll be left out, is that what you want?" Auntie Dusya demanded angrily.

"Don't you worry, we'll squeeze ourselves in too somehow!" Women shouted defiantly. "You'd better get those three cars here quickly!"

The sun was getting hotter and hotter.

The waiting crowd had drunk up all the lemonade and eaten up all the icecream on sale in the square and the nearby streets. People queued up waiting their turn at the water taps in the yards along Ligovsky, Staro-Nevsky and Vosstaniye streets. Valya stood in line with their kettle in one hand and the milk-can in the other, while Lucy clutched her little mug in her hands.

When their turn came, they drank their fill, and then wetted their handkerchiefs, knotted them at the corners, and put them on their heads. The handkerchiefs made very pleasant, cool caps, but they dried too quickly.

Mother was sitting on their basket, with all their belongings piled at her knees where she could keep a hand on them. Beside her on a large suitcase sat a fat old woman with a big sallow face and very black eyes. She wore a blue polka-dot dress and a white silk scarf draped over her shoulders. As she chatted with Mother she fanned herself with a folded newspaper.

"You have handsome children," she said.

Mother was delighted, naturally.

"They take after their father," she said. "He also has this fair hair, and a slender bone structure."

"Lovely girls," the old lady said, and gave Lucy and Valya a chocolate each.

"Lucy, say thank you," Mother admonished her. "You see, Valya said thank you, didn't she? You must always remember to say thank you. Now offer Granny a drink of water. Do have some."

There were lots of girls there of Valya's own age, and she made friends with them. A bevy of them went wandering up and down past the tall buildings which gazed down upon them from their thousands of windows, criss-crossed with strips of white paper.

The girls walked into a large shop to see what they had on sale there.

There were various hats, fabrics, furs, furniture, anything you wanted. The display windows, though, were boarded up with plywood, and so all the lamps were on.

What do we want this furniture for anyway? Valya was thinking. We've left our own behind, and we don't know if it'll be safe.

Nice dress material, but we've nowhere to put it, our knapsacks are stuffed full as it is.

But that hat over there I'd gladly take if it were bought for me. That dream of transparent straw trimmed with flowers I'd take alright. I'd put it on right away. What beautiful flowers. Can't tell them from real ones.

The girls left the shop in single file, and continued on their stroll.

The bolder, perky girls among them talked and laughed in loud lilting voices to attract the attention of the passersby.

But the passersby went past without taking any notice. They'd glance up absently and walk on.

Perhaps they were on their way to the enlistment office, perhaps they'd been called up.

Or else a man might have just come back from the trenches and was hurrying home to eat and take a wash, with a million other things to do besides. What were these loitering girls to him?

6.

There was one girl among the lot. There is always just one. She was still silent. She was still sort of sizing you up from afar, wondering if you two would get along and have fun together. As for yourself, you already knew that of all your friends this girl was going to be your dearest, truest friend!

"What's your name?"

"Valya. And yours?"

"Svetlana. Let's go and buy some icecream."

"Let's."

"I'll go and ask my mother for money."

But their mothers shouted at them.

"Stop running around! Can't you keep still for a minute? If they tell us to board where are we to find you?"

It was fun sitting on bags with your bosom friend.

"What books have you read?"

"Oh, what a book I've just read! You see, he was in love with her. And she was in love with him...."

"Your braids are so thick and long...."

"And I prefer a bob. Like yours."

"Have you seen the film 'The Great Waltz'?"

A woman was telling about the German air-raids on Moscow.

Another one was telling about the air-raids on Pskov. But mostly the talk revolved round some place called Mga. You heard it all the time—Mga this, and Mga that.

"Oh Lord, I hope there's no air-raid alarm while we're sitting here," Mother was saying. "How could we go into the shelter with all these bags?"

"Let's hope there won't be an alarm," the fat old woman said and, suddenly, pulling the scarf off her shoulders she waved with it and shouted: "Sasha! Sasha!"

A bald-headed gent was picking his way to her carefully. He had an egg-shaped head, the bald spot like the pointed end of an egg. His eyes were as black as the fat old woman's. He had his sleeves rolled up, and carried a briefcase.

"So you're still here," he said. "Have you had any water to drink?"

"I have," she replied. "Don't worry about me."

"Have you eaten anything?"

"Oh I have, I have. Don't worry."

"Shall I bring you something? Icecream. Shall I go and hunt up some icecream?"

"I don't want anything, just stay with me for a little. What's new?"

They talked in low voices. He stood bending over her, while she held his hand, his thin, sinewy hand that sprouted dark hairs and had a watch on a leather strap at the wrist.

"Will you come again, Sasha love?"

"I'll try."

"Our departure may not be soon. Supposing it's not until late evening?" She just could not let him go. "Do come again, just in case."

"I'll try."

Stepping like a stork, he made his way out of the crowd.

"Your son?" Mother asked.

"And what a son, if you only knew!" replied the old woman. Tears trickled down her big face. "He's such a busy man, yet he's found the time to come and see me here. And he'll come again, my darling child, I know he will!"

Valya and Svetlana exchanged glances. Fancy calling that bald-headed gent a child.

Lucy fell asleep in her mother's lap, and the fat old woman made her newspaper into a sort of tent to shield the child from the sun.

Valya and Svetlana also lay down on the knapsacks, hiding their heads in the short shadow cast by the old woman. The stone wall gave off heat like an oven.

The shadow shifted, and Valya sat up, startled and dizzy.

There was a roar overhead, swelling in rolls like thunder, and two planes flew past, low over the roofs. Lucy jerked in her sleep.

"Sleep, my baby, sleep," Mother said, rocking her. "They're our planes."

They flashed past with a scorching gleam. They seemed to be even hotter than the stone wall. They were red-hot like the sun. And their roar, too, was hot and furious.

Ligovka and Nevsky Prospekt were a merry-go-round as always. People and cars were hurrying along. A traffic officer stood swinging his stick. All this had nothing to do with the people who were sitting or sprawling here, outside the railway station, they were no longer in town, sort of. They had already started on their journey.

Now this tramcar No. 25, Valya was thinking, would go rumbling and jingling along the streets, over the bridge, and on to Vyborgskaya Side to their house. In no more than twenty minutes the tram would run past their street. And there, in their street, was their house and their room which they had swept that morning and left the broom and dustpan in a corner.

It was nice and quiet in their street.

Hopscotch squares were chalked on the asphalt in front of the house. *Their* hopscotch squares. Someone else was playing there now.

It was only twenty minutes to go if you took this tram, this tram No. 25.

People were boarding the tram.

And they wouldn't. They had begun their journey, goodbye. Their house was far away. Their quiet street was far away. At world's end.

7.

A big girl came with her mother and her brother. The mother and the brother sat down and began to eat and drink, but the girl did not want anything. She did not even want to sit down. She stood before them, looking about her with an angry face and saying mean, angry things to her mother:

"Oh, you're hot, are you! Oh, you don't like it here! And whose idea was it, mine and Victor's perhaps? Victor and I will return home this minute. Gladly! Oh, you don't want to return, do you? Very well then, as you like. Only please don't tell us how hot you are because it's your own fault!"

Her brother kept silent. He was a cripple on crutches: one of his legs had been amputated above the knee. He sat silent, with drooping head. Now their mother addressed her plaints to the old couple sitting next to them.

"I brought her up with such care, I denied myself everything for her sake, and she, look how she talks to her mother!"

"What are you doing to me? Where are you taking me?" the girl's voice rang with despair. "You hate me! You're killing me! You're doing to me what only an enemy would do and not my own mother!"

The brother now spoke up too.

"All right, stop it!"

And their mother asked the old couple:

"See?"

The old couple got up and started brushing each other's clothes.

"Be so kind, keep an eye on our things," they said. "We'll go and have some lunch with a relative of ours. We have a relative who lives quite near here, on Vtoraya Sovetskaya Street."

"How convenient for you. But what if the train leaves without you?"

"Oh well, it will mean we're fated to stay," said the old lady. "You see, we want to take a shower before lunch."

"And lie down for a bit afterwards," added the old gentleman.

Everyone watched them walking away with mincing steps, the husband leaning on his cane and the wife holding his arm.

"Isn't it all the same to them where to die—in the rear or here in Leningrad? No, they still want to go somewhere, heavens above!" somebody said.

"Everyone wants to live," people protested.

A young woman held her little red-cheeked boy close to her breast, and kissing his red cheeks said over and over again:

"How long will it be before you and I come back, Vasil, my pet?"

A steam engine screamed a warning. One more train was leaving, taking away people. Everyone stood up nervously, and then Auntie Dusya appeared, looking somewhat dishevelled, the inevitable cigarette stuck in the corner of her mouth.

"It won't be long now, women," she said. "The train has been promised soon."

Their steam engine was screaming: I'm here! I'm working hard! I'll do everything I can!

8.

The people from the chemical plant left.

The opera and ballet theatre people left.

The old couple had their lunch at their relative's, a shower, and a nap, and came back to the railway station.

That big girl stopped quarrelling with her mother and fell silent. She was sitting on a bag, clutching her knees with her sunburnt arms, staring glumly before her, and her face was dark from dust and anger.

The women buzzed, fretting because the evacuation was going so slowly.

"What's in the last broadcast? Did you listen to the news this afternoon?"

"They say people were leaving Gatchina on foot, driving their cows along."

"We're not going via Gatchina. We're going via Mga."

"Yes, Mga."

In the meantime Svetlana was saying to Valya:

"I knocked and asked: may I come in? He said: come in. I went in. He said: what can I do for you? I said: please try me for the part of the Snow Maiden. He said: we don't take girls under sixteen. I said: I beg your pardon, but doesn't talent count for anything? He said: we'll talk about talent when you're in the eighth form. I almost burst into tears. I said: sorry, and left quickly. Two more years to wait, can you imagine it?!"

Svetlana had narrow shoulders, and arms and legs like sticks. She wore sandals on her feet. And blue bows in her braided hair.

"Will you write to me?" Valya asked.

"How can I when I don't know where you're going to be? And you won't know where I am either."

"Write to my Leningrad address, and I'll write to your Leningrad address. When the war's over we'll come back and find each other."

"I'm sick and tired of this war something awful!" said Svetlana.

9.

The day dragged endlessly. There was no counting the trips they made for water, the times they tried to doze on their bags, the number of faces they saw, the different conversations they heard, and the amount of words they spoke themselves.

At long last the dazzling sunlight began to mellow a little. You could already look up without squinting. The sky was turning a lilac colour and was no longer heavy.

The fat old woman was in despair because her son hadn't come again, and kept saying: "But he promised to come, he promised."

She watched for every arriving tramcar with sad and eager eyes, rising a little from the suitcase she was sitting on and craning her neck. This was the tram on which her son was sure to come.

"Maybe he'll come yet," the women tried to console her.

"Supposing he's been transferred to barracks and can't leave?" the old woman fretted. "Maybe he's gone off to dig trenches? How can I find out? Should I go home?"

But it was already five minutes to ten on the station clock. And after ten there was curfew. It was too late for her to go home. And too late for her son to come.

Night slowly descended on Ligovka and Nevsky Prospekt.

It was no longer a white night: the season of white nights was over. It was lilac coloured at first, and then simply dark.

No street lamps, not a sliver of light anywhere. Just the blue lamp bulbs and the stars beginning to show in the fathomless heights.

Was this Ligovka Street, or what?

Where were they sitting under the stars?

Valya closed her eyes, and in her sleep she saw the Sahara desert.

"Valya, child, have something to eat, dear," she heard her mother's voice very close.

She must have dreamt of the Sahara desert because she had read a book about it the other day.

"You haven't eaten all day," her mother's voice went on. "Come, dear, have this egg."

The sounds with which the egg-shell was broken was loud enough for the whole of the Sahara desert to hear. For the stars to hear.

Someone else was having a snack quite near: wrapping paper rustled, a milk-can clattered. Someone was asking for a thermometer.

"Do you happen to have a thermometer? I beg your pardon, but I wonder if you have a thermometer? Anybody has a thermometer? Thermometer?"

The fat old woman was telling about her son.

"Since he was a little tot it was Mummy, Mummy, all the time. He wasn't so loving with his father, it was always Mummy, Mummy. And now, too, he says—you must go away, Mummy, I can't bear the thought that you might be exposed to danger."

Through the knapsack stuffed with clothes (was she imagining it? No, she wasn't), through the knapsack (there it went again) Valya felt faint jolts. As though there was an earthquake somewhere far away. Why, of course, it was an air-raid. How could it be an earthquake? Bombers came and dropped bombs. They were far away: there was no sound at all, only the earth shuddering soundlessly. They were far away....

The crowd was hushed.

With a metallic rumbling, a black lorry rolled past on thick tyres.

A man in uniform was coming this way.

This soldier who was permitted to walk about at night now crossed the street from where the hotel was.

The fat old woman raised her head. She probably thought it was her son. But this man was in uniform.

He walked down the line of people, looking for someone. He would make a step and stop to look.

Who was he looking for?

Suddenly a girl's slim dark figure rose over the piles of luggage.

She rose and stretched out her hands. Not a word was spoken. Valya blinked just once—and there the girl was beside the man. She blinked a second time—and the two were already walking away. Keeping step so nicely.

The soldier's boots thudded on the pavement, and the girl beside him seemed to be walking on air. And she laughed softly in the deep of night.

She laughed with such a carefree laugh in the darkness of this wartime night, with not a sliver of light anywhere and only the stars high above, as if only happiness lay ahead of her. As if there were no bombers dropping bombs, no guns aimed to kill her happiness.

10.

The night ended. Valya stood up and looked about her.

It was early morning, the hour at which they left home the day before. The sun shone softly once more, and the shadow cast by the house was cool.

A street-flushing car appeared, and watered the asphalt with wide cool sprays.

Sparrows chirped and hopped about with no fear of the sprays. These quick brown little birds would fly over to the pavement and peck at the crumbs around the bags and people's feet.

The mothers were combing out their daughters' hair. A young woman was nursing her baby, her scarf draped over her shoulder and breast.

Lucy awoke too. This is how she always awakened: first, her eyelashes began to tremble lazily because she was still in dreamland; then her eyes opened a little, slowly and lazily because they were still seeing dreams; and at last they opened wide, and were so very, very clear and bright.

Lucy awoke and it was obvious that she had forgotten everything: where they were and why. She sat up and looked to right, to left, and up into the sky.

Their pretty new dresses which their mother had made and ironed with such care had become crumpled and dirty, with all the flounces and bows dropping like rags. What a pity! They had looked so nice only yesterday!

11.

Oh, what an exciting piece of news, it was breathtaking! Do you know who went off with the soldier in the night? That big girl who kept quarrelling with her mother. It was clear now why she lost her temper and wrung her hands: her mother was taking her away, and she wanted to be where her lover was. And that's why she was so cheeky to her mother.

"But why did she agree to go in the first place?"

"She may have lost touch with him, and didn't know where he was."

"He may have been away from Leningrad."

"And her mother made her come."

This was how the girls, Valya and Svetlana's age, saw it. They had flocked together to discuss the happening, embroidering imaginatively on the little they knew.

"He came to their house and they'd already left."

"He was told where they'd gone."

"And so he came to the railway station just in case she was still here."

"And she *was* still here!"

"And he kidnapped her."

"Why kidnapped, when she ran to him herself?"

"It's a kidnapping just the same because he did it on the quiet."

"Her mother was fast asleep. She couldn't sleep at first, she told people, and just before this happened she dropped off."

"Was the brother asleep too?"

"Maybe he was and maybe he wasn't."

"He was not asleep. I saw him."

"He says he was."

"That woman over there saw them go off. She was nursing her baby. She saw them and didn't tell."

"I should hope not. Would you tell?"

"Not for anything in the world!"

"Nobody would," said Svetlana. "I don't know what kind of person one must be to tell."

The mother of the girl was weeping.

"Maybe she'll come back," the women comforted her. "She'll think better of it and come running back."

"Not she, she won't come running back," the mother sobbed.

"You could report him," one woman said. "They won't pat him on the head for such doings, believe me."

"But where can I report him?" wailed the fugitive's mother. "I don't even know his surname, all I know is that he's Kostya!"

The other women worried that the girl had gone off without her passport—it was in her mother's keeping.

And the girls said:

"She's beautiful!"

"Who, she? She's not beautiful at all."

"A most ordinary girl."

But it was obvious to all—to those who talked and those who kept their silence—that this fugitive, this rude girl, was certainly not ordinary, for whether beautiful or not she was the only one in the whole enormous crowd to be sought out by her lover and to run to him with outstretched arms.

"Her eyes are so very, very blue."

"They're not blue! They're hazel."

"You're all wrong. They're grey one minute, and green the next, you can't tell the colour."

"Did you see her go or not?" the mother pestered her crippled son. "Were you asleep or not?"

The boy made no answer for a long time, and finally he snapped:

"Oh, get off my neck!" And suddenly he looked very much like his sister. "Let someone in this family have a real life!"

"And what if it's death and not life?" sobbed the mother.

"That's all right too," replied the crippled boy. "A real death in war is not bad either."

He rose with difficulty, picked up his crutches and hobbled away. He had been run over by a tramcar when he was a little boy and played in the middle of the street forgetting his mother's warning. His shoulder-blades stuck out under his shirt, and his long untrimmed hair lay in strands on his thin neck.

The women were saying:

"Fancy going off without her passport, without her ration cards, and just in the clothes she stood in!"

And the girls said:

"Oh, how she wrung her hands! How broken-hearted she was!"

"And how happy she must be today!"

"Are you glad for her sake?" Svetlana asked.

"Oh, yes!" Valya replied.

"Wonderful, isn't it?"

"Marvellous!"

They squeezed each other's hands furtively and quickly.

What a romantic story to happen on a dark, wartime night! And what an unexpected bit of excitement for the girls bored with waiting for their train!

12.

And suddenly it all vanished. There was none of it left.

"Svetlana! Goodbye!"

She couldn't see Svetlana, and only heard her weak little voice ringing in answer: "Bye-bye! Bye!"

It sounded weaker and weaker: "Bye! Bye!"

Hitching their bundles on their backs, the crowd streamed forward.

Valya was carried like a chip of wood in this stuffy stream. You had to trudge on and on. You couldn't pause or look back. There was a bag on her left and a bag on her right, and it hurt when they jolted her—they might be filled with stones. Valya's own knapsack squashed her vertebrae and pulled at her neck. They trudged on and on. She couldn't see where they were going, they just trudged on. For a moment she thought she would suffocate, but she moved on readily and without fear for that was what she must do. That's what this journey of theirs required of people. The main thing was not to lose hold of Lucy's hand. Their mother was holding her other hand—it was all right, they were all there, Lucy couldn't get lost....

...They boarded the train. You couldn't see a thing for the luggage and the crowd. Valya, Lucy and two more little children were sitting on the top bunk. Someone's bundles had been put there with them. Below there was a crush of people, a sea of heads.

"Thank God, we got in," their mother said.

The car was full up, but people still kept arriving with more bundles and bags, and it was a wonder how they all squeezed in. The earlier arrivals grumbled:

"What are they doing, we're suffocating as it is!"

The fat old woman with the black eyes went on with her lament, addressing no one in particular:

"He didn't come. Oh Lord, I so wanted to see him once more, and I won't now!"

Vasil, the small red-cheeked boy, lay on his mother's jacket spread out on the lower bunk opposite. He was ill. It was his mother who had been looking for a thermometer all night, and now everyone was talking: "He has thirty nine and three! Thirty nine and three! Must be measles! Diphtheria! Scarlet fever! Chicken pox!"

A white coat with a red cross surfaced from the crush and asked in a loud voice:

"Who has thirty nine and three?"

Aunt Dusya appeared behind the white coat.

"Heavens, Nina, something always goes wrong with you! And at the last minute, too."

Vasil's young mother replied defensively: "How could I have helped it, Aunt Dusya? One might think I'd done it on purpose!"

"You should have told me earlier," Aunt Dusya said angrily. "You needn't have put a sick child in with well ones. Where's your sense of responsibility towards your own child and towards the community? Which are your belongings? Here, I'll help you."

The woman in a white coat carried Vasil away. His mother came behind them, laughing and crying at the same time.

"Here we are, Vasil, returning to Leningrad already!"

There was a sharp whistle, and the clang of metal under the car. The station buildings shifted, and slowly moved past the dim window.

Valya sat on her top bunk and looked out.

There was Aunt Dusya standing on the platform and waving. She floated past, and vanished.

A man with an egg-shaped bald head was running down the platform, swinging the briefcase in his hand and kicking his grey-trousered legs high. His face was turned to their train as he ran.

"There's your son, Granny! There's your son!"

"Where? Where is he? Where?" the old woman cried.

"There! Over there!" Valya shouted.

But the old woman could not see him from where she was, and there was no getting to the window.

He disappeared from view.

...The train ran as through a tunnel between two other trains standing on the lines. It was a long, dark tunnel, but suddenly the blue expanse of the sky was flung open before them, and beneath them was a strange street with houses, fences and green tousled trees, and there they were moving along a high embankment above the street and the trees, heading for the blue open space beyond. The train was gathering speed. And the wheels were starting their song.

Svetlana had stayed behind in Leningrad. Or had she left too? There had been so many trains at the station. Svetlana, where are you, did you leave or not? We never had a real talk, we haven't really talked our fill and learnt everything about each other. And we were going to be best friends for life!

Mother was building a nest on that side of the shelf where Valya and Lucy were sitting.

She spread something on the bunk to make it softer for them to sit, she took off Lucy's sandals to make it easier on her feet and, pouring a bit of water from the can on a wash-rag, rubbed the dusty little feet with it. Next, from her shopping-bag she took out some bread, cucumbers, a knife and salt. She did not dump the food down just anywhere, but first spread a clean dishtowel on Valya's knees. The towel was embroidered in cross-stitch with roosters and horses in red and black thread, and anyone who saw that towel was sure to say:

"What a beautiful dishtowel!"

And Mother would reply:

"Its from my mother's trousseau, she embroidered it herself."

Nobody admired the dishtowel here. They could not be bothered with dishtowels. They could not be bothered with homely, pretty things.

But Mother went on building her nest just the same.

"I wish I could change you into clean frocks," she said.

She had built her nest under a roof, in a freshly papered room. She had built it as best she could under the open sky, on the pavement outside the railway station. And now she was building it on the bunk of a railway carriage.

Now that her children had been made comfortable and fed, she could sit down on the suitcase of the fat old woman with the black eyes who made room on it for her, and doze off, exhausted by her efforts and the excitement of boarding the train, with her head bowed down on her hands. Valya, sitting cross-legged on the bunk above, looked down on her mother's small brown head with the white parting.

13.

She taught her little girls all the good she knew herself. It wasn't her fault that she did not know much. She had not had the time to learn. She had a full-time job at the factory, and after work there was everything to be done at home—cooking, cleaning, sewing, washing. She was the latest to bed and the earliest to rise: the family would still be fast asleep, and she would already be up and about— making soup, or ironing a shirt for her husband.

When there was something special for dinner, she'd divide it up among the three of them, and tell them that she'd already eaten.

When her husband had a drink too many, she'd put him to bed, tuck him up, persuade him not to sing, and tell the neighbours that he'd had a hard day at work, and was resting.

She always shouldered the hardest jobs, and was always run off her feet.

It was her joy to do everything for those she loved.

Valya was too young to appreciate or even understand any of this.

She had not had the time to understand anything. She had not had the time to appreciate her mother as she deserved. She thought it only natural that her mother should get up first and do everything for them.

Oh, how stupid, how stupid it was of me to think about Svetlana when you were there beside me, but I wasn't thinking about you, I was thinking about Svetlana! I would have understood later when I was older, when I had more sense! Oh, Mummy darling, I would have kissed your feet in gratitude!

14.

The train was going to Mga.

True, it did more standing than going. It would roll on, quite briskly sometimes, and suddenly stop, and remain, standing for three or even four hours.

The Neva was visible from the train on some stretches of the road, and then it would vanish from sight.

Men and women were digging trenches. Deep-black and reddish-brown earth flew off their shovels. And people in the train were saying:

"They're already digging right outside Leningrad."

Blocks of something were stacked on the swamp—people said it was peat.

They said that Mga was very near, a stone's throw away, but there was still no sight of it. It was always farther ahead, Mga was.

But they were approaching it. Cramped and miserable, with their legs gone numb, falling into a heavy, nightmarish slumber from the stuffiness and waking with moans—they were approaching Mga, the last outlet from the town besieged by murderers.

She would always remember these swamps and these people digging trenches.

The trenches would be gone, but she would remember them.

Night was approaching, and they were approaching Mga. It was unavoidable on their route, this Mga place.

1.

Ksenia Ivanovna packed some medicines into an old chocolate box and told them:

"If it's a cut or a scratch, paint it with iodine. If it's a sore throat, here's some streptocide, take a pill three times a day. And I'm putting in some valerian drops, just in case."

Ksenia Ivanovna regarded valerian drops as a cure-all, and loved treating everyone with this wonder-drug.

"Don't go out at the stops because you might stray too far and the train will leave, and what will you do then? But if you do go out and miss the train, go straight to the railway militia office. They'll find some way of sending you on."

"We shan't go out," Lucy assured her. "We'll stay in the train all the time."

"And, Valya, you are a big girl now, and I must give you a word of warning," Ksenia Ivanovna said, dropping her voice. "Keep away from strange young men on the train. Do not, under any circumstances, strike up any chance acquaintances. All they have on the brain when travelling is starting a flirtation with a girl. First they'll start a conversation with you, then they'll fetch you some hot water for tea, and after that they'll sit beside you and start making up to you. And that is improper. You are only a little girl. It's improper altogether, even for grownups. This is what you must do: if he brings you some water, tell him that you've no need of his services, thank you very much, and that you'll get your tea from the train attendant. Once I was travelling by train, this was before the war, and there was a man in a felt hat in the compartment with us. We were three girls, and he flirted with all of us. But I told him: stop it, I know all these tricks, I won't fall for them, not me! And cases have been known," Ksenia Ivanovna continued, ominously narrowing and then widening her eyes, "when a young man would pretend to be flirting, and then he'd pinch your suitcase, and that would be that!"

"Was yours pinched too?" asked Lucy.

"No, mine wasn't," replied Ksenia Ivanovna. "But this did happen to the daughter of one of our teachers. It isn't so

simple to pinch anything from me. I don't let my suitcase out
of my sight when I travel. At night I put it behind my pillow,
so I can feel it with my head all the time even in sleep."

"We'll lie down like that too," Lucy said. "We'll lie down
so that we can feel things with our heads."

The other teachers would have liked to give Valya some
sound advice as well. But as they could not clearly picture
what life was like in Leningrad just then, they did not know
what advice to give to someone going there. They let the
words of advice they had begun to speak trail sadly. Not so
Ksenia Ivanovna. She never doubted that the advice *she* gave
people would come in useful under any circumstances.

2.

"Valya, Lucy, get up, it's time to go!" she shook them
awake with nervous impatience.

Valya jumped out of bed. The light dazzled her. Ksenia
Ivanovna stood there fully dressed with a wet fox collar on
her shoulders and holding the lamp high in her hands. Valya
began to dress, grabbing the wrong things and shivering from
the night's cold. Many of the girls had risen from under their
grey blankets, and were dressing in silence. Lucy sat up in
bed and was finishing her sleep, with her eyes closed and
steam rising from her open mouth.

"Wake up," Valya told her.

"I want to sleep," said Lucy, rocking from side to side.

"Get dressed, girls, get dressed," Ksenia Ivanovna repeated
over and over, and left the room in a state of high
excitement. Her felt boots made dark prints on the floor,
much like the figure 8. In the middle of the night she had gone
to the collective farm stables to make sure that they were
harnessing the horses for the girls.

The sledge was there at the front door. The older girls and
the teachers had come out to see Valya and Lucy off. A
storm lantern illumined the front porch. Uncle Fedya,
moving clumsily on his artificial leg, arranged their luggage in
the sledge and tucked Lucy into the straw, with Aunt Nastya
helping him. After this, they wrapped Lucy up into a smelly
black sheepskin coat, and everyone came up to kiss her
goodbye. She was such a sweet little thing, and everyone had
pampered her.

The girls who were staying behind felt sad.

"Valya, write! Hope you get a good job!"

"Muffle up your mouths properly or you'll catch cold!" This from Ksenia Ivanovna.

"Mind you go easy on the bottle," Aunt Nastya said to Uncle Fedya.

The sledge moved off.

Slowly moved off the sledge, and slowly receded the Children's Home—a lone, dark building with a cluster of people on the porch, and a storm lantern hanging from a nail in the bare timber wall above it.

All this retreated slowly into the night and vanished, when the lantern was carried inside. It was so dark that they could not make out even the trail left by the runners on the snow, there was not even this trail left to connect them with what had gone forever....

The frosty air was pure and motionless. The far-scattered villages slumbered in this motionless frost. In the Children's Home, too, everyone must have gone back to sleep after seeing Valya and Lucy off. And here they were riding away in a sledge, muffled up in scarves, with their eyeballs freezing.

We had lived in this Children's Home for three years, three months and three days.

It was there that we received the notification that Daddy had been killed at Schlüsselburg. Lucy hardly remembered him and did not cry.

We were taught school subjects here.

We grew up.

Our house in Leningrad had been destroyed by a bomb. It felt strange, and yet it was not really strange, when you came to think of it. The house existed when there were Mummy and Daddy. It stopped existing when they were no more.

But we were going to Leningrad anyway. Aunt Dusya had arranged it. She had written us long ago, during the hunger and the bombing: "The factory won't forsake you, wait." We waited, our waiting was rewarded, and here we were on our way back home.

The horses snorted. Good animals, horses. It was cold and dark, yet they went on pulling our sledge, snorting now and then.

It was growing light. Before us there was a huge frozen river down below that looked like so much milk spilled from here all the way to the horizon. We drove down to the river. The road we were to take made a thin black chain across the white expanse.

I suppose we appeared very small amid this white, icy morning, rising from the night. Just a tiny black beetle crawling across the boundless white plain. But in actual fact there were two big horses, a sledge, two girls, a man in an army greatcoat and a woman driver—a broad, severe woman, bundled up in shawls, and her eyebrows and eyelashes white with hoarfrost.

3.

Chilled to the marrow, they gasped in the warmth and the shag smoke inside the train coach. Shag smoke and music! The gramophone was playing a waltz. A sailor boy, quite ignoring the gramophone, was playing something else on a guitar with a big blue bow. He had borrowed the guitar from the girl in the white fluffy beret. He played and sang: "Last night, as I left home to fight in countries far away...." The refrain: "My darling, my sweet girl," he addressed to the girl, causing her to glance at her watch, tuck her hair in place under the beret, turn away to look out of the window, and fidget generally.

All the berths were crowded, from floor to ceiling. Three or four people sat on each of the lower bunks. Packed like sardines, they drank tea, played dominoes, and walked about the car. A rosy, early-morning sun showed in the windows.

They were off.

Having settled Valya and Lucy in, Uncle Fedya now gave them their breakfast. He had filled a kettle with boiling water at the station. People were curious to see what the girls were eating. They looked at their dresses made from stiff khaki cloth, and commented approvingly:

"From a Children's Home, are they? The Home has certainly provided them well for the journey. These new dresses."

"Overcoats too," said Uncle Fedya. "The overcoats are also new, they weren't sent off just any old how."

"Your daughters?" somebody asked.

"As good as," Uncle Fedya replied with a wink at Lucy, his pet. "I'm going on business of my own, and I agreed to look after them."

Naturally, people wanted to know what this business of his was.

Uncle Fedya began from the very beginning, and related

how his unit recaptured Ropsha, how he was wounded and taken to a hospital in Leningrad.

"And now," he said, "I want to live only in this highly cultured city, and my wife, who is the Children Home cook at the present time, is of a like mind with me."

"I see," one of the listeners said.

"I see," said another.

"A Major I know was demobilised in Leningrad," continued Uncle Fedya, "and was given quite a good room on the Karpovka embankment. True, it's an attic room, but a proper bathroom has been installed and electricity has been put in."

"That's because he's a Major," one of the privates there said. "And who're we to get flats in Leningrad?"

To this Uncle Fedya objected that rank didn't come first, there were other things counted far more: supposing a man had lost a leg, fighting for Leningrad, eh?

Another private agreed that this was so indeed. They got to talking, and it transpired that he and Uncle Fedya both hailed from Vologda. Uncle Fedya brought out a bottle filled with some cloudy liquid that looked like kerosene, and said:

"Let us permit ourselves a drop for this good reason. It's home-made, nice and fresh."

He and the private touched their tin mugs and drank.

The train rumbled on.

Facing Valya sat an officer and a girl. They were holding hands, and their fingers were intertwined and restless. Every so often one of them would turn and look into the face of the other, and immediately the other would start and turn as well, and they would gaze bemused into each other's eyes, the officer whispering something, moving his lips tenderly, and the girl blushing a bright red.

"I'm sorry," she said.

"Sorry about what?" he asked, leaning towards her.

"The little house."

"Our house?"

"Yes. The porch. The path. The little window."

"Why sorry?"

"Because I'll never see it again."

"Are you very sorry?"

"Very."

A look into her eyes. She blushed a bright red.

"And you?" she asked after a moment.

"I've taken our little house along. I have it here."

With his free hand he patted his field bag. The girl smiled. She was happy.

"Did you take everything?"

"Everything."

"You didn't forget the path?"

"How could I forget it?"

"You didn't forget that the little window was red?"

"And the pine trees black."

"And the new moon over the pines."

"Such a thin, young crescent. Here it is. And the pines are here. Everything's here. See what a great load? It's hard to go away from you with this load."

"You'll come back," she said, closing her eyes and gripping his fingers. "You'll come back, you'll come back!"

"You'll meet me," he said. "I'll open the bag and get everything out. The little house, the crescent moon, the path."

But she wept. Why was she crying so bitterly? He must have been on leave, and now he was going back to the war. And people didn't always come back from the war.... Here's music! The gramophone was playing a rhumba. And the sailor boy was playing "Sunlit Meadow" on the guitar with the blue bow.

4.

I like it when there's music. And when people have untroubled, pleased faces.

It's so nice when the talk is polite and friendly.

What I like especially is when people talk beautifully about love. Honestly, what is she crying for, she has this great love and she's crying!

Look what you've done, you went and ruined a beautiful conversation with your tears! Silly, silly girl.... I knew another girl, that one laughed. She went off with him without her passport, without her ration cards, just in the clothes she stood in, and she was laughing.

By and large, I'm sick of tears.

Of course, you can't do without tears when there's a war on.

But, if possible, please let there be more beautiful words and feelings, and let the music play!

Uncle Fedya was taking off his boots to show his artificial leg to his Vologda friend. Why show it, I don't understand. "I

say, Lucy, come here. I'll read you a book if you like.
There's nothing for you to see there. Come, I'll read you the
'Why?' book."

5.

They read the "Why?" book.

After that Valya read "Rainbow" to herself, not aloud. It
was about the war.

Uncle Fedya and his Vologda friend were relating their
wartime experiences, and everybody listened. There was one
more soldier travelling on the top bunk: he was asleep, and
his legs shod in blue wool socks stuck right across the aisle.
He woke up now, sat up with his feet dangling, and also
related a war experience.

War, war, blood, and pain!

After that the women told about bad, unfaithful wives.

One woman told about dreams that came true and visions.

Uncle Fedya's Vologda friend said that it was only the
mentally unhinged who had visions, but what people really
did have sometimes was premonitions.

The sailor boy said that premonitions were just a
superstition too. He laid aside his guitar, and read them a
small lecture. The soldiers approved of his learnedness, and
decided that the state money spent on his education had not
been wasted. His lecture finished, the sailor boy played a
crashing chord on the guitar, and began to sing his love songs
again with new force. The girl in the fluffy beret, impressed
by his lecture, now listened with a smile and did not turn
away. Honestly, it does mean a lot when a man who shows
an interest in you can deliver a lecture.

In the meantime the December day, the first day of their
journey, had dimmed. A yellow streak of sunset had lingered
in the window for a long time, and when it had melted away
the light was put on and the lamps right under the ceiling
glimmered yellowly through the clouds of smoke. Everyone
quieted down, the singers, the talkers, and the chap who had
been playing the gramophone since early morning. A hush
fell on the travellers, and only at the very far end of the car a
monotonous voice went on talking tirelessly. Lucy fell
asleep, nestling against Valya. And Valya suddenly began to
float away and away. She lurched against the woman beside
her, and woke up. The soldier in the blue wool socks was
standing before her and nudging Uncle Fedya awake.

"Comrade, I say, Comrade," he was saying very quietly. "Wake up and listen: I'm getting off the stop after next, so go and grab my bunk for the kids, you hear me?"

Uncle Fedya heard him, sprang to his feet and without a word lifted Lucy up into the upper bunk. Lucy mumbled in her sleep: "I'll tell Valya on you", and stretched out luxuriously, her tousled fair head touching the soldier's small trunk.

"You climb up too, young lady," he told Valya, and taking her vacated seat beside Uncle Fedya said: "Let's have a smoke, Comrade."

Clouds of acrid smoke rose ceilingward at once.

"So you want to get settled in Leningrad," said the soldier.

"I'm an enchanted wanderer," Uncle Fedya replied. "Leningrad has enchanted me."

"And I," said the soldier, "I'll go back home to my Kursk region when this is all over. Our cherry trees are a sight in blossom time."

"Hitler's done a lot of damage in your Kursk region."

"We'll repair it."

"Won't be long now," said Uncle Fedya's Vologda friend. "Everyone will go each his own way. It's a question of months now, and soon it will be a question of days."

"What I did learn in the army is driving a car," said Uncle Fedya. "I'm quite well up in motors, so I'm going to try and get a driver's license."

"Now, a salesman's job has its advantages too," said Uncle Fedya's Vologda friend.

"Oh no," Uncle Fedya sighed. "I'm no salesman, I wouldn't make a go of it. I'm a lumberjack, I'm a carpenter, I'm a lover of birds, an enchanted wanderer I am, I tell you."

6.

The second day on the road. They were almost halfway there.

The soldier in the blue wool socks got off. And so did the girl, the one who had wept. The girl's officer travelled on alone with a sombre frown on his face and never a glance at anyone.

They came to a large station. The trains standing on the lines were hung with icicles. Many of the passengers got out to stretch their legs and get a breath of fresh air. Uncle Fedya got out too: he had again permitted himself a drop that morning, and had a splitting headache.

"We are not going out because Ksenia Ivanovna told us we mustn't," Lucy was telling her neighbours. "Because we might stray too far and the train will leave, and what shall we do then? And if we get a sore throat we shall take streptocide three times a day."

She was speaking more and more absently and slowly, and her face grew pensive. Gazing pensively into space, she began to swing her foot which she always did when she was in difficulties.

Valya followed her gaze, wondering what difficulty Lucy could be in now.

There stood a young man, or rather a big boy, in a padded jacket, fur hat, and with a half-empty knapsack flung over his shoulder.

He had a clean and, perhaps, handsome face. The beginnings of a dark moustache shadowed his upper lip.

The boy saw them looking at him, and asked politely:

"Are all the seats here occupied?"

"I believe so," Valya replied, feeling shy and awkward because she had to deny a person hospitality. But then what did this person expect, couldn't he tell from the piles of luggage that there wasn't a single vacant seat?

"Well, when people return I'll get up," said the boy, and sat down on the edge of the bunk.

"He sat down," Lucy said.

"What?" Valya asked.

"He sat down!" Lucy repeated triumphantly. "And he's wearing a hat!"

Swinging a foot, she asked:

"Is it really a hat you've got on?"

"What did she say?" the boy was puzzled. "What did you say?"

"It *is* a hat!" Lucy cried, delighted that Ksenia Ivanovna's warning was coming true. "And now he'll start making up to you."

"Sure it's a hat, what else," said the utterly baffled boy. "D'you want me to make up to you?" His smile was strangely mirthless. "You funny little girl. You're a very funny little girl. How shall I make up to you? If you like, I'll go and fill the kettle and you'll have some tea."

"Thank you," said Lucy, swinging her foot. "We have no need of your services, thank you very much, we'll get our tea from the train attendant."

"Look at that," said the boy. "Where did a smartie like you come from?"

He was joking, but his eyes were stern. They lit up for a very, very brief moment, and became sombre once more.

"What's your name?"

"Lucy, Ludmilla in full," Lucy replied in a thin voice like a well-mannered girl. "And yours?"

"My name's Volodya. How d'you do," he held out his hand and Lucy put her fingers in it.

"Your sister?" he asked Valya. "Are you going to Leningrad?"

Valya was not used to speaking with strange boys, in fact she did not know many boys well—just a few village youngsters, and so she mumbled "yes", blushing and hating herself for her awkwardness. And just so he shouldn't think that she was a completely stupid boor, she asked:

"And you?"

"Me too. Where do you live in Leningrad?"

"We used to live on Vyborgskaya Side," Valya told him. Mentally she went on to say that their house had been destroyed by a bomb, but she did not venture to say it out loud, for their conversation was becoming much too lively.

"And we live on Degtyarnaya. Do you know Degtyarnaya Street?"

Valya did not, and truth to tell she did not know much of the city outside her neighbourhood. She saw streets in her dreams sometimes, and believed they were Leningrad streets, but maybe she was imagining them up in sleep.

Mentally she told him all this, but aloud she uttered just one word: "No."

The passengers who had gone out to stretch their legs came back. Uncle Fedya returned holding in one hand a bottle of baked milk topped with a brown skim, and in the other—a large, freshly baked, magnificent potato bun. He bore his purchases with care and dignity and was naturally displeased to find his place occupied.

"Shove off, fellow," he told the boy.

Volodya got up meekly. Satisfied, Uncle Fedya broke the bun in two and handed a half each to Lucy and Valya, saying: "Here's a treat for you."

"I'll eat it later," Valya said.

Because the boy was looking at the bun. She'd give him half of her piece. Even the whole piece. But how give it to him? If she said: "Here, take it," he'd feel offended, and if she asked: "Want some?" he'd say, "No thanks."

He had turned away. He sat on someone's bag and looked the other way. Purposely, so Valya could eat her bun in peace. Much she cared for that bun!

The ticket collector appeared. He was a little old man wearing spectacles, and he was preceded by the train attendant who called out: "Your tickets please!"

All the passengers got their tickets out. Uncle Fedya delved in his breast pocket for theirs. And the boy also delved in his breast pocket. The ticket collector examined everybody's tickets carefully and asked to see some of the passengers' papers, punching the tickets with a loud click, and once a ticket has been punched its owner could rest assured that he was travelling according to all the rules and could continue to his destination.

The ticket collector punched the tickets of Uncle Fedya, of his Vologda friend, of the woman who had told them about dreams that came true, of the sailor boy, the girl in the fluffy beret, and all the rest of the passengers, and now he turned to the boy in the padded jacket and fur hat who was sitting on somebody's bundle. The boy showed his papers.

"Your ticket," said the little old man.

The boy stood up and said nothing.

"No ticket?" asked the little old man, looking at the boy angrily through his glasses.

"I have to get to Leningrad," said the boy.

"And where's your permit?" asked the ticket collector.

"I simply have to get to Leningrad," said the boy.

"This bundle yours?" shrilled the train attendant. "Which is your luggage anyway? Are all these things yours?"

The boy made no reply. Nobody spoke while the ticket collector examined his papers.

"I see," he said when he had finished. "Come along."

Without looking at anyone, the boy followed the train attendant out. Behind them came the ticket collector. Everyone began to speak at once.

"The nerve of travelling without a ticket!"

"Were you never in the same soup? Don't you know why a person travels without a ticket?"

"He's an ordinary crook, that's what! He meant to steal something, but didn't get away with it."

Lucy asked Valya: "Was he going to steal somebody's suitcase?"

"Don't talk nonsense!"

"Is he a crook, Valya?"

"No."

"He's simply a young man," Lucy said in a conciliatory tone, wanting to comfort Valya and please her.

Valya picked up her novel. She felt sad. They had almost two more days to go. Weren't some people mean! A crook couldn't have a face like that boy's.

7.

...I have that little window and the crescent moon above the black pines on the mind. Someone else's window.

The thin crescent shines in the dark. The window shows red. And the path running to the little house calls you on....

What will I have, what? What kind of love am I fated to know?

What feats, what changes of fortune?

Does it happen to everyone or only to me that the people I need keep leaving me or I keep leaving them?

And this boy too—he sat beside me for a minute, and now he's gone, he's been taken away.

Will I meet someone to last, for ever?

8.

What a lot of chimneys people had built here! Numbers of them stuck out from under the snow. A stove once went with each chimney: people warmed themselves before it and cooked food on it. And now the homeless chimneys had a wild, naked look. Everything had collapsed all around, walls and stoves lay buried under the snow, but the chimneys still stuck there.

The train was pulling in.

People had long been standing about in their overcoats, feeling hot and raising the heat in the car unbearably. Uncle Fedya in his army great coat and the ear-flaps of his hat tied under his unshaven chin, stood like a rock behind Valya and Lucy. With a jolt the train stopped, and the passengers began to pour out of the car.

Fresh air cooling the face, a post, a clock....

Was this Leningrad?

The crowd streamed down the platform.

"Hold tight!" Uncle Fedya shouted to Lucy, as he swung their luggage on to his back. Lucy clutched his coat with a mittened hand. There was an iron gate at the end of the platform, and there by the gate stood Aunt Dusya—yes, it was Aunt Dusya, an older and darker Aunt Dusya with her bobbed hair falling in strands down her cheeks, the inevitable cigarette stuck in the corner of her mouth, and one eye screwed up from the smoke.

9.

In Aunt Dusya's house, they washed their hands and faces over the sink in the large and dark kitchen, and then had dinner. There was soup and gruel, and also a sweet liqueur which everybody had a drop of, even Lucy, let alone Uncle Fedya, wishing each other never to have to go through such an experience again, even if they lived to be a hundred, and good health!

The table had been laid and the dinner served by a beautiful young woman whose name was Manya. She worked at the factory with Aunt Dusya. Her mother had died during the blockade.

Aunt Dusya told them how Manya had been putting out the fires and how she caught a traitor sending up rocket signals.

"She grabbed the scoundrel by the scruff of his neck."

Manya laughed merrily. It was not difficult at all to picture this girl with the plucked eyebrows and golden locks grabbing the scoundrel by the scruff of his neck. She looked such a great sport that nothing was too difficult to picture about her. She ran about the roofs amid the dancing tongues of fire, so what? There was nothing she could not do. How smartly her black sweater fitted her, a sight for sore eyes!

"What are your plans?" Auntie Dusya asked Valya when they had finished dinner, when they were done with their recollections and when Uncle Fedya had gone off to see some friends of his.

Valya had a plan she had nursed for a long time.

"What I'd like to do," she said, stumbling over the words because she herself thought her plan too fantastic, although any number of fantastic things happened in the world. "If I may, I'd like to go to Mga, and try to find Mummy's grave. Daddy's couldn't be found, of course...."

"Amazing!" said Aunt Dusya. "It's amazing that you people should have not the slightest notion about anything. You came past it in the train: did you see the place? Can anyone's grave be found there? Mga, of all places!

Everything has been blown up in Mga, it's still chockfull of mines. And she's going to look for a grave there!"

"But I remember where it is," Valya protested. "The ditch we ran to goes like this, and here...."

"And why are you in the mood for graves, I'd like to know?" Aunt Dusya demanded wrathfully. "You're young, you've got to live! Get started at the shop where your mother used to work—that's what I'd call beautiful, that would be something! And just now, take Lucy and go to the bathhouse with her, there's nothing like a good scrub after a train journey."

When Valya had got their clean underwear, towels and things together, Aunt Dusya came to her and kissed her.

"You have mettle, and no mistake," she said. "I was afraid you were a nervy sort like your mother, but no, you have mettle. D'you remember where the bathhouse is? If you don't Manya will take you there."

"No need to take us there, I remember the way."

She and Lucy had a good scrubbing, and then she suggested:

"Let's go and see what's left of our house. It's quite near."

The street lamps were burning. A fine snow whirled, sparkling, round the lamps. Valya stared about her — memories emerging from the flying snow thronged her mind. The signs, the front doors, the jingling of the tramcars, the brightly illumined entrance of the cinema, the doll with curled hair in the hairdresser's window, all were reminders. But strangely Valya was not thinking of the days when she walked here as a little girl, but remembered again her train acquaintance, the young man whose name was Volodya and who had been taken away by the ticket collector.

"He'll get to Leningrad just the same," she was thinking. "And I might come across him. Why, I might even come across him now, why not, it's not that impossible!"

And she looked at all the passersby, just in case.

People came down the street, they went into the shops and came out from the shops. A man without legs came past walking on his hands and deftly flinging up his short, thick body over the snow-covered pavement. His dark, bloated face dived out unexpectedly before Lucy, making her spring back in horror.

"Valya," she begged, "I don't want to go and see where our house was. Let's go back to Auntie Dusya."

"We're almost there," Valya told her. "That's our corner over there. That one where the bakery is. See it? With that tall porch where we used to buy our bread."

They came to the bakery and turned the corner.

All the houses were there. All save one, and in its place there was a boarding. To the left stood the catering complex — a lot of snow had drifted round the stone pillars. To the right rose a tall dark house with only a few of the windows showing a light. And in between was a gap, as though a tooth had fallen out. A gap and a boarding.

"Good heavens!" Valya sighed.

They stood there for a while, looking at the fence.

"This is where the gate was," Valya said.

"Maybe it's not our house," Lucy said. "How d'you know?"

"Oh, but I do know!" Valya said. "This is where the yardkeeper always stood. Her name was Aunt Olga. You went into the yard and the second window on the right was ours."

"Come on, let's go," Lucy said.

The going was easier the other way, with the wind blowing in their backs. Through the whirling snow they could see now a green now a red light going on at the crossing.

10.

"You're nice and clean," Aunt Dusya said. "Hang your coats closer to the radiator. We'll have tea now."

Manya was hanging up a wash of stockings and bras on a line in the kitchen, and singing: "Came the young lad riding 'cross the great Don steppe". She sang, hung up her laundry, and washed the basin very efficiently, with obvious pleasure, and it was nice watching her. "I'll do all my wash tomorrow too," Valya said to herself.

A kettle was wheezing on the oil stove. Aunt Dusya broke up a large lump of sugar into smaller pieces with a sugar-cracker, cut the bread, took a tin out of the cupboard and told Manya:

"Open it, will you, it's pork and beans."

"Oh, Aunt Dusya, it's not pork and beans, it's liver paste."

"How can it be liver paste when it's pork and beans?" Aunt Dusya demanded.

"But how can it be pork and beans when it's liver paste?" cried Manya, holding up the tin in her small hands, puffy from soap and hot water, and with a ring on one of her pink fingers.

They argued a bit more before opening the tin. It was liver paste. They sat down to tea. Lucy ate everything she was given and sipped the hot tea from her saucer, a bloom spreading over her face, while Valya ate very little for fear that there wouldn't be enough left for Aunt Dusya and Manya who had starved so terribly during the blockade. She looked at Manya and thought: "Isn't she beautiful!" She wanted to have a sweater and a hairdo like Manya's. And to be as brave and quick. "She speaks with Aunt Dusya as with an equal," Valya was thinking. "That's because she had been putting out fires and rescuing the dying."

There was a knock on the door, and a woman came in.

"Nyura's girls have arrived," Aunt Dusya told her. "Remember Nyura?"

"What Nyura is that?" asked the woman.

"But you must remember her—she worked in the second shop, a smallish woman."

"A bit pock-marked, was she?"

"No, that was Sonya," said Aunt Dusya, and Manya confirmed: "That was Aunt Sonya."

"How come I don't remember Nyura?" the woman wondered.

Another neighbour came in—a sickly, glum woman. Aunt Dusya asked her the same thing:

"Do you remember Nyura? These are her kids."

"Nyura's kids, are they?" the woman said. She stood leaning against the door frame and looked hard at Valya and Lucy.

"They don't look like Nyura," Aunt Dusya said. "They take after their father, I knew him, a fair-haired chap he was."

"They don't look like Nyura," the woman echoed glumly.

She turned away and, in profile, Valya recognized her. Heavens, how she had changed! She had been little more than a girl when she was to be evacuated with her baby son Vasil and got on the train with them at Moscow Station. Her face had grown thin and grey, and her features had become so different that it was a wonder Valya guessed who she was at all.

Valya did not tell her she had recognized her, and did not ask about Vasil. She understood that she must not ask. People would tell you what they could tell without your prying questions. You had to keep quiet and wait till they told you.

The neighbours left. Aunt Dusya and Manya made the preparations for the night. Aunt Dusya took Lucy into bed with her, and Manya made up a bed on the floor for Valya and herself, propping the pillows up against the radiator. The light from the street filtered into the room through the window.

"Move up into the middle, there's plenty of room," Manya said.

"I'm fine, thanks," Valya replied.

Each tried tactfully to leave the other more space.

"If they offer you a job at the tramcar place, or a course of training at the builders' technical school or some such thing, turn everything down. That's my advice to you. We've wonderful people at the factory, and you can't know about the other places. That's for one thing. And for the other—our people remember your mother. So you won't be just anybody, but one of our own hereditary workers."

"You listen to Manya," Aunt Dusya spoke from across the room. "She's talking sense."

"Was your house hit, too?" Valya asked Manya in a whisper.

"No. When my mother died, Aunt Dusya took me in, and I've lived with her since. It will be three years soon. I have a room of my own, and not a bad one."

Manya twisted and turned for a bit, making herself comfortable, and then fell asleep, whistling softly through her nose. Aunt Dusya also snored. Valya lay awake, breathing lightly. The radiator gave out a pleasant warmth. The light from the street was reflected in the dark, gleaming surface of the mirror on the chest of drawers.

"Have I arrived?" Valya asked somebody. "Hullo! No, I'm still on my journey, I'll be on a journey all life long."

Manya mumbled sleepily: "It's fourteen square metres. In case I decide to live on my own I have where to live."

"I'll show you, living on your own!" Aunt Dusya said. "Sleep now."

A lorry went past. All the houses on that street were there, all except one, and in its place—a boarding.

"Well, I never!" said Uncle Fedya.

"We'll repair it," said the soldier in the blue wool socks.

"We'll get our tea from the attendant," said Lucy.

"Your tickets, please!" said the train attendant.

There was music. Someone was singing: "Came the young lad riding 'cross the great Don steppe." The young lad had on a fur hat and a padded jacket. And he looked at Valya with his dark eyes.

1959

VOLODYA

1.

When the ticket collector told Volodya to come along, Volodya went without any fuss. He had not done anything wrong, so he had nothing to fear. Of course he had no permit, but how could he have one if his father had not sent him the affidavit. And without a permit they would not have sold him a ticket anyway, even if he had the money for it.

Just formalities, really. Who could prevent him from returning to the town where he was born and where he had lived right up to the war? He had made up his mind to return, and return he would. If he came back two or three days later, it did not matter.

Carrying his light, half-empty knapsack he patiently made his way between the bundles, suitcases and baskets cluttering up the corridor. The attendant walked ahead of him shouting out: "Tickets, please. Tickets, please, citizens."

The ticket collector came behind, and Volodya heard his puncher clicking with a crisp sound behind his back.

"They'll put me off the train at the next stop," he was thinking, as he stepped over the bundles and bags. "They might hand me over to the militia. No, hardly that I'm not a thief, after all. Well anyway, let's suppose they do. And what will the militia do? At worst they'll draw up a statement, but they won't detain me, because why should they want to feed me? No, they won't even draw up a statement, wasting time on such a trifle. They'll give me a talking to and a warning, and I'll ask them to help me board the next train going, because what's the good of my hanging about that station? If the militia is not brought into this business, I'll get on the next train anyway. Maybe I've a better chance of slipping through unnoticed if I change trains often, and make it in short laps? Maybe, but I must find out if there are suitable trains. I'm a fool, it's my own fault that I got nabbed. I ought to have travelled outside, on the step. You'll never get anywhere if you're scared of the cold wind. What I'd like to know is where my next meal is coming from?" The thought made him swallow hungrily. He pictured a big rosy bun, the colour of baked milk, like the one that soldier bought the girls.

"Get a move on," the ticket collector gave Volodya a shove.

They got through the crowd of women waiting at the lavatory door, and stepped on to the gangway between the cars—two metal shields thrown across a rumbling void. A gust of icy wind tore at the collar of Volodya's jacket, flipped it up and pressed it to his cheek, and Volodya gulped a lungful of this cutting wind with an admixture of engine smoke. He could see the rails flashing past in the slits between the metal shields.

The next car was as packed, the air as grey and thick with smoke and human exhalations, and the train attendant moved ahead of him as before, only it was another woman now, and behind her came Volodya, while the ticket collector with his puncher brought up the rear. The going was as slow with mountains of luggage blocking the way. They crossed another connecting bridge, and went through yet another car, stuffed full of bags and baskets, grownups and children, some crying, some sleeping.

The train ran on at a good, steady pace; outside the windows there was the grey, darkening sky and telegraph wires, and then an occasional telegraph pole sailed past, solitary and unhurried.

"Are they going to walk me to the end of the train?" Volodya wondered.

But in the next car they came to, the ticket collector left him in charge of the two train attendants, and went off, taking Volodya's papers with him.

2.

The older of the train attendants was a fat short-legged, broad-shouldered woman with a large white face topped by a small black beret. She wore an expression of morose self-importance.

The other was skinny and quite young, though her sallow forehead was already lined with long horizontal wrinkles. Bony hands protruded from the sleeves of her uniform coat. Her eyes were very bright, and her thin red lips curled in a smile all the time, as though she kept remembering something funny.

"A fare dodger, is it?" she said in a loud, shrill voice, staring at Volodya when the ticket collector had gone. "Look at the lamb, Varya! He's got a black moustache!"

She burst out laughing, giving peal after nervous peal. As she laughed she showed her long yellow teeth and pink gums. Volodya squirmed from this laughter, and from the woman's bared gums, teeth, and look. He turned away and stared through the window.

He saw telegraph wires, poles and forest. It was growing dark, and the forest took on a sombre look. Smoke from the engine plastered the window only to be blown away at once by the wind.

The forest seemed only an arm's length away, and then it fell back. A grey, logwood village came into view, and drifted away like a snatch of dream. The village children had made a huge snowman, and it stood there facing the railway, saluting with its broom, and through the gathering dusk Volodya caught it looking at him out of the little black coals it had for eyes.

Railwaymen stood at the small stations, holding up their little flags, but the train did not stop, it only slowed down and then went on.

"After all, it's got to stop somewhere!" Volodya thought.

He was alone in the end section of the car where the toilet was. There were no passengers crowding here, so it must be a sleeper. A lieutenant came from one of the compartments and threw an empty tin and some oily paper into the dustbin; Volodya caught the smell of pork fat, bay leaf, and satiation. He glanced through the open door: it was not an ordinary sleeper, it was a first-class sleeper, and there was a runner on the floor all the way down the corridor. Two officers stood there smoking. Gosh, there were some lucky fellows who travelled in first-class sleepers, whom nobody had the right to put off the train, and who ate tinned pork! That man had eaten a whole tin of pork!—and thrown that divinely smelling tin into the dustbin, apparently without even wiping it clean inside with a piece of bread first.

"Stop thinking about it!" Volodya told himself sternly. "Will a tin drop down from the skies if you brood on it?" He knew from past experience what harm such futile brooding did you: you became despicably envious and selfpitying, you weakened, and Volodya did not want to be weak.

The names of the stations along this road had a non-Russian sound: Kez, Cheptsa, Pibanshur, Tuktym. What language were they in, Udmurt? Were they passing through

Udmurtia? Or had these names perhaps remained from the tribes which inhabited this part of the country in ancient times? What were they now? Chud, Merya, Muroma ... (Volodya liked history, and liked reading historical books). And some of the stations which had Russian names had a hopelessly sad, tragic sound. The stations had probably taken these names from the closest villages in tsarist times. How much grief and trouble the people must have suffered to call their settlements like that!

He certainly would like to know where they were going to put him off the train.

He'd prefer it to happen before it grew quite dark, and at a decent station where they had electricity and the practice of heating the passenger waiting room once a day at least.

"Is this Balesino?" someone asked. And the younger of the train attendants shouted in answer: "Balesino! Balesino!"

The train was slowing down.

That's it, then. In a moment the ticket collector would come and tell him: "You have arrived, get off."

The compartment doors began to click. Lights went on at the exit end of the train. Passengers crowded there, waiting for the train to stop. All officers, without exception.

The night outside the window became pitch dark when the lights were put on.

"Where is that ticket collector?" Volodya thought.

"Make way, please," said the fat train attendant importantly as, lantern in hand, she squeezed her way through the throng.

The little lights in the dark window slowed their movement, and stopped altogether. Metal grated and clanged under the floor. Catching diamond sparks in the snow-encrusted window pane, the illumined station sign hit the eyes—BALESINO.

3.

"Young man," said a self-important voice, and the older train attendant touched Volodya on the elbow: "Come this way, will you."

He followed her to the narrow service compartment and on the small table he saw a glass of tea and some rye rusks.

"Sit down and have a bite."

He sat down. It was only when he began to crunch a rusk and had its delicious, saltyish taste on his tongue, that he fully realised how ravenous he was.

"Eat," the woman told him. "Eat them all, don't be shy."

She refilled his glass from a large, merrily steaming samovar.

The train was going at full speed. Balesino was left dozens of kilometres behind. And the ticket collector had never turned up.

While Volodya ate, the woman stood unsmiling beside him, with her small beret perched above her large face, and a serious look in her little colourless eyes with no eyebrows above them.

"Is your mother living?" she asked.

"Yes."

"What does she do?"

"She works in the savings bank."

"And your father?"

Volodya took a gulp of tea.

"I have no father."

"Any brothers or sisters?"

"One sister."

"Big sister?"

"No, a little sister."

"And what did you work as?" she asked, looking at his hands.

"As a fitter."

"Not bad!" she nodded.

The younger woman came in with some empty tea glasses on a tray.

"Hullo, lambkin!" she said with her big yellow-toothed, pink-gummed smile. "He's eating, the darling!" And again she went into peals of high-pitched laughter, causing the glasses to jump and tinkle on the tray.

"Mind you don't smash them," the older woman said sternly.

Volodya finished his tea without raising his eyes. He knew this reasonless feminine laugh and this desperately bright feminine look. His mother had them.

"Lie down now," the older woman said to him. "Get a spot of sleep."

She motioned to the top bunk, ready and waiting with a striped mattress and a pillow.

Volodya took off his felt boots and padded jacket, and climbed in. It was very warm up there, but he gladly pulled

the prickly thick blanket up anyway. When he started out on
this journey he did not count on any sort of convenience, and
now he readily and gratefully   accepted all the good things
that came his way. "That ticket collector seems to have
forgotten about me," he thought. "Good, I'll have a good
sleep before he remembers." He stretched out deliciously,
relishing the thought of sleep. The two women were rinsing
the glasses. After that they got out their knitting and sat
down on the lower bunk. The single lamp burnt wanly, and
the car rocked and swayed. But, obviously accustomed to
this, they sat and calmly knitted lace, deftly wielding their
crochet hooks. Fits of laughter came over the younger
woman, taking her off her work.

"Better start a song," the older one said. "Honestly, you
can't hold yourself in hand at all, Kapitolina!"

The younger woman started a song, and the older one se-
conded her.

"Marusya was washing her white, pretty feet," the younger woman sang in a breaking voice as though she were
gasping for breath, while the older one boomed quietly:
"She was washing her feet, her white pretty feet...."

An officer resplendent with decorations walked past
their door. The younger woman got up and took a look at
Volodya.

"Is he asleep?" asked the older woman.

"Sleeping like a top, our pretty lambkin," replied the
younger woman, revealing her gums and teeth in a smile of
sheer bliss.

The older woman also stood up to throw a sternly tender
look at the boy sleeping under their roof. He lay with his
cheek pressed into the pillow with the railway laundry mark
on it; there was a tranquility in his black eyelashes, and his
chest rose and fell rhythmically. The women sat down again,
knitting lace and singing, as though they were there to guard
over the sleep of the strange boy.

"And grey geese came swimming up to Marusya," they
sang very softly to the accompaniment of the knocking
wheels, quickly manipulating their crochet hooks. "A flock
of grey geese, grey-blue geese with bright yellow beaks."

4.

Just before leaving Leningrad in the summer of '41,
Volodya had gone with his mother to see his father.

"We must say goodbye to him," his mother had said. "We may not be fated to meet again, who knows...."

They had been there twice already, only to learn that he was in hospital. The second time they were received by father's wife, the woman whom Mother always spoke of as *she*, without a name, and who in Volodya's childish concept was a dangerous, predatory, shameless creature who broke into people's homes and robbed them. This creature had broken into their home and robbed it of Volodya's father when Volodya was only two and his mother was very young and impractical, which she remained till this day.

It was bad manners to stare, and so Volodya averted his eyes after every quick look. However, nothing escaped his hostile scrutiny. The woman was plain! How strange that Father should leave Mother for this slant-eyed woman with the projecting cheekbones, with such long, skinny arms, and wearing a plain grey dress—there couldn't be a plainer one! There was simply no comparing her to Mother in looks, Volodya thought with pride and bitterness. And Mother dressed ten times better too. She always had on something pretty—a silk scarf, a lace collar, or a bow, and her dresses were bright and gay. She was prettier than ever that day, all dressed up, her hair freshly permed and set, and her eyes shining with excitement and fear.

Yes, Mother was afraid of this woman. She quailed before her so terribly that she became quite dithery, stumbling over her words and saying the silliest things. Volodya felt ashamed. The other woman stood looking now at his mother, now at Volodya with her slanted eyes, and spoke in a low voice. She asked them to come back in the evening when Father would be home. Of course, they must say goodbye to him, she said and gave Volodya a long, pensive look. She had a great favour to ask them. She had never told Oleg, her son, that he had a brother, and Oleg did not know. She'd like him to hear it from her own lips ... and, at the right time. If Oleg hadn't gone to bed yet, when they came that evening. He might overhear something. She was asking Volodya too, after all he was a big boy.

"No, no, Volodya won't talk, don't worry!" Mother assured her in panicky haste, as if this wish voiced by the other woman, long known to all and implicitly obeyed for some reason, was not silly, mean, and really outrageous.

They did come back in the evening, and found Father at home. He received them politely, if glumly. With his eyes wearily half-closed, he kept up the conversation. It was an effort to pretend that he was interested in their problems. Tears rose to his eyes when he controlled his great, tearing yawns. He kept repeating himself and getting confused. It seemed to surprise him that Volodya had grown, and he expressed his surprise several times. Afterwards, the memory rankled with Volodya.

Suddenly his father wanted to know with what marks Volodya had passed to the next, seventh form. The idea! He never gave a thought to Volodya's school marks even in peacetime. Having asked his question, he placed his hand on his son's shoulder — a large, surgeon's hand with the skin grown thin and red from constant washing. Volodya blushed, his face was literally aflame from this show of tenderness from which he could not escape and to which he did not know how to react.

They were sitting in his father's study. Volodya looked at the desk, the bookcase, and the book shelves. It was a clean, pleasant flat in a new building. "He sleeps here on the couch," Volodya surmised. A small table had been pushed up to one end of the couch. On it was a reading lamp, some newspapers, and an alarm clock. "He turns off the big light, switches on the lamp on the little table and reads the papers before he goes to sleep, and in the morning the alarm clock goes and he gets up."

His stepmother came and went very quietly, serving them tea. She brought three cups: for Mother, Volodya and Father. She did not have tea with them. The first time she came in bringing jam and biscuit dishes, Father gave her a look as if to ask: "Is this necessary?" She did not glance at him once as she set the dishes down on the table, but her whole look, composed and determined, seemed to say: "Yes, it is necessary."

They came late, and so her son Oleg had either been put to bed already or else she had hidden him somewhere out of harm's way.

Mother had a shrinking, apologetic look, sitting there with her feet tucked under her armchair, and afraid to take a biscuit. Volodya signalled to her with his eyes again and again: "Let's go home!" but she stayed on and assiduously helped Father to carry on this futile and humiliating conversation.

Towards the end Father told them how hard it was for him to make both ends meet, it was quite a struggle, in fact. Still, he did give Mother some money when they were taking their leave.

Their leavetaking was cool and embarrassing for all.
Father wished them all sorts of things, thinking meanwhile:
"They're leaving at last (yawn), thank God, and I shall be
able to go to bed (yawn)."

Mother began to cry when they were out in the street.

"He thought I came because of the money."

Volodya twitched an angry shoulder.

"We shouldn't have gone. We never went before, and we
shouldn't have gone now."

She walked along and cried.

"If we never meet again I, for one, won't weep," Volodya said in an outburst of rancour.

But Mother, blowing her nose, objected meekly:

"No, there was much that was good and happy too, once
upon a time, you know...."

Two days later they left, they travelled a long time, and
finally arrived in N.

5.

They were accommodated in a room together with two
Latvian women who had fled from Riga. It did not embarrass
them to dress and undress in Volodya's presence—he was
only a kid.

The Latvian women went about in fur coats and wore
glittering rings on their fingers. In the morning, before going
to work, they slipped off their rings and put them in the small
cloth bags they wore on a chain round their necks. They
worked at the transhipping base where they sorted the
potatoes and washed the barrels used for pickling. When
they came home they rubbed coldcream into their chapped
and reddened hands. Occasionally they were given several
pickled cucumbers or a jar of sauerkraut at the base. They
shared the food with Volodya and his mother. They always
shared the little they had.

Volodya noticed that they treated him to these delicacies
with pleasure, and his mother with some reluctance and only
because it would be awkward not to offer her any. Volodya
felt hurt for his mother, but kept his silence—for what was
there to say?

The big, dark-green cucumbers with the squashed sides
and dripping with brine were delicious.

The Latvian women offered to get Volodya's mother a
job at the base which paid more than the savings bank, but

she said: "Oh no, not scrubbing those barrels!" She was used
to the work at the savings bank, it was clean work, and she saw
a lot of people. The Latvians said no more, they were taciturn
by nature and spoke rarely, exchanging a few words
in their own language. Their presence in the room never
interfered with Volodya's homework or reading. His
mother's did, though. When she came home from work she
immediately began relating her experiences of the day in a
small, tired voice, asking them countless questions and going
into peals of laughter.

She never complained or grumbled about life's hard-
ships. Just sometimes, sitting down to a meal, she would
say in passing, without any resentment: "Ugh, soup again,"
or would tell them, also in passing, how rudely a client had
spoken to her. In those days she still took everything lightly,
certain that the best in her life was still ahead. She told the
Latvian women about it, her eyes sparkling brightly.

"It can't be that everything is over for me so soon," she
said one night. "No, no, I feel it that I'll fall in love yet and be
loved in return."

The Latvian women pursed up their lips.

"Your boy can hear you," one of them said.

"Never mind, there's nothing wrong in this," Mother
said in a carefree voice. "I'm going to know real happiness,
nothing like I had before. That had been happiness too, but it
was over so quickly, I never noticed it going. Just think, I was
nursing our son, and he started an affair with *her*. No, it can't
be, life can't be all over!"

"You have your son," the other Latvian said. "You have
someone to live for."

"Yes, of course," Mother agreed half-heartedly, and
said no more.

How her eyes had sparkled! She had such a delicate
neck, it looked so thin and white in her much-laundered lace
collar. She wore a fashionable hairdo, piling up her hair in the
shape of a little nest.

6.

During the summer holidays Volodya went with the
school to a state farm to gather in the hay and do the
weeding. The country was beautiful and so peaceful as if
there was no war on in the world, just these wide fields
inviting leisurely meditation, the deep and cool forest, full of

life and mystery, and the lake in its very heart—cold, mauve water, moss-grown stones, and pines all round, straining their dark crowns skyward. The boys and girls fished in the lake; they boiled or baked in coals the fish they caught, and it tasted wonderful.

There was a girl Volodya took a fancy to — she also came from town, but she went to another school, not Volodya's. Many of the boys were in love with Alyonka, but it was to Volodya she said when their stay in the country was over:

"Come and see us. Promise?" She dropped her voice when she said: "Promise?" She told him her address, and he wrote it down. They returned to town. Every day, he tried to work up the courage to go and see her, he was dying to go, her "Promise?" spoken in a low voice, her lowered eyes, came to him in dreams, but he flinched: supposing he went, what would he say to her, what would she say to him? After that "Promise?" what sublime words must be spoken! What a radiance of light must burst forth from under her lowered eyelashes! *If* the unspoken joyous promise made at that moment was to come true. *If* he were not to leave with the horrible feeling of destruction and emptiness....

But the calls he heard at night were strong, and finally he did work up the courage to go.

And now he discovered that his trousers were terribly short and his sleeves too—he had grown out of everything! He did not notice himself growing, and suddenly his trousers barely covered his shins. No, he could not go to see her looking like that. He had no other pants. He could not go anywhere looking like that.

The Latvian women ascribed his growing up to the country air and the freshly caught fish he ate there.

They stopped going half-dressed in his presence. They procured some chintz somewhere, and curtained off their part of the room. And when Volodya had to go to bed or get up, they retired behind this curtain.

"I'm twice as strong as Mother," Volodya was thinking as he chopped wood in the shed. "I'm three times as strong, yet I let her support me. I cook the soup and chop the wood which has been delivered for the Latvians, and I go about looking like a scarecrow."

His father gave them money before the war, but after leaving Leningrad they never heard from him once. Their letters remained unanswered. Maybe he wasn't in Leningrad any more. Maybe he was dead.

"I've been a child long enough," Volodya said to himself, furiously attacking the next log with the axe.

Then he flung the axe aside and looked at his right hand: not a big hand, but strong; the muscles were well developed and there were callouses on the forefinger and the pink palm earned at the collective farm; a man's hand, nothing to be ashamed of.

On a rainy morning in October he set off to look for work.

Big boards with Manpower Wanted notices were hung up at the entrance to the park. His hands in the too-short sleeves thrust into the pockets of his too-short trousers, Volodya stopped and read all the notices tacked on the dark, sodden plywood.

7.

There was a man at the town Soviet in charge of juvenile employment, and he arranged for Volodya to take a course of training as a metal worker. The trainees were soon assigned to a munition factory.

This factory was situated a long way from town. First they had to go by train, and then by bus through woods and copses. The "bus" was actually a lorry with a tarpaulin top and benches along the sides; you grabbed a seat, or squatted on the floor.

Volodya was issued a pair of padded trousers, a padded jacket, felt boots and a soldier's fur hat. He handled parts of mechanisms that had no name: they said, for instance, that what they had worked on that day was No. 16 for unit B-7. The shop where Volodya worked was called Shop No. 2.

All this sounded mysterious and important, but very often the boys were called away from this world of meaningful numbers to do the most ordinary plumbers' jobs. Something would go wrong with the water system at the workers' settlement, and Roman would say:

"Come on, Volodya, let's go and see what's up."

And off they'd go to solder pipes.

When the bathhouse-cum-laundry was being built, a team of young plumbers was sent there to lay on the water pipes under Roman's supervision.

Destruction was going on everywhere in the world, and here they were engaged in construction.

The bathhouse-cum-laundry was a large, magnificent place, like a Palace of Culture.

It was while working there that Roman got married. Zena, his bride, was a plasterer. They decided to make their temporary home in this building until it was finished. There was a little room upstairs. Zena plastered the walls, Roman installed an iron stove, and made a couple of trestles—one for their bed, and the other for the table. Roman also made some stools—there wasn't anything he couldn't make, and there was any amount of material. They sat on the stools and drank tea; their room was hot and damp, and the unpainted floor was stamped all over with whitewash footprints. When work on the interior began, they said, they'd move to the technical school, it was already roofed and would be livable soon. And after that, they'd see. Maybe they'd go to Leningrad, or to Zena's folks in Sorochintsy, the village described by Gogol. They were happy, and invited everyone to come and see them.

And then Zena fell ill and died in hospital. She was buried in a small graveyard on the edge of the forest. It was a big funeral, with beribboned wreaths brought from town. During the speechmaking, Roman stood before the open grave, numb from cold and grief, his boyish face stony and blue, and his hat crushed in his hands. He had no luck—the whole family had died in Leningrad, his father was reported missing, and Roman himself, for all his spunk and dash, had a heart disease. His wife, whom he had loved dearly, had been a little older than himself. And he was only eighteen.

When they came back from the funeral Roman lay down on his trestle bed and turned away to the wall. The boys sat down, and did not speak. One of them went out to collect some chocks and shavings, and started a fire in the stove. Zena's green village-style trunk stood against the wall, and someone said in a muted voice: "That trunk ought to be sent to her mother, I suppose."

Approaching footsteps resounded with an amplified thud in the doorless corridors and spacious rooms, and Bobrov came in. He gave the boys a nod, warmed his hands over the roaring stove, and went close to Roman.

"Roman, I say, Roman...."

"What d'you want?" Roman asked hoarsely.

"You mustn't just lie there."

"What's it to you?"

"Let's go where there are people, Roman."

He gently patted Roman on the back with his one hand, and a strand of fair hair escaped from under his fur hat as he leaned over.

"How about it, Roman? Let's go to the hostel, shall we? Come on, now."

Roman got up with the same wild-eyed look on his frozen face, and went with Bobrov. The boys, of their own accord, picked up Roman's things and Zena's little trunk and carried them after Roman.

8.

Volodya's life, his interests and friendships, were all centred on the factory now.

He seldom remembered Alyonka, and there was a taste of bitterness in the memory.

He wrote to his mother occasionally, but it was some time before he went home to see her.

He came for May Day. The first people he saw were the two Latvian women, who were cooking in the kitchen. They smiled in welcome and asked how he was. Then, he entered the room where his mother lived. She looked at him with alarm and entreaty. She had a guest, a captain. A not very young, balding captain. There was vodka and food on the table.

"This is my son," Mother said, blushing hotly.

The captain filled a glass with vodka for Volodya. Mother asked him about this and that, but she heard his answers with such a faraway look that Volodya doubted if she really understood what he said. And he, the idiot, had imagined that she'd be beside herself with joy when he came home.

She couldn't be bothered with him just then. He had crashed into their tête-à-tête and prevented them from pursuing their intimate conversation. Some phrases from this stillborn conversation, which would have been so thrilling had Volodya not barged in, broke through, and Mother laughed, her eyes flashing sparks, although there was nothing really funny. He squirmed from embarrassment for her, he did not like the captain with the balding head and puffy cheeks, but he could not get up and leave because it would show that he understood everything.

At last he said: "I think I'll go to the pictures."

Mother was overjoyed. But to keep up pretences, she objected:

"You'll hardly get a ticket now."

The captain sat blowing smoke and watching Volodya's movements out of the corner of his eye.

There were no tickets, and so Volodya spent the rest of the day at a school friend's. When he returned home he found his mother alone, wandering about the room with a sad and lost air. They talked for a bit, and went to bed.

He had to catch the 5 a.m. train. With his alarm-clock faculty for waking up when he had to, Volodya got up at four. It was already light. The Latvian women were busily snoring behind the curtain. His mother slept with her head resting on her meekly folded hands. Her hair was in paper curlers. As he left, Volodya looked with a twinge of resentment and pity at her face and her emaciated arms.

It was not until autumn that he came to see her again. She was away, and the Latvian women told him that she had gone to a health home.

"She has not been feeling well," they said.

The Latvian women pursed up their lips, saying this. They each had only one ring—a wedding ring—left, having sold the others for food. Their fur coats were not as good as they once were. But they were in an excellent spirits.

"It won't be long now before we can go home," they said. "Oh, Riga! The most beautiful town in the world, our Riga! When you're back in Leningrad, come and visit us in Riga, it's not far to go, it's quite near."

From this remoteness it did seem that Riga was quite close to Leningrad, practically its suburb.

"When you're back in Leningrad...." The thought was uppermost in the minds of Volodya, Roman, and all the Leningraders there. Few people said: "I want to stay on here." They loved their home town with a love that had become really exalted in those years, but apart from this the urge to go back to Leningrad had a psychological basis. They left it at a bad, grim time, when the enemy was tearing on over land and air, and seizing town after town. The evacuation from Leningrad signified disaster, insecurity, and a smash-up of life's routine. The nazis were now being pushed back to the west. When the singing, playing or talking loudspeaker fell silent, people fell silent too, and turned in the direction whence the silence came. And then came the soft call sign—the opening bars of the song "Our Country is a Land of Beauty", they were repeated three times, inviting everyone to come and listen, and then a familiar voice announced on a solemn and commanding note: "This is Radio Moscow". He read out the orders of the Supreme Command, and they rang with victories. Again town after town was mentioned and you heard not sorrow, wrath or dismay, but a victory salute fired from a hundred guns! Poltava had just been liberated. Kiev's turn would come soon. The return home meant that the evil days were over, the worst was over and done with, they could begin from there and get on with living, they were back where they belonged, everything was all right!

That's why everyone was so eager to return home, Volodya and Roman reminisced as they lay in their beds at the hostel, talking far into the night.

"Listen, remember how Nevsky looked when it was illuminated for a holiday?"

"Why only then? It doesn't need any illumination, it looks fine in rain and sleet too. All kinds of weather suit it."

"And remember those pennants on the bridges on holidays? Red pennants fluttering in the wind...."

"And the Sphinxes on the Neva? They're real sphinxes, not sham. They were brought from Africa."

"Yes, I know, they're thousands of years old."

"Did you ever fish from the spit of Vasilyevsky Island? I did. And did you ever swim just outside Peter and Paul Fortress? I did."

"We live in a different part of town. It's far from us. But then the Smolny is quite close. What cinema did you go to mostly? The *Velikan*, I suppose?"

Roman could not live without attachments, he was that kind of person. After Zena's death he became attached to Volodya. The age gap did not impede their friendship. Roman's face — a small face with small features — was more childish than Volodya's, and he was shorter, too.

Half-sitting up in bed, and propping up his head with his small fist, Roman was saying:

"There are the dead. The wounded. The blockade. The missing. The death camps. Plus the people driven off to Germany by force. Add it all up."

"Well?"

"It gives you the creeps to think how *many*."

"Well?"

"What d'you think, what consequences is all this going to have?"

"What d'you mean?"

"For countries. For people."

"Hitler's finished, fascism's finished, isn't that enough?"

"Is fascism finished?"

"Sure it is."

Roman thought and said:

"It isn't enough for me."

"For Chrissake! Fascism's finished, and we're going to build communism now, aren't we?"

"We have been building communism before the war too," Roman replied. "What I asked you was something else: what do you think, did people pay in full with this war for future security, so there won't be any more wars?"

"Oh, come on, Roman, go to sleep," one of their roommates begged. "Deliver a lecture about it at the club tomorrow."

"Or haven't they paid in full?" Roman persisted, dropping his voice to a whisper. "Will they have to pay more, d'you think?"

"I don't know," Volodya replied thoughtfully.

A letter arrived from his father at long last. Although Volodya's mother had written to him and tried to find him, the letter was addressed not to her, but to Volodya at the factory. Volodya's striking out on his own (of which his mother had written in one of her letters) was approved by his father, for he himself had become self-supporting at an early age. He trusted that while following his independent course Volodya would not forget that he must continue his education. About himself, his father wrote that he was working at the same hospital as before. He did not say a word about his family. It had nothing to do with Volodya or his mother, he believed, and so no information was called for. Oh well, he was probably right.

9.

A daughter was born to his mother.

The captain vanished from the scene well before the event. His wife had arrived. She came again and again to Mother's place, tearfully complaining to the landlady and the neighbours, until they were all up in arms against his mother for breaking up a happy family. The Latvian women could not endure the rows, and found elsewhere to live. The landlady's husband was away at the front, and she held that bad women used the war for their own ends, they liked it when husbands were parted from their wives, they profited by the war, these women did, and human blood was shed for their dirty pleasure.

It was she who told Volodya everything. He hurried away from her and her talk, but he failed to defend his mother. Indeed, how could he know what to say in a woman's defence in such cases? And how defend her, when he also accused her in his heart, and far more sternly than these simple women had done.

His mother wandered about the room in a state of helpless confusion, while vainly struggling for nonchalance.

"You see, Volodya darling, what news I have for you," she said almost casually.

"What's her name?" Volodya asked.

There was nothing for it, accuse her all you wished, but the thing was done, you had to accept it and live with it.

"Tamara, Tommy for short. A pretty name, isn't it?"

"Very pretty."

He did not understand it. A beautiful, tender thing like Alyonka could be loved. But a bald captain with puffy cheeks definitely could not. The thought that his mother had loved this bald captain and this child was the fruit of their love outraged his youthful, wholesome and tremulous concept of love, and the beauty of love. (That which sometimes went on at the hostel didn't count, it was just one of those things.) Eyes dropped shyly, kisses, daydreaming—this was for young people, for beautifully fresh bodies and souls. When people were older, let there be mutual respect and liking, a comradeship, if you like! But love, no!

His mother asked him to run down to the pharmacy, but he was ashamed to go out into the street. This street where everyone knew everything about each other! Still he ventured abroad with a sullen gleam in his dark eyes.

The landlady was in the kitchen when he returned.

"How d'you like it?" she said, and then raised her voice for all the neighbours to hear: "There you're working for defence, and she, was she thinking about you? No, it's men friends she was thinking about, that's what!"

"Oh, stop it," Volodya said.

His mother was kneeling at the bed and crying. "I've done wrong to all of you," she sobbed. "I've done you wrong, and her, too."

She meant her baby girl. The baby lay unswaddled on the bed, kicking up her crooked and trembling little legs.

"Oh, Volodya," his mother sobbed out loud. "You're angry with your father, but if you only knew how much wrong I did him too!"

Clutching his hands and pressing her wet face to them, she told Volodya what a miserable life she was living. Early in the morning she took the baby to the crèche which was very far away, at the other end of the town. She came to work feeling dead tired and dizzy, she could not think clearly and made mistakes. She would be discharged, she would have been discharged already if she were not a nursing mother. And the horrible thing was that instead of owning to her mistakes and begging pardon, she lost her temper when her mistakes were pointed out to her, and talked back very rudely. It wasn't like her at all, was it? But she had become such a nervous wreck. Imagine being rude to people who were sorry for her and kept her on, when she should have been dismissed long ago. And here, in the house, everyone hated her. When she came to get water from the pump, the women made way for her and watched her in hostile silence while she filled her pail, and then when her back was turned she heard the things they said about her. If she put on lipstick, they all began to say that she was about to go husband-snatching again! Oh, if only she could leave this place! If only she could go back to Leningrad where nobody knew about her! People had suffered such horrors there, no one would even ask, they would probably even be glad that here was a little baby, a new life where so many had been lost.

"I don't want to go on living! I don't want to go on living!" she screamed as in delirium.

"The first thing to do is move to another place," Volodya said, horrified to feel with his hands the throbbing of the hot veins in her temples.

"You think it's easily done? You think I haven't tried? Nobody wants a tenant with a baby. Or else they want too much money. And anyway that woman will come there too. She goes everywhere and sets everyone against me, as if she couldn't have been lonely too, she could have, couldn't she?"

"What about writing to Father about it?"

"No. I can't."

"There's nothing to it: just ask him to send you one of those affidavit things."

"He'll refuse," she said with despair. "He's glad we're here, he's glad we're not in Leningrad."

The baby's feet diverted her at last. She began to catch them with her lips and kiss them, laughing through her tears and keeping her laughter low for fear that the landlady might hear and condemn her for it. And Volodya was thinking—how was she to go on, what was he to do with them.

10.

He wrote to his father telling him that his mother had a very hard time of it in this town, that she was unwell and run down, and asking him to send her a guarantee and her train fare. Once back in Leningrad she'd sell some of her furniture and pay him back the money.

The reply came rather quickly. It was an ill-humoured letter. Leningrad was not a sanatorium, and life there was not adapted to the requirements of convalescents. There were excellent hospitals and doctors in the town they were in, and every known illness might be treated there. As for being run down, wasn't everyone? By and large, the best thing was for Volodya not to meddle in the relations between his father and mother which had shaped as they did for reasons which Volodya could not know.

Volodya wrote back: very well, he wasn't going to meddle, but he asked his father to send him the required affidavit made out in his, Volodya's, name, and on return to Leningrad he would himself take care of his mother's affairs.

There was no answer, and so Volodya wrote the same thing again and sent the letter by registered post.

In the meantime, Roman had gone back to Leningrad. He obtained his permit on the strength of a guarantee from an uncle twice removed who lived there—this uncle twice removed was certainly a brick—and Roman left, torn in two by his exalted devotion to Leningrad and his attachment to the factory and the workers' settlement where he had known happiness and grief, and where he was abandoning the grave of the girl he loved on the edge of the forest, beyond the airfield. Volodya still expected to receive a reply from his father, but his mother had given up, she was already past expecting anything good from anyone.

She became a prey to all kinds of ailments, she was ageing fast, and the light had gone out of her eyes. It was an effort to get up in the morning, and she had fits of asphyxia. She still took the baby to the crèche every morning, and then trudged the long way to work, barely able to drag herself along.

Little Tommy was a sweet, jolly baby with dimples on her pink, plump body, the result of the extra nourishment and vitamins she was given at the crèche.

Volodya decided to go to Leningrad without a permit. He would not have been released from work at a moment like that when every pair of hands was needed, but after several unsuccessful attempts to get his resignation okayed, it occurred to him to speak to Bobrov, and the matter was quickly settled. Possibly it could have been settled at other levels, and earlier too, because after all Bobrov was not the biggest noise there. But then he was the person to whom Volodya could give a candid answer to the question: "Why do you want to resign?"—"I have to get my mother back to Leningrad. She's in a fix." And when Bobrov asked: "What kind of fix?" he did not clam down, and told him what kind of fix it was, whereas he had clammed down before everyone else, for the words had got stuck in his throat.

"At home, the very walls are healing, is that how the saying goes?" Bobrov said. "Good, come and see me in a day or two and I'll tell you what to do."

He was the sort of person you could tell all your troubles to, and what is more he would take your case up with your chief, with the highest chief, and say: "The lad must be allowed to leave, comrades. We must let him go. We must be considerate wherever we can. It's our duty to people, it's good management, look at it from any point you like, but considerate we've got to be."

Everybody needs to have a person like Bobrov to go to when up against the wall.

Volodya put such faith in Bobrov that he immediately wrote to Roman: "I'm coming soon. How about a job? I'll try to leave two or three days from now." But it took Bobrov all of ten days to persuade the management, and then it took as long to wind up all the formalities.

"Well, the best of luck to you," Bobrov wished Volodya at parting. "Give us, Urals people, a thought sometimes. Write and tell us if you got there safely and where you found employment, and give our regards to Roman."

When Volodya came home, he announced to his mother: "Well, I'm off."

She started, and then her face lit up, for Volodya's departure for Leningrad was a happy event, filling her with hope that she, too, might now expect a change for the better in her own life.

"Will you write me at once?"

"And what do you think?"

"Oh, how I'll wait for your letters!" She gazed up at him with trust and adoration, like a little girl at a grownup.

That night they whispered till late, making all sorts of plans. His mother went over Volodya's clothes, mending them, and packed his knapsack.

11.

He boarded the train without a ticket, and at first everything went well, but then the ticket collector took away his papers and handed him over to the two train attendants in the officers' car, where he travelled for two days, all the time expecting to be put off at the next station.

It was only when they reached Volkhovstroi and the ticket collector came in and returned Volodya's papers to him without a word, that he realised that he need not have been afraid, for here they had brought him all the way to Leningrad.

12.

The old house in Degtyarnaya Street had grown even older since he'd seen it last. It stood there shabby and morose, giving Volodya no welcome, and not even noticing his approach. Almost all the windows were boarded up; in those that were not the surviving panes were pasted across with strips of paper which had yellowed to a deep brown, as though scorched by fire. Those paper ribbons had been pasted on by the tenants who either left town after Volodya and his mother or died there.

The staircase was pitch dark, you couldn't see a thing. But Volodya remembered that there were five steps first, then eleven to each flight, and went up to the fourth floor, never touching the bannisters.

He rang. The doorbell did not work.

He knocked. He knocked once more. No one answered.

He found his keys and, gropingly, unlocked the door. In complete darkness, he entered the empty, cold flat.

The light did not go on when he pressed the switch. The bulb had burnt out or been removed, or perhaps there was no current.

He took a big step to where the door of their room was, and looked at it in the tiny flame of his lighter.

What was that padlock doing there? He and his mother had simply turned the key in the door to lock it when they left. They had never even owned a padlock. Nor had they ever had those staples put into the door.

The flame of his lighter danced and wavered.

Maybe it was the wrong door?

Of course not. It was their door, and their front hall. He had lived in this flat all his life.

He dug one of the staples out with his penknife, and the door swung open. Someone had entered their room in their absence, breaking in, and when this someone left he had fixed on the padlock. It was not a burglar. A burglar would have left the door open, what did he care, he wouldn't bother to drive in the staples and hang the padlock when he was finished with his business.

But the room was empty as a barn. Whoever had entered it had carried away the furniture, all except Mother's bed. Someone slept in this bed and left it unmade. There was an indentation in the pillow, and the blanket lay in an untidy heap.

Someone must be living here....

Yet the neglected look of the room, his loudly echoing steps, the desolately stripped walls, and the hoarfrost in the window recess, all said: heavens, no! How could anyone live here?

The window was boarded up. The panes in the transom, pasted across with strips of paper, were intact but so dirty that they barely let the light through.

In the faintly glimmering light Volodya saw that both the blanket and the pillow were covered with a thick layer of fluffy dust.

It was old dust; it would become matted into a ball of grey felt if you touched it with a broom.

Someone had lived in this room, a long time ago.

This someone had forced the door. He had brought his own blanket along (it wasn't theirs, they had taken theirs with them), and made this room his home. He tried to keep the place habitable at first: he boarded up the window and swept the broken glass into the corner where it still lay in a dusty little heap.

And then, perhaps, he had died on this bed.

The people who took his body away and buried it probably thought that there was no one to claim his belongings. And so they decided to take possession of his furniture and use it while they themselves were living.

They must have felt squeamish about touching the dead man's bedding, and that's why they left it behind.

What Volodya could not understand was why drive in the staples and hang the padlock on the door when they had cleaned out the room?

He was no slave to things, that least of all. He had seen such devastation from the train window, that it would be ridiculous weeping over some old sticks of furniture. All the same, when he pictured his mother arriving with the baby and finding the room stripped bare except for the bed, his head began to spin.

He heard shuffling steps behind him. He swung round and saw an old woman. He did not know her.

"I'm sorry, but I heard someone walking here. Who are you, might I know?"

"I've just returned home. Do you live here?"

"My room is next door. Are you Volodya Yakubovsky?"

"Yes, I'm Yakubovsky. Who lived in our room, d'you know?"

"No, I don't, son. No one, since I've been here. I didn't touch anything in your room. I was even afraid to go in. I cleaned out my room when I moved in, that was a month ago. My son got the room for me. My son is an invalid of this war. He married and lives at his wife's place, and he got this room for me. I come from Krasnoye Selo, and all through the war I've been moving from one house to the other, in different parts of town. You see, I had my own little house in Krasnoye Selo, and it's there no more. A terrible battle was fought there, when our troops recaptured it. People say that our tanks came on and on all night long, so how could a little house survive? My son tells me, don't cry, wait a bit, just let us get our breath back and we'll build you a new one." The old woman did not cry, but rather took pleasure in telling her story. "I went down to the bakery, and when I came back I heard someone walking about here, so I thought it must be my neighbour. Someone left a note for you. A young man came in the day before yesterday and left the note."

The young man must be Roman.

Indeed, the note was from him, and upon reading it Volodya cheered up at once.

"Hullo, Volodya," wrote Roman. "Too bad that something's holding you up. Your personal presence is essential to secure the job. Your room's in a state of filthy neglect, and this problem will have to be solved urgently. Come over *at once*. I'm on second shift this week, so you'll always find me at home in the daytime, and if I'm out get the key from the top of the cupboard in the hall, go into my room and make yourself at home. I happened to have a padlock and a couple of staples in my pocket, and so I locked up your room because it stood wide open and ownerless. I'm leaving the key with the granny next door. Let this padlock make the beginning of your settling in. Cheers. R."

"And here's the key," said the old woman.

Roman lived in Pushkarskaya Street. He also had plywood in place of glass in the window, but a lamp was burning brightly, the floor was freshly scrubbed, the iron stove was going, on it a kettle was hissing, and the radio was playing the Torreador song with a verve. Roman had furniture, and Roman had firewood which lay neatly stacked between the couch and the book-shelf.

"Gosh, you've a proper household!" Volodya exclaimed.

"Never say die, friend! We'll now have tea. You are the guest of a Kirov Works man. Apart from the fact that we're given decent rations, there's no end of people everywhere who can't do a damned thing for themselves. How do they manage to exist, can you tell me? They can't change a fuse even, the idiots! Yesterday I did a bit of plumbery for a learned bloke who lives on the third floor, and he gave me a share of his special ration, A or B, I don't know which."

Roman made the tea, sliced sausage and bread, and all in a matter of seconds!

"You'll go and see the foreman today, let's strike the iron while it's hot. See him before he goes on shift, let him take a look at you and ask you the questions he wants to ask. I have spoken to him. He's not a bad old chap. He knows Kalinin personally. Did you know that Kalinin had once worked at our plant?"

He went on to tell Volodya what the plant did during the blockade.

"I must go," Volodya said. "There's someone I have to see."

"Look, Volodya, stay with me until you're fixed up."

"Maybe I will."

"Your place is less than habitable, speaking frankly. So you'd better stay here. We'll get hold of some packing cases and I'll make you any kind of furniture you want."

They agreed to meet at the entrance gate of the Kirov Works at seven p.m.

The hospital Volodya's father worked was in Kirochnaya Street, next to the Suvorov Museum.

It was visiting hour. A lot of women carrying shopping nets and packages stood about in the vestibule. Volodya went up to the cloakroom attendant and asked her how he could get to see Dr. Yakubovsky.

"He's not here today. Doctor Yakubovsky is ill," she said.

"Seriously ill?"

"That we don't know. And who're you?" She peered at Volodya curiously.

"A relative," he replied.

"Well, I saw it right away. You might be his son, you're so much like him."

The wintry sky was overcast. Powdery snow was falling, and there was a chill little wind.

The streets were strangely desolate, there were few people about and few cars.

Wooden boarding had been put up round the ruined houses, and some of them peeped over the edge with their burnt-out eyes.

The snow had been swept up into a tall barrier along the railing of the Fontanka embankment.

The locked up Summer Garden looked bare and sombre. Volodya remembered that there were some old lime trees there whose hollows had been filled like teeth. As a little boy he used to pause before these fillings, curious and touched by people's kindness to the ageing trees. And now, walking past, he smiled at the bare, chilled trees on the other side of the grille. One had to be a man to put fillings in the tree hollows. One had to be a man to let a boy without a ticket get safely home. One had to be a man to say to a friend: "Stay with me."

The wind blew harder, and the snow whirled thicker and faster.

Volodya was about to enter the house on Moika where his father lived when his stepmother came out. They all but collided in the front door. She was wearing a flat fur hat. He had only seen her once before, and she had no hat on then. But he instantly recognized the narrow face with the high cheekbones and the narrow, slanted eyes, as it flashed past him in the mesh of snow.

She did not recognize him, and went on her way. Volodya was glad she was gone and would not be in and out of the room with tea things all the time, listening to his conversation with his father.

13.

His father opened the door himself. He had on a smoking jacket and soft slippers. He had lost weight.

"Volodya?" he said, surprised. "Come in. Well, how are you?"

They shook hands.

"Have you been back long? Good of you to call."

He needn't have said that, need he? After all, this was his son and not just a casual caller. Wasn't it natural for a son to come and see his father?

Volodya hung up his wet padded jacket on the hall tree, and followed his father into the study.

"You *have* grown! You're quite a man!" his father said when they had sat down. "And how is your mother?"

"Mother's alive. Did you receive my letters?"

"Yes. I have been ill, as you can see. I am better now, to be sure. Well, tell me all about yourself."

As on the previous occasion there was this painful awkwardness between them, and they could not surmount it. His father sat with half-closed eyes, and Volodya did not believe that his life interested him at all, and the words stuck in his throat as they had done when he tried to tell strangers of his family troubles. And he still resented his father for leaving his mother, although they could never have made a go of it, he now realised.

"And how have you been?" Volodya asked his father.

"I? Oh well.... I lived through the blockade here. You know, of course, you've heard what it was like. I lived at the hospital and hardly ever came here, and you can see for yourself what the place looks like." He made a helpless gesture, motioning at the cracked, dark ceiling and the torn wallpaper. "We did procure some glass for the windows though, thus solving a most difficult problem. Yes indeed. Working in industry is a very useful thing; when I was your age I also worked in industry, those are my happiest memories. Yes indeed. I didn't send you the affidavit because, you see, I simply did not imagine that it was so urgent. I teach, you see, besides working at the hospital, and so I do not have much time left for my personal affairs, and then I was ill, you know, but I meant to do it as soon as I was well, and had already done something in that direction, finding out how one went about it. But you managed to get here without any formalities, and that's all the better. Is your record in order? No tails, I hope?"

"What tails?"

"You didn't get into trouble? Did you resign from the factory or bolt?"

"I resigned."

"All clean?"

"All clean."

"Is your room safe?... You need money, naturally, but at the moment I.... But in a couple of days I'll.... What are your plans for the immediate future? Will you go back to school? Or go to technical school?"

"Not back to school, I don't think," Volodya replied. "I'm going to work in any case." It was a relief, a joy to realise that he did not depend on his father, that he needn't even take any money from him, he'd manage, Roman would see him through till his first pay. No, he must take the money, and send it to Mother. "There's a chap here who's promised to help me get a job at the Kirov Works."

"Why some chap," his father said. "If you wish, I can help you find employment, in any case I might try."

"Thanks. But it's not me who wants helping just now."

"Oh yes, your mother is unwell, you wrote," Volodya's father sighed. "What is it, actually? What is she ill with?"

With his eyes lowered, and a grimace of distaste on his face, his father heard out Volodya's terse story. He made it very obvious that he would prefer to know nothing of this.

Of the captain he said: "What a bounder."

Quite possibly, his former wife's plight would not have impressed him much, but the news that her room had been robbed penetrated his armour. It made the whole picture clear to him, so to say. His eyes opened, quite literally. And he moaned with fastidious horror: "Good Lord!"

"May I smoke?" Volodya asked when he had told everything.

"Yes, of course," his father started up, pushed the ashtray up to Volodya and, taking some tobacco and cigarette paper from his son, lit up too.

They sat in armchairs facing one another, their legs crossed, father and son. The son resembled the father in appearance, in stature, and even in the way he smoked. He saw the resemblance, and it both pleased and strangely annoyed him. He wondered if his father noticed the resemblance too.

"Ah yes. A pretty mess. But what can I do?"

Volodya had a ready answer, for he had thought everything out a long time ago.

"You must, first, give her a chance to come here where she has a room of her own, but you will guess, of course, that she has no money for the journey. You must, second, help her find work that would enable her to exist. It's not just a question of wages, you see, but mainly of having the baby put in a day-and-night crèche, as that's the only way to rescue Mother, she's really ill, and just now that would be her only salvation."

"How awful!" Father said. "To make such a mess of her life. Awful, really."

He began pacing the cluttered room, a few steps each way.

"It was not all her own doing. People always helped her to mess up her life."

"I must object!" Father said. "Volodya, I don't want you to judge me too sternly. She was always an unfortunate, irresponsible person."

"Perhaps. Most probably so. Unfortunate is right. So what does it mean? That she must be denied help and abandoned to her fate?"

"Listen to me. I did not have a softly carpeted path in life. I worked at a factory, finished a workers' high school, and when I enrolled in the medical college I worked as a stevedore, often the whole night through, so that when I came to the dissecting room in the morning, I couldn't hold the scalpel, my fingers were so stiff. I worked for you, so you wouldn't starve. My state allowance would have done for me alone, you may be sure of that. All I wanted was to study and become a surgeon, plain bread was enough for me. And she?! She did not appreciate anything, she never took an interest in anything, never took a book in her hands — I don't want to say more, I do not feel I decently can, but...."

"Things are so bad for her just now, they could not be worse," Volodya cut in. "You and I are sitting here and discussing her, and she? It's too awful to picture. She has to be helped up to her feet, understand? Put back on her feet, because otherwise.... I won't manage by myself, understand? We have to do it together."

"But why do I *have to*?" his father shouted. "By what

law must I straighten out the mess she got herself into, and, mind you, we've been separated for fourteen years! It's a laugh, really!"

14.

In the room next to the study, Oleg Yakubovsky — a sickly boy with curly fair hair, a narrow face and narrow eyes—sat at the table, doing his homework.

He did his homework with the carelessness of a gifted pupil who knew that if he made the slightest effort the sum would be solved, his hands untied for more exciting things, and the excellent mark to make his parents happy — assured.

He could grant his parents this happiness at little cost to himself, and so he did grant it them with indulgent generosity.

However, a good mark was desirable, if not essential, for his own peace of mind as well. He was not excessively vain, but had no wish to lay himself open to reproach over trifles. And doing his homework and receiving good marks were indeed trifles not worth talking about.

Besides, quite a lot of people relied on his doing the homework sum. Boys who found it too difficult or were too lazy to tackle it themselves would be able to copy it from Oleg in school next morning and also get top marks.

For the sake of these boys he always came to school a little earlier than he had to. It was no trouble to get up half an hour earlier for his friends. And he didn't care for sleep. The time he spent in bed always seemed a waste. He had not done anything in life yet. It was shameful, and he always urged himself on, saying it was time to begin.

Begin what? He did not know. He liked biology, physics, and geography. Everything relating to outer space and interplanetary communication stirred him so deeply that a lump rose in his throat. He was not admitted to the public library because he was under age, but through friends he obtained the scientific magazines he needed to be up on the latest problems and discoveries.

He was as interested in literature — literature as such, and also all the debates revolving round it, all the developments and happenings in this complex sphere of art. He wrote poems, short stories and plays, and thought that under any circumstances, no matter what profession he chose in life, he would at the same time be a writer.

It was also possible, he believed, that chess would be one of his main occupations—he already had the first rating, which wasn't so bad.

If all this were combined plus many other things which had not occurred to him yet, perhaps it would suffice for Oleg Yakubovsky's lifetime.

Because of such a multiplicity of interests and because of the overpowering fascination of the treasures strewn over his road, he was always in a state of nervous excitement and his narrow, slightly slanted grey eyes glittered feverishly.

Since he could remember himself he was provided with everything that might further his physical and mental development. He was never pestered with wheedlings to "eat just one more spoonful", but in order to strengthen his health, weak from birth, a keenness for outdoor games, skiing and physical exercises was cultivated in him. It was his mother who did it when they were evacuated from Leningrad during the war. Loving but not sentimental, attentive but not indiscreet, she tried not to miss anything that might give him physical strength, knowledge, and people's liking. She cultivated in him a taste for wholesome pleasures, taught him to read good books, took him to concerts and art exhibitions, wishing to fill his life with those spiritual delights which formed the supreme joy of her own existence.

At the same time he enjoyed complete freedom. He always had his own inviolable little corner and when, a year before the war, they moved into this three-room flat, he was installed in a room all his own, to which he had so gladly returned not so very long ago. The room was furnished modestly, but with such loving care! He must never want to go loitering in the streets, and wherever he was he must always be drawn home—this was the thought Oleg's mother had in mind when choosing the furnishings for his room, and it was the thought which underlay the whole set-up of the family's life. As much respect was shown for Oleg's work as for his father's. If sometimes he talked childish rubbish, he was responded to patiently and seriously. He could always bring his friends home, and if there were girls their coming never made the subject of that idiotic and insulting teasing indulged in by other, less intellectual families.

It was Oleg's mother who laid down the law, his father readily obeyed her, and a spirit of decorum and mutual assistance reigned in their home.

Oleg's mother had more culture than his father, for all that she was titled so modestly—a housewife. His father, for instance, had rather a poor knowledge of music. He might explode for no good reason, or have tantrums just like a woman. And the expressions he used were too slangy sometimes. Oleg's mother was faultless. Her faultlessness inspired a tender pride in Oleg, but his affection for his father did not suffer from this comparison. Oleg was sufficiently wise and broad-minded to overlook the small things in which his father was perhaps wanting. Did it matter so very much that he had a poor knowledge of music? He was doing important work, everyone thought highly of him, and those people with the well-known and esteemed names who supplied Oleg with scientific magazines and answered his difficult questions—those people were his father's patients who became their family friends. Father was the cornerstone of their family, the base on which Mother built her pedagogical construction.

Oleg was perfectly aware that his mother's pedagogical methods were intended to beneficially influence not just himself but also his father, and this rather amused him and brought him even closer to his father, put as they were on the same footing. They were two men who, voluntarily and good-naturedly recognizing the woman's moral superiority, had entrusted themselves to her guidance (needless to say, within reason and not letting her overstep the line where a man's calling and a man's independence began). Oleg thought it all very beautiful and right, and in his eyes this relationship raised the three of them to a new height.

He was sitting and doing his sum. The desk lamp with its olive-green paper shade lit up his narrow face with the narrow eyes and sharp cheek-bones.

The sum was done. Feeling thirsty, he went into the dining-room and as he poured himself a glass of water from the teapot on the sideboard, he heard someone talking in his father's study. There was his father's voice and another strange voice that obviously belonged to a young man. Oleg listened.

Their voices rose, and some words caught his attention. The young voice had said: "You must give her a chance to come here."

Oleg didn't know a soul in the world who could have spoken so casually and confidently to his father.

"Volodya, I don't want you to judge me too sternly," Father said, and he sounded distressed.

Now, who could be judging his father, and why should his father sound so distressed and self-defensive?

"She was always an unfortunate, irresponsible person."

And the young voice said inexorably: "Perhaps. Most probably so. So what does it mean? That she must be denied help and abandoned to her fate?"

Oleg went closer to the door.

"Listen to me. I did not have a softly carpeted path in life."

Now Father would be off about those ships he loaded. Telling people about his stevedore past was one of his little weaknesses.

"I worked for you, so you wouldn't starve...."

"And she?! She did not appreciate anything...."

Again the young voice: "Things are so bad for her just now, they could not be worse.... She has to be helped up to her feet, understand? Put back on her feet, because otherwise.... I won't manage by myself, understand? We have to do it together."

"But why do I *have to*?" Father shouted. "By what law must I straighten out the mess she got herself into, and, mind you, we've been separated for fourteen years! It's a laugh, really!"

"It may be a laugh for you, but it isn't funny for her, and that's why you've got to help!" the young man said angrily.

Oleg stood at the door. He wasn't eavesdropping, he simply felt it imperative to listen to this conversation. And, standing there before the closed door with his hands thrust into his pockets he heard the conversation to the end, ruffled yet determined.

"When shall I phone you?" asked the young voice.

"What's today? Call me on Friday," Father said meekly.

"Goodbye," said the young man.

"All the best, Volodya."

Oleg retreated into his room. It would be extremely stupid and tactless to get in their way just then.... The front door banged shut.

When Oleg returned to the dining-room, his father was just entering it from the front hall, after seeing his visitor off.

"Who was it?" Oleg asked. "Daddy, who was it?" he repeated the question, following his father into the study.

"A business call," his father replied brusquely, standing with his back to Oleg and lighting a cigarette.

"Why did he call you Father?"

"You're imagining things."

"Oh, Daddy, what nonsense. Is he my brother?"

His father swung round. The hand holding the cigarette before his lips was trembling.

"I forbid you to ask questions! Who, what and why! Poking your nose in everything. Not a shred of respect. Nice upbringing!" His father shouted angrily and incoherently. "Leave me, I'm busy."

Oleg's blood was up too. Intelligent, grown-up people, suddenly turning liars and hysterics!

Very well. He'd act as he thought right. Who could forbid him? And could he act differently anyway?

Leaning over the bannisters he called down the stairwell: "Volodya!"

15.

Oleg raced down the stairs and out into the street. The wind and whirling snow assailed him. Clutching his unbuttoned coat to his chest, he peered about him.

The wind drove the snow along the embankment, and in the light of the street-lamps he saw dark figures hurrying away to the right and to the left. Which of these could be his brother? Oleg shouted into the slanting white mist of snow: "Volodya!"

He shouted with all his might.

Two of the figures turned their heads, and one of them stopped. Oleg ran to the waiting figure.

"Are you Volodya?"

"Yes, why?" Volodya responded coolly.

"Hullo! I'm Oleg Yakubovsky."

Each peered hard into the face of the other.

Volodya held out his hand, and said: "And I'm Volodya Yakubovsky."

"Look, we've got to have a talk," Oleg said, gasping with excitement yet speaking in an urgently business-like tone.

"Are you sure we've got to?"

"Yes, quite sure."

"What about?"

"I must tell you something. Something very important."

Volodya's guardedness was causing Oleg almost physical pain.

"It's important, is it?" Volodya said. "All right, walk me to the tram stop. I'm on my way to the Kirov Works."

"Do you work there?"

"I'm going to."

"Look, how old are you?" Oleg asked, his questions tumbling from his lips impatiently.

"Sixteen. And you must be fourteen, right?"

"You know? You mean you've known about me? You knew that I existed?"

"Yes."

"Have you known long?"

"I always knew."

"You don't say! And I never knew anything about you. What are they doing it for? What do you think?"

"Doing what?"

"Well, I mean, keeping me in complete ignorance about you. Why are they keeping it a secret? D'you know? For pedagogical reasons, or what?"

"I don't know," Volodya said, shrugging. He never could understand why his father and stepmother wanted to make a mystery of it, and apparently Oleg was taking it as badly as he did himself.

"Are they protecting our youthful souls? Or afraid we might get too close?"

"Both, probably."

"They're afraid that I might judge Father. Poor things. Must be awful to go in constant fear of being judged, don't you think?"

"I should say so! That's why they shouldn't have made a secret of it."

"Of course! Frankness is always best. If everyone got together and talked things over, no one would have to be afraid of anyone."

They walked along the edge of the Field of Mars, buried in snowdrifts. The wind blew in their backs and did not bother them.

"Don't run so," Oleg begged. "I want to say something. Just because something went wrong between them, or something happened anyway, it shouldn't prevent us from being brothers, should it? I don't mean in name only, I mean real brothers, you see what I mean?"

"Of course it shouldn't," Volodya agreed with bigbrotherly condescension. "Did I say it should?"

"No, but you're trying to get away from me."

"Please don't think that I have anything against you, any ill feelings or anything like that," Volodya assured him. "I never did, why should I? A chap's waiting for me, that's all."

"What chap?"

"We worked together at the factory."

"Did the factory make tanks?"

"The name of the director was comrade Golovanov, that's all I can tell about that factory."

"I see.... Look, is it your mother who's in such a bad way? I heard you talking. Is she very ill?"

"Let's not talk about this," Volodya told him.

"All right. I'm sorry. Listen, where do you live? D'you have a place to live?"

"I have a place to live," Volodya replied somewhat haughtily, suspecting Oleg of trying to patronise him. "Come over, if you like."

Oleg realised that he had hurt Volodya, and said contritely: "Thanks. I will if you let me."

At the tram stop he asked: "May I come with you?"

It worried him that they had said so little to each other, terribly little even for a first brief meeting.

"I'll come with you to the works, if you don't mind."

"Come along, I don't mind," Volodya replied. His inner resistance was broken, and it rather pleased him that Oleg was asking his permission so humbly, as befits a younger brother. He wondered how they'd get along if they had grown up together.

The tram smelt of wet coats and fur. They stood squashed into a corner, hastily exchanging information about each other. What form were you in when you left school? Where were you during the war, and what was it like in Sverdlovsk, not bad? Do you play games?

"In a small way," Volodya replied, watching the play of expression on the nervous, triangular face before him, with the narrow eyes flashing up with excitement. This was a nature that vibrated excitedly in response to everything under the sun, his whole being becoming fired at once.

"He looks like *her*," Volodya was thinking.

"Gosh, he's the very image of Daddy!" Oleg thought.

"Was it *she* who brought him up to be like this?" Volodya wondered. "But what do I know about *her*? Or Father?"

They were father and son, meeting after a long separation. But they had met like strangers and they had talked, resenting one another, about depressing, mundane matters. "And it will probably always be like that, why should anything change? I'm a burden to him, a boring nuisance, nothing else." Oleg had nothing to do with it. He was a hundred percent sincere, he had nothing to do with it.

The tham passed under a bridge, and stopped at a long wall. The tall gate loomed darkly in the snow-whirl.

Roman stood waiting there, doing a tap dance to keep his feet warm.

"This is Roman, my friend," Volodya said to Oleg. "And this is Oleg," he hesitated, and then added: "My brother."

This statement made no impression on Roman. People called their cousins brothers sometimes, and there were even such relatives as uncles twice removed.

"How do," he said grumpily. "Come on, Volodya, I thought you were never coming. Got your papers with you?"

They went into the gate. Oleg stood looking after Volodya. His brother! His elder brother, locked out of his family and home through no fault of his, striding like a stranger, apart from them, down his own road! With all the ardour of his nature, Oleg wanted to be admitted to Volodya's life, to offer him a shoulder to lean on.

He stood alone before the factory wall, which was scarred and nicked like a fortress wall that had withstood a siege.

And this was, indeed, a fortress, for it had been a fighting front only a short while ago, fires were blazing all round, but the fortress had stood firm against the siege, and the enemies retreated, leaving their dead without number at the approaches to the factory. And the factory was alive, its slender chimneys rose skyward through the whirling snow, and a warm, live hum came from it.

The snow fell slantwise in such tiny particles that it looked like white smoke. The street was foggy with this flying snow. It was as if the barns up in the sky where they stored this light, white grain had been flung open, and down it came pouring freely and inexhaustibly. Oleg raised the collar of his coat, and strode on, smiling, squinting in the blinding snow and whispering.

The dark lines of the roofs and the blurs of the street lamps showed through the snowstorm. His beloved city! Everything whirled upward and flew, sweeping Oleg along, and he rapturously succumbed to the mood.

People hurrying home that evening along the endless, whirling street noticed a strange-looking boy. He alone was walking calmly, untroubled by the avalanche from the flung-open skies, as though he were taking a pleasant stroll in fine weather. The passersby thought: "He must be mad!" but immediately guessed that he was feeling happy, he must be if he could behave as strangely as he did. He made up verses as he went along, wishing to immortalise his beloved city which, he did not think, was sufficiently immortalised in poetry.

There was the Arch of Triumph and the boy beside it, completely lost in its magnificence, as though there was no boy in the square at all, nothing but the Arch of Triumph.

But who knows — maybe he really will immortalise his beloved city in his poems! What if he achieves what none have achieved before him? Who knows what and which of these boys and girls will attain? What they will grow up to be. Who knows, who knows....

1959

SERYOZHA

Some Stories from the Life
of a Very Small Boy

To my children—Natalia, Boris and Yuri.

WHO SERYOZHA IS AND WHERE HE LIVES

Now, they've taken it into their heads he's like a girl! That's as silly as silly can be. Girls wear frocks and Seryozha hasn't worn one for ages. And when did a girl ever have a catapult? But Seryozha has one, he can shoot stones with it. Shurik made it for him. And in exchange Seryozha gave Shurik all the old cotton reels he'd been collecting his whole life long.

And if his hair's like that, well, it's been cropped with the clippers ever so many times and Seryozha endured it all, he sat quiet till they'd finished, and all the same it grew again, just like it had been.

But to make up for that, he's very clever for his age, everyone says so. He knows no end of books by heart. If they read him a book two or three times, he can say it all off. He knows his letters, too, but reading things by himself takes such a long time. The books are all thickly daubed with crayons, because Seryozha likes to colour the pictures, and if they are already coloured he changes them to suit his own taste. Books don't look new for very long, they soon start falling to pieces. Aunt Pasha mends them, she sews pages in and sticks together the ones torn at the edges.

If some page gets lost Seryozha hunts for it and knows no peace until it is found. He loves his books, although in his heart of hearts he does not take everything in them really seriously. Animals can't talk, and the flying carpet can't fly because it hasn't got an engine, you'd have to be very silly not to know that.

Anyway, how can you believe stories when they read you one about a witch and then say: "But there aren't really any witches, Seryozha."

All the same, he can't bear hearing how the woodcutter and his wife took their children into the forest so that they'd get lost and never come home again. And although Tom Thumb saved them, still, you just can't listen to things like that. He never lets them read that book to him.

Seryozha lives with Mummy, Aunt Pasha and Lukyanich. There are three rooms in their little house. Seryozha and

Mummy sleep in one, Lukyanich and Aunt Pasha in another, and the third one is the dining-room. They have meals there when visitors come, but when they are alone they eat in the kitchen. There is a veranda and a yard, too. And in the yard there are chickens, onions and radishes grow in two long beds. To keep the chickens out of the beds dry prickly branches are pushed into the ground all round, and when Seryozha has to pull up a radish he always scratches his legs.

People say their town is a small one. Seryozha and his friends are quite sure that's all wrong. It's a big town. It's got shops and some water-towers and a monument and a cinema. Mummy takes Seryozha to the pictures sometimes. And when the lights go down Seryozha says: "Mummy, if you understand anything, tell me."

Lorries drive along the road. Timokhin gives the children rides in his. But that doesn't happen very often. Only when Timokhin hasn't been drinking vodka. Then he frowns and doesn't talk, smokes, spits and gives them all rides. But if he's looking gay, it's no good asking—he'll just wave his hand through the window and call out: "Hullo, kids! I can't take you. Wouldn't be right. I've had a drink!"

Seryozha's street is called Dalnaya Street. But that's just a name, because it's close to everything. Vaska says it's only two kilometres to the square, and Vaska says the Bright Shore State Farm's even closer.

There's nothing more important than the Bright Shore Farm. That's where Lukyanich works. Aunt Pasha goes to the shops there to get pickled herrings and cloth. And Mummy's school is on the farm, too. On holidays she takes Seryozha with her to the school parties. That's where he met red-haired Fima. She's awfully big, eight years old. She's got braids wound round over her ears, and ribbons plaited in them and tied in bows. Sometimes the ribbons are black, sometimes blue, or white, or brown. She's got an awful lot of ribbons. Seryozha might not have noticed them, but Fima told him herself: "Have you seen what a lot of ribbons I've got?"

LIFE'S LITTLE HARDSHIPS

She was quite right to tell him. You can't notice everything, you simply haven't got enough to notice in you. There are so many things all round. The world is packed with things. How can you possibly notice them all?

Almost all the things are very big. Doors are terribly high, and people (except children) are almost as high as they are. Not to speak of lorries and harvester combines, or those great railway engines that whistle so loudly you can't hear anything else at all.

But they aren't really dangerous. People are kind to Seryozha, they stoop down if he wants them to, and they never tread on him with their great feet. Lorries and combines won't hurt you either if you don't run in front of them. The engines are a long way off, at the station. Seryozha went there once or twice with Timokhin. But right beside him in the yard there lives a terrible creature. It has nasty, angry, suspicious little eyes, a great crop that you can see breathing, a chest as round as a cart-wheel and an iron beak. It stands scratching the earth with a warty claw. When it stretches out its neck it's as tall as Seryozha. And some day it may peck Seryozha just like it pecked the silly cockerel from the next yard that flew over to pay a visit. Seryozha always makes a wide circle round that savage creature, trying to look as though he doesn't even see it, and the creature lets its red comb hang down on one side and gobbles something threatening while it follows him with a watchful, malicious eye.

Cocks peck, cats scratch, nettles sting, boys fight, the ground grazes your knees when you fall—so Seryozha is always covered with scratches, bumps and bruises. Almost every day something bleeds somewhere. And things are always happening. Vaska climbed the fence and Seryozha wanted to climb up, too, but he fell down and bumped himself. They dug a trench in Lida's garden and all the children began jumping across it, but when Seryozha jumped he fell in. His foot got all swollen and hurt him. So Seryozha was put to bed. And the first time he got up and went outside to play with his ball the ball flew up on the roof and got itself stuck right behind the chimney, so he had to wait for Vaska to get it down again. And once Seryozha was almost drowned. Lukyanich took the children out on the river in a boat—Seryozha, Vaska, Fima and a girl called Nadya. But Lukyanich's boat was no good at all, when the children moved it started to rock from side to side and they all fell into the water, all but Lukyanich. The water was just terribly cold. And it went into Seryozha's nose and mouth and ears, into his stomach, even, he hadn't time to call out. Seryozha got all wet and heavy, and something seemed to be pulling him down. He was terribly frightened, he'd never been so frightened before. And it was all dark, too. And it went on and on and on like that. But then, suddenly, something lifted him up. He opened his eyes and there was the river right by his face, and he could see the bank, and everything was sparkling in the sunshine. All the water that had been inside Seryozha came out again and he breathed air; the bank came closer and closer, and then Seryozha was crouching on all fours on the firm sand, shivering with cold and fright. It was Vaska who'd thought of getting hold of him by the hair and pulling him out. But what if Seryozha hadn't had such long hair, what then?

Fima swam out by herself, she knew how to swim. But Nadya nearly drowned. It was Lukyanich who saved her. But while Lukyanich was saving Nadya the boat floated away. Some people on a collective farm down the river found it and telephoned to the office for Lukyanich to come and get it. But Lukyanich never took the children in a boat any more. He said: "I'll be damned if I ever take you in a boat again."

With so much happening and so much to see, Seryozha gets very tired. By evening he is quite exhausted, his tongue will hardly move and his eyes roll up like a bird's. They wash his hands and feet and put on a night-shirt and he doesn't even fill it; his clock has run down.

He sleeps, his head thrown back, his thin little arms flung wide, one leg stretched out, the other bent as though he were climbing stairs. His soft, light hair falls back in two waves from his brow, with its stubborn bumps over the eyebrows, like you see on a calf. The eyelids with their fluffy fringe of lashes are closed firmly. The middle of his mouth is a very little bit open, the corners glued in sleep. He breathes imperceptibly, like a flower.

He sleeps, and you could beat a drum, fire a gun beside him and Seryozha would know nothing of it; he is gathering strength to go on with the job of living.

CHANGES IN THE HOME

"Seryozha," said Mummy, "you know what?... I want us to have a Daddy."

Seryozha raised his eyes to her face. He had never thought about that. Some children had Daddies, others hadn't. Seryozha had no Daddy, his had been killed in the war. Seryozha had never seen him, only his photograph. Sometimes Mummy would kiss it, and give it to Seryozha to kiss

too. He was quite ready to press his lips to the glass, misty
from Mummy's breath, but he did not really feel any love.
How could he love someone whom he'd seen only on a
picture?

Now he stood between Mummy's knees looking inquiringly into her face. And very slowly it began getting pink — the
pink started on her cheeks, and then it spread to her forehead
and ears.... Mummy gripped Seryozha tight with her knees,
put her arms round him and laid her hot cheek on his head.
Then all he could see was her arm in a blue sleeve with white
dots.

"After all, it would be nicer with a Daddy," she whispered.
"It would, wouldn't it, Seryozha?"

"Ye-e-es," he answered, whispering too, although he did
not know why.

Actually, he was far from sure of it. He said "yes" simply
because she wanted him to say "yes". And he turned it over
quickly in his mind—which is better, to have a Daddy or not
to have a Daddy? When Timokhin gave them rides in his
lorry all the children got in the back but Shurik; he sat in
front with Timokhin, and they envied him but no one
disputed his right, because Timokhin was Shurik's Daddy.
But then, if Shurik was naughty Timokhin gave him the
strap, and Shurik went about tear-stained and gloomy, and
Seryozha was sorry for him and brought out all his toys to
comfort Shurik. But all the same, perhaps it was better if you
had a Daddy. When Vaska teased Lida not long ago she told
him: "But I've got a Daddy and you haven't, yah!"

"What's that bumping?" Seryozha asked suddenly, noticing the dull thud-thud in Mummy's chest. Mummy laughed,
kissed Seryozha and hugged him closer.

"It's my heart."

"And have I got one, too?" he asked, bending his head to
listen.

"Yes, you've got one, too."

"No. I can't hear it bumping."

"But it does. It's just that you can't hear it. But it's beating
all the same. You couldn't live if it didn't."

"And does it always go like that?"

"Yes, all the time."

"Even when I'm asleep?"

"Yes, even when you're asleep."

"And can you hear it?"

"Yes, I can. And you can feel it with your hand, too."
She took his hand and laid it on his ribs.

"Now can you feel it?"

"Yes.... Oooh, isn't it banging! Is it big?"

"Shut your hand, that's right. It's about as big as that."

"Let me go," he said, wriggling out of her embrace, evidently full of some sudden idea.

"Where are you going?" she asked.

"Wait a minute," he said and ran out into the street, his hand pressed against his left side. There he saw Vaska and Zhenka, and ran to them.

"Look, would you like to feel? That's my heart. I can feel it with my hand. Would you like to feel, too?"

"Huh, your heart," scoffed Vaska. "Everyone's got a heart."

But Zhenka said: "No—really?" and put his hand on Seryozha's side.

"Can you feel it?" Seryozha asked.

"M'yes," said Zhenka.

"It's as big as my fist," said Seryozha.

"How do you know?" asked Vaska.

"Mummy told me," Seryozha said, and suddenly remembering, he added: "And I'm going to have a Daddy!"

But Vaska and Zhenka did not hear him, they were too busy with their own affairs. They were taking medicinal herbs to an office where they were collected. There were lists on all the fences saying which kinds were needed, and the boys wanted to earn some pocket-money. They had been gathering herbs for two days. Vaska had asked his mother to clean his and sort them out and wrap them in a clean cloth, now he was taking a big, neat bundle to the office. But Zhenka had no mother, his cousin and aunt were at work, and he couldn't bother with all that himself; so he was taking his herbs in an old, torn potato sack, together with the roots and even the soil clinging to them. But to make up for that he had a lot—much more than Vaska. When he heaved the sack up on his back he had to bend double to carry it.

"I want to go with you," cried Seryozha, running after them.

"You can't. Go back home," said Vaska. "We're busy."

"Can't I just walk along with you?" Seryozha begged.

"Go home, I tell you," said Vaska. "This isn't play. There's nothing for kids like you to do where we're going."

Seryozha stopped. His lip trembled, but he wouldn't cry. Lida was nearby, she'd start teasing him with "Cry-baby! Cry-baby!"

"Wouldn't they take you?" she asked. "Too bad!"

"I can get as many herbs as that if I want," said Seryozha, "and I'll heap them up higher than the sky."

"Higher than the sky—ha, ha!" laughed Lida. "Nobody can make a heap higher than the sky."

"But I'm going to have a Daddy, he can," said Seryozha.

"That's a story," said Lida. "You're not going to have any Daddy at all. And he couldn't get as much as that anyway. Nobody could."

Seryozha looked up at the sky, his head thrown far back. Could anyone gather enough herbs to reach higher than the sky, or not? While he was still thinking about it, Lida ran home and came back with a coloured scarf her mother often wore, sometimes on her head and sometimes round her neck. Lida started to dance, waving her arms so the scarf floated out and kicking her feet and singing something to help. Seryozha stood watching her. Lida stopped for a moment.

"Nadka's a story-teller, she says she's going to learn to dance in the ballet."

She danced a little more, then went on: "They teach you to dance in the ballet in Moscow and Leningrad."

She saw the admiration in Seryozha's face, and said condescendingly: "Well? What are you looking at? Shall I teach it you? Watch me and do the same as I do."

He started copying her, but without the scarf it was not the same. She told him to sing, but it didn't help.

"Give me the scarf," he begged. But all he got was: "Anything else you'd like?"

So she didn't give it to him.

Just then a car stopped at Seryozha's gate. A woman was driving. She got down, and Aunt Pasha came out of the gate.

"Here you are," said the driver. "Dmitri Korneyevich sent these."

There was a suitcase in the back, and piles of books fastened together with a string. And there was something thick and grey, rolled up—it turned out to be an army greatcoat. Aunt Pasha and the driver began carrying the things inside. Mummy looked out of the window and then disappeared.

"Well, that's all—not much of a dowry, I'm afraid," said the driver.

"He might at least have bought a new overcoat," said Aunt Pasha mournfully.

"He'll get one," the driver reassured her. "All in good time. And here's this note, give it to her, please."

She handed over a letter and drove away. Seryozha raced into the house.

"Mummy! Mummy! Korostelev's sent us his soldier's coat!"

(Dmitri Korneyevich Korostelev used to visit them. He brought toys for Seryozha and once, in the winter, took him for a sleigh ride. His army coat had no shoulder-straps on it, it was left over from the war. Seryozha found it difficult to get his tongue round the full name and patronymic— "Dmitri Korneyevich," so he simply called the visitor Korostelev.)

The greatcoat was already hanging on the rack, and Mummy was reading the letter. She did not answer at once; but when she had quite finished reading she said: "I know, Seryozha. Korostelev's going to live here with us. He's going to be your Daddy."

Then she started reading the letter all over again, once evidently was not enough to remember what it said.

"Daddy"—that word had made Seryozha think of someone strange, unknown. But Korostelev—why, he was an old friend, Aunt Pasha and Lukyanich called him "Mitya", what had come over Mummy?

"But why?" Seryozha asked.

"Now look here," said Mummy, "are you going to let me read this letter or not?"

So she never answered him. She seemed to have an awful lot of things to do. She took the string off the books and arranged them on the shelves. And she wiped every book with a cloth. Then she changed the places of all the things in front of the mirror on the chest of drawers. Then she went into the garden, picked some flowers and arranged them in a vase. Then for some reason she had to wash the floor, although it was quite clean as it was. And then she started baking a tart. Aunt Pasha taught her how to make dough. And Seryozha got some dough and jam, too, so he could make a little tart all his own.

When Korostelev arrived Seryozha had forgotten all his puzzlement and cried: "Korostelev! Look I've made a tart!"

Korostelev stooped down and kissed him several times. And Seryozha thought: He keeps on kissing me so long because he's my Daddy now.

Korostelev unpacked his suitcase, took out Mummy's picture in a frame, got a hammer and nail from the kitchen and hung the picture up in Seryozha's room.

"Why bother with that," asked Mummy, "when the real me'll always be here with you?"

Korostelev took her hands, they drew closer—but then they looked at Seryozha and their hands dropped. Mummy went out of the room. Korostelev sat down on a chair.

"Well, so here we are, Seryozha. I've come to live with you. You've no objections, I hope?"

"Have you come for always?" asked Seryozha.

"Yes," said Korostelev, "for always."

"And will you give me the strap?"

Korostelev looked surprised. "Why should I give you the strap?"

"When I'm naughty," Seryozha explained.

"No," Korostelev answered. "I think using a strap that way's stupid."

"Yes, it *is* stupid," Seryozha agreed. "And it makes you cry."

"We'll manage to settle things man to man, without any strap, you and I."

"And what room are you going to sleep in?" asked Seryozha.

"It looks as if I'll sleep in this one," Korostelev answered. "Yes, that's what it looks like, kid. And on Sunday we'll go—you know where we'll go?—to the shop where they sell toys. And you shall choose whatever you like. How's that?"

"Ooh!?" said Seryozha. "I want a bicycle. Is it long to Sunday?"

"No, it's quite soon."

"How many days?"

"Tomorrow'll be Friday, then comes Saturday, and then Sunday."

"As long as that!" cried Seryozha.

They were three for supper — Seryozha, Mummy and Korostelev. (Aunt Pasha and Lukyanich had gone out somewhere.) Seryozha felt sleepy. Grey moths circled and circled round the lamp, bumped against it and fell down on the tablecloth with their wings fluttering, and that made him still sleepier. Suddenly he saw Korostelev carrying his bed away somewhere.

"Where are you taking my bed?" asked Seryozha. But Mummy said: "You're almost asleep. Come and wash your feet."

When Seryozha woke up in the morning he could not make out at first where he was. Why were there three windows instead of two, and on the wrong side of his bed? And with different curtains? Then he realised—this was Aunt Pasha's room. It was a very pretty room, there were flowers on the window-sills and a peacock's feather tucked in behind the mirror. Aunt Pasha and Lukyanich had gone already, their bed was made, with the pillows piled neatly one on top of the other. The early sunshine was playing hide-and-seek in the bushes by the open window. Seryozha climbed out of bed, took off his long night-shirt, put on his shorts and went into the dining-room. The door of *his* room was closed. He turned the handle, but it did not open. And he simply had to get in, all his toys were inside. That new spade was there with them, and he suddenly felt he wanted most awfully to dig. "Mummy!" Seryozha called out. "Mummy!" he called again.

The door remained shut. Everything was quiet.

"Mummy!" he yelled with all his lungs.

Aunt Pasha came running in, picked him up and carried him to the kitchen.

"What's this, what's this!" she whispered. "What d'you want to scream like that for? You mustn't do that, you're not little any more. Mummy's asleep, and let her sleep, why d'you want to wake her?"

"I want my spade," he said excitedly.

"You'll have it, it won't run away. Mummy'll get up and then you can take it," said Aunt Pasha. "Look, here's your catapult. You go and play with that for the present like a good boy. If you like I'll give you a carrot, you can clean it for yourself and eat it. But the first thing respectable people do is to get washed."

Kind, sensible talk always had its calming effect on Seryozha. He let her wash him and drank a mug of milk. Then he took his catapult and went outside. A sparrow was sitting on the fence the other side of the street. Seryozha sent a stone at it from his catapult without aiming properly and of course missed. He shot without aiming on purpose, because however much he aimed he always missed, for some reason. But if he aimed then Lida would tease him and now she'd no right to tease him because anyone could see he hadn't been trying, he'd simply wanted to send the stone somewhere, it didn't matter where.

Shurik was beside his own gate.

"Seryozha, come to the wood," he called.

"Oh, bother the wood!" said Seryozha.

He sat on the bench by the gate swinging his leg. He felt ruffled and upset again. Passing through the yard he had seen the shutters closed at his windows. He hadn't paid any attention at the moment. But now in occurred to him that the shutters were never closed in summer, only in winter when there was a hard frost. So his toys were locked in on all sides. And he wanted them so badly, he could have thrown himself down and howled. Of course he wouldn't throw himself down and howl, he was too big for that now, but being too big didn't make him feel any better about it. And Mummy and Korostelev didn't care a bit that he needed his spade this very minute.

As soon as they wake up, thought Seryozha, I'll take every single thing into Aunt Pasha's room. I mustn't forget that building block that rolled under the chest of drawers, it's still there.

Vaska and Zhenka came up and stood in front of Seryozha. Lida came, too, carrying little Victor. They all stood and looked at Seryozha. And he sat swinging his leg and said nothing at all.

"What's the matter with you?" asked Zhenka.

"His mother's got married," Vaska explained.

Another silence.

"Who's she married?" asked Zhenka.

"Korostelev, the director of the Bright Shore," said Vaska. "And didn't he get it in the neck at the last meeting!"

"What for?" asked Zhenka.

"Because he deserved it, I suppose," said Vaska and pulled a crumpled packet of cigarettes from his pocket.

"Give me a smoke," said Zhenka.

"I'm nearly out of 'em myself," said Vaska, but he gave one to Zhenka all the same, lighted his own and offered Zhenka the burning match. The tiny flame was transparent and invisible in the bright sunshine. You couldn't see what made the match twist and turn black, and smoke rise from the cigarette. The sun was shining on the side of the street where the children had gathered, while the other side was still in shadow, and the leaves of the nettles by the fences, washed by the dew, were wet and dark. And it was the same with the dust in the middle of the street—on the other side it was cool, on this side warm. There were two caterpillar tracks in the dust, someone had driven a tractor down the street.

"Seryozha's in the dumps," Lida told Shurik. "He's got a new father."

"Don't worry about that," Vaska said to Seryozha. "He looks all right. You'll just go on the way you always have, what's it matter to you?"

"He's going to get me a bicycle," Seryozha suddenly remembered last night's talk.

"Has he promised, or do you just think he will?" asked Vaska.

"He promised. We're going to the shop together. On Sunday. Tomorrow'll be Friday, then comes Saturday, and then Sunday."

"A bicycle or a tricycle?" asked Zhenka.

"Don't take a tricycle," Vaska advised him. "What good's that to you? You'll soon be big, what you need's a proper bicycle."

"He's just making it all up," said Lida. "He's not going to get a bicycle at all."

Shurik was pouting. "My Daddy's going to get me a bicycle, too. Next time he's paid he'll get me one."

THE FIRST MORNING WITH KOROSTELEV.
GOING VISITING

There was a rattle of iron in the garden. Seryozha looked in through the gate—Korostelev was outside, drawing the bolts and opening the shutters. He was in a stripped shirt and blue tie, his hair was wet and combed smooth. He opened the shutters, Mummy pushed the window open from inside and said something to Korostelev. He replied, resting his elbows on the window-sill. She reached out and took his head in her hands. They did not see the children watching them from the street.

Seryozha went into the yard.

"Korostelev! I want my spade!"

"Spade?" Korostelev repeated.

"And all my things," Seryozha added.

"Come in and get what you want," said Mummy.

There was a new smell in Mummy's room — tobacco and strange breath. And strange things lay here and there — clothes, a brush, and cigarette boxes on the table. Mummy was unplaiting her hair. When she loosed the long braids it fell like a lot of little chestnut snakes down below her waist. And then she brushed it till it poured down straight like rain in summer.

"Good morning, Seryozha," said Mummy from behind the chestnut snakes.

He did not answer, he was busy looking at the cigarette boxes. They were fascinatingly new and alike. He picked one up but it was pasted together and would not open.

"Put that down," said Mummy, who could see everything in the mirror. "I thought you came for your toys?"

The building block under the chest of drawers was right at the back. Seryozha could see it when he crouched down, but he could not reach it, it was too far away.

"What are you puffing and panting about?" asked Mummy.

"I can't get it," Seryozha answered.

Korostelev came in.

"Will you give me those boxes when they're empty?" asked Seryozha. (He knew grownups always give boxes to children when what's inside them is smoked or eaten.)

"Here's one to begin with," said Korostelev. He tipped the cigarettes out of their box and gave it to Seryozha.

"Would you help him?" asked Mummy. "There's something of his behind the drawers."

Korostelev took hold of the chest of drawers with his big hands—the old chest creaked and moved forward, and Seryozha got his block without any difficulty at all.

"Ooh!" he said, looking admiringly up at Korostelev.

Out he went, hugging his box, his block and as many other toys as he could hold. He took them all into Aunt Pasha's room and dumped them on the floor between his bed and the cupboard.

"You've forgotten your spade," Mummy called after him. "You were in such a hurry for it and now you've left it behind."

Seryozha took his spade in silence and went out into the garden. Somehow, he didn't want to dig any more, it had just occurred to him he'd like to put his collection of coloured wrappers from sweets in the new box, but he had to dig just a little, at least, after Mummy said that.

Under the apple-tree the soil was loose and easy. He tried to drive his spade a long way down—to the top of the blade. He worked really hard, panting with the effort, the muscles tensing on his arms and on his bare, narrow back, golden with sunburn. Korostelev stood smoking on the veranda, watching him.

Lida came up carrying Victor.

"Let's plant some flowers," she said. "It'll look pretty."

She seated Victor on the ground with his back against the apple-tree so he would not fall. But all the same he slumped down sideways.

"Sit up, can't you!" Lida cried, giving him a shake and setting him more firmly. "You little silly! Other babies can sit by themselves at your age!"

She said it all very loudly so that Korostelev should hear it on the veranda and understand how sensible and grownup she was. With side glances at him, she brought some marigolds and pushed them in the ground where Seryozha had dug it up.

"Now then, see how nice that is," she said.

Then she brought some red and white stones from the gutter and arranged them round the marigolds. She smoothed out the ground with her fingers and patted it with her palms, so that her hands became quite black.

"Now, isn't it pretty?" she asked. "Only tell the truth, don't just say it."

"Yes," Seryozha admitted, "it's very pretty."

"There, you see," Lida triumphed. "You can't do a single thing without me!"

At that moment Victor fell down again, this time on his back.

"All right, lie there, if that's all you can do," said Lida.

Victor did not cry, he simply sucked his thumb and gazed with a look of surprise at the leaves stirring overhead. Lida unwound the rope from her waist where it had been serving as a belt and started skipping in front of the veranda, counting loudly: "One, two, three...." Korostelev laughed and went inside.

"Look," said Seryozha, "there are ants running over him."

"Ugh, you little silly!" cried Lida, irritated; she picked Victor up and started clearing the ants off him, smearing dirt over his frock and his bare legs in the process.

"They wash him and wash him all the time," said Lida, "and he's dirty just the same."

Then Mummy called from the veranda.

"Seryozha! Come and change, we're going visiting."

Seryozha ran in eagerly—you don't go visiting every day! And visiting was lovely; people gave you sweets and showed you all sorts of toys.

"We're going to Granny Nastya," Mummy told him, although he had not even asked. What did it matter where they were going, if only they went visiting?

Granny Nastya was stern and serious. She always wore a white dotted kerchief on her head, tied beneath her chin. She had a medal which she sometimes wore, and it had a picture of Lenin on it. And she always carried a black bag that fastened with a zipper. She would open the bag and give Seryozha something good to eat. But he had never been to visit her.

They all put on their best clothes—he, and Mummy, and Korostelev, and then set off. Korostelev and Mummy took his hands, but he soon tore himself away, it was much more fun walking by himself. He could stop and look through cracks in fences into yards with terrible dogs on chains and geese waddling about. Or he could run on ahead and back again. He could be a puffing engine. He could pull acacia pods and whistle through them. He could pick up a golden copeck someone had lost. But when people held his hands, then they just got hot and sticky and there was no fun at all.

They came to a little house with two little windows facing the street. The yard was little, too, and so was the room. They went into the room through a kitchen with a huge brick stove in it, the old-fashioned Russian stove. Granny Nastya came out to meet them.

"All my very best wishes," she said.

So it must be a holiday. Seryozha answered as Aunt Pasha always did: "And the same to you."

He looked round about. There were no toys, not even the little figures people stand here and there for ornaments, only dull things for eating and sleeping.

"Have you any toys?" Seryozha asked. (Perhaps they were put away somewhere.)

"I'm afraid I haven't," answered Granny Nastya. "I've no children here, so I've no toys either. Here's a sweet for you."

A blue glass bowl of sweets stood in the middle of the table among the plates of cakes and buns. Everybody drew up chairs and sat down. Korostelev pulled the cork from a bottle and poured dark-red wine into little glasses.

"None for Seryozha," said Mummy.

It was always like that. They drank themselves, but they wouldn't give him any. As soon as it was something extra good, he mustn't have it.

But Korostelev said: "I'll just give him a drop. So he can drink to us, too."

He poured out a tiny glassful, and Seryozha felt it was going to be all right with Korostelev.

Then they all clinked glasses, and Seryozha clinked glasses as well.

There was another Granny with them. But they told Seryozha she wasn't just a Granny, she was a Great-Granny, and that's what he must call her. Though Korostelev called her just "Granny" without any "Great" at all. Seryozha didn't like her a bit.

She said: "He'll spill it on the cloth."

He actually did spill a drop of wine when they clinked glasses.

Then she said: "There, you see," and sprinkled salt from the salt-cellar on the wet spot, breathing heavily, which sounded very cross. And after that she watched Seryozha all the time. She wore glasses. And she was most awfully old. Her hands were brown and wrinkled and knotted; she had a big nose that turned down and a bony chin that turned up.

The wine was sweet and very nice and he drank it at a gulp. They gave him a bun, he began to eat it and made some crumbs.

Great-Granny said: "Don't you know how to eat properly?"

He felt uncomfortable on his chair and wriggled.

Great-Granny said: "Don't you know how to sit properly?"

Then he felt all hot in the middle and wanted to sing. So he did sing.

Great-Granny said: "Don't you know how to behave?"

But Korostelev took Seryozha's part. "Let him alone. Give the boy a bit of peace."

Great-Granny said ominously: "You wait a bit, he'll show you something yet!"

She had drunk wine, too, and her eyes sparkled frighteningly behind her glasses. But Seryozha shouted boldly: "Go away! I'm not afraid of you!"

"Oh, how awful!" said Mummy. "Rubbish," said Korostelev. "It'll pass over in a minute. He only had a drop."

"I want some more!" cried Seryozha, holding out his glass and overturning the empty bottle. There was a crash of dishes. Mummy gasped. Great-Granny brought her fist down on the table with a bang and cried: "There you are, fine goings-on!"

But Seryozha felt he wanted to rock. So he started rocking from side to side. And the table with the buns rocked in front of him, and so did Mummy, and Korostelev, and Granny Nastya, they were talking and rocking as if they were all in rocking-chairs, it was awfully funny and Seryozha had to laugh. Suddenly he heard someone singing. It was Great-Granny. She held her eye-glasses in her knotted hand and waved them from side to side and sang about Katyusha who went down to the shore. And while Great-Granny was singing Seryozha fell asleep, his head on a piece of bun.

When he woke up Great-Granny was not there, and the others were drinking tea. They smiled at Seryozha.

"Well, feel all right now?" asked Mummy. "You won't brawl any more?"

Was I brawling, thought Seryozha.

Mummy took a comb out of her bag and combed his hair. And Granny Nastya said: "Here's a sweet for you."

In the next room, behind a faded coloured curtain, someone was snoring — Hrrr! Hrrr! Seryozha cautiously pushed the curtain aside, peeped in and saw Great-Granny asleep on the bed. He walked sedately away from the curtain.

"Let's go home," he said. "I'm tired of visiting."

When they were saying goodbye he heard Korostelev call Granny Nastya "Mother". Seryozha had never known Korostelev had a mother, he had thought he and Granny Nastya just happened to know each other.

Seryozha found the way back very long and very dull. Korostelev ought to carry me now, he's my Daddy, he thought. He had seen other fathers carrying their sons on their shoulders. The sons looked very proud of themselves, and they must be able to see a long, long way all round. So Seryozha said: "I'm tired."

"It's not much further now," said Mummy. "You can manage it."

But Seryozha ran in front of Korostelev and clutched his knees.

"A big boy like you asking to be carried," said Mummy, "you ought to be ashamed!" But Korostelev picked Seryozha up and settled him on his shoulders.

Seryozha felt awfully high up. But he wasn't a scrap afraid, because a giant who'd moved a whole chest of drawers like that couldn't possibly drop him. And he could see over the fences, he could see everything happening in the yards and even on the roofs. It was wonderful! This interesting view of things kept Seryozha absorbed all the way home. Proudly he looked down on other boys who had to walk on their own feet. And it was with a feeling of a new, wonderful superiority that he finally arrived home—on his father's shoulders, as a son should.

BUYING A BICYCLE

On those same shoulders he set out on Sunday to buy the bicycle.

All of a sudden Sunday was there, much sooner than he

had expected, and when he knew it had come, Seryozha was
wild with excitement.

"You haven't forgotten, have you?" he asked Korostelev.

"Of course not, I'd never forget an important thing like
that," Korostelev answered. "We'll go as soon as I've
finished one or two things I have to do."

But that was just a story, about having things to do. He had
no things to do at all, he only sat and talked to Mummy. It
was stupid talk, and dull, but they seemed to like it because
they went on and on. Mummy especially, and she'd keep on
saying the same word over and over again for some reason.
And Korostelev got it from her. Seryozha hovered round
them, too excited to say anything, filled with one single
thought, waiting and waiting for them to get tired of their talk
and stop.

"You understand everything," said Mummy. "It makes
me so happy that you understand everything."

"To tell the truth," Korostelev answered, "I didn't
understand very much about things like that till I met you.
There was a lot I didn't understand, and I only started to
understand when—well, you understand."

Then they took hands as if they were going to play Oranges
and Lemons.

"I was just a girl," said Mummy. "I thought I was madly
happy. And then I thought I'd die of grief. And now it all
seems like a dream."

She'd got a new word now and kept on and on with it,
covering her face with Korostelev's big hands.

"I just dreamed it, you understand? Like a dream you have
when you're asleep. It was all a dream. I was dreaming. And
now I'm awake and there's—you."

Korostelev interrupted her.

"I love you."

But Mummy didn't believe him.

"Really and truly?"

"I love you," Korostelev insisted. But still she didn't
believe him.

"You really love me?"

Seryozha thought: Why doesn't he say "word of honour"
or "cross my throat and die", then she'd believe him.

Korostelev seemed to have got tired of answering, he said
nothing and just looked at Mummy. And she looked at
him. They went on and on looking at each other maybe for a
whole hour. Then Mummy said: "I love you." Like that game
where they all say the same thing one after the other.

When will they stop? thought Seryozha.

Yet short as his life experience was he knew he should not pester the grownups when they were taken up with their own talk. That was something they just couldn't stand. They might get really angry and then who knows what they'd do. He could only try to remind them of himself by staying around and sighing noisily now and then.

But the end of his torment came at last.

"I'll have to go out for an hour or so, Maryasha," said Korostelev, "Seryozha and I have something important to do."

He had long legs, Seryozha had hardly time to look round before they were there on the square where the shop stood that sold toys. Here Korostelev set Seryozha down and they went over to the shop.

A doll with round cheeks smiled in the window, her feet in real leather shoes spread wide apart. A family of blue bears sat on a red drum. A bugle gleamed golden. Seryozha was breathless with anticipation. Music came from inside the shop. A man was sitting on a chair holding an accordion. But he wasn't playing it, only pulling it out now and then, so that it gave a mournful wail and then stopped again. The gay music came from somewhere else, from the counter. Some men in Sunday suits and ties were standing listening to it. Behind the counter stood an old shop assistant.

"What do you want to see?" he asked Korostelev.

"A child's bicycle."

The old man leaned over the counter and looked at Seryozha.

"A tricycle?" he asked.

"No, no, not a tricycle!" cried Seryozha, his voice trembling with anguish.

"Varya!" the old man shouted.

Nobody came, but the old man seemed to forget all about Seryozha, he went over to the men and did something or other. The gay music stopped at once and something slow and sad started instead. To Seryozha's alarm, Korostelev, too, seemed to forget all about why they had come, he went over to the men and they all stood without moving, staring in front of them, never thinking of Seryozha and his palpitating expectation. Seryozha couldn't stand it, he pulled Korostelev's jacket. Korostelev seemed to wake up, he sighed and said: "That's a grand record."

"Will he give us the bicycle?" Seryozha asked loudly.

"Varya!" the old man shouted again.

Evidently it all depended on Varya whether Seryozha would get his bicycle or not. And at last Varya appeared through a low door between the shelves behind the counter. She had a bread-ring in her hand and she was chewing. The old man told her to bring a bicycle from the store-room. "For this young man," he said. Seryozha liked being called that.

The store-room must have been at the other end of the world because it took Varya an age to come back. That man with the accordion had time to buy it, and Korostelev bought a gramophone. That was a sort of box, you put a black plate on it, then the plate turned round and round and played—gay music or sad music or whatever you wanted. It was this box which had been playing on the counter. And Korostelev bought a lot of those plates in paper envelopes as well, and two little boxes of something he called needles.

"That's for Mummy," he told Seryozha. "We'll take her a present."

All the men watched the old man wrap the things up. And then Varya came back from the end of the world, bringing a bicycle. A real bicycle with spokes and a bell and handle-bars and pedals and a leather saddle and a tiny red lamp! And it even had a number at the back, four figures on a yellow tin plate!

"You've got something worth having here," said the old man. "Turn the front wheel. Ring the bell. Press on the pedals. Go on, press hard, what's the use of just looking at them? Well? Aye, that's a really good article, not just any sort. You'll thank me for it every day of your life."

Korostelev conscientiously tested the steering, rang the bell and pressed on the pedals, while Seryozha watched in something like terror, mouth open, breathing in little short gasps, hardly daring to believe all this glory was going to be his.

He rode home on his bicycle. That is to say, he sat on the leather saddle, sensing its pleasantly springy feel, holding the bars with uncertain hands and trying to get his feet on the rebellious, elusive pedals. Korostelev, bent nearly double, pushed the bicycle and kept it from falling. Red and panting, he brought Seryozha as far as the gate and leaned him and his bicycle against the bench.

"Now, try by yourself," he said. "I'm just about steaming."

He went into the house. Then Zhenka, Lida and Shurik came up to Seryozha.

"I've learned a little already," Seryozha told them. "Get out of the way or I'll run over you!"

He tried to ride away from the bench and fell off.

"Oh!" he cried, getting out from under the machine and laughing to show it was all nothing much. "I turned the bars the wrong way. And it's awfully difficult to find the pedals, too."

"Take off your shoes," Zhenka advised. "It's much better barefoot. You can grip the pedals with your toes. Here, let me try. Hold it still a minute." He got up on the saddle. "Hold it firmer."

But though all three held him, he fell off as well, together with Seryozha who had been holding him more enthusiastically than any.

"Me now!" said Lida. "No, me!" cried Shurik.

"The dust's too thick here," said Zhenka, "you'll never learn on that. Come to Vaska's Lane."

That was what they called a short blind alley that ran behind Vaska's garden. On the opposite side was a timber-yard with a high fence. Short, soft, curly grass covered it; it was a wonderful place to play, with no grownups round to interfere. And although its blind end came up to Timokhin's fence and two mothers—Vaska's and Shurik's—both threw slops over the fences on the grass, still nobody ever disputed that the really important person there was Vaska; and so it was called Vaska's Lane.

That was where Zhenka wheeled the bicycle. Lida and Shurik helped him, arguing about who would learn to ride first, while Seryozha ran behind, trying to catch the wheel.

Zhenka announced he would be first because he was the oldest. Then came Lida, and after Lida—Shurik. Then they let Seryozha try but very soon Zhenka said: "That's enough! It's my turn now!"

Seryozha wanted terribly to go on, he clung on to the bicycle with hands and feet. "I want to ride some more! It's my bicycle!"

But of course Shurik turned on him at once.

"Ugh—stingy!"

And Lida added in a nasty jeering voice: "Stingy-mingy!"

To be stingy-mingy was an awful disgrace. Seryozha got down without another word and moved away. He went to Timokhin's fence, turned his back on the children and cried. He cried because it wasn't fair, because he couldn't stand up for himself, because there was nothing in all the world he

wanted but that bicycle and they were just great big bullies
and didn't unterstand it.

They paid no attention to him. He could hear their loud
squabbles and the metallic clang of the falling bicycle.
Nobody called him, nobody said: "Your turn now." They
were riding the third time already! And he stood there crying.
Then suddenly Vaska appeared on the other side of the
fence.

He was stripped to the waist, in trousers a size too
long—to allow for growth—kept up by a tight belt, and a cap
with the peak behind—strong and wonderful. He looked over
the fence and took in the situation at once.

"Hey!" he shouted. "What d'you think you're doing?
Whose bicycle is it—yours or his? Come on, Seryozha!"

He vaulted over the fence and took the handle-bars with a
commanding grasp. Zhenka, Lida and Shurik fell back
respectfully. Seryozha came up, wiping his tears away with
his arm. Lida tried squeaking: "You're both stingies!"

"And you're a greedy guts," Vaska answered. He called
her some other names, too. "Couldn't wait to let the little one
learn." Then he said to Seryozha: "Get on."

Seryozha got on, and rode a long time, and all the children
helped him, except Lida; she sat on the grass making a
dandelion wreath and pretending she enjoyed that much
better than riding a bicycle.

Then Vaska said: "Now I'll try," and Seryozha made way
for him willingly, he would have done anything in the world
for Vaska. Then Seryozha rode alone, without anyone
helping him, and he didn't fall very often, but the bicycle
kept wobbling every way and somehow or other he got his
foot in the wheel and four spokes came out. But it didn't
matter, the bicycle would still go just the same. Then
Seryozha began to be sorry for the other children.

"Let them ride, too," he said. "We'll take turns."

A little later Aunt Pasha came out into the garden and
heard Seryozha crying. She opened the gate and saw a
procession advancing in single file. First came Seryozha
carrying the handle-bars. Vaska carried the frame, Zhenka
the two wheels, one on each shoulder. Lida the bell and
Shurik trotted at the tail with a bundle of spokes.

"Great heavens!" gasped Aunt Pasha.

"He did this himself," said Shurik in a deep bass. "He got
his foot in the wheel."

Korostelev came out and stared.

"Made a thorough job of it," he observed.

Seryozha cried bitterly.

"Cheer up, we'll get it mended," said Korostelev. "We'll take it to the workshop, they'll make it as good as new."

But Seryozha only hung his head and went to cry in Aunt Pasha's room. Korostelev was just saying it to comfort him. How could anyone ever put all those pieces together so as to have that beautiful gleaming bicycle again, just as it had been? To ride on and ring the bell, with spokes that sparkled in the sunshine? No, it was impossible, quite impossible! It was gone, gone for ever!

Seryozha mourned all day, he found no joy even in the gramophone which Korostelev started going specially for him. The box with its plates made merry music for the whole street to hear; Seryozha heard it, too, but paid no attention, he was deep in despondency and there was no gleam of brightness in life.

But what do you think? They really did mend the bicycle. Korostelev hadn't been making it all up after all! The mechanic at the Bright Shore Farm mended it. Only the bigger children mustn't ride it, the mechanic said, or it would break again. Vaska and Zhenka heeded, and after that only Seryozha and Shurik rode it, and Lida when there were no grownups about; but Lida was thin and not so very heavy, let her ride.

Seryozha learned to ride splendidly, he even learned to freewheel down a hill with his arms folded, as he had seen a trick cyclist do. But for some reason he no longer felt that wonderful joy of possession, the breath-taking delight of those first blissful hours.

And then he got tired of the bicycle. It stood there in the kitchen with its red lamp and silver bell, handsome, all in order, but Seryozha went about his various affairs on foot, indifferent to its splendour. He was tired of it, that was all, and there was nothing you could do about it.

THE DIFFERENCE
BETWEEN KOROSTELEV AND THE REST

What a lot of unnecessary words grownups used! For instance, Seryozha happened to upset his tea. And Aunt Pasha said: "What a careless boy you are! I can never wash tablecloths fast enough for you! You're not a baby now!"

All those words were unnecessary, in Seryozha's opinion. In the first place he had heard them a hundred times already.

And besides, he knew himself that he oughtn't to spill his tea, as soon as it was spilled he knew at once he'd done wrong and felt bad about it. He was so ashamed he only wanted her to take the wet cloth away as quickly as possible, before anyone saw it. But she kept on talking and talking.

"You never seem to think that somebody washed that cloth and starched it and ironed it, and that it's all work for somebody."

"I didn't mean to do it," Seryozha explained. "The cup sort of slipped from my fingers."

"The cloth's old," Aunt Pasha went on implacably, "I mended and mended it, a whole evening I sat over it, look at all the work I did."

Just as though you could spill all you wanted on a new tablecloth.

And Aunt Pasha would end indignantly: "Didn't mean to do it—I should think not, indeed! A pretty thing it would be, if you did it on purpose!"

It was the same thing when Seryozha broke anything. But when they broke glasses or plates themselves, that was quite all right.

And then there was the way Mummy always made him say "please", when the word didn't even mean anything.

"It means you're asking politely," said Mummy. "If you ask me for a pencil, you must say 'please' to show it's a request."

"Why, didn't you understand I was asking for a pencil?" asked Seryozha.

"Yes, I understood, but without 'please' it's not polite, it's not the way well brought-up little boys talk. What does it sound like—'Give me a pencil!' It's quite different if you say: 'Give me a pencil, please,' that's polite, and I'm glad to give it to you."

"And if I don't say 'please' will you be sorry to give it to me?"

"I shan't give it to you at all," said Mummy.

All right, "please", Seryozha would give them their "please". Their ideas might be queer, but they were strong, they ruled children, they could give Seryozha a pencil or not give it to him, just as they liked.

Korostelev, now, he didn't bother about little things, never even noticed whether Seryozha said "please" or not.

And if Seryozha was busy in his own corner and did not want to be disturbed, Korostelev never interrupted his play, never said stupid things like "come here, let me kiss you", as

Lukyanich did when he came home from work. Lukyanich would kiss Seryozha, pricking him with his rough beard, and then give him a chocolate or an apple. That was very nice, of course, but why did he have to interrupt a person's play which was much more important than the apple? Seryozha could have eaten the apple afterwards.

All sorts of people came to the house, usually to see Korostelev. The one who came the most often was Uncle Tolya. He was young and handsome with long black eyelashes and white teeth and a shy smile. Seryozha looked at him with fascinated respect, because Uncle Tolya could make up poetry. When they asked him to read his latest verses he would look uncomfortable at first and refuse, then he would get up, go away to the side and recite them. He'd made up poems about all sorts of things—about war and about peace, about the collective farm, about the fascists, about spring, and about some woman with blue eyes whom he waited and waited for but all the same she didn't come. Wonderful poems! Just as smooth and musical as the ones in books. Before he began to recite Uncle Tolya would cough and push his black hair back, then he would recite in a loud voice, looking up at the ceiling. Everybody would praise him and Mummy would pour out tea for him. Then while they were having tea they would talk about sick cows—Uncle Tolya was the cows' doctor at the Bright Shore Farm.

But it wasn't everybody who was so interesting and so nice. There was Uncle Pyotr, for instance—Seryozha tried to keep out of his way. He had a nasty face and a smooth pink bare head like a celluloid ball. And he had a nasty kind of laugh too—"He-he-he!" One time when he was sitting with Mummy on the veranda—Korostelev was not there—Uncle Pyotr called Seryozha and gave him a chocolate—a wonderful big chocolate in paper. Seryozha politely said: "Thank you," opened the paper and found there was nothing inside. It was empty. Seryozha felt ashamed—of himself for having believed in it, and of Uncle Pyotr for having deceived him like that. And Seryozha could see Mummy felt ashamed, she had believed it, too.

"He-he-he-he!" sniggered Uncle Pyotr.

Then Seryozha said without anger, regretfully: "Uncle Pyotr, you're a fool."

He was sure Mummy thought the same. But she cried: "What do you mean by that! Beg Uncle Pyotr's pardon this very minute!"

Seryozha stared at her in surprise.

"You heard what I said?" asked Mummy.

He did not answer. Then she took his hand and led him into the house.

"Don't you dare come near me," she said. "I don't want to talk to such a rude boy."

She stood a moment, waiting for him to say he was sorry, to ask her to forgive him. But he pressed his lips together and looked away with eyes turned sad and cold. He did not feel he had done wrong. Why should he beg pardon? He had simply said what he thought.

She went away. He trailed into his room and began turning over his toys, unconsciously trying to forget what had happened. His fingers trembled. As he turned over the figures cut out of old playing-cards, he tore the head off a lady in black. Why had Mummy stood up for that silly Uncle Pyotr? There she was, talking and laughing with him; but she didn't want to talk to Seryozha.

In the evening he heard her telling Korostelev all about it.

"Well, he was right," said Korostelev. "That's what I call fair criticism."

"But how can you let a child criticise adults?" Mummy objected. "If children start criticising us, how can we educate them? A child must respect adults."

"But what on earth should he respect that ass for?" said Korostelev.

"He has to respect him. It never ought even to enter his head that an adult can be an ass. Let him wait till he's grownup to Pyotr Ilyich's age, then he can criticise him."

"To my mind," said Korostelev, "if it's a question of sense, he's grown well beyond Pyotr already. And no pedagogical rules on earth say you must punish a kid for calling a fool a fool."

About criticism and pedagogical rules Seryozha didn't understand much, but that remark about a fool he understood splendidly, and felt very grateful to Korostelev.

In general, Korostelev was grand, it was queer to think there had been a time when he had not lived with Seryozha, when he had lived with Granny Nastya and Great-Granny, and only came now and then to visit them.

He took Seryozha down to the river to bathe, and taught him to swim. Mummy was afraid Seryozha would drown, but Korostelev laughed at her. He took the rails off the sides of Seryozha's bed. Mummy was afraid Seryozha would fall out of bed and hurt himself, but Korostelev would hear nothing of it.

"What if he has to go on a long train journey? And sleep on the top berth? Let him learn to sleep like a grownup."

So now Seryozha did not have to climb over the rail in the morning and evening. He undressed sitting on the edge of his bed. And slept like a grownup.

Once, they told him, he did fall out of bed. It was in the middle of the night, they heard him fall and put him back into bed again. In the morning they told him what had happened. But he couldn't remember it and he wasn't hurt anywhere. And if he wasn't hurt and didn't even remember it, then it didn't count.

Then there was that time he fell down in the yard, scraped the skin off his knee so it bled hard, and came home crying. Aunt Pasha exclaimed and ran for a bandage. But Korostelev said: "Cheer up, Sonny. You'll be all right in a minute. What if you're soldier and get wounded some time, what'll you do then?"

"When you were wounded, didn't you cry?" asked Seryozha.

"Why, how could I, all my pals would have laughed at me. We're men, that's our part in life."

Seryozha stopped crying and said: "Ha, ha, ha!" to show his manliness. And when Aunt Pasha came with the bandage, he said recklessly: "Go on, bandage it up, it doesn't hurt a bit."

Korostelev told him about the war. And after that, Seryozha felt proud as he sat beside Korostelev at the table. If there was a war, who would go and fight? Why, he and Korostelev! That was their part in life. And Mummy and Aunt Pasha and Lukyanich would stop here and wait till the war was won, that was their part in life.

ZHENKA

Zhenka was an orphan, he lived with his aunt. The aunt had a daughter; during the day that daughter went to work and in the evening she ironed. She was always ironing her frocks. She would fuss about in the yard with a big charcoal iron. She'd blow on it and spit on it and put the samovar pipe over it to make it burn hotter. And she'd have her hair twisted round bits of metal so it looked as if her head was covered with little sausages.

When she'd finished ironing her frock she'd put it on and let down her hair and prink a bit and then go to the club to

dance. And the next evening she'd start fussing about with
the iron all over again.

The aunt worked, too. She complained that she was both
cleaner and messenger, but they only paid her as cleaner, and
the rules said there ought to be a paid messenger. She would
stand a long time with her buckets by the water tap at the
corner telling the other women how she'd put the manager in
his place and what she'd written in the complaint she'd sent
in.

Zhenka's aunt was always cross with him because he ate a
lot and didn't do anything to help in the house.

But he didn't want to do anything. He got up in
the morning, ate what was left out for him and then went to
join the other boys.

He would spend the whole day in the street or with
neighbours. Aunt Pasha always gave him something to eat
when he came. A little while before his aunt came back from
work, Zhenka would go home and sit down to his lessons. He
had a lot of holiday tasks because he was behind. He had
stopped a second year in the second form and in the third and
he would be a second year in the fourth, too. When Zhenka
first went to school Vaska had been quite little, but now
Vaska had caught up with him, although Vaska, too, had
stopped a second year in the third form.

And Vaska was even taller than Zhenka now, and stronger,
too.

At first the teachers used to worry about Zhenka, they
would send for his aunt or go to see her. But she would say:
"My bad luck wished him on to me, do as you like with him,
he's eaten me out of house and home already if you want to
know."

Then she would complain to the women: "They tell me to
give him a special corner for himself, to do his lessons. It's
not a corner he wants, it's the stick, laid on well, only I'm
sorry for him because he's my dead sister's."

Then the teachers stopped coming. And they even praised
Zhenka—a very orderly, well-behaved boy, they said; others
might talk during lessons, but he always sat quietly; only it
was a pity he was absent so often and didn't know anything.

They gave Zhenka top marks for conduct, and for singing,
too. But for everything else his marks were as bad as they
could be.

In front of his aunt Zhenka pretended to work at his
lessons so she wouldn't scold him so much. When she came
home he would be sitting at the kitchen-table with its load of

dirty dishes and greasy rags, writing down figures, doing his arithmetic.

"You lazy brat," she would start, "I see you haven't brought the water again, and not got the lamp oil either. Not done a thing. How long have I got to stand your good-for-naught ways?"

"I've been doing my lessons," said Zhenka.

His aunt would go on scolding, he would sigh reproachfully, put down his pen and pick up the oil can.

"What are you doing, making a mock of me?" his aunt would scream in a frenzy. "The shop's shut now, and well you know it, you devil's brat!"

"All right, it's shut," Zhenka would agree. "What are you yelling about, then?"

"Go and chop the wood!" she would scream with such fury it sounded as though her throat would burst. "Get out, and don't come back without the wood!"

She would snatch up the buckets from the bench and go off screaming to get the water, while Zhenka went unhurriedly to the shed to chop the wood.

Zhenka was not really lazy. Not at all. If Aunt Pasha asked him to do something, or one of the children, he would do it at once. And if people praised him he tried his very best to do it well. One time he and Vaska together chopped and stacked a whole cubic metre of wood, a huge pile.

He wasn't stupid, either, whatever they said. When Seryozha was given a meccano set, Zhenka and Shurik made such a railway signal that the boys came all the way from Kalinin Street to look at it. It had red and green lights. Shurik helped a good bit, of course—he knew a lot about machines, because his father was the lorry-driver Timokhin, but it wasn't Shurik who thought of taking coloured lamps from Seryozha's New Year Tree decorations and putting them on the signal, that was Zhenka's idea.

Zhenka made little men and animals out of Seryozha's plasticine—not at all bad, really, quite life-like. Seryozha's mother saw them and bought him a box of plasticine for himself. But his aunt scolded, said she wouldn't let him waste his time on such rubbish, and threw the plasticine away.

Zhenka learned to smoke from Vaska. He had no money to buy cigarettes, so he smoked Vaska's, and if he saw a cigarette end lying in the street he picked it up and smoked it. Seryozha was sorry for him, so he, too, picked up any ends he saw lying around and gave them to Zhenka.

Zhenka never put on airs with the little ones as Vaska did, he was ready to play with them any time, at anything they liked, soldiers or militiamen or lotto. But because he was the oldest he always wanted to be the general or the chief of militia. And when they played lotto and he won, he was glad; but if he lost he sulked.

He had a kind face with a big mouth, and big ears that stood out, and tails of hair down his neck because his hair wasn't cut very often.

One day Vaska and Zhenka went to the little wood and took Seryozha with them. There they made a fire to bake potatoes. They had brought the potatoes, some salt and some spring onions. The fire burned badly, with a lot of acrid smoke.

Vaska said to Zhenka: "Let's talk about what you're going to do."

Zhenka sat hugging his knees; his narrow trousers had slipped up showing his thin legs. He gazed without blinking at the dense column of grey and yellow smoke rising from the fire.

"You've got to finish school, whether you like it or not," Vaska continued; you would have thought from his tone that he had top marks in everything and was at least five forms higher than Zhenka. "What good will you be to anyone without an education?"

"That's sure," Zhenka agreed. "I'm no good to anyone if I haven't got that."

He picked up a stick and stirred the fire to make it burn more brightly. The damp twigs hissed, the sap oozed out and they caught fire slowly. Birch, aspen and alder-trees grew thickly round the glade where the boys were sitting. In their games this thicket was always the primeval forest. In the spring there were a lot of lilies-of-the-valley, and in the summer a lot of mosquitoes. Now most of the mosquitoes had retreated before the smoke, but a few of the bolder ones penetrated through it and bit, and then the boys loudly slapped their legs and faces.

"Put your aunt in her place, that's all," Vaska advised.

"Just you try it," Zhenka said. "Try putting her in her place!"

"Take no notice of her, then."

"I don't. But I'm sick of her. You know yourself, she's always at me."

"And Lucy—what about her, is she all right?"

"Yes, she's all right. She's going to get herself married."

"Who'll she marry!"

"Oh, somebody or other. She's got an idea she'll marry an officer, but there aren't any here. Maybe she'll go away somewhere where there are officers."

The fire burned up, it conquered the damp and caught a pile of twigs and leaves, mischievously putting out flaming tongues. Something snapped like a shot. The smoke had all gone.

"Go and get some dry twigs to put on," Vaska told Seryozha.

Seryozha ran off to do as Vaska said. When he came back Zhenka was talking, while Vaska listened with serious attention.

"I'll live like a lord," said Zhenka. "Just think— come back to the hostel in the evening, there's your bed waiting, and a night table beside it. You can lie there and listen to the radio, or play draughts, and nobody yells at you. Lecturers come, and entertainers. And they give you supper at eight o'clock."

"Yes," said Vaska, "it sounds fine. But will they take you?"

"I'll send an application. Why shouldn't they take me? They will, for sure."

"How old are you?"

"I was fourteen last week."

"Your aunt's not against it?"

"No, she's nothing against it, only she's afraid if I go away I won't help her later on."

"Oh, to hell with her," said Vaska and added a few more expressive words.

"I'll go away anyway, I guess," said Zhenka.

"What you've got to do is make up you mind what you're going to do, and do it," said Vaska. "You keep saying you guess, but the school year'll start soon and then it'll be the same thing all over again."

"Yes, I guess I'll make up my mind and do it," said Zhenka. "You know, Vaska, I often think about it. And when I remember that it'll soon be September—ugh, I get real down."

"I don't wonder," said Vaska.

They talked about Zhenka's plans until the potatoes were baked through. Then they ate them, burning their fingers, their teeth crunching the juicy stems of the onions, and lay down to sleep. The sun began to sink, the trunks of the birches turned pink, and shadows spread over the little glade where invisible sparks still lay concealed beneath grey

ash in the middle. The boys had told Seryozha to drive away
the mosquitoes, so he sat conscientiously waving a twig over
them as they slept, thinking as he did so: why should Zhenka
give money to this aunt when he's working? Why, all she
does is scream at him! That wouldn't be fair. But soon he,
too, fell asleep, snuggled in between Vaska and Zhenka. He
dreamed of officers and of Luska, Zhenka's cousin, with
them.

Zhenka was not particularly resolute by nature, he would
sooner daydream than act, but September was near, repairs
and decorating work were finished at the school and the
children were already going there to get their textbooks and
exercise books. Lida was boasting about her new uniform.
The new school year with all its troubles was just round the
corner, and Zhenka made up his mind. If the vocational
school would not take him, then perhaps a factory school
would, he said. Anyway, he was going.

Most people thought he was right and tried to help him.
The school gave him a recommendation, and Korostelev and
Mummy gave him some money, and even his aunt baked
buns for the journey.

The morning he left, his aunt said goodbye to him without
screaming, and asked him not to forget all she had done for
him. He said: "All right, Auntie," and even added "Thank
you." After that she went to the office where she worked,
and he started preparing for the journey.

His aunt had given him a wooden suitcase painted green.
She had hesitated over it for a long time, she didn't want to
part with it, but all the same she gave it him in the end,
though she said: "It's like cutting off my hand." In that
suitcase Zhenka put his shirt, a pair of socks all holes, a worn
towel and the buns. The children watched him pack.
Seryozha with a sudden start rushed off and came back
holding the railway signal with the green and red lamps.
Everyone had liked it so much; it had not been taken apart; it
had stood on the table and been shown to visitors.

"Take it with you," he told Zhenka. "Take it, I don't want
it, it just stands there."

"What'll I do with that?" said Zhenka, looking at the
signal. "I'll have fifteen kilograms to carry as it is."

Seryozha rushed away again and came back with a box.

"Take this, then," he said excitedly. You'll be able to make
things there. It's quite light."

Zhenka took the box and opened it. It held pieces of
plasticine. Zhenka looked pleased.

"All right," he said, "I'll take it." He put the box in his suitcase.

Timokhin had promised to take Zhenka to the station. It was thirty kilometres away, there was no railway line to the town yet. But just the evening before, Timokhin's lorry had gone on strike; there was something wrong with the engine, Shurik said, it was being repaired, and Timokhin was asleep.

"It doesn't matter," said Vaska. "You can get a lift."

"You could go on the bus," said Seryozha.

"Clever, aren't you," Shurik objected. "He'd have to pay for the bus."

"I'll go to the road and get a lift," said Zhenka. "Someone'll take me."

Vaska gave him a packet of cigarettes. But he had no matches, so Zhenka took his aunt's. Then they all went out of the house. Zhenka padlocked the door and put the key under the steps. They set off. The suitcase weighed like lead— not because of what was in it, it was heavy in itself. Zhenka carried it first with one hand, then with the other. Vaska carried Zhenka's coat, and Lida carried little Victor. She thrust out her stomach to take part of the weight and kept shaking him, saying: "Be quiet, can't you! What d'you want now?"

It was very windy. They went to the highroad that ran past the town. The dust rose in whirling columns and got in their eyes. The greyish grass and faded cornflowers by the roadside were trembling, flattened down by the wind. Round white clouds sailed calmly in the blue sky overhead, without a shadow of malice in them, but further away a heavy black one advanced rapidly, reaching out ragged claws; it was as if the wind came from it, carrying through the dust a sharp freshness that made the breath light. The children stopped, set down the suitcase and waited for a lorry. But as though for spite, they were all going the wrong way, from the station to the town. At last one appeared going the way they wanted. It was loaded to capacity with boxes, but there was nobody beside the driver. The children raised their hands. The driver looked out, and drove past. Then a black car appeared, almost empty—there was only one man in it besides the driver. But it went past, too.

"Oh, hell!" Shurik swore.

"What d'you all want to put up your hands for," said Vaska. "That's daft. They think the whole lot wants to go! Let Zhenka get in front and put his hand up. Here's another old trundler."

The children did as he said, and when the trundler came close nobody put up their hands except Zhenka and Vaska, who went against his own orders. Big boys always did the things they told the little ones not to do.

The car shot past and then stopped. Zhenka ran after it with his suitcase and Vaska with the coat. The door handle clicked, Zhenka disappeared inside and Vaska after him. Then a cloud of dust rose and hid everything. When it settled there was neither Zhenka nor Vaska and the car was already a long way off, almost out of sight. So that's what Vaska had up his sleeve. He'd not told anyone, never even let a word drop, that he was going to the station with Zhenka.

The other children went home. The wind was now at their backs, pushing them forward and slapping strands of Seryozha's long hair stingingly in his face.

"She never made him any clothes," said Lida. "He always wore rags."

"Her manager's an old devil," said Shurik. "He doesn't want to pay her as messenger. And she's a right to it."

But Seryozha thought, as the wind pushed him along—how lucky Zhenka was, he'd ride in a train. Seryozha has never been in a train in all his life. The sky became dark and suddenly a quick savage flash jabbed across it, then thunder rolled like guns overhead, and the next moment down came the rain. The children ran, slipping in the mud that lay thick in an instant, while the rain lashed them till they bent nearly double, the lightning danced over the whole sky and through the rolling, crashing thunder they could hear little Victor crying.

So Zhenka was gone. Soon afterwards two letters arrived, one for Vaska and the other for Zhenka's aunt. Vaska told nobody about what Zhenka had written, and acted as though the letter contained all sorts of secrets between men. But the aunt kept nothing back, she went about telling everyone that Zhenka, God be praised, had been taken at the vocational school. He lived in the hostel. They'd given him a suit of clothes. "So I've got him settled after all," said the aunt, "he'll get on now, and who's to thank for it but me!"

Zhenka had never been a natural leader, a lad of ideas, and the children soon got used to doing without him. When they remembered him they were glad he was so well off, that he had a night-table by his bed and entertainers coming to amuse him. If they played soldiers, Shurik and Seryozha took turns at being the general.

GREAT-GRANNY'S FUNERAL

Great-Granny was ill and they took her to the hospital. For two days everyone said they ought to go and see her, and on the third day when only Seryozha and Aunt Pasha were at home, Granny Nastya came. She was even straighter and sterner than usual, and she carried her black bag with the zip fastener. After a few words of greeting, Granny Nastya sat down and said: "My mother's dead."

Aunt Pasha crossed herself and said: "Peace be to her soul!"

Granny Nastya took a plum from her bag and gave it to Seryozha.

"I took some things for her, and they told me she'd died two hours ago. Eat it, Seryozha, it's washed. They're good plums. Mother was fond of them, she'd put them in her tea, let them get soft and eat them. Here, you can have them all." She poured the plums out on the table. "Keep some for yourself," said Aunt Pasha.

Granny Nastya began to cry.

"I don't want them. I bought them for Mother."

"How old was she?" asked Aunt Pasha.

"Eighty-two. People live longer than that. Some live to ninety."

"Have a glass of milk," said Aunt Pasha. "It's nice and cold, I've just brought it up from the cellar. We're still got to eat, whatever happens."

"All right, thanks," said Granny Nastya, blew her nose and began to drink the milk. When she had finished it she said: "I can see her just as if she was standing there. She was so wise, and she'd read so many books, it was amazing. It's an empty house I've got now.... I'll take a lodger."

"Eh, dear me," sighed Aunt Pasha.

Seryozha took as many plums as he could hold, went out into the yard, into the warm sunshine, and pondered. If Granny Nastya's house was empty, that meant it was Great-Granny who was dead. They had lived together. So Great-Granny had been Granny Nastya's mother. Now, thought Seryozha, there'd be no one to nag and scold him when he went to see Granny Nastya.

He knew what death was. He'd seen a mouse that Zaika the cat had killed; before that the mouse had run about and Zaika had played with it, then suddenly Zaika had made a spring and jumped back again, and the mouse had stopped running, and Zaika had eaten it, lazily shaking his fat face.

And Seryozha had seen a dead kitten, like a bit of dirty fur; he had seen dead butterflies, their wings torn and transparent, with all the dust rubbed off; he had seen dead fish thrown up on the bank, and a dead chicken on the kitchen-table. Its neck was long like a goose's, and there was a black hole with blood dripping from it into a basin. Neither Aunt Pasha nor Mummy could kill chickens, they always had Lukyanich do it. He shut himself up with the chicken in the shed, the chicken squawked and Seryozha ran away so as not to hear it. When he went through the kitchen later he would glance with disgust and involuntary curiosity at the blood dripping down. They told him he needn't be sorry for the chicken any more. Aunt Pasha would pluck it with her large, skilful hands and say comfortingly: "It can't feel anything now."

Seryozha had once touched a dead sparrow. It was so cold that he snatched his hand away, frightened. It was as cold as an icicle, the poor little sparrow—lying there with its claws up under a lilac bush warmed by the sun.

Stillness and cold—that was what death must mean.

When they found the sparrow Lida said: "Let's have a funeral!"

She brought a cardboard box, lined it with rags, made a little pillow out of some more scraps, and then put lace round it. Lida really could do a lot of things, you had to give her that. She told Seryozha to dig a hole. Then they laid the box with the sparrow inside at the bottom of the hole, put the lid on and covered it with earth. Lida smoothed over the tiny mound and stuck a twig in it.

"See what a fine funeral we've given him," she crowed. "He never dreamed of having one like this!"

Vaska and Zhenka wouldn't take any part in the funeral. They sat a little way off, smoking, watching morosely. But they didn't laugh at it.

People sometimes died, too. Then they were put in long boxes called coffins and carried along the street. Seryozha had seen it from a distance. But he had never seen a person who was dead.

Aunt Pasha filled a soup plate with boiled rice, white and fluffy, and arranged red sweets round the edge. In the middle, on top of the rice, she put some more sweets, in a pattern that wasn't quite a flower and wasn't quite a star.

"Is that a star?" Seryozha asked.

"It's a cross," Aunt Pasha answered. "We're going to Great-Granny's funeral."

She washed Seryozha's face, hands and feet, put on his socks and shoes, his sailor suit and sailor cap with the ribbons—an awful lot of things she put on him! She, too, wore something special—her black lace scarf. She tied up the plate of rice in a white napkin. She had a bunch of flowers, too, and she gave Seryozha some flowers to carry—two dahlias with thick stems.

Vaska's mother was going for water with buckets on the yoke. Seryozha called out: "Good morning! We're going to Great-Granny's funeral."

Lida stood at her gate holding little Victor. Seryozha called to her, too: "I'm going to Great-Granny's funeral!" and she followed them with looks of envy. He knew she wanted to come but felt she couldn't because he was in his best clothes and she was in a dirty frock and barefoot. He was sorry for her, so he turned and called back: "You come as well! It's all right!"

But Lida was too proud, she said nothing and she didn't go with them, she only stood watching them till they turned the corner.

They went along one street, then another. It was very hot. Seryozha got tired of carrying the two heavy flowers.

"You hold them, it'll be better," he said to Aunt Pasha.

She took them. Then he began to stumble. He'd trip and stumble when there weren't any stones at all.

"What's the matter with you?" asked Aunt Pasha.

"It's because I'm so hot," he said. "Take all these off. I want to go in just my trousers."

"Don't be silly," said Aunt Pasha. "Who'd ever let you go to a funeral with only trousers on? We're nearly at the stop, then we'll get on the bus."

That cheered Seryozha and he stepped out more readily along the endless street, past the endless fences with trees hanging over them.

Some cows were coming towards them in a cloud of dust.

"Hold my hand," said Aunt Pasha.

"I want a drink," said Seryozha.

"Don't be silly," said Aunt Pasha, "you don't want a drink at all."

She was wrong, he really did want a drink. But when she said that, he stopped wanting it so badly.

The cows went by, slowly nodding their serious heads. All their udders were full.

Seryozha and Aunt Pasha took the bus on the square, and sat down in the places reserved for children. Seryozha didn't often ride in a bus, so it was a treat for him. He knelt on the seat, looking out of the window and glancing at his neighbour. The neighbour was a fat boy, smaller than Seryozha, who was sucking a sugar cock on a stick. His cheeks were smeared with it. He looked back at Seryozha, that look said: "I've got a sugar cock and you haven't, aha!" Then the conductor came up to them.

"Do I have to pay for the child?" asked Aunt Pasha.

"Come and be measured, little boy," said the conductor.

There was a black mark on the side of the bus for measuring children. If they had grown as high as that mark, they had to be paid for, Seryozha raised himself a little on tip-toe.

"Yes, pay for him," said the conductor.

Seryozha looked triumphantly back at the boy. They don't take a ticket for you, but they do for me, aha!—that look said. But the boy came off best in the end, because when it was time for Seryozha and Aunt Pasha to get out, he went on further.

In front of them was a white stone gateway, and beyond it were long white houses, with young trees round them; and the tree trunks were painted white, too. People in dark-blue dressing-gowns were walking about or sitting on benches.

"What's this?" asked Seryozha.

"It's the hospital," Aunt Pasha answered.

They went to the very last house, turned a corner and Seryozha saw Korostelev, Mummy, Lukyanich and Granny Nastya. They were all standing by a big, open door. There were three old women with kerchiefs on their heads as well.

"We came in the bus!" Seryozha announced.

Nobody answered, but Aunt Pasha said: "Ssssh!" and he understood he mustn't talk here. They were talking themselves, but quietly. Mummy said to Aunt Pasha: "Why on earth did you bring him?"

Korostelev stood holding his cap in the hand hanging down by his side, his face quiet and thoughtful. Seryozha looked into the doorway. There were steps inside leading down to a cellar, and the darkness below breathed out a cold dampness. All went slowly forward and down the stairs, Seryozha with them.

After the daylight it seemed quite dark at first in the cellar. Then Seryozha saw a broad bench running along the wall, a white ceiling and a rough cement floor. High up in the middle was a wooden coffin with muslin round the edges. It was cold and there was a smell of earth and something else. Granny Nastya went with long steps to the coffin and bent down over it.

"Oh dear, what's this?" said Aunt Pasha under her breath. "Look how the hands are laid. Dear Lord in Heaven— down by her sides."

"She wasn't a believer," said Granny Nastya, straightening. up.

"That makes no difference," said Aunt Pasha, "She isn't a soldier to appear before the Lord like that." Turning to the old women she added: "What were you thinking of!" The old women sighed.

Seryozha could see nothing from below. He climbed on to the bench, stretched out his neck, and looked down into the coffin.

He had thought Great-Granny was in the coffin. But it was something strange that lay there. *It* was a bit like Great-Granny—the same sunken mouth and bony chin sticking up. But *it* wasn't Great-Granny. He didn't know what *it* was. People never have eyes closed like *that*. Even when they're asleep, their eyes are closed differently.

It was most awfully long. But Great-Granny had been quite short. *It* was enveloped in cold, gloom and quietness, in which those standing by the coffin whispered fearfully together. Seryozha felt frightened. But if *it* had suddenly come to life, that would have been even more frightening. If *it* suddenly went "Hrrr", for instance. At that thought Seryozha screamed.

He screamed, and as though in answer, from above, from the sunshine, came a sharp, live sound, familiar and gay — a motorhorn. Mummy picked Seryozha up and carried him out of the cellar. A lorry stood by the door with a side down. Men walked about smoking. Aunt Tosya was at the wheel, she was the driver who had brought Korostelev's things when he came to live with them, she worked at the Bright Shore Farm and sometimes came to fetch Korostelev. Mummy put Seryozha down on the seat beside her, told him: "Stay here," and shut the door.

"So you've come to see Great-Granny buried, have you?" asked Aunt Tosya. "Were you fond of her?"

"No," said Seryozha honestly. "I didn't like her."

"Why've you come, then?" asked Aunt Tosya. "If you didn't like her, then you shouldn't see it."

The light and the voices had dispelled the horror, but Seryozha could not forget it all at once, he wriggled uneasily,

looked about him, thought hard, and at last said: "What does
it mean—to appear before the Lord?"

Aunt Tosya laughed scornfully.

"That's just a way of talking."

"But why do they talk that way?"

"It's just the old ones talk that way. Don't listen to it. It's
silly."

They sat there in silence. Then Aunt Tosya narrowed
her green eyes and said: "Yes, we'll all be there some day."

There—where?—thought Seryozha. But he felt no desire
for more exact information, so he did not ask. When he saw
the coffin carried up from the cellar he looked the other way.
There was relief in the fact that the lid was on the coffin now.
But it was very unpleasant indeed to know it was on the
lorry.

At the cemetery they took the coffin off and carried it
away. Seryozha and Aunt Tosya did not get out, they
stopped in the driver's cab. All round he could see crosses
and wooden pillars with red stars on them. Reddish ants kept
crawling out of a place where the earth had cracked on a
mound nearby. On other mounds weeds grew. Could she had
meant the cemetery when she said we'll all be there some
day, thought Seryozha. Then the ones who had gone away
came back without the coffin, and the lorry started off.

"Have they covered her with earth?" asked Seryozha.

"Yes, kiddie, they've covered her up," said Aunt Tosya.

When they got home he found Aunt Pasha had stopped at
the cemetery with the old women.

"Pasha just had to treat folks to funeral meats the old
way," said Lukyanich. "Well, after all, she bothered with
making it."

Granny Nastya took off her kerchief and smoothed her
hair.

"No need to quarrel with them about it. Let them eat their
rice and say their prayers if it makes them happy."

They were talking in their ordinary voices again, they even
smiled.

"Our Aunt Pasha's got a million superstitions," said
Mummy.

They sat down to table. But Seryozha could not eat. The
very thought of it nauseated him. He sat quietly, looking at
the faces of the grownups. He tried not to remember *it*, but *it*
kept coming back to him—long, frightening, enveloped in
cold and the smell of earth.

"Why did she say we'll all be there?" he asked.

The grownups broke off their talk and turned to him.

"Who said that?" asked Korostelev.

"Aunt Tosya."

"Don't you listen to Aunt Tosya," said Korostelev. "Why d'you want to listen to everybody?"

"But shall we all die?"

They looked as uncomfortable as though he'd asked one of those things you mustn't talk about. But he looked at them and waited for what they would say. Korostelev replied.

"No. We shan't die. Aunt Tosya can do as she likes, but we shan't die, you especially, that I'll guarantee."

"I won't ever die?" asked Seryozha.

"Never!" Korostelev answered firmly, triumphantly.

Seryozha at once felt light and happy again. He got quite red with happiness, then crimson, and started laughing. He suddenly felt most terribly thirsty — after all, he'd wanted a drink a long time ago, and then he'd forgotten. So he drank a lot of water, drank and drank, gasping with enjoyment. He hadn't even the tiniest grain of doubt in Korostelev's word. How could he have lived if he'd known he was going to die? And how could he not believe it when he was told—you'll not die!

THE MIGHT OF KOROSTELEV

They dug holes in the ground, they stood tall posts in them and fastened a wire to the posts. The wire turned and crossed Seryozha's yard, then went in through the wall of the house. And a black telephone appeared on the little table in the dining-room, beside the railway signal. It was the first and only telephone on Dalnaya Street, and it belonged to Korostelev. It was for Korostelev they had dug holes in the ground, and put up posts, and fastened the wire to them. Because other people could do without a telephone, but Korostelev had to have one.

When you took off the receiver some woman you couldn't see said: "Exchange." Then Korostelev would say, like an officer giving orders, "Bright Shore!", or "Party Committee!" or "Give me the Regional State Farm Board!" Then he would sit, swinging a long leg, talking into the telephone. And when he was doing that, nobody must disturb him, not even Mummy.

Sometimes the telephone would ring with a silvery trembling voice. Seryozha would run to it, pick it up and say:

"Hallo!" Then a voice would ask him to call Korostelev.
What a lot of people needed Korostelev! It wasn't often
people wanted Lukyanich or Mummy, and Aunt Pasha and
Seryozha — never.

Early each morning Korostelev left for the Bright Shore
Farm. Aunt Tosya sometimes brought him home for dinner.
But usually not. Mummy would ring up the Bright Shore and
they would tell her Korostelev had gone to one of the
sections and wouldn't be back for a long time.

The Bright Shore Farm was most awfully big. Seryozha
had never thought it could be as big as that till Korostelev
took him along one day in the car when he had some things to
see to. They kept on driving and driving and driving. Great
wide expanses rushed to meet the car and fell away on either
side—great, tall haystacks on huge sweeps of autumn
meadows reaching out to where the world ended in pale lilac
haze, yellow stubble, black velvet plough-land misted with
the fresh green of winter crops just coming up in thin lines.
Endless roads like grey ribbons unrolled and criss-crossed.
Lorries and tractors pulling trailers ran along them.

"Where's this?" Seryozha would ask. And he always got
the same answer: "The Bright Shore."

Three big groups of farm buildings stood lost in the
vastness, a long way from each other—one had a fat
silo tower, another big machine sheds. A drill buzzed and a
welding lamp hissed in the workshop. Sparks shot up in the
dark depths of the smithy and a hammer thudded. And
wherever they stopped, people came out to speak to
Korostelev, and he looked at everything, and asked a lot of
questions, gave instructions, then got back into the car and
they went on. Seryozha understood now why he was always
in such a hurry to go to the Bright Shore—how would they all
know what to do if he didn't come and tell them?

There were no end of animals on the various farm
sections—pigs, sheep, hens and geese, but mostly cows.
While the weather stayed warm the cows had grazed on the
pastures; the makeshift shelters where they had spent the
night in bad weather were still standing there. But now they
were in the cow-houses. They stood quietly side by side,
fastened to a wooden beam with chains round their horns,
and ate out of a long trough, waving their tails. They didn't
behave themselves very well; every now and then someone
would come and clear away the dung. Seryozha was ashamed
to look at them when they behaved so badly; he walked along
the slippery planks through the cow-house, his hand in

Korostelev's, without raising his eyes. But Korostelev took no notice, he slapped the cows' spotted flanks and gave instructions.

One woman started arguing about something, but he interrupted with: "All right, that's enough. Get on with it." And the woman stopped talking and went to do as he had said.

There was another woman in a blue cap with a pompon like Mummy wore; to her he snapped: "Who's responsible for it? Do I have to look after little things like that, too?"

She stood there all upset and kept saying: "I don't know how I forgot it, how I didn't think of it. I just can't understand."

Lukyanich appeared from somewhere holding a paper. He gave Korostelev a fountain-pen and said: "Sign this, please." Korostelev hadn't finished scolding the woman, he said: "All right, afterwards." But Lukyanich insisted.

"Afterwards is no good, they won't give it to me without your signature, and people must get their wages."

Think of that, now, if Korostelev didn't sign that paper, they wouldn't get their wages!

When Seryozha and Korostelev were picking their way among the yellow pools to the car, a young man confronted them—a young man most wonderfully clothed in low rubber boots and a leather jacket with shining buttons.

"Dmitri Korneyevich," he said. "What shall I do now, they won't give me a place to live, Dmitri Korneyevich!"

"Huh—did you think they'd got a house all newly built and waiting for you?" Korostelev snapped.

"It means the end of my getting married," the young man pleaded. "Dmitri Korneyevich, please cancel the order!"

"You ought to have thought of that before," snapped Korostelev still more sharply. "You've got a head on your shoulders. Use it."

"But Dmitri Korneyevich, I'm asking you, as one man to another, can't you understand? I'm new to it all, I hadn't had experience, Dmitri Korneyevich, I didn't understand all these relationships."

"But working on the side—you understood that all right," said Korostelev, his face darkening. "Neglecting your own sector, deserting, to earn money on the side—you'd experience enough for that!"

He turned to go. But the young man persisted.

"Dmitri Korneyevich! Dmitri Korneyevich! Think of my

position! I know I did wrong. I realize it. Give me another chance. Let me go on working here. Dmitri Korneyevich!"

"Well, all right. But remember," said Korostelev grimly, "if it ever happens again, even once—!"

"I was a fool ever to bother with them, Dmitri Korneyevich! They only promise me a bed in a hostel, and God knows when that'll be, too. I've had enough of them, Dmitri Korneyevich!"

"You selfish bastard," said Korostelev, "individualist, miserable whelp! For the last time—get off to your work, and to hell with you!"

"Yes, right away!" cried the young fellow eagerly and turned to go, winking at a girl with a kerchief on her head who stood nearby.

"It's not for your sake I'm doing it, it's for Tanya's. Lucky for you she's in love with you!" Korostelev called after him, and he, too, winked at the girl as he passed. And the girl and the young fellow looked after him, smiling, holding hands.

So that was Korostelev—if he'd wanted, it would have been bad for the young fellow and Tanya. But he didn't want that because he was not only all-powerful, but kind, too. So he made them glad, and left them smiling.

How could Seryozha help being proud that his Korostelev was like that?

It was quite clear. Korostelev must be wiser than anybody else and better than anybody else, if he was put over them all.

THINGS IN THE HEAVENS AND ON EARTH

You couldn't see the stars in summer. When Seryozha went to bed and when he woke up it was always light outside. Even if it was cloudy or raining it was light just the same, because the sun was shining the other side of the clouds. In a clear sky he could sometimes see a light transparent patch as well as the sun, it looked like a piece of frosted glass. That was the moon during the day when no one needed it; it hung up there and then melted in the sunshine, melted away and disappeared, and only the sun was left to reign in the great blue vastness of the sky.

But in wintertime the days were short. Darkness came early. Long before supper-time Dalnaya Street with its quiet snow-covered gardens and white roofs lay under the stars. There were thousands of them, perhaps millions. There were big ones and little ones. And there were the tiniest stars of all, like sand, melting together to make light milky patches. The big stars shone blue, white and gold. Sirius had rays like eyelashes. And in the middle of the sky there were big stars and little stars and star-dust that all joined together to make a thick, frostily-sparkling mist, a fantastic, vague strip flung right across like a bridge over a street—the Milky Way.

Seryozha had never noticed the stars before, they hadn't interested him. That was because he hadn't known they all had names. But then Mummy showed him the Milky Way. And Sirius. And the Great Bear. And red Mars. Every star had its name, Mummy said, even those no bigger than grains of sand. And besides, they only looked tiny because they were so far away, they were really very big, Mummy said. On Mars there were very likely people living.

Seryozha wanted to know the names of all of them, but Mummy couldn't remember; she had known them once, but she'd forgotten. To make up for that, she showed him the mountains on the moon.

Nearly every day it snowed. People cleared paths, trampled them hard, and then more snow came and covered everything with fluffy white cushions. The fence posts wore white caps. The trees had fat white caterpillars along their twigs and round clumps of snow where the branches divided.

Seryozha played with the snow, he built with it and fought battles with it, and went sledging down the hills. Then the day died in purplish-pink behind the timber yard. It was evening, and Seryozha came home pulling his sledge behind him. He stopped to take a look at the familiar stars, his head flung back. The Great Bear had crawled almost to the middle of the sky, its tail flung cheekily out. Mars winked a red eye.

If Mars is so big there may be people on it, thought Seryozha, then perhaps there's a boy just like me standing there now with a sledge just like mine, and perhaps he's called Seryozha, too. That was a wonderful thought, he wanted to share it, but not with just anybody; some people wouldn't understand, they often didn't; they made jokes of things, and Seryozha hated those jokes, they offended him. So he chose a moment when nobody else was near and told Korostelev—because Korostelev never laughed. He didn't laugh this time, either. He thought a moment and said: "Well, why not?"

Then for some reason he took Seryozha by the shoulders and looked at him very seriously, almost fearfully.

You come home on winter evenings, tired with playing and cold, and there's the stove burning, sending out heat all round. You get warm, sniffling a bit, while Aunt Pasha puts your trousers and felt boots on top of it to dry. Then you sit down at the kitchen-table with the grownups for supper, you drink hot milk, listen to their talk and think of tomorrow, when you're all going to besiege and capture the snow fortress you made today. A fine thing, winter.

Yes, winter's a fine thing, but it lasts too long. You get tired of heavy clothes and biting winds, you want to run out of the house in shorts and sandals, to bathe in the river, to lie on the grass, to go fishing—it doesn't matter that you never catch anything, it's fun just to be there all together, to dig for worms, to sit with rod and line and shout: "Look out, Shurik, you've got a bite!"

Agh—another blizzard, and yesterday everything was thawing! You're sick of the beastly winter!

Then fat tears run slantingly down the window, and instead of snow the street is covered with a thick black mass, with firmer paths trodden here and there. Spring! The ice cracks on the river. Seryozha and the other children go to see it floating down and away. First come big dirty-looking chunks, then a grey mush. Then the river overflows its banks, and the willows on the far side stand in water half-way up their trunks. Everything is blue, water below and sky above, and grey and white clouds sail over the blue in both.

And when has the grain grown up so tall and thick in the fields beyond Dalnaya Street? How did Seryozha miss seeing it? When did the rye manage to flower and form ears? Busy with the job of living, Seryozha never noticed it, and now the ears have filled, ripened, and rustle richly over his head when he walks along the path. The birds have brought up their fledglings, the mowing-machines have gone out on to the meadows to cut down the flowers that make the far bank so gay. School has closed for the holidays, it is real summer again, and Seryozha forgets all about snow and stars.

Korostelev called Seryozha, and stood him between his knees.

"There's a question we've got to discuss," he said. "Which do you think it would be better for us to get—a little boy or a little girl?"

"A little boy," Seryozha answered at once.

"Yes, but you've got to look at it all round. Of course, two boys are better than one. But on the other hand, we've got a boy already, maybe we ought to have a girl now, eh?"

"All right, if you like," Seryozha agreed without any great eagerness. "We could have a girl. Only a boy would be better for me to play with, you know."

"But a little girl—you'd look after her and stand up for her as an elder brother. See the boys didn't pull her hair."

"Girls pull your hair, too," Seryozha remarked. "And they pull hard." He might have told Korostelev how Lida had pulled his hair not long ago, but he didn't want to be a telltale. "They pull it so hard they make boys yell."

"Yes, but ours will be quite tiny," said Korostelev. "She won't pull hair."

"M'yes—but all the same, let's have a boy," said Seryozha, after thinking it over a moment. "A boy'd be better."

"Are you sure?"

"Boys don't tease and girls—that's all they ever do, tease you."

"Oh? H'm. That's a point. Look here, we'll discuss it all again, shall we?"

"All right."

Mummy listened, smiling. She was sitting beside them sewing. She'd made herself an awfully wide dressing-gown, Seryozha wondered why it was so wide. But it was true, she'd got fatter. And now she had something very tiny in her hands, she was sewing lace round it.

"What's that you're making?" asked Seryozha.

"A baby's cap," said Mummy, "for a little boy or a little girl, whichever you both decide to get."

"Will he have a head as little as that?" asked Seryozha, examining the doll's cap—that was what it looked like—and thinking within himself: Gosh—give a good tug to a head like that, and you might pull it off!

"At first, yes," said Mummy, "but then he'll grow. You can see how Victor's grown. And the way you grow yourself. He'll grow just the same way."

She put the tiny cap on her hand and looked at it; her face was clear and happy. Korostelev carefully kissed her forehead, just at the place where the soft shining hair started.

They were quite serious about it—about getting a little boy or a little girl. They bought a tiny bed and a quilt. They could use Seryozha's old bath for the little boy or girl; it was too small for him, it was a long time since he'd been able to stretch out his legs when he sat in it, but for anyone with a head to fit that cap it would be just right.

He knew where people got babies, of course—they bought them at the hospital. The hospital supplied them. One woman had bought two at once. Though why she had got two just alike he couldn't understand. People said she could only tell them apart by the mole, one had a tiny mole on the neck and the other hadn't. It was queer, why she'd got two alike. She'd have done better to get them different.

But though Korostelev and Mummy had started off as if they meant it, they delayed for some reason. The bed was there, but no sign of a little boy or a little girl.

"Why don't you go and buy one?" Seryozha asked Mummy.

Mummy laughed—and goodness, how fat she'd got!

"There aren't any just now. But they say there'll be some soon."

Well, that did happen sometimes. You wanted something and it wasn't there in the shop. All right, they could wait, Seryozha wasn't in any hurry.

Babies grew very slowly, whatever Mummy might say. You could see it by Victor. He'd been alive a long, long time, and still he was only eighteen months old. So how long would it take before he could play with the big children? That meant the time when a new little boy or girl would be able to play with Seryozha was so far off that you couldn't even guess at it. And until that time came he, Seryozha, would have to protect the baby and take care of it. Of course that was very fine and important, Seryozha knew it, but it wasn't nearly as interesting as Korostelev seemed to think. Lida found it very hard bringing up Victor—carrying him about and amusing him and punishing him. Not long ago her father and mother had gone to a wedding, but Lida had stopped at home and cried. If there hadn't been Victor, she could have gone, too. But with him it was like being in prison, Lida said.

But—well, all right, Seryozha was ready to help Korostelev and Mummy. They could go to work, and Aunt Pasha could boil and bake, and he, Seryozha, would take care of the helpless little thing with a head like a doll's that couldn't do anything if it wasn't looked after. He'd give it gruel and put it to bed. He and Lida would go and visit each other and take the babies, it would be easier to look after them if they were together — while the babies were asleep they could play.

One morning when he got up they told him Mummy had gone to the hospital to buy a baby.

Although he had been expecting it, his heart gave a little jump. After all, it was a big event.

He expected Mummy back soon, he stood by the gate waiting for her to come round the corner with a little boy or a little girl, so he could run to meet her. At last Aunt Pasha called him.

"Korostelev wants you on the telephone."

He ran into the house and picked up the black receiver lying on the table.

"Hullo?" he called. Korostelev's voice answered, a laughing, delighted voice:

"Seryozha! You've got a brother! You hear me? A brother! With blue eyes! He weighs four kilograms, fine, isn't he? Are you pleased?"

"Yes—yes!" cried Seryozha, hesitant, confused. The telephone was silent.

"Blue eyes, takes after his father," said Aunt Pasha, wiping her eyes on her apron. "Well, the Lord be praised! It's a happy hour."

"Will they soon be home?" asked Seryozha. He was amazed and disappointed to hear that it would be only in a week and perhaps more — because the baby would have to get used to Mummy, and they'd teach him that in the hospital.

Korostelev went to the hospital every day. They wouldn't let him go in and see Mummy, but she sent him notes. Our boy's a beautiful baby. And unusually clever. She'd quite decided on his name—Alexei, and they'd call him Alec for short. She was very bored, she missed them, she was longing to come home. She sent love and kisses to everyone, especially Seryozha.

A week passed, even more, and then one day when Korostelev left, he told Seryozha: "Wait for me, we're going today to fetch Mummy and Alec."

He came back in Aunt Tosya's car, carrying a great bunch of flowers. They drove to the same hospital where Great-Granny had died. They went to the first house near the gates, and suddenly they heard Mummy's voice.

"Mitya! Seryozha!"

She was looking out of an open window and waving to them. Seryozha cried: "Mummy!" She waved again and disappeared. Korostelev said she'd come out in a minute or two. But it was a long time before she came—they had time to walk up and down the path, and look into the door with a spring that screeched, and sit a while on a bench under a thin young tree that cast hardly any shade. Korostelev got restless, he said the flowers would be wilted before she came. Aunt Tosya left the car outside the gate and joined them. She told Korostelev it always took a long time.

At last the door screeched and Mummy came out, carrying a blue bundle. They ran to meet her and she said: "Careful, careful!"

Korostelev gave her the flowers and took the bundle. He turned back a corner of lace and showed Seryozha a tiny little face, pink and important, with closed eyes. Alec, his brother. One eye opened a little, a vague blue something peered out of the crack, then the face twisted. Korostelev said in a kind of weak voice: "Ah—you!" and kissed him.

"Mitya, you mustn't!" said Mummy sternly.

"Why, mustn't I?" asked Korostelev.

"He's susceptible to any infection," said Mummy. "They wear muslin masks here whenever they come near him. So please, Mitya."

"All right, I won't do it again," said Korostelev.

When they got home Alec was put on Mummy's bed, she unwrapped him and Seryozha could see the whole of him. But why on earth had Mummy said he was beautiful? His tummy was all swollen, and his arms and legs were thin as little sticks, not like proper arms and legs, and they moved about without any aim or purpose. There was no neck to be seen at all. And nothing to show he was clever. He opened an empty toothless mouth and started to cry, a queer, complaining cry, weak, and tiresome, going on and on.

"Now, now, my wee one," said Mummy, "I know what it is, you're hungry, my boy's hungry, that's it. Just a moment, only a tiny moment."

She spoke loudly, moved quickly and wasn't fat any more, she'd got quite thin there in the hospital. Korostelev and Aunt Pasha tried to help her, and ran as fast as they could to do all she asked.

Alec's nappies were wet. Mummy put on dry ones, sat down with him on her lap, unfastened her dress, and put Alec's mouth to her breast. He gave one last cry, seized the nipple with his lips and began to suck, choking with greed.

What a little pig, thought Seryozha.

Korostelev guessed his thought.

"He's only nine days old," he said softly. "Nine days, that's all, what can you expect of him?"

"Uhuh," Seryozha agreed, shamefaced.

"Later on he'll be a fine chap, you'll see."

But how long will that be, thought Seryozha. And how can I look after him when he's like jelly, even Mummy's careful when she touches him.

Alec, well fed, slept on Mummy's bed. The grownups sat in the dining-room talking about him.

"You'll need a nurse," said Aunt Pasha, "I'll not be able to manage alone."

"No, I'll do without," said Mummy. "It's holidays now, I can look after him myself, and then I'll put him in a nursery, there are real nurses there and proper care."

That's fine, let him go to a nursery, thought Seryozha, relieved. Lida was always wishing they'd send Victor to a nursery. Seryozha clambered on to the bed and sat down beside Alec, hoping to get a good look at him while he wasn't crying or screwing up his face. It seemed Alec had real eyelashes, only very short ones. The skin was soft, like velvet. Seryozha touched it with the tip of his finger.

"What are you doing?" cried Mummy, entering. It was so sudden Seryozha started and snatched his hand away.

"Get down this minute! What d'you mean by touching him with dirty hands?"

"They're clean," said Seryozha, slipping down from the bed in alarm.

"And in general, Seryozha," said Mummy, "keep away from him while he's so little. You may push him off by accident—you never know what can happen. And another thing—don't you start bringing the children in, or he may pick up some illness from them. In fact, let's go out of here," Mummy ended affectionately but firmly.

Seryozha followed obediently. He was very thoughtful. Nothing had turned out the way he had expected. Mummy hung a shawl over the window so the light should not shine on Alec, followed Seryozha and shut the door quietly.

VASKA AND HIS UNCLE

Vaska had an uncle. Lida would certainly have liked to say he hadn't any uncle at all, he was making it all up, but this time she had to keep quiet. For there was an uncle, his photograph stood on the whatnot, between two vases of poppies made of red shavings. Uncle had been taken standing under a palm. He was all in white, and the sunshine was white, too, so blindingly white that you couldn't properly see either his face or his clothes. The only things that came out really well were the palm tree and two short black shadows — one from Uncle, the other from the tree.

The face didn't matter, but it was a pity you couldn't make out how Uncle was dressed. He wasn't just Uncle, he was the captain of an ocean vessel. It would be interesting to see how captains of ocean vessels dressed. Vaska said the photograph had been taken in Honolulu, on the island of Oahu. Sometimes parcels came from him. Vaska's mother would say: "Kostya's sent me two more lengths."

What she called lengths were just pieces of material. But sometimes there were fine things in the parcels, too. A crocodile in a bottle of spirit, for instance, tiny as a fish, but still—a crocodile. It could stand there in spirit for a hundred years and it would never spoil. No wonder Vaska thought a lot of himself. All the finest things other boys had were rubbish compared with that crocodile.

One parcel had a big shell in it, grey outside, rosecoloured inside, with rosy edges open like great lips; if you put your ear to it you could hear a quiet murmur that seemed to come from a long, long way off. When Vaska was feeling kind he let Seryozha listen. And Seryozha would press the shell to his ear, his eyes wide and fixed, holding his breath, listening to the quiet, unceasing murmur that came from the depths of the shell. What was it? Where did it come from? And why did it make him restless, why did he feel he could go on listening and listening?

And that Uncle, that wonderful, amazing Uncle—after seeing Honolulu and all sorts of islands, he was coming to stay with Vaska! Vaska mentioned it when he came out—mentioned it casually, keeping a cigarette in the corner of his mouth and screwing up one eye against the smoke. He mentioned it just as though it were the most ordinary thing in the world. And when Shurik, after a silence, asked in a deep voice: "Which uncle? The captain?" Vaska answered: "Who else? *I* haven't any others."

He said "*I* haven't" with a kind of emphasis, as much as to say—*you* may have uncles who aren't captains, but not *me*. And all admitted that he was right.

"Will he come soon?" asked Seryozha.

"In a week or two," Vaska answered. "Well, I'm off to buy some chalk."

"What d'you need that for?" asked Seryozha.

"Mother's going to whitewash the ceiling."

Of course—with an uncle like that coming you have to have the ceiling freshly whitewashed!

"He's making it up." Lida couldn't keep quiet any longer. "There's nobody coming at all."

She moved hastily back with the last word, expecting a buffet. But this time Vaska had none for her. He didn't even say "fool", he simply walked away, swinging the basket with the bag for chalk inside. And Lida was left looking silly.

They whitewashed the ceiling and papered the walls. Vaska smeared paste over the pieces of wallpaper and passed them up to his mother, and she put them on. Children peeped in from the entry—Vaska told them to keep out of the room.

"You'll mix everything up in here," he said.

Then Vaska's mother scrubbed the floor and laid down runners. They all had to walk on the runners and keep off the floor.

"Sailors like everything shining clean," said Vaska's mother.

The alarm-clock was taken into the back room where Uncle was to sleep.

"Sailors do everything by the clock," said Vaska's mother.

Everyone waited for Vaska's uncle with seething impatience. If a car turned into Dalnaya Street they held their breath—was it Uncle coming from the station? But the car would pass by, no Uncle came and Lida was glad. She had her own peculiar ideas of enjoyment which the others could not share.

When Vaska's mother came home from work in the evening, she would get through her household jobs and then stand by the gate talking to the neighbours, boasting of her brother the captain. And the children would stand nearby listening.

"He's at a health resort just now," said Vaska's mother. "He's taking a cure. His heart's not too good. He was sent to the very best sanatorium, of course. Then, when he's finished his treatment, he'll come here."

"He used to be a wonderful singer," she said another time. "The way he used to sing in our club—better than Kozlovsky! Of course, he's got stout now, and short of breath, and with all the trouble in his family—you don't feel much like singing."

She lowered her voice and said something not for children to hear.

"...and all of them girls," she went on. "One's fair, the second dark, the third red-haired. Only the eldest's like

Kostya. And he goes off to sea and worries all the time. She's got luck, having only girls. It's easier to bring up ten daughters than one son."

The neighbours looked at Vaska.

"He's my brother, he'll be able to advise me," said Vaska's mother. "A man's decision. Because I sometimes think I'll go clean crazy."

"Aye, it's a hard time you have with boys till you get them on their feet," sighed Zhenka's aunt.

"Depends on the boy," Aunt Pasha objected. "Take ours. He's a real loving little fellow."

"They're all like that when they're little. It's when they get bigger they lead you a dance."

Uncle-captain arrived late at night. In the morning the children looked into Vaska's garden and there was Uncle standing on the path, all dressed in white just like the picture—a white tunic, white trousers with creases in front, and white shoes. And gold broid on the tunic. He stood there with his hands behind his back, and talked in a soft voice, slightly nasal and a very little bit breathy.

"How really lovely it is here. Beau-tiful. A real rest after the tropics. You don't know how lucky you are, Polya, to live in a place like this."

"Yes, it's not bad here," said Vaska's mother.

"Ah, a starlings' box," cried Uncle yearningly. "Starlings on a birch-tree! Do you remember our school reader, Polya, there was a picture in it just like this—a birch-tree and a box for starlings."

"Vaska put it up," said his mother.

"A splen-did boy!" said Uncle.

Vaska was there, too, well-washed, quiet, without a cap, his hair smoothed as if it were May Day.

"Come to breakfast," said Vaska's mother.

"I want to breathe some more of this air," the captain demurred. But Vaska's mother took him away. He mounted the steps—massive, like a white tower with gold on it, and disappeared into the house. He was stout and handsome, with a kind face and a double chin. The lower part of his face was brown and his forehead white, there was a clear line where the sunburn ended.

Vaska went to the fence, where Seryozha and Shurik had their faces wedged in the gaps.

"Well," he said graciously, "what d'you want, kids?"

They only sniffed.

"He's brought me a watch," said Vaska. Yes, there was a

watch on his left wrist, a real watch on a strap. He raised his hand and listened to it ticking, then wound it a bit.

"May we come in?" asked Seryozha.

"All right, come in," Vaska permitted. "But quiet, mind. And when he lies down to rest, and when the family come, then out with you both at once. There's to be a family council."

"What's that?" asked Seryozha.

"They're going to talk about what's to be done with me," Vaska explained.

He went into the house and the boys followed him in silence, and stood by the door of the room where the captain was sitting.

Uncle-captain buttered a piece of bread, put an egg in an egg-cup, cracked the top with a tea-spoon, carefully cut it off and sprinkled salt on the egg. He took the salt from the salt-cellar with the point of his knife. But there was something missing, he looked about, here and there, and his pale brows were knitted in suffering. At last he asked delicately, in his soft voice: "Excuse me, Polya—may I have a table-napkin?"

Vaska's mother hurried away all in a fluster, and brought him a clean towel. He thanked her, laid the towel across his knees and began to eat. He bit off tiny pieces of bread, and you could hardly see at all that he was chewing or swallowing. Vaska sniffed, and his face expressed contending feelings—chagrin that there had been no table-napkins in the house, and pride in his most cultured Uncle who couldn't eat his breakfast without one.

Vaska's mother put all kinds of different foods on the table, and Uncle took a little of everything; but all the time it looked as if he was eating nothing, and Vaska's mother kept groaning: "You're not eating, you don't like it!"

"Everything's excellent," said Uncle, "but I have to keep to a diet, so don't be angry, Polya."

He refused vodka.

"I'm not allowed it. Once a day a small shot of brandy," with a graceful gesture he held up finger and thumb to show the size of the shot, "just before dinner, to assist in expanding the vessels. That's all I can have."

After breakfast he invited Vaska to go for a walk, and put on his cap—also white with gold braid.

"Go home now," Vaska told Seryozha and Shurik.

"Oh, let's take them," said Uncle through his nose. "Splendid little boys! A beautiful pair of brothers!"

"We aren't brothers," said Shurik in his deep voice.

"They aren't brothers," Vaska upheld him.

"Really?" Uncle was surprised. "I thought they were. They're alike some way—one fair, the other dark. Well, not brothers, then—it doesn't matter, come for a walk."

Lida saw them going down the street. She would have run after them, but Vaska gave her a look over his shoulder; so she turned and ran with little skips in the other direction.

They walked in the woods and Uncle was enraptured by the trees. They walked through the fields and he was enraptured by the wheat. To tell the truth, they got a bit tired of his raptures. He'd have done better to tell them about the sea and the islands. But all the same he was wonderful. It dazzled you to look at his gold braid glittering in the sunshine. He walked with Vaska, while Seryozha and Shurik sometimes followed behind, and sometimes ran on ahead so as to admire Uncle from in front. They came to the river. Uncle looked at his watch and said it would be fine to have a swim. Vaska looked at his watch, too, and said—why not. So they undressed on the clean, warm sand.

Seryozha and Shurik were disappointed to find that Uncle did not wear a striped sailor's singlet under his tunic, just an ordinary white shirt. But when he raised his arms and pulled it off over his head they stared, thunderstruck.

The whole of Uncle's body, from his neck to his waist, all that broad, evenly brown body with its fat creases was thickly covered with patterns done in blue. Uncle stood up and stretched, and the boys saw they were not patterns, but pictures and words. On his chest there was a mermaid with a fish-tail and long hair; an octopus was crawling down to her from the left shoulder, with twisty tentacles and terrible human eyes; the mermaid had her hands stretched out towards him and her face turned away, begging him not to seize her—a terrible picture! On the right shoulder something long was written, and down the right arm, too—you might say Uncle was written all over on that side. On the left arm, above the elbow, two doves were kissing, and over them was a garland and a crown; below the elbow was a turnip with an arrow through it, and underneath the name MUSYA in big letters.

"Gosh!" Shurik said to Seryozha.

"Gosh!" sighed Seryozha.

Uncle went into the water, dived, came up again with wet hair and a happy face, snorted and swam up against the stream. The boys followed him, enchanted.

And how Uncle could swim! He moved through the water

as easily as if he were playing, and just as easily it supported his massive body. He swam to the bridge, turned on to his back and floated down again, steering with very small movements of his feet. And the mermaid on his chest moved under the water as though she were alive.

Then Uncle lay down to rest on the bank. He lay on the sand, on his stomach, with a blissful smile, while they examined his back which had a skull and cross-bones like the transformer hut, and the moon and stars, and a woman in a long dress with bandaged eyes sitting on clouds with her knees apart. Shurik plucked up courage.

"What's that you've got on your back, Uncle?" he asked.

Uncle laughed, sat up and began brushing sand off himself.

"It's to remind me of the time when I was young and foolish," he said. "You see how it is, dear boys, once upon a time I was so foolish, I covered myself with all sorts of silly pictures, and unfortunately, it's for ever."

"And what's that written on you?" asked Shurik.

"What does it matter," said Uncle, "what kind of nonsense is written on me? What matters is a man's feelings and his actions, what do you think, Vaska?"

"Yes," said Vaska.

"But the sea?" asked Seryozha. "What's it like?"

"The sea," repeated Uncle. "The sea? Well, what can I say? The sea's the sea. There's nothing more beautiful than the sea. It's something you have to see for yourself."

"And when there's a storm," said Shurik, "is it very terrible?"

"A storm is beautiful," answered Uncle. "On the sea everything is beautiful." Shaking his head thoughtfully, he recited:

> *What does it matter, he said, which is best?*
> *Quietest of all in the water you rest.*

Then he began putting on his trousers.

After their walk he lay down to rest, and the children gathered in Vaska's Lane to talk about Uncle's tattooing

"They do it with gunpowder," said a boy from Kalinin Street. "They make the drawing, and then they rub gunpowder in it. I read about it."

"But where could you get gunpowder?" another boy asked.

"In the shop, of course."

"I see them letting you have it! They don't sell cigarettes to anyone under sixteen, let alone gunpowder."

"We could get it from the hunters."

"Don't you hope they'll give it you!"

"But what if they do?"

"And what if they don't?"

Then a third boy chimed in.

"They used powder in the old days. Now they do it with Indian ink or ordinary ink."

"Will it gather if it's done with ink?"

"It will, and how!"

"Better with Indian ink. It'll get more inflamed with that."

"You'll get all you want with ordinary ink, too."

Seryozha listened, and tried to picture Honolulu on the island of Oahu, where palms grow and the sunshine is blindingly bright. And snow-white captains with gold braid stand under the palms to be photographed.... And I will, too, some day, thought Seryozha. Like all those boys discussing the comparative merits of gunpowder and ink, he believed without the faintest shadow of doubt that everything in all the world was before him—including being a captain in Honolulu. He believed it, just as he believed that he would never die. He would try everything, see everything in a life that would have no ending.

Towards evening he became impatient to see Vaska's uncle again; but Uncle kept on resting and resting—he had been travelling all night and hadn't slept. Vaska's mother ran out on high heels, and told Aunt Pasha as she passed that she was going for brandy, Kostya never drank anything else. The sun sank. Relatives arrived. The electric lights went on in the house. And there was nothing to be seen from the street except curtains and geraniums. Seryozha was glad when Shurik called him; in Shurik's garden there was a lime-tree, you could see everything if you climbed it.

"He did exercises when he woke up," said Shurik, trotting along in a business-like way beside Seryozha. "And when he shaved he sprayed perfume on himself through a tube. They've had supper now. Come through the lane, or Lida'll want to tag on."

The old lime-tree grew close to the fence separating Timokhin's kitchen-garden from Vaska's garden. The fence was close to Vaska's house but you couldn't climb it because the wood was rotten, it cracked and crumbled. The lime had a hollow in it, one summer hoopoes had lived there, and now Shurik used it to hide things better kept out of sight of the grownups—cartridge cases and a magnifying glass which he used to burn words on fences and wooden seats.

Scraping their legs on the rough, cracked bark, the boys climbed up and settled themselves on a twisted, knotted branch, Shurik holding on to the trunk, and Seryozha holding onto Shurik.

They were up among the silkily rustling, stroking, tickling, fresh, aromatic leaves. High overhead the canopy of leaves was gilded by the sunset, down below was the thickening dusk. A branch with dark leaves swayed in front of Seryozha but did not hide the inside of Vaska's house. The electric light shone brightly, and there was Uncle-captain sitting among the family. Seryozha could hear all they were saying.

Vaska's mother was speaking, waving her arms about.

"...so they write a receipt for a fine of twenty-five roubles paid by me for unseemly behaviour in the street...."

One woman laughed.

"I don't find it funny," said Vaska's mother. "Then two months later they summon me to the militia station again, and show me a charge, and then they write down that I've paid fifty roubles for a broken display-case at the cinema."

"What about when he fought the big lads?" said another woman. "And what about when he burned holes in the quilt with cigarettes, and nearly burned the house down?"

"And where does he get the money for cigarettes?" asked Uncle-captain.

Vaska was sitting there, his elbow on his knee, his chin on his hand, quiet, his hair combed till not a single hair jostled its neighbour.

"Worthless brat," said Uncle in his soft voice. "I'm asking you—where do you get the money?"

"Mother gives it me," said Vaska with a sniff.

"Excuse me, Polya," said Uncle, "but I don't understand."

Vaska's mother broke out sobbing.

"Show me your school report book," Uncle told Vaska.

Vaska got up and brought it. Uncle turned page after page, his eyes narrowed. Then he said gently: "You rascal. You good-for-nothing."

He slammed the report book on the table, took out a handkerchief and began to fan himself with it.

"Yes," he said, "it's bad. If you want anything to come of him, you must keep an ab-so-lute-ly firm hand on him. Look at my Nina. She's brought up my girls beau-tifully. Obedient, and learning to play the piano. And why? Because she always keeps a firm hand."

"With girls it's easier," chorussed the relatives. "It's always easier to bring up girls than boys."

"You must remember, Kostya," said the woman who'd told tales about the quilt, "if she doesn't give Vaska money, he takes it himself from her handbag, without asking."

Vaska's mother sobbed more loudly.

"Where else can I take it?" asked Vaska. "From strangers?"

"Get out of here!" cried Uncle through his nose and stood up.

"He'll give him a belting," Shurik whispered. Then there was a loud crack and the branch on which they were sitting fell down with a loud scraping. With it fell Seryozha, carrying Shurik with him.

"Don't you dare cry!" said Shurik from the ground where he was lying.

They got up, rubbing their bumps. Vaska looked through the fence and understood it all.

"I'll give you spying!" he said.

A white figure rose up behind Vaska glittering with gold in the light cast from the window.

"Give me your cigarettes, blockhead," it said.

Limping, Seryozha and Shurik left the garden but before that they saw Vaska give his uncle a packet of cigarettes and they saw Uncle tear them up, break them, crush them to powder, and then take Vaska by the collar and lead him into the house.

The next morning a padlock hung on the door. Lida said they'd all gone away as soon as it was light to relations on the Chkalov Collective Farm. They were away all day. The next morning Vaska's mother, sobbing, hung the padlock on the door again and went to work in tears. Vaska had gone away that night with his uncle. He had gone for good, Uncle had taken him along to send him to a Nakhimov Naval School and make a man of him. So a wonderful thing had happened to Vaska, and all because he'd taken money from his mother's handbag and broken the display-case at the cinema!

"It's because of those relations," Vaska's mother told Aunt Pasha. "They talked of Vaska so it sounded as if he was a real criminal. And he wasn't such a bad boy really, remember how he chopped and stacked a whole metre of wood? And he helped me put up the wallpaper, too. And what'll happen to him now, without me there...."

She started to cry.

"They don't care, it's not their boy," she sobbed, "and there's never an autumn without he gets boils on his neck, and who'll bother about that now...."

She couldn't see a boy wearing his cap with the peak backward without starting to cry. She'd ask Seryozha and Shurik in and talk to them about Vaska, and what he'd been like when he was little, and show them the photographs her brother the captain had given her. There were pictures of seaports, banana groves, ancient buildings, sailors on the deck, people riding elephants, a motor boat cutting through the waves, a black dancing-woman with bracelets on her ankles, black children with thick lips and curly hair—strange things, things you had to ask about to know what they were, and on almost all the pictures there was the sea, stretching out endlessly till it merged with the sky, living, rippling water, with a gleaming mist of foam—and all that unknown world sang a deep, enticing song like the rosy shell when you laid it to your ear....

But Vaska's garden was silent and empty. It became a kind of everyman's land, you could go in and play there all day, nobody scolded you, nobody sent you away. The master of the garden had gone into that singing rosy world where Seryozha, too, would go some day.

WHAT CAME
OF KNOWING VASKA'S UNCLE

Secret relations had come into being between Kalinin Street and Dalnaya Street. There were negotiations. Shurik went back and forth, was very busy, and brought Seryozha news. His plump, sunburned legs carried him about quickly, and his black eyes darted quick looks on all sides. That was a way they had—when Shurik got some new idea his eyes always kept darting right and left, so everyone knew at once he was up to something. His mother worried, and his father, the lorry-driver Timokhin, threatened him with the strap. Because Shurik's ideas were always mischief. So his parents were alarmed because after all they wanted a son alive and healthy.

But Shurik didn't care a bit about the strap. What did an old strap matter when the boys on Kalinin Street were going to tattoo themselves! They made efficient, business-like preparations. And think of it—they'd got all the details out of Shurik and Seryozha, every bit of it, what pictures Vaska's Uncle had and where, they'd made their drawings just as Shurik and Seryozha told them, and now they didn't want to let Shurik and Seryozha be in it, they said: "It isn't for kids like you." The nasty sneaks! It was as unfair as ever it could be!

And you couldn't complain to anyone, either, you'd promised you wouldn't say a word to anyone in the whole world — that is to say on Dalnaya Street. Because on Dalnaya Street there was a famous telltale — Lida. She'd go and tell the grownups at once, just for spite — for what good would it do her? — and they'd make a fuss, and there'd be trouble at school, you'd be called to teachers' meetings and parents' meetings, and instead of a business-like operation there'd be all sorts of fuss and bother.

So because of that Kalinin Street kept its plans secret from Dalnaya Street. But you couldn't keep much secret from Shurik. And besides, he'd seen the drawings. Wonderful drawings on cartridge paper and parchment paper.

"They've thought some up for themselves," Shurik told Seryozha. "They've drawn an airplane, and a whale making a fountain, and printed a lot of mottoes. They put the sheet of paper on you and then prick you with a pin right through it all along the drawing. It ought to come out fine."

Seryozha shuddered. A pin!

But if Shurik could stand it Seryozha could, too.

"Yes," he said with assumed nonchalance. "It ought to come out fine."

But the Kalinin Street boys not only refused to give Shurik and Seryozha a whale, they wouldn't give them even the tiniest little motto. Shurik tried them one after the other, argued and pleaded, but it was all no good. They just said: "Don't bother us. What, kids like you? Scram!"

So they just sent the two away. Things looked very black indeed until Shurik managed to get Arsenti on to his side.

Arsenti was the kind of boy all parents held up as a model. He always got top marks, pored over his books, was clean and neat, and was much respected. But what mattered most was that he understood fair play.

After trying to joke them out of it he said: "After all, they do deserve something. Let's make them one letter each. Their initials. What d'you say to that?" he asked Shurik.

"No," said Shurik, "we don't agree to just one letter."

"Beat it, then," said that big strong Valeri from the fifth form. "You won't get anything."

Shurik went, but he'd no choice, he came back again and said—all right, one letter. Only it must be made properly, not just any old way. The whole thing was to be done the next day, at Valeri's place, because his mother was away.

Shurik and Seryozha arrived at the time they had been told. Lariska, Valeri's sister, was sitting by the door with her embroidery. If anybody came to the house she was to say there was no one at home. The children gathered in the yard by the bath-house—boys from the fifth form and even the sixth, and one stout, pale girl with a very serious face and a thick, pale, pendulous lower lip. One had the feeling that it was because of this lip she had such an earnest, impressive look, if she had pulled it up she wouldn't have looked earnest or impressive at all. This girl — her name was Kapa — was cutting bandages into lengths with a pair of scissors and arranging them on a stool. Kapa was a member of the hygiene commission at her school. Over the stool she had spread a white cloth.

Just inside the door of the small, smoky bath-house with its dim window up under the roof stood a broad low wooden block, and the drawings were on a bench, rolled up into tubes. All the boys picked up these drawings when they arrived, looked at them, argued gaily about them, cursing with satisfaction, and choosing which ones they wanted. There was no quarrelling because the same drawing could be used for any number of boys. Shurik and Seryozha admired the drawings from afar, but did not dare take liberties with them—those other boys were so very big and splendid and masterful.

Arsenti came straight from school, still carrying his satchel because there had been six lessons that day. He asked to be done first because he had a lot of homework—a composition and a big chunk of geography. The others agreed, out of respect for his diligence. He put his satchel carefully on the seat, pulled off his shirt with a smile and sat down on the bench, his naked back to the entry.

The big boys all surrounded him. Seryozha and Shurik were pushed out into the yard, and however much they jumped they could see nothing. The talk died down, there was the rustling and crackling of paper and then a little later Valeri's voice.

"Kapa! Go to Lariska, ask her for a towel."

Serious Kapa ran past, her lower lip bobbling, brought back a towel and threw it to Valeri over the intervening heads.

"Why do they want a towel?" asked Seryozha, jumping. "Shurik! What's the towel for?"

"Maybe he's bleeding," said Shurik eagerly, trying to push his head in between the boys to see what was going on.

A tall boy turned a stern face to him and said with quiet menace: "Now then, stop that fooling!"

The silence went on and on, the uncertainty weighed on them endlessly. Seryozha had time to get tired, to get bored, to catch a grasshopper and to look at Valeri's yard and at Lariska. At last the big boys began to talk, to move, they separated and Arsenti came out—oh! not to be recognized, terrible, purple from neck to waist; where was his white chest, where was his white back? And the towel tied round his waist was spotted with ink and blood! And he was as pale as pale, but all the same he was smiling, that hero Arsenti! He walked firmly to Kapa, took off the towel and said: "Bandage me tightly."

"We'd better let the kids go next, before they make themselves a real nuisance," said someone. "What about it?"

"Where are you, kids?" asked Valeri, coming out of the bath-house with purple hands. "Not changed your minds? All right, quick, then."

How could you say you'd changed your mind? How could you pluck up courage to say it when Arsenti was standing there, all blood and ink, looking at you with a smile?

One letter won't take long, thought Seryozha.

He followed Shurik into the empty bath-house. The big boys were all watching Kapa bandage Arsenti. Valeri sat down on the broad bench.

"Shall I need a towel?" asked Shurik.

"You'll be all right without," said Valeri. "I'll do it on your arm."

He took Shurik's arm and pricked it with a pin just below the elbow.

"Oh!... "

"If it's oh, off you go," said Valeri and gave another prick. "Just try to think I'm taking out a splinter," he said helpfully, "then it won't hurt."

Shurik set his teeth and did not make another sound, he only jumped from foot to foot and blew on his arm where crimson points of blood were appearing one after the other. Then Valeri scratched the skin between the points—Shurik jumped again, beat with his heels and blew with all his lungs, while the blood trickled down. Oh, isn't Shurik brave, thought the pale Seryozha, he isn't making a sound, I won't make a sound either, oh, oh, oh—I can't run away, they'd all laugh at me, and Shurik would call me a coward.

Valeri took a bottle of ink from the bench, dipped a paint brush in it and drew it along the line of blood.

"Finished!" he said. "Next?"

Seryozha marched up and held out his arm....

That was at the end of the summer when school had only just begun, and days were warm and golden with sunshine. Now it was autumn, outside the windows the sky was a dirty grey and Aunt Pasha had put cotton wool and glasses filled with salt between the double panes to prevent the glass from getting steamed and then pasted strips of paper over the cracks to keep out draughts in the winter.

Seryozha was in bed. By the bed were two chairs. On one of them lay a pile of toys, on the other he played. But it was difficult to play on a chair. There was no room for tanks to turn round properly, and nowhere for enemies to retreat—they'd get as far as the back of the chair and that was all, the battle was over.

The illness started when Seryozha came out of Valeri's bath-house, his right hand supporting his left arm—swollen, burning, inky. He came out into the light, and black circles swam before his eyes, he smelt the smoke of someone's cigarette and vomited. He lay down on the grass, his bandaged arm aching and burning. Shurik and another boy took him home. Aunt Pasha did not notice anything because he was wearing a long-sleeved shirt. He went into the house without a word and lay down on his bed.

Soon, however, came vomiting and fever. Aunt Pasha was frightened and telephoned Mummy at school, Mummy hurried home and the doctor came. They undressed him, took off the bandage, exclaimed, and asked questions. But he had no answer for them; he was tormented by dreams, dreadful, sickening dreams of something big, in a red vest, with bare purple arms that smelt horribly of ink, a wooden block and a butcher cutting meat on it, and around him boys cursing and all stained with blood. He talked about the things he saw, unconscious of what he was saying. So the grownups did find out all about it.

They were loving and kind to Seryozha, but they tormented him worse than Valeri. Especilly the doctor, who kept ruthlessly pouring penicillin injections into him; and Seryozha, who had not cried for pain, sobbed from the humiliation, from his helplessness against the humiliation, and from the offence to his modesty. But the doctor was not content with that, he sent a woman in a white smock, a nurse, who pricked his finger with a special machine and squeezed out drops of blood. And after inflicting all this torment the doctor joked and stroked Seryozha on the head—adding insult to injury.

Seryozha got tired of playing, he lay back and thought of his sad lot. He wanted to find the first, original cause of all the trouble.

I got ill because of the tattooing, he thought. But I wouldn't have been tattooed if I hadn't seen Vaska's Uncle. And I wouldn't have seen him, if he hadn't come to visit Vaska. Yes, if he'd never thought of coming nothing would have happened, and I'd have been well.

He felt no resentment against Vaska's Uncle. It was simply the way one thing led to another, you could never guess where trouble might be coming from.

They tried to find things to amuse him. Mummy gave him an aquarium with little red fishes inside. Plants grew in it, too. You had to feed the fishes with powder from a little box.

"He's so fond of pets," said Mummy, "this'll keep him interested."

It was true, he was fond of pets. He was fond of the cat Zaika, and his tame jackdaw. But fish weren't pets.

Zaika was warm and fluffy, and it was great fun playing with him until he got old and gloomy. The jackdaw was gay and amusing, it flew about the room, stole spoons and came when Seryozha called it. But what could fish do except wag their tails? And why couldn't Mummy understand that!

What Seryozha wanted was the other children, good games, good talk. Most of all he wanted Shurik. Once, when the windows had still been open, Shurik came and called in through them.

"Seryozha! How are you?"

"Come in," cried Seryozha, jumping up on to his knees. "Come here!"

"They won't let me in," said Shurik. (The top of his head could just be seen over the window-sill.) "Get better and come out."

"What are you doing all the time?" Seryozha asked excitedly.

"Daddy's bought me a schoolbag, I'm to go to school," said Shurik. "They've got my name down. And Arsenti's ill, too. But none of the others are. And I'm not either. And Valeri's been sent to a different school, he's got an awful long way to go now."

All that news!

"Goodbye! Come out quick!" Shurik's voice was already further off, Aunt Pasha must have come into the yard.

Oh, if only Seryozha could have gone, too. With Shurik. Out into the street! How lovely everything had been before he got ill. Just think of all he had had, and all he had lost.

BEYOND UNDERSTANDING

At last Seryozha was allowed to get up, and then to go out. But they would not let him go far away from the house or to other houses, they were afraid something might happen to him again.

Anyway, they only let him go out in the mornings, when all his friends were at school. Even Shurik was at school although he was not yet seven. His parents had sent him because of the tattooing, so as to have him under someone's eye and keep him busy and out of mischief.... But it was no fun for Seryozha to play with the little ones.

Coming out into the yard one day, he saw a strange man in a worn cap with ear-flaps, sitting on the logs piled up by the shed. His face was like a brush, his clothes torn. He was smoking a very tiny cigarette, so small it could hardly be seen in his yellowish-black fingers, and the smoke seemed to come straight from them—how could he do that without burning himself? His other hand was bandaged with a bit of dirty rag. His boots were fastened with string instead of laces. Seryozha took it all in, then asked: "Have you come to Korostelev?"

"What Korostelev?" the man asked. "I don't know any Korostelev."

"It's Lukyanich you want, then?"

"I don't know Lukyanich either."

"They're not at home anyway," said Seryozha. "There's only Aunt Pasha and me. Doesn't that hurt?"

"What d'ye mean?"

"You're burning your fingers."

"Ah."

He drew on the tiny end for the last time, dropped it and put his heel on it.

"And your other hand—did you burn that before?" asked Seryozha.

The man didn't answer, only bent a grim, ruminative kind of look on Seryozha. Why's he looking at me like that? the boy thought.

"How ye off here? Live well?" the man asked.

"Yes, quite well, thank you," answered Seryozha.

"Plenty of stuff here?"

"What sort of stuff?"

"Well, what sort of things have ye got?"

"I've got a bicycle," said Seryozha, "and I've got toys. All sorts of toys, mechanical toys and ordinary ones. But Alec hasn't got very many, only rattles."

"And materials—got much of those put away?" the man asked, then probably thinking Seryozha might not understand, he explained: "You know—stuff for making coats and suits."

"We haven't any here," said Seryozha. "But Vaska's mother has, she's got a lot."

"Where does she live—Vaska's mother?"

What further talk there might have been one could not say; at that moment the latch of the gate clicked. Lukyanich came into the yard and saw the stranger.

"Who are you? What do you want?" he said.

The man rose from the logs and stood there looking humble and miserable.

"I'm looking for work, Master," he said.

"Why do you look for it in other people's yards? Where do you live?"

"Nowhere, just now," the man said.

"And where've you been living?"

"Where I used to live—that's gone. A long time ago."

"Just out of prison, eh?"

"A month ago."

"What were you in for?"

The man shuffled from foot to foot.

"Well, they said I was sort of careless about what was my own and what wasn't. But I didn't do it. It was all a mistake."

"Well, why didn't you go home when you came out, why are you hanging round?"

"I did go," he said, "but my wife wouldn't have me back. She'd got herself another man, a counter-jumper.... Now I'm tramping to where my Ma lives, she's in Chita."

Seryozha listened, open-mouthed. So he'd been in prison! In a prison with iron bars and bearded guards armed to the teeth with swords and pole-axes just as he'd seen them in the picture books, and the man had a mother in some place called Chita, and very likely she cried about him, poor mother.... She'd be so glad when he came. She'd make him a suit and a coat. And she'd buy laces for his boots.

"Chita, a good way," said Lukyanich. "Well, and what next? Will you earn your living honestly, or will it be the same thing over again—careless with thine and mine?"

The man snuffled.

"Give me your wood to saw, Master."

"All right," said Lukyanich and fetched a saw out of the shed.

The talk had brought Aunt Pasha out, and she stood listening on the steps. Then for some reason she called the chickens into the shed although it was still early for them to go to sleep, and locked the shed door. And put the key in her pocket. And told Seryozha quietly: "While you're out here keep an eye on that man, so he doesn't go off with the saw."

Seryozha circled round and round the man, staring at him with curiosity, doubt, pity and a certain fear. He could not pluck up courage to talk to him any more, out of respect for the man's strange, mysterious life. And the man said nothing either. He sawed with energy, only stopping now and then to sit down, roll a cigarette and smoke it.

Seryozha was called in to dinner. Korostelev and Mummy were not at home, so there were only the three of them. After dinner Lukyanich told Aunt Pasha: "Give that tramp my old felt boots."

"You could wear them a bit more yourself," said Aunt Pasha. "He's got boots."

"He'll never get to Chita in those," said Lukyanich.

"I'll give him something to eat," said Aunt Pasha. "I've a lot of yesterday's soup left."

After dinner Lukyanich lay down to rest, and Aunt Pasha took the cloth off the table and put it away in the cupboard.

"Why've you taken off the table-cloth?" Seryozha asked.

"Good enough for him without," she answered. "He's filthy dirty."

She heated up the soup, cut some bread and called the man in a melancholy voice.

"Come and get your dinner."

The man came, and wiped his feet for a long time on the mat. Then Aunt Pasha poured out water and he washed his hands. There were two pieces of soap on the little shelf, one pink, the other grey—washing soap. The man took the grey soap, maybe he didn't know the pink soap was for your hands, or maybe it wasn't proper for him to have it, just as it wasn't proper for him to have a table-cloth or today's soup. In general he seemed shy and humble, and walked through the kitchen awkwardly, carefully, as though afraid of breaking the floor. Aunt Pasha kept her eye on him all the time. When he sat down, the man crossed himself. Seryozha saw that pleased Aunt Pasha. She filled his soup plate to the very brim and said kindly: "Eat your fill."

The man ate the soup and three pieces of bread without a word and all in a minute, working his jaws vigorously and sniffing noisily every now and then. Aunt Pasha gave him some more soup and a tiny glass of vodka.

"Now you can have a drink," she said. "But on an empty stomach it's bad."

The man raised the glass. "God give you good health, Mistress."

He threw back his head, opened his mouth and in the twinkling of an eye all that had been in the glass disappeared into the cavern. Seryozha looked — there was the glass on the table, empty.

He gazed in admiration.

The man ate more slowly now, and started to talk. He told Aunt Pasha how he had come home to his wife and she wouldn't let him in.

"And she wouldn't give me anything either," he said. "And we'd quite a lot of stuff, too, a sewing-machine and a gramophone and all sorts of pots and dishes.... But she wouldn't give me a thing. Get back where you came from, she said, you jail-bird, she said, you've spoiled my life. I begged her—give me the gramophone at least, we bought it together, we both earned the money for it. But not even that. She'd made a costume for herself out of my suit. And she'd sold my coat in a commission shop."

"And how did you get on before? Were you happy together?" asked Aunt Pasha.

"As happy as doves," the man said. "She was crazy over me. But now she's got that counter-jumper there. I saw him, he's not worth looking at. A shrimp. What did he get her with? With being a counter-jumper, plain enough."

Then he talked about his mother, about the pension she had and the parcel she had sent him. Aunt Pasha was completely melted, she gave him a piece of boiled meat, and tea, and let him smoke.

"Of course," the man said, "it would have been better if I could have brought something with me when I go to my Ma— even the gramophone."

Of course it would be better, thought Seryozha. They could play records on it.

"Maybe when you start working, everything will be all right," said Aunt Pasha.

"Yes, but they're not overfond of taking on our sort," the man answered, and Aunt Pasha sighed and shook her head as though sympathising both with the man and with those who didn't like taking on his sort at work.

"Yes," said the man. "I could have been a counter-jumper, too. I could have been anything. But I've just wasted my time."

"But that's your own fault, if you've wasted your time," said Aunt Pasha in an admonitory tone. "Why did you do it? It would have been better if you'd used it properly."

"What's the good of thinking of that now, after all that's happened?" said the man. "Now it's no good talking. Well, thank you kindly, Mistress. I'll go and finish the sawing."

He went back into the yard, but Aunt Pasha did not let Seryozha go out again because a drizzle had started.

"Why's he like that," said Seryozha, "that man out there?"

"It's because he's been in prison," Aunt Pasha told him. "You heard what he said."

"But why was he in prison?"

"Because he lived badly, that's why. If he'd lived properly no one would have put him in prison."

Lukyanich had finished his after-dinner nap and was going back to his office. Seryozha transferred the questions to him.

"If people live badly, are they all put in prison?"

"Well, you see it's this way," said Lukyanich. "He stole other people's things. Suppose, for instance, I work and work and earn money and buy something with it—and he comes along and steals it. Is that good?"

"No."

"Of course not, it's bad."

"Is he bad, then?"

"Of course he is."

"Then why did you tell Aunt Pasha to give him your felt boots?"

"I was sorry for him."

"Are you sorry for people that are bad?"

"Well, it's this way," said Lukyanich, "it's not because he's bad I was sorry for him, but because his boots were through and he'd soon be barefoot. And in general, you don't

like seeing a man down and out. Well, and then. Of course
I'd have liked giving him the felt boots much better if he were
good. Goodbye. I've got to go," said Lukyanich and hurried
away.

That's all just silly, thought Seryozha, I can't understand a
word he's said.

He looked at the drizzle outside the window and tried to
make sense of Lukyanich's words. Then the man in the worn
cap went down the street carrying the felt boots, the shaft of
one thrust down the shaft of the other so that there was one
shaft with a foot at either end. Mummy came home, bringing
Alec wrapped in a red quilt.

"Mummy," said Seryozha, "you remember when one of
the children at school stole an exercise book; did they put
him in prison?"

"Why, of course not," said Mummy.

"But why not?"

"He's only little. He's eight."

"Are little ones allowed to, then?"

"Allowed to—what?"

"Steal."

"No, little ones mustn't steal either," said Mummy. "But I
spoke to him seriously, and he'll never steal anything again.
But what's set you thinking about that?"

Seryozha told her about the man who'd been in prison.

"Yes, there are some people like that, unfortunately,"
said Mummy. "We'll talk about it again, when you're
a little older. Go and ask Aunt Pasha for my darner,
please."

Seryozha brought the darner.

"Why did he steal?" he asked.

"He didn't want to work, that's why."

"But didn't he know he'd be put in prison?"

"Of course he did."

"And wasn't he frightened? Mummy! Isn't it at all terrible,
prison—not even a little bit?"

"Now, that's enough," Mummy sounded quite cross. "I've
told you already, you're not old enough to understand things
like that yet. Think of something else. I don't want to hear
another word about it."

Seryozha looked at her frowning face and stopped asking.
He went into the kitchen, got some water from the bucket
with the dipper, poured it into a glass and tried to drink it all
at once, in one swallow. But however much he threw back
his head, however wide he opened his mouth, all he did was

to get himself wet. Even the back of his collar was wet and water trickled down his spine. But he said nothing about his wet shirt, or they'd have started their fussing and made him change and scolded him. And by the time he had to go to bed the shirt was dry again.

The grownups thought he was asleep and talked quite loudly in the dining-room.

"All he wants is a plain yes or no," said Korostelev. "If you give him something in between, he can't understand it."

"I simply ran away," said Lukyanich. "I couldn't answer him."

"Each age has its own difficulties," said Mummy, "and we shouldn't try to answer every question a child asks. Why discuss things beyond his understanding? What good will that do? It will simply cause confusion in his mental processes and induce thoughts for which he is in no way prepared. It's enough for him to know that the man committed a crime and was punished for it. And I must ask you not to talk to him about these things."

"Do we talk to him about it?" Lukyanich protested. "He does the talking."

"Korostelev!" Seryozha called from the darkened room.

Silence fell.

"Yes, here I am," said Korostelev, coming in.

"What's a counter-jumper?"

"Now see here, young man, why aren't you asleep?" said Korostelev. "Just you go to sleep this minute."

But Seryozha's eyes were wide open, turned expectantly to him in the dim light. And in a hasty whisper (so that Mummy shouldn't hear and be angry) Korostelev answered his question.

BOREDOM

Then he was ill again. For no reason at all he suddenly got tonsilitis. The doctor said: "Glands." And thought up a fresh torment — cod-liver oil and poultices. And told them to take Seryozha's temperature.

They'd smear some stinking black ointment on a rag and lay it on your neck. On top they put some stiff paper that scratched. Then cotton wool. Then they wound bandages round it all, right up to your ears, so your head was like a nail sticking out of a board—you couldn't turn it either way. Try living like that.

At least they didn't make him stay in bed. And when his temperature was normal and it wasn't raining, they let him go out. But that didn't happen very often. Almost always there was either a temperature or rain.

They kept the radio on, but not everything interested Seryozha, far from it.

And they were so lazy, those grownups—whenever you asked them to read to you or tell you a story, they'd say they were busy. But when Aunt Pasha was cooking only her hands were busy, her tongue was free, she could quite well have told you a story. Or take Mummy. When she was at her school or changing Alec's nappies or correcting exercise books that was one thing, but what about the time when she stood in front of the mirror pinning her hair first this way, then that, and smiling at herself — was that being busy?

"Read me a story," Seryozha begged.

"Wait a little, darling," she said. "I'm busy."

"Why are you taking it all down again?" asked Seryozha, looking at the braids.

"I want to do my hair differently."

"Why?"

"No special reason."

"And why are you smiling like that?"

"No special reason."

"Why's there no special reason?"

"Oh, dear, Seryozha. Don't get on my nerves."

Why do I get on her nerves, Seryozha wondered. After a moment's thought he said: "But all the same, read me a story."

"Wait till I come home this evening," she said, "I'll read to you then."

But when she came home in the evening she would nurse Alec and talk to Korostelev and correct exercise books. And again she'd avoid reading.

But here was Aunt Pasha, she'd done all her work and sat down to rest on the little sofa in her room. She was sitting quietly, her hands clasped on her lap, there was nobody at home—this time she couldn't get out of it.

"Now you can tell me a story," said Seryozha, turning off the radio and sitting down beside her.

"Oh dear, oh dear," she said wearily, "what d'you want a story for? You know them all off by heart."

"That doesn't matter. Tell me one."

How lazy she was!

"Well," she started, "once upon a time there lived a Tsar and Tsaritsa. And they had a daughter. Now, one fine day—"

"Was she beautiful?" Seryozha asked vigilantly.

He knew very well that the daughter was beautiful, everyone knew it. But why did Aunt Pasha leave it out? You mustn't leave out anything when you're telling a story.

"Yes, she was beautiful. So beautiful that ... well, one fine day the princess decided to get married. And many suitors came to pay court to her...."

The story followed its familiar course. Seryozha listened attentively, gazing into the dusk with big, serious eyes. He knew every word of it, but the story was none the worse for that. On the contrary.

Just what ideas he got from the words "suitors" and "pay court" he could not have explained; but he understood everything—in his own way. For instance, "the horse stood rooted to the ground," and then galloped off—well, they'd cut off the roots.

The dusk deepened into darkness. The windows were blue and the frames black. There was nothing to be heard in all the world but Aunt Pasha's voice telling him about the trials of the suitors who came to pay their court to the princess. Quietness filled the little house on Dalnaya Street.

It was dull for Seryozha in all that quietness. The story would soon come to an end, and Aunt Pasha would never agree to tell him a second however much he begged or argued. Yawning, sighing, she would go into the kitchen and he would be alone. What could he do? He'd got tired of all his toys while he was ill. He was tired of drawing. You couldn't ride a bicycle indoors, there wasn't room enough.

Boredom took the life out of Seryozha more than illness, it made him languid and dulled his mind. Everything was so tiresome.

Lukyanich came home with a parcel, something he had bought. It was a grey box tied round with string. Seryozha looked at it eagerly, he waited with impatience for Lukyanich to get the string off. Why didn't he just take a knife and cut it? No, Lukyanich stood there breathing hard, undoing the tight knots; the string would come in for something; if he cut it, then it would be spoiled.

Seryozha stood on tiptoe, devouring the parcel with his eyes. But the grey box, big enough for something really interesting and splendid, only contained a pair of big black cloth-topped overshoes with rubber soles.

Seryozha himself had overshoes like that, with the same kind of fastenings, but made only of rubber, without any cloth on top. He hated them, and there was no pleasure or excitement at all in looking at this pair.

"What are those?" he asked wearily, in bored contempt.

"Overshoes," said Lukyanich. "Folks call them 'Farewell to Youth'."

"Why?"

"Because young men don't wear this kind."

"Are you old, then?"

"If I'm putting these on, it means I am."

He stamped his foot in the overshoe and said: "Comfortable!" Then he went to show them to Aunt Pasha.

Seryozha climbed on to a chair in the dining-room and switched on the electric light. The fish were swimming about in the aquarium, staring stupidly. Seryozha's shadow fell on them and they came to the top and opened their mouths, expecting to be fed.

I wonder if they'd drink their own sort of oil, thought Seryozha.

He took the cork out of the cod-liver oil bottle and poured a few drops into the aquarium. The fish stood on their tails with their mouths open, but did not swallow it. Seryozha poured in a few more drops. The fish swam away....

They don't like it, Seryozha thought, without any interest.

It was so dull, so *dull*! Boredom led him into senseless naughtiness. He took a knife and scratched the paint off the doors in the places where it had risen in bubbles. It wasn't that he enjoyed it, it was just something to do. He took the ball of wool with which Aunt Pasha was knitting herself a jamper and unwound it right to the very end, so as to wind it all up again—in which he did not succeed. And every time he knew that he was being naughty, that Aunt Pasha would scold and he would cry — and she did scold and he did cry, but all the same he found a certain satisfaction even in that. She had scolded, he had cried—at least something had happened.

It was better when Mummy came home and brought Alec. The house came to life. Alec cried, Mummy nursed him and changed his nappies. Then she'd give him a bath. He was more like a real person than when he was first born, only he was far too fat. He could hold a rattle, but that was all he was good for. All day he lived his own life in the nursery, and Seryozha had nothing to do with him.

Korostelev came home late and everyone wanted him for something. He'd begin talking to Seryozha or agree to read to him, then the telephone would ring. Mummy would interrupt every minute, she always had something she wanted to say, and she couldn't wait till people had finished what they were doing. Alec would cry before he went to bed, and Mummy would call Korostelev, it had to be Korostelev and no one else, to walk up and down the room with Alec and hum to him. And then Seryozha would be sleepy, and all his talk with Korostelev would be put off till some other time, he didn't know when.

There were, however, wonderful evenings, too — not very often, but sometimes—when Alec quietened down early, and Mummy was busy correcting exercise books; then Korostelev put Seryozha to bed and told him a story. At first he was bad at stories, he didn't know at all how to tell them. But Seryozha helped him and taught him the proper way, and now Korostelev would start off quite confidently.

"Once upon a time there lived a Tsar and Tsaritsa. And they had a beautiful daughter, a princess...."

Seryozha would listen and correct the story when it went wrong, until he fell asleep.

In those dull days when he didn't know what to do with himself, when he had no energy and could only tease or be naughty, he came to love still more Korostelev's fresh, healthy face, his strong hands, his manly voice. Seryozha would fall asleep glad that he, too, had had something of Korostelev, not only Mummy and Alec.

HOLMOGORY

Holmogory. That was a word Seryozha began hearing all the time when Korostelev and Mummy were talking.

"Have you written to Holmogory?"

"Maybe I shan't be so busy in Holmogory, then I can take my political-economy exam."

"I've had an answer from Holmogory. There's a place in the school."

"They've rung up from the personnel department. It's all settled about Holmogory."

"Why take that to Holmogory? It's all worm-eaten." (About the chest of drawers.)

Holmogory. Holmogory.

Holmogory. It must be something very high up. Hills and mountains, like you saw in .pictures.[1] People would climb from mountain to mountain. The school stood on a mountain. Children went sliding down the mountain on sledges.

Seryozha drew it all with red pencil, humming "Holmogory, Holmogory" to a tune that had come into his head specially for the word.

We must be going to live there, because they talked about the chest of drawers. Grand! The very best thing in all the world! Zhenka went away, Vaska went away, now we're going away. That makes us much more important, that we're going somewhere and not stopping in the same place all the time.

"Is Holmogory a long way off?" Seryozha asked Aunt Pasha.

"Yes, indeed it is," said Aunt Pasha and sighed. "A very long way."

"And are we going to live there?"

"Eh, I don't know, Seryozha, I don't know all your arrangements."

"Do you go there on a train?"

"Yes, a train."

"Are we going to Holmogory?" Seryozha asked Korostelev and Mummy. They ought to have told him themselves, they must have forgotten.

They looked at each other, and then looked away somewhere, and Seryozha tried to meet their eyes and couldn't.

"Are we going? We are, aren't we?" he insisted, puzzled. Why didn't they answer?

Then Mummy said in careful sort of voice: "Daddy's being transferred to work there."

"And are we going with him?"

That was a plain question and he waited for a plain answer. But Mummy started talking round and round, as she so often did.

"How could I let him go alone? Look how bad it would be for him, all alone. He'd come home and nobody there—everything untidy—nobody to get him anything to eat—nobody to talk to. Poor Daddy would be quite miserable."

Then at last came the answer.

"So I'm going with him."

[1] *Holm* — hill, *gora* — mountain.— *Tr.*

"And me?"

Why did Korostelev keep looking at the ceiling? Why did Mummy say nothing for such a long time, only caress Seryozha?

"And me?!" he cried in panic, stamping his foot.

"First of all, don't stamp," said Mummy, and stopped caressing him. "That's no way to behave. Don't let me ever see it again! And secondly—let's talk it over. How could you go just now? You've only just been ill. You're not properly well yet. The least little thing, and your temperature's up again. We don't know what it'll be like there, how we'll arrange everything. And the climate isn't right for you, either. You're just go on getting ill again and again and never pick up properly. And who'd I leave you with then? The doctor said you mustn't go just yet."

Long before she had finished he was sobbing, tears streaming down his face. They weren't taking him! They'd go themselves, and leave him behind! He hardly heard her last words through his sobs.

"Aunt Pasha and Lukyanich will stop here with you. You'll go on living just the same way you always have."

But he didn't want to go on living the same way he always had! He wanted to go with Korostelev and Mummy!

"I want to go to Holmogory!" he cried.

"Now listen, dear, stop, hush, don't go on like that," said Mummy. "What do you want with Holmogory? There's nothing special there."

"There is!"

"Why do you talk to Mummy like that? Mummy always tells you the truth. And you won't stop here all your life, you little silly, now hush, that's enough. You'll spend the winter here, and then in the spring or perhaps the summer Daddy'll come for you, or I will, and we'll take you there, just as soon as you're properly well and strong we'll take you, and then we'll all be together again. Just think, how could we leave you for long?"

Yes, but what if he didn't get strong again by the summer? And was it nothing, to wait the whole winter? Winter— why, there was no end to it. How could he bear it when they went away and he was left behind? They'd live there without him, a long, long way off, and they didn't care a bit, not a bit! And they'd travel in a train, and he'd have travelled in a train, too—but they weren't taking him! Everything mingled into one dreadful knot of infury and misery. But he could put it all only into the most simple words.

"I want to go to Holmogory! I want to go to Holmogory!"

"Give me a glass of water, Mitya, please," said Mummy. "Here, drink a little, Seryozha. Why, you mustn't get into such a state. However much you cry, it won't help. If the doctor says you mustn't go, that's the end of it. Now hush, now be a sensible little boy, hush, hush now.... Why, how often have I gone away without you, don't you remember when I was studying and took my exams? I went away and came back again, didn't I? And you were quite all right here. And you never cried when I went away. Because you were quite happy without me. Don't you remember? Why are you making all this fuss now? Can't you do without us for just a little while, when it's for your own good?"

How could he explain? It had been quite different then. He had been little and silly. When she was not there he forgot about her, and had to get used to her again when she came back. And she had gone away alone, now she was taking Korostelev away from him. Then came a new, piercing thought—will they take Alec? He had to know. In a choked voice, through swollen lips he asked: "And Alec?"

"But he's tiny," said Mummy reproachfully, and got red. "He can't do without me, don't you understand? He has to have me. And he's not ill, he doesn't get temperatures or swollen glands."

Seryozha hung his head and cried again, but quietly, hopelessly.

He might have borne it if Alec had been left behind, too. But it was *only him* they were leaving. It was *only him* they didn't want.

"Left to my fate," he thought in the words of the fairy-tale about Tom Thumb.

His feeling of injury against his mother—a feeling that would leave a lifelong scar—was mingled with a sense of inferiority. It was his own fault, of course he was worse than Alec, his glands got swollen, so they were taking Alec and leaving him behind.

"Oh," groaned Korostelev and went out of the room. But he came back at once.

"Seryozha, come for a walk. In the woods."

"In this damp! We'll have him in bed again!" cried Mummy. Korostelev shrugged his shoulders.

"He's in bed half the time as it is. Come on, Seryozha."

Still sobbing, Seryozha followed. Korostelev helped put his outdoor things on, except for the scarf, he had to ask

Mummy to help with that. Then hand in hand they went to the woods.

"You know," said Korostelev, "there's a little word— 'must'. Do you think I want to go to Holmogory? Or Mummy? We don't. It's upset all our plans, everything. But we must—so we're going. And that's happened to me a lot of times."

"Why?" asked Seryozha.

"That's what life's like, Sonny."

Korostelev spoke seriously, sadly, and Seryozha felt just a tiny bit better because he seemed sad, too.

"When Mummy and I get there, well—we must start right away with our work and everything new to us. And there'll be Alec. We must get him into a nursery at once. But what if the nursery's a long way off? Then we must look for a nanny. And that's no joke either. And I've got exams hanging over my head, I must sit for them if I bust. Wherever you look, everywhere it's 'must'. But there's only one 'must' for you—to wait here just for the present. Why should we make you share all those difficulties with us? You'd only get ill again, and worse than ever."

They needn't *make* him. He would be willing, glad, he longed to share all their difficulties. He could do the same as they did. And in spite of the earnest persuasiveness in that voice, Seryozha couldn't rid himself of the thought that they weren't leaving him behind just because he'd be ill, but because if he was, he'd be a nuisance. And his heart knew already that nobody really loved could be a nuisance. And the doubt of their love pierced deeper into his heart, ripe for understanding.

They came to the woods. Everything was empty and dreary. The leaves had fallen, the dark nests on the bare boughs looked from below like badly rolled balls of black wool. Seryozha's boots squelched in the wet layer of leaves as he walked hand in hand with Korostelev, thinking. At last he said tonelessly: "It's all the same, anyway."

"What's all the same, anyway?" asked Korostelev, bending over him.

Seryozha did not answer.

"It's only till the summer, Sonny," said Korostelev awkwardly after a pause.

What Seryozha wanted to say was something like this: I can think what I like, I can cry as much as I like, it'll all be the same. You grownups have the power, you can allow or forbid, you can give presents or punish, and if you say I've got to be left behind you'll leave me behind whatever I do. That is what he would have answered had he had the words. The feeling of helplessness when faced with the tremendous, boundless power of grownups crushed him.

From that day he became very quiet. He hardly ever asked: "Why?" He often went off alone, sat on Aunt Pasha's sofa with his feet tucked under him whispering to himself. He was still not allowed out very often. The autumn dragged on, damp and unpleasant, and his illness dragged on with it.

Korostelev was hardly ever with them. In the morning he would go away to "hand over". (That was what he always said now: "I'm handing over to Averkiev.") But he didn't forget Seryozha. One day there were new building-bricks beside the bed when he woke up, another time it was a brown monkey. Seryozha dearly loved the monkey. It was his little daughter. And she was as beautiful as the princess. He said to her: "Well, Sonny." He went to Holmogory and took her with him. Whispering to her, kissing her cold nose of plastic, he put her to bed.

THE EVE OF DEPARTURE

A lot of strange men came, they moved all the furniture about in the dining-room and Mummy's room and packed it in bast matting. Mummy took down the curtains and pictures. The rooms looked dismal and hideous with bits of string littering the floor and with darker patches on the walls. Only Aunt Pasha's room and the kitchen were homely islands amid all this depressing ugliness. Bare electric bulbs shed a harsh light on bare walls, bare windows and scraps of reddish bast. Chairs were stacked one on top of the other, their scratched legs pointing to the ceiling.

At any other time it would have been wonderful for hide-and-seek. But not now.

It was late when the men went away. Everyone was tired and went to bed. Alec fell asleep, too, after his usual evening cry. Lukyanich and Aunt Pasha whispered and blew their noses in bed for a long time, till at last they were quiet, too; then came snores from Lukyanich and a thin nasal whistle from Aunt Pasha.

Korostelev, however, still sat alone in the dining-room by the bast-covered table, writing under the bare lamp. Suddenly he heard a sigh behind him. He looked round, and there stood Seryozha in his long night-shirt, barefoot, with bandaged throat.

"What are you doing here?" whispered Korostelev.

"Please," said Seryozha, "Korostelev, dear Korostelev, take me with you, please take me, too, please, please!"

He broke out in heavy sobbing, trying to hold it back so as not to waken other people.

"But look here, Sonny, what's this," said Korostelev, picking Seryozha up in his arms. "You know you mustn't run about barefoot on this cold floor. You know it, don't you? And haven't we talked it all over and agreed about it?"

"I want to go with you to Holmogory!" Seryozha sobbed.

"Why, your feet are quite cold, you see now," said Korostelev. He wrapped the bottom of the night-shirt round Seryozha's feet, and gathered up the little shaking body. "What can we do when things turn out this way? You see, you're not well."

"I won't be ill again!"

"But as soon as you're really well, I'll come for you right away at once."

"Will you *really*?"

"I've never lied to you yet, Sonny."

No, he hasn't, thought Seryozha, but of course he does lie sometimes, they all do.... What if this is the time when he's lying to me?

He clung to that firm masculine neck, prickly under the chin, as his last refuge. Here, in this man, was his main hope and protection and love. Korostelev carried him up and down the room and whispered—all that nocturnal talk was in whispers: "I'll come for you, and then we'll go in the train. The train goes very quickly. And the coach is full of people. And before we know it we'll see Mummy waiting for us. The engine will whistle."

. He'll have no time to come for me, and Mummy'll have no time, either. Every day people will come to him, or they'll telephone him, and he'll always have to go to work, or take exams, or walk up and down with Alec, and I'll go on waiting and waiting for ever.

"—there's real forest where we're going to live, not just little woods like here. With mushrooms and berries growing wild."

"And wolves?"

"That I can't say. I'll find out about the wolves and write you a letter. And there's a river, we'll go bathing. I'll teach you to do the crawl."

But what if it really will be like that, thought Seryozha, weary of doubts. Perhaps it will.

"We'll make fishing rods and go fishing. Why, look out there, it's snowing!"

He carried Seryozha to the window. Great white flakes were floating gently down, some of them smashing softly on the glass.

Seryozha looked at them. Worn out, he quietened his feverish cheek pressed to Korostelev's face.

"Here's winter come at last. You'll be able to play out of doors all the time, and go sledging, the time'll pass so quickly you won't notice it."

"Oh, but—" said Seryozha, wearily worried—"the rope on my sledge is awful bad, will you put a new one on for me?"

"Right you are. I'll see to it. And you, Sonny, promise me one thing, not to cry any more. It's bad for you, and it upsets Mummy, see? And anyhow, it's not proper for men. I don't like that sort of thing. Now, promise—you won't cry any more, will you?"

"Uhuh," said Seryozha.

"That's a promise? Word of honour?"

"Uhuh."

"Well, remember. A man always keeps his word!"

He carried the exhausted Seryozha, slumping heavily in his arms, back to Aunt Pasha's room, put him into bed and tucked him up. Seryozha drew one more long, quivering sigh and fell fast asleep. Korostelev stood looking at him. In the light from the dining-room his face looked very small and pale. Korostelev turned away and went out on tiptoe.

THE DAY OF DEPARTURE

Then the day of departure dawned.

It was a dull, dreary day, without either sunshine or frost. The snow on the ground had melted in the night and only a thin layer remained on the roofs. The sky was grey. Underfoot it was wet and muddy. Sledging? Why, it was unpleasant even to go out into the yard.

How could you hope for anything in weather like that? How could there ever be anything good again?

But all the same, Korostelev had put a new rope on the sledge. Seryozha looked into the entry and saw it.

But Korostelev himself had disappeared.

Mummy sat nursing Alec. She kept on and on. And she smiled and said to Seryozha: "Look what a funny little nose he has."

Seryozha looked. Just an ordinary nose. She likes his nose because she loves him, thought Seryozha. She used to love me, but now she loves him.

So he went to Aunt Pasha. She might have a million superstitions, but she would stay with him and she would love him.

"What are you doing?" he asked dully.

"Can't you see for yourself?" she said. "I'm making rissoles."

"Why are you making such a lot?"

Raw meat rissoles smothered in bread-crumbs filled the whole kitchen-table.

"So there'll be enough for dinner for us all, and plenty for them to take on the journey, too."

"Will they go soon?"

"Not very. In the evening."

"How many hours is that?"

"Oh, a lot. It'll be getting dark when they go. As long as it's light they'll still be here."

She went on making rissoles, and he leaned his forehead against the edge of the table, thinking. Lukyanich loves me, too, and he'll love me more, he'll love me an awful lot. I'll go with Lukyanich in a boat and I'll get drowned. Then they'll bury me in the ground, like Great-Granny. And Korostelev and Mummy'll hear of it, and they'll be so sorry, they'll say — why didn't we take him with us, he was so clever for his age, and such a good boy, he never cried and never got on your nerves. A million times better than Alec. No, I don't want them to bury me in the ground, I'd be frightened lying there all alone. And we'll have a good time here, too. Lukyanich'll bring me apples and chocolates, and I'll grow up and be a sea captain, and Mummy and Korostelev will be down and out, and they'll come here and say: "Give me your wood to saw," and I'll tell Aunt Pasha: "Let them have yesterday's soup."

Here Seryozha felt so unhappy, so sorry for Korostelev and Mummy that he began crying. But Aunt Pasha had barely time to say: "Oh, heavens above!" when he remembered he'd given his word to Korostelev.

"I won't cry any more," he said quickly.

Granny Nastya came with her black bag.

"Is Mitya at home?" she asked.

"He's gone about a car," said Aunt Pasha. "Averkiev doesn't want to give him one, just think, what a brute."

"Why a brute?" asked Granny Nastya. "In the first place, he needs the car for the farm. And secondly, he's given them a lorry. That's far better, because of the luggage."

"For the luggage, of course," said Aunt Pasha. "But a car would have been better for Maryana and the baby."

"People are spoiled these days," said Granny Nastya. "In my young days we didn't have cars or lorries either to take children about, and we reared them just the same. She can sit with the baby beside the driver, and they'll be quite all right."

Seryozha listened, blinking slowly. He was filled with the sense of this parting, a parting which nothing could alter. It was as though everything in him was tensely prepared to endure the approaching grief. Whether in a car or a lorry, soon they would go, they would abandon him. And he loved them.

"Why's Mitya gone so long?" said Granny Nastya. "I wanted to say goodbye to him."

"Aren't you going to see them off?" asked Aunt Pasha.

"I have a conference," said Granny Nastya and went to Mummy. Then everything was quiet. The day outside became a deeper grey and the wind rose. It made the window-panes rattle and shake. Thin ice with white lines covered the puddles. The snow started again, whirling quickly in the wind.

"How many hours now?" asked Seryozha.

"A little less," Aunt Pasha answered. "But still quite a lot."

Granny Nastya and Mummy stood talking in the dining-room, among the piled-up furniture.

"Where on earth can he be all this time," said Granny Nastya. "I want to say goodbye to him, who knows if I'll ever see him again."

She's afraid, too, that he'll go away for ever, thought Seryozha, and never come back any more.

Then he saw it was nearly dark, soon they would have to put on the lights.

Alec began to cry. Mummy ran to him, almost bumping into Seryozha on the way.

"Why don't you find something to amuse yourself with, Seryozha dear?" she asked kindly.

He would have been glad to amuse himself; he tried conscientiously to play with his monkey, then with his bricks, but it was no good. It wasn't interesting, nothing seemed to matter. The kitchen-door banged, there was a stamping of feet and Korostelev's loud voice.

"Let's have dinner. The lorry'll be here in an hour."

"Didn't you get the car then?" asked Granny Nastya.

"No. They can't spare it, they say. What's it matter? We'll just go on the lorry."

Habit gave Seryozha a feeling of gladness on hearing that voice, he wanted to run in, but then came the thought: Soon there'll be nothing more of all this—so once more he started moving his bricks aimlessly about on the floor. Korostelev came in, his face red with the cold outside and said apologetically: "Well, Seryozha?"

They had a hasty dinner. Granny Nastya went away. It got quite dark. Korostelev went to the telephone and said good-bye to somebody. Seryozha leaned against his knee, hardly moving, and Korostelev drew his long fingers through Seryozha's hair as he talked.

Then Timokhin came in.

"Well? All ready?" he asked. "Give me a spade to clear the snow away, or we won't get the big gates open."

Lukyanich went with him to open the gates. Mummy picked up Alec and started busily wrapping him in a quilt.

"There's no hurry for that," said Korostelev, "he'll get too hot. Time enough yet."

He and Timokhin and Lukyanich began carrying out the packed things. Every now and then the open door let in a cold breath. They all had snow on their boots, nobody wiped his feet and Aunt Pasha did not scold them, she knew there was no sense in wiping your feet just now. Pools of water gathered on the floor, it was wet and dirty. There was a smell of snow, straw and tobacco mixed with an animal smell from Timokhin's sheepskin. Aunt Pasha ran about giving advice. Mummy, still holding Alec, went up to Seryozha, put one arm round him, pressed his head to her. He moved away. Why did she bother to hug him when she wanted to go away without him!

Everything was carried out, the furniture, the suitcases, the basket of provisions, the bundle of Alec's nappies. How empty the rooms looked! Nothing left but some scraps of paper and an empty medicine bottle lying on its side. You could see the house was old, the paint on the floor was worn off, it looked new and fresh only in the places where the what-not and chest of drawers had stood.

"Here, put this on, it's cold outside," Lukyanich said to Aunt Pasha and handed her a coat. Seryozha jumped in alarm and ran to him.

"I'm going out, too! I'm going out, too!"

"Of course, of course, you shall," said Aunt Pasha smoothingly, and helped him on with his outdoor things. Mummy and Korostelev were getting theirs on, too. Korostelev put his hands under Seryozha's arms, lifted him up and kissed him hard.

"Goodbye for the present, Sonny. Get well, and remember what we agreed."

Mummy started kissing Seryozha and crying.

"Seryozha! Say goodbye, darling!"

"Goodbye, goodbye," he said quickly, breathless with haste and agitation, looking at Korostelev. And he had his reward.

"Good lad, Seryozha," said Korostelev.

Mummy was still crying. She said to Aunt Pasha and Lukyanich: "Thank you for everything."

"Nothing to thank us for," said Aunt Pasha mournfully.

"Take care of Seryozha."

"You needn't worry about that," said Aunt Pasha still more mournfully, and suddenly cried: "You've forgotten to sit down! We must all sit down a minute!"

"But where?" asked Lukyanich, staring about.

"Oh, heavens above," cried Aunt Pasha, "come into our room, then."

They all went in, sat down here and there for some reason and waited in silence for the traditional few moments. Aunt Pasha was the first to rise.

"Well, God be with you," she said.

They went out and down the steps. It was snowing and everything was white. The big gates were wide open. A lantern with a candle inside hung on the shed wall, and the snowflakes whirled in its light. The loaded lorry stood in the middle of the yard. Timokhin was covering everything up with canvas. Shurik was helping him. A good many people were standing about—Vaska's mother, Lida and a lot more, all came to give Korostelev and Mummy a send-off. Seryozha felt as though he were seeing them all for the first time. Everything round him seemed strange, unknown. Voices sounded strange. The yard was not like his own yard. It was as if he had never seen that shed before. As if he had never played with those children. As if this man had never given him rides on this same lorry. As if nothing of it all had ever been *his*, and nothing ever could be, for he was abandoned.

"It's going to be bad, driving," said Timokhin in his stranger's voice. "Slippery."

Korostelev put Mummy and Alec in the seat in front and wrapped a shawl round them. He loved them more than anyone else, he took care of them, he saw to it that they would be warm and comfortable. He himself climbed into the back and stood there, tall as a statue.

"Get under the canvas, Mitya," Aunt Pasha called out. "Under the canvas, or you'll have the snow in your face."

He took no notice.

"Seryozha, move back there a bit," he said, "or we'll run over you."

The lorry snorted. Timokhin got in. The lorry snorted more and more loudly, trying to move. There, it gave a jerk, then slipped back; then it went a little bit forward and back again. Now it would go, the gates would be shut, the lantern would be put out, and it would all be over.

Seryozha stood on one side, under the falling snow. With all his strength he remembered his promise and only sobbed now and then—long, desolate, almost soundless sobs. And one single tear forced its way out of his eye and shone in the light of the lantern, a difficult tear, not a baby tear, but the tear of a boy, a bitter, burning, proud tear.

No, he could not wait there any longer, he turned and walked to the house, bent with grief.

"Stop!" Korostelev called in a desperate voice, and drummed on the back of the driver's cab. "Seryozha! Come on! Quick! Get your things together! You're coming with us!"

He jumped down.

"Hurry up! Bring them along clothes, toys, what else? Won't take a minute. Come on!"

"Mitya, what are you thinking of! Mitya, think what you're doing! Mitya, you're crazy!" said Aunt Pasha from the door and Mummy from inside the lorry. He answered angrily:

"Oh, rubbish. What d'you think this is? Can't you understand? It's like vivisection. Do as you like, but I can't stand it. That's flat."

"Oh, heavens above, it'll kill him there!" cried Aunt Pasha.

"Rubbish," said Korostelev again. "I'll take the responsibility, understand? It won't kill him at all. That's all your nonsense. Come on, come on, Seryozha."

He ran into the house.

Seryozha could not move at first. He could not believe it, he was afraid to believe it. His heart beat so loudly he could hear it. Then he dashed inside, ran panting through all the rooms, caught up his monkey as he passed, then had a sudden desperate fear that Korostelev might change his mind, Mummy and Aunt Pasha might talk him round, and rushed back to him. But Korostelev hurried to meet him saying: "Quick, quick!" And they began collecting Seryozha's things. Aunt Pasha and Lukyanich helped. Lukyanich folded Seryozha's bed up.

"It's right what you're doing, Mitya," he said, "you're absolutely right, good lad!"

Seryozha feverishly scooped up any of his treasures that came to hand and tossed them into the box Aunt Pasha gave him. Quick! Quick! Or they might go! You could never know what they might do the next minute. His heart seemed to be beating in his throat, so it was hard to breathe or hear anything. "Quick, quick!" he cried while Aunt Pasha bundled him up. He tugged to get away, looking for Korostelev. But the lorry was still standing there, and Korostelev had not even got in, he told Seryozha to say goodbye to everybody.

Then he picked Seryozha up and pushed him in beside Mummy and Alec, under Mummy's shawl. The lorry began to move, now he needn't be afraid any more.

It was crowded in the driver's cab—one, two, three, four people, think of that! There was a strong smell of sheepskin. Timokhin was smoking, too. Seryozha coughed. He sat wedged in between Mummy and Timokhin, his cap was down over one eye, his scarf was too tight round his neck, he could see nothing but the snow dancing in the light of the headlamps. It was cramped and uncomfortable, but who cared? We're going, we're going all together, our Timokhin's taking us, and at the back there, high up, there's Korostelev, he loves me, he takes the responsibility for me, he's out there in the snow but he put us in the cab, he'll take us all safely to Holmogory. Oh, heavens above — we're going to Holmogory, how wonderful it is! I don't know what's there, but it must be lovely if we're going there!... Timokhin's horn sounded warningly, and the gleaming snow rushed straight towards Seryozha.

1955

PROGRESS PUBLISHERS
PUT OUT RECENTLY

PROGRESS. SOVIET AUTHORS LIBRARY SERIES

Bondarev Y. *The Hot Snow*
(A novel)

December 1942. Manstein's panzer armadas are ramming their way to Stalingrad in an attempt to rescue the surrounded army of Field Marshal von Paulus. Their last barrier on the way to Stalingrad proves to be a small river lost in the steppe and bound by severe December frosts. From the East, to meet them, hurry the divisions of General Bessonov's army, overcoming the last laps of an exhausting non-stop march to take up positions on the same river.

Thus begins the new novel by the Soviet writer Yuri Bondarev.

Yuri Bondarev was seventeen when the Great Patriotic War began. The soldier's hard roads, the endless lines of trenches from the Volga to the Czechoslovak border, all this left an indelible impression on his young mind.

"The time has come in our literature," Bondarev said, "for a thorough investigation of the nineteen forties and fifties. We have accumulated enormous experience of life connected with this period and our study should embrace both the heroic and the tragic, the courage and the character of the Soviet people."

PROGRESS PUBLISHERS
WILL SOON PUBLISH

PROGRESS. SOVIET AUTHORS LIBRARY SERIES

Ostrovsky N.
How the Steel Was Tempered
(A novel)

Most of the novel's characters have real proto-
types and the fate of Pavel Korchagin, the main
character, repeats the author's life. Nikolai Ostrov-
sky (1904-1936) lived a short and heroic life. After
being seriously wounded in the Civil War he found
himself a permanent invalid at the age of twenty
with failing sight. It was then that he wrote his
wonderful book about youth, love and struggle,
about his Komsomol friends of the '20s. The
creation of *How the Steel Was Tempered* was a great
human exploit; this novel is popular with young
people all over the world. It is translated into 48
foreign languages, and published in 42 countries.

PROGRESS PUBLISHERS
WILL SOON PUBLISH

PROGRESS. SOVIET AUTHORS LIBRARY SERIES

Leonov L. *The Russian Forest*
(A novel).
In two volumes. Volumes 1 and 2

Leonid Leonov (b. 1899) is a veteran Soviet writer, an eminent artist and a celebrated public figure.

The action of *The Russian Forest* (1953) begins at the turn of the century and passes through the vital events of the 20th century: the First World War, the October Revolution and the Great Patriotic War. This is a novel about the continuity of the generations, the conflict between moral attitudes and the struggle between the forces of conscious creativity and the forces of destruction.

The Russian Forest itself, taken in an historico-philosophical sense, is the leitmotif of the novel, and it is this which organises the novel's social, scientific, moral and ethical problems.